Erik's blood coursed so hard the p
caught himself before he leaned too f
the velvet of the armchair, he imagin
whispering his adoration into her ear, a
in ways he only dreamed.

Yes, I gave you it all, Christine. I would have lassoed the moon for you.

"And you gave nothing in return?" Anna said. "He loved you."

The memory of how he'd shunned Anna wrapped around his heart like a rope of thorns. The raw passion he felt for her tightened those binds until he swore his heart would puncture. He forced such passion away. He didn't want it. Not now. He clamped his teeth in an attempt to govern the thoughts tumbling drunkenly in his mind. The velvet shredded beneath his fingers.

Damn it, you little minx. Stay out of my mind.

Christine wandered the empty stage staring out across the seats. "There was nothing I could give. Least of all love."

Ridges plowed into Anna's brow. "Why?"

"He was horrifically deformed. He frightened me. I was put through so much horror."

"Then why did you continue with the lessons?" Anna demanded sharply. "If you knew he loved you and you couldn't give that in return, why torment him?"

"I wanted to know the music for I had never experienced anything like it. I deeply respected the Angel of Music and cared for him, but I could never truly *love* him. Not in the way he wanted. His affections were so powerful—they frightened me." Christine shook her head. "A woman such as you could never comprehend the situation. He was a distorted soul, a madman. I couldn't be expected to look on that with love. No one could."

No one could? That? Respected? Rejected!

Erik tensed as he shook from head to toe. His hands crushed to his mask. He cursed his ugliness. Looking at the two women, he recognized the confusion Anna had mentioned. With all his being, he tried to control his demons. His inability to do so was not *his* fault. Man made him this way.

He turned his attention to the woman beside her. Erik leaned forward avoiding the urge to fold himself over the velvet railing and scream to the women below.

Anna, make her understand me.

Madrigal:

A Novel of Gaston Leroux's The Phantom of the Opera

Jennifer Linforth

Highland Press Publishing
Florida

Madrigal

For information, please contact
Highland Press Publishing,
PO Box 2292, High Springs, FL 32655.
www.highlandpress.org

ISBN: 978-0-9815573-3-5

HIGHLAND PRESS PUBLISHING

Excalibur Imprint

Dedication

For Joseph who believed from the

beginning,

For Tony who believed in me,

For Hannah who believed when I could not,

For Lisa who believed when I would not,

And for Abigail who simply...believed.

Senior Editor – Patty Howell

Junior Editor – Amber Wentworth

Acknowledgements

Writing a novel with a multi-faceted character as Erik required a great deal of research, but more importantly the enthusiasm of many.

Endless thanks to my critique partners, author Nina Pierce—cohort, sidekick and best friend, and author Ronna Hochbein who stood by me through thick and thin. Both women are incredible sources of support in my career.

Thanks to my editor, Amber Wentworth, who was thrust into the jaws of a student of Leroux and survived. I appreciate her patience and willingness to work with me. Senior Editor, Patty Howell has major kudos for her encouraging words and her editorial work on this project. I owe Sandra Andrés Belenguer of *ladyghost.com* thanks for sharing her knowledge and rare photos of the Opera Garnier and especially for the resulting friendship.

Undying gratitude to artist Ken Altobello for the cover that stopped my heart...

Thanks to Amanda Ashley and Kathryn Johnson for their support. Nothing strengthens a new writer's confidence more than the encouragement of fellow authors.

Many of my views on Erik were echoed in a book I stumbled across, *The Undergrounds of The Phantom of the Opera: Sublimation and the Gothic in Leroux's Novel and its Progeny* by Dr. Jerrold E. Hogle. I appreciate what this text offered as well as the subsequent question and answer emails that resulted between the author and me.

I can also never adequately express my appreciation to the numerous faceless friends and Phantom fans I have met over the years through various forums and blogs because of *Madrigal*. Those who have supported me with their laughter, and even more so with their love, are worth more than I can ever express.

My husband has my deepest gratitude for his unparalleled belief in my abilities. It was his first kiss, in the wake death that gave me my words and my freedom. And finally...to Lisa Schmidt and Hannah Phillips, two women who stood by me insisting if I *Let It Be* The Madrigals would become the vision I desired—even without ice in the burgundy.

I think the posse will be pleased.

~Jennifer Linforth

Author's Note

"And, now, what do they mean to do with that skeleton? Surely they will not bury it in the common grave! I say that the place of the skeleton of the Opera ghost is in the archives of the National Academy of Music. It is no ordinary skeleton."

~Gaston Leroux: The Phantom of the Opera.

A good story transcends time and a gripping opening hook rolls off the tongue years later. No opening line is as closely defended or debated as—*The Opera Ghost really existed.*

A writer cannot expand a timeless classic without an impending sense of doom. Doing so challenges readers to view beloved characters in new and compelling ways. Through the years Leroux's original novel has had numerous progenies. Fans of Phantom of the Opera are faithful to the versions they love whether it be the musical adaptation of Ken Hill or the film starring Lon Chaney. One thing it seems all Phantom fans appreciate is a deep respect for Gaston Leroux and his vision of a sensual madman.

Leroux's novel was an incredible synthesis of themes, ideas and plot twists. His book did for me what good literature should. It left behind questions. Did Erik truly die, or was that another trademark plot twist of the author? Was Erik not a trickster who enjoyed manipulating the world that shunned him? Could he not have manipulated his death? Why was Christine compelled to bend to Erik's will, a man she adamantly feared to the point of attempted suicide? Was it because she loved him, feared him, or a combination of both? Leroux mentioned in a speech in Nice shortly before his death that one of his goals as a writer was to mislead the reader. That haunted me...

I kept returning to one question in particular. Who was Philippe de Chagny, beyond the haughty aristocrat with "an excellent heart and an irreproachable conscience"? His mysterious role and untimely death drew me deeper into the story and kept bringing me back to study more. With these questions in mind, the idea for my series mushroomed until there was no controlling the need to write it. Though not seen in *Madrigal*, Philippe and his death play a large role in forthcoming books. As a result, certain elements of Leroux's novel have been adjusted to suit my imagination, primarily in the timing of Philippe's demise and the characters' perceptions of Erik.

Leroux's unmasking was a pivotal turning point in the original novel and written entirely though Christine's point of view. Here we have the description of the Phantom as seen by a woman looking to rediscover a lost link in her life, so much so to the extent of equating Erik to a living 'dead' version of her father, with his yellowed skin, his death head skull and the scent of death upon his hands. Leroux's descriptions of what Christine saw, felt and smelled were anything but objective. Therefore, who is to say what the perceptions of Erik were to others involved in the story when all the reader was given were impressions solely based on Christine's needs and ideas, and rumor? What were they seeing and reacting to in Erik and what did they need to pull from his persona? Subtle changes to his character served to eliminate this closed point of view and open Erik up to several different and necessary perceptions.

I did not take these changes lightly, knowing how deeply respected Leroux's novel is. I kept that respect in mind as I worked with Leroux's ideas and molded characters of my own to enhance them.

It is my hope that Gaston Leroux's extraordinary and passionate story will pass from one generation to the next and continue to leave in its wake many more questions than answers.

~Jennifer Linforth

There is no past that we can bring back by longing for it. There is only an eternally new now that builds and creates itself out of the best as the past withdraws—

Johann Wolfgang von Goethe

Prologue: Paris four years later—1885

Paper. Ink. Figs.

The contents were nothing if not consistent. He never asked for any of it, but who was he to refuse them? The package was always there, the first of every month...consistent in every way—a small bundle painstakingly wrapped in plain brown paper and tied with twine. Sighing, he picked it up. The paper had turned moist from humidity. He rotated it several times and found what he always found. No markings, no card, no indications whatsoever of where it had come from or who had left it. It was a package, and like him, wrapped in complete anonymity.

He wouldn't open it this time, as there was no real need. He had enough paper to last for some time, and the packaging kept the pages from getting too soiled. The ink would dry if the seal was cracked. He could wait. Alas, but the figs couldn't. Those blasted wretched figs.

Long fingers nimbly unwrapped a corner. The figs were always in the same spot. The whole thing was maddening in its consistency. Removing an inner brown bag tied with another piece of twine, he paid no regard to the other contents nestled neatly inside. He fumbled slightly with the knot. Even the string was damp.

Water seeped through the walls around him. Paris had been unusually rainy this spring. It invaded everything in his labyrinthine home, making the floors slick, moss grow thick on the rock, and the waters of the lake deepen. No matter to him. He was used to the water, the damp, the darkness. What he wasn't used to were packages.

He was perfectly capable of tending to his own needs. The packages had been arriving now for months and for whom else could they be left? Some other hunted man living below Paris? Some other misunderstood outcast? No. They were for him. The paper gave it away long ago—being immaculately lined for a Maestro's notes.

Lengthening his strides propelled him past the steps that curved upward toward the opera house. He had stopped pausing to listen there long ago. The stairs he would follow led deeper into the labyrinth, further from the place he wanted to be and closer to the place fate forced him to be. One angry twitch snapped the string around the figs. He threw the tiny parcel into a murky corner. The rats would eat them, as they always did.

He hated figs.

Chapter One

"More treats for him, Anna?"

Anna tripped over her feet, nearly plowing headfirst into an abandoned push cart. She glanced left to right, scanning the fog covered street and spotted the elderly woman hugging the wall of an alleyway. Anna's wind-burned cheeks plumped with her smile. "Yes, Madame." She tapped her parcel. "Paper, ink and figs."

"Who is he? Lover?"

Anna laughed as she scampered across the road to share the dark alley. Mud splattered from her boots and bedecked the hem of her dress. No cobbles in this area of Paris. Nothing noteworthy existed in this quarter. Nevertheless, before darting into the alley, she checked to make certain no one took note. Unlikely they would. In this neighborhood on the opposite side of the green-hued Seine, the poor were in limbo. They didn't rule like in the heart of the Saint-Antione, rather darted like bedraggled rats out of sight of wary eyes. Anna fished in her coat for the remains of her morning bread and gave it to the old woman.

"I have no idea who he is," she replied. "You are well aware of that. Stop making him into some fanciful gentleman." Her smile grew at the woman's toothless grin and her eagerness to steal the package. Lifting it above her head, Anna kept it from her reach.

"How many does this one make?" The woman swiped at the parcel.

"I have lost count."

Laughter tumbled around them. How many years had she entertained the hag in this way? Anna was well-known around the streets of Paris, among the rejected and lonely. Most outcasts regarded her as one of their own. While not rich, Anna had a roof over her head and her needs attended. What she didn't need she gave to others.

A roof. How ridiculous. Contempt poured past her eyes as she glared in the direction of the Académie Nationale. The place was more prison than home. Anna knew nothing about music, nor did she fit in with the bourgeoisie that seemed attracted to the arts. The debt her family owed the management ran too deep to allow her to leave. Every day her routine followed the same unrelenting pattern. She worked like a slave for the administration. Her meager salary went right back into their pockets with the exception of the few coins permitted her.

"What does he look like?" the woman said, both hands swatting the air in between nips at bread. "Handsome, I bet."

"You think so?"

"Handsome, handsome, handsome!"

A wind gust knocked Anna's locks into her face. She placed the parcel on the ground, careful not to set it in mud, and gingerly put her foot atop it. Grabbing fistfuls, she whisked her hair into a long braid. She sighed. Not that arranging it mattered. Only twenty-three years old and lightning would strike her before she caught the eye of a handsome man.

What does he look like? Just as the woman leaping about her like an overly excited frog, Anna reasoned the recipient of her parcels must have some form of dementia. She had seen firsthand the prejudices forcing the infirm and imbecilic into hiding. Surely, she reasoned, he must be such, for why else would a gentleman wear a mask?

His living arrangement didn't shock her. She'd seen the desolate live in many places—under bridges, on rooftops, or in crates on the street. Yet something about so commanding of a man struck her.

Anna picked up her parcel and hugged it to her chest. *How could a man like him live so far from the finery of such a city?* The night she'd followed him deep into the cellars of the opera house remained as fresh as if it had happened minutes ago. Though she'd quickly lost sight of him, she'd uncovered enough to label him more miraculous genius than imbecile.

That night, his awesome emptiness played on the maddening notes of music. A composer like no other, hidden from the world...

Watching the occasional well-to-do and clearly misplaced resident hustle past, she admired the seemingly graceful and uncomplicated world she thought he could command.

Jealousy hummed through her veins. Anna would give anything to taste the life of an elegant lady, have a gentleman upon her arm, and go about her days feeling as if she had some worth in the world.

"Bloody hell," she groaned, staring at a fetching young couple.

"Anna's sad again." The old woman clawed at the package.

Anna swatted her away, and nodded toward the couple. "Can you see me upon his arm?" She teased herself. "Thank-you for your company, Monsieur, but I must tell you—before you charm me further by your affections—I am desired not only by you, but by the English authorities, the German authorities, the Belgian authorities..." She moaned. "Yes, *definitely* the Belgian authorities."

"Anna has been bad."

Anna made light of the statement with a well-practiced contrite smile. Such a past was not her doing. The life of crime was forced upon her. She could understand why someone would not wish to be seen in society. Time waned, so she patted the elderly woman upon the hand and assured her she would be passing by the first of next month as usual.

Stepping into the street, she pulled her threadbare coat close around her, intent on heading toward the Garnier. What a contrast between Anna's two Paris'—the cold and desolate outskirts, and the prosperous inner city.

Such distinctions made her shuck her coat and drape it around the woman's shoulders before she left in earnest.

The cold spring air hastened her through the streets. Dodging and weaving her way in and out of the hustle of carriages and crowds, she didn't stop until she reached the Rue Scribe. She halted at a small stone archway at the entrance of a sewer. Pretending to fumble with the lace on her muddy boot, she knelt, looking about to make certain no one took notice.

Anna smiled slyly at the parcel. She confessed to knowing nothing about music or the social class of which her mystery man appeared to be a part. But the music he wove spoke to every unwanted soul and uplifted the spirit. If she couldn't walk equal among the women she passed, maybe such a great Maestro as he could. And perhaps her parcels would help.

Once certain she was undetected, she shoved the package between the grates of the archway. She jerked up, darting her eyes around the area. The authorities would be quick to question someone of her class lurking so near the Garnier.

Should she wait and see if he came? It had been awhile since she'd seen him.

"Absolutely ridiculous." Her mind was made up. Help whomever she could and move on. Attachments meant trouble and she was far too versed in that.

"You must know!" Although exceedingly late, the weary droop to Madame Giry's shoulders didn't deter Erik's questioning.

"I do not know, Monsieur. Please leave."

"No. You are the concierge, Madame. It is your duty to know everything that goes on in this theater. I know you know."

Folding his arms, he leveled a stone-hard stare at her and

watched with gathering dismay as the older woman tried to focus on anything but him. The office was dark enough, he assumed his golden eyes shone through the depths of his mask. Their unusual color must have made her uneasy, for she jigged as if standing on hot coals.

"Monsieur, I know no more than you. A stranger is reaching out and thinking of you in kindness. It is a random act. Leave it be."

He stopped pacing. Not many in the opera house knew the intimate details of his life. Appalled at how blasé Madame Giry seemed, considering the circumstance, he changed tactics. "It would be wise if you told me what you know, Madame Giry. A stranger taking interest in what lurks in this opera house could arouse suspicion. Would you rather another investigation?"

The old woman's white face stood out remarkably against her faded black dress. It amused him, but only for a moment. He quickly regretted frightening her.

"I do not wish another investigation."

"Nor do I, Madame. What makes you think I want to see my peace disturbed?"

When the old woman jerked back, Erik instantly repented his sharp tone, but a part of him was unable to apologize. Far too long he'd been labeled a monster and a madman. Kindness confounded him, being a luxury rarely extended his way. "The investigations into the Phantom of the Opera are over. But if you know something to the contrary—"

"I told you, Monsieur, I know nothing."

"Then why is this occurring? Why would anyone pay attention to *me*?"

He was a condemned man—fate had seen to that. The burden of the atrocities Paris suffered was firmly stacked upon his shoulders. Erik faded away into the great, unsolved mystery of the Paris Opera House. After the investigations into his former crimes closed, no one had bothered to look for him. He blocked off all entrances to his residence on the underground lake beneath the theater and sealed himself away to live in a tomb. His only contact was Madame Giry, theater concierge and box keeper.

"You are every bit as entangled in this as I," he continued. "The very nature of you keeping my anonymity makes you an accomplice. I know nothing of this stranger's intent. I—"

Stopping abruptly, he swallowed additional rebuke. What was the point of threats? She had no say in the events which condemned him to wallow in the cellars of the Opera Garnier.

"My apologies, Madame, you are not deserving of my rants. I bid you good-night." Erik bowed. He was almost at the door when her whisper stopped him.

"Why can I not deny you? I damn fate for bringing you into my life."

Turning, he noted her fear. She covered her mouth with her hand as soon as the confession slipped through her lips. It made his shoulders sag.

"Fate, Madame? Fate had nothing to do with it. You serve me because it is what you wish."

"You are mistaken, Monsieur."

"I am not mistaken," Erik snipped. "Have you not been kindly compensated for tending to my eccentricity? Have I not rewarded you for serving my necessity to live as a recluse? A franc here, a box of English sweets there? And do not forget all I have done to promote the dancing career of your daughter."

Fanning his cloak aside, he leaned in toward her. Madame Giry swallowed and the feathers of her hat swayed as she trembled. He had driven his point home.

"Very well." She squared her shoulders. The air of bravery was well performed, but notes of mistrust trembled in her voice.

He'd given her control of too many of his secrets, and it pained him to see her just as vulnerable to them as himself. Erik knelt in front of her. One by one his long, slender fingers came to rest on the back of her hand. As intimate a gesture as he could display.

"Madame Giry, who?"

Erik followed her gaze to the back of her hand. Uncertainty wrapped around him. Ashamed, he lifted his fingers and coiled them into his palm. Rarely touched in his life, what right had he to intimacy? He heard her indecisiveness as she took a breath, and he found he held his as well.

"There is a woman. Her name is Anna. She has worked for Messieurs Laroque and Wischard for two years now. Not many pay mind to her unless something is needed. When she is not here, she spends her time administering to the homeless. I believe you are one of her charges."

Erik stood. Charity? Pity? He neither needed nor wanted either. "Good-night, Madame."

The uncomfortable feelings stirring in him hastened him to the door. Who was this Anna? Why bother to show him small kindnesses? He didn't ask for it. The world was an uncompassionate place, wrapped first in the swaddling clothes of his infancy, then later disguised as the dark vaults of an opera house. He didn't know how to react to such news. Quickening his pace, Erik moved deeper into the familiar sanctuary of the darkness. He couldn't bear history to repeat itself.

He wouldn't allow it.

The answer was simple, but the consequence of such haunted him.

Anna must die.

Even with her vivid imagination, Anna could never conjure up such a fantastic realm as the backstage of the Opera Garnier. The atmosphere buzzed like a hive of bees drunk on sugar. Everyone fed off the excitement whether they wanted to be in the limelight or a part of the support making the magic happen.

Anna wanted nothing to do with it—especially on gala evenings.

"Mademoiselle, please!"

"Pardon, Monsieur, my mistake." Scooping up the top hat and brushing it clean, she sheepishly handed it back to the gentleman.

He swiped it out of her hand and continued in the opposite direction. Anna always moved against the flow. The gentlemen she passed this evening had one destination in mind—the only place in the Opera Garnier she both avoided and wasn't invited.

The salons—elegantly appointed rooms well-suited for the comfort of the aristocracy—filled each night with gentlemen enjoying the company of dancers. Anna often fantasized about being a part of the parties she only heard about in stories.

Just as well. She had her reasons for disliking aristocracy.

But it wasn't out of need to escape all the finery that hastened Anna through the crowd.

"Anna!"

"Bloody hell."

She didn't need to turn around to confirm Jacob Wischard's approach. He always used a stick to walk, so his footfalls were accompanied by a metallic clack of a steel-tipped cane against the wood flooring.

"Where are you going with such urgency?"

"Any place you are not."

"Watch your tone, Mademoiselle," Jacob snapped. The tip of his cane rested against her bosom. He backed her toward a secluded area of the hall.

Anna knocked the offending sword away. "What do you want, Monsieur?"

"Stay out of the way of my patrons. You are to be worked, not seen. Why are you roaming about on a gala evening?"

Gala evenings meant mindless work. She'd had enough of that for one day.

"I have no reason," she lied, pushing down her hatred for Jacob Wischard and his partner Edward Laroque.

"You best watch your behavior, Anna. You are here out of the kindness of my heart."

Anna snorted.

He snatched her arm and hauled her aside. As he leaned in close, Anna recoiled from the stench of cigar and scotch. "Listen to me you meddling little wench. You are only here as payment until your bloody father gets me the money he owes. Were it Edward's choice, you would still be living on the streets."

"Much preferred, Monsieur." Clamping down on her teeth muffled her grunt when Jacob shoved her against the wall.

"Spare me your tongue. I know you long to be a part of the grand parties and elegant balls."

Anna followed Jacob's hand as it wiped imaginary dirt from her shoulders.

"You are small and ordinary. There is no chance of you ever receiving the attentions of such fine men. Your rightful place is astride me, or cowering from Edward."

The muscles in her back seized when Jacob knocked his cane against her breast. "I suggest you be in your bed this evening. I might call on you. You wouldn't want your father to find you were naughty and not there for Jacob, now would you?"

Anna waited until she saw his back before spitting at him. She rushed off in the opposite direction. Tonight, she'd spend away from her meager blanket and bed.

Sleeping on the floor was better than waiting for Satan to arrive.

The cellars of the Garnier were tremendous as the opera itself. Totaling five, they supported the layout of the stage with a network of traps, hatches, winches, counterweights and revolving doors.

Anna often found respite among the wheels and pulleys of the sub-stage level. She enjoyed wandering among the giant machinery. When lucky, she could watch the teams of horses as they rotated the wheels which operated the hatches that moved scenery. Sometimes, she even sneaked a pat of a muzzle or two. No horses were employed this evening, so Anna contented herself with roaming free from the demands of the managers.

One could easily make a wrong turn in the maze and get lost in the cellars. She was certain this was the case upon spotting a shadow moving along the wall. The swift sense of motion seemed out of sorts.

"Lost, Monsieur?" Anna moved around a huge wheel. "The way from the first cellar toward the salons is just around the corner. You should take care and travel with caution; it is easy to get disoriented."

The gentleman kept his back to her and refused to answer.

"I beg your pardon, Monsieur…" She squinted in the darkness. Anna didn't approach, perching in such a manner that if he proved a threat, she could make a swift escape. She scowled and turned in a small circle.

Was she going mad? He'd been here a moment ago. "Monsieur?"

Silence.

An arm came from the shadows and hooked around her shoulders.

Anna screamed.

She bucked and thrashed against the grip threatening to paralyze her with more than fear. Her assailant caged her against his length with arms of iron.

Fingers, extraordinarily long and thin, stifled her cries. She thrashed her head. The more she wrestled, the harder her assailant held her—and the angrier she became.

Too many times in her life she'd experienced the darker side of men and their intentions. Her life of crime made her a tasteful lady for those of malicious minds. It honed her instinct to fight. Anna drew her knees to her chest and squirmed with every ounce of strength she had. She whipped her head from side to side, managing a breath to scream.

"If it is your intent I be a vessel for your filthy needs, then be done with it already!"

Her breath slammed out of her lungs as she hit the floor. Rolling to her feet, Anna scrambled out of the way. Her eyes darted toward every corner, searching for her attacker.

"Be done with it I say." She dared not question why she'd been dropped. "Do what you need. Have no mercy if you must, but let it be a scar on your heart what you would do to a lady who was merely concerned."

The shadows poured unfathomable disbelief into the air around her.

"I have done many things in my deplorable, wretched life, Mademoiselle, but I will not even address the filthy assumption you just passed. I assure you, *that liberty* I will not take unless it is freely given. But be wary. This is my kingdom in which you so boldly trespass."

Her heart thumped against her ribcage. "I beg your pardon, Monsieur," she spat to a random shadow.

The cellars would offer her no respite tonight and unwilling to return to her bed, Anna bolted.

Erik's eyes narrowed to slits as he watched her storm off. He took a deep breath, sucking in air between his teeth. Tossing his head backward, he settled the flutter in the pit of his stomach. He only killed when he found it necessary to protect his secrets. Each time plunged him into a gloomy pit of self-abhorrence. Too many years traversing Europe as a highly skilled assassin had seeped loathing into his soul. The genius in him contorted to a darker being as his hands were forced to do the bidding of malicious men. The power deflected a world that abused him as a degraded and repugnant freak. He spread his fingers across his mask and slammed his head against a wheel.

He never asked for the blood upon his hands. It had become a necessary means of survival.

Music and noise rose in his mind. The blessing and curse often worked against each other to create a chaos of indecipherable emotions. Squeezing his eyes, his gut panged like fingers angrily plucking a violin.

Damn!

He despised being associated with the vermin who'd force themselves upon a woman, but what was he to do? Manipulation served as his only means to communicate his deepest desires. His only means until her comment made him drop her. He banged his head again, ignoring the pain that raced up his neck. What caused such a reaction?

This woman couldn't wander freely about his cellars. His secrets were his only sanctuary, solitude the vice that draped a veil over his demons.

Wasn't it?

To safeguard his seclusion, all he need do was follow. Yet something fixed Erik to his spot. All he desired was peace.

Wasn't it?

Years ago, gala evenings were a source of entertainment. Carefully cloaked, Erik studied the patrons as they filled his theater. He'd glare at nobles and the feeble-minded members of bourgeois as they jostled for rank and prestige; listened as they made pompous attempts at besting one another on the subjects of music and kings. Erik loathed them, knowing the airs they painted were a self-inflicted mask. In the past he might have desired a sword upon his hip to partake in the air of forced fraternity, but such frivolity waned through the years. He no longer envied them.

Back then, Erik had controlled everything in the Opera Garnier and had done so in complete anonymity. He'd had no need to cajole himself to the classes.

This evening's gala was different. War and revolution had long ago stunted the crowds and squelched the groveling he used to enjoy. This republic was a confused beast, a paradoxical political regime he found oddly still monarchial. Now, so few were the patrons, it seemed unnecessary for him to wander in shadow. His past forced his caution. Anger over being seen by Anna, and confounded as to why he simply hadn't killed her, launched him into a morose mood. To calm himself, Erik attempted to do what he'd avoided for years—view the evening's opera from his box.

The fact he couldn't indulge himself in the pathetic rendition of *La Traviata* angered him further. A man of peculiar habits, he expected, despite the passing of time, for things to remain the same.

When he arrived at his destination, he kicked the door open with such force Madame Giry shrieked in pitches usually reserved for the reigning diva.

"Why is my box rented?" Erik panted like a bellows.

He had Madame Giry collapsing into a chair within two strides.

"Your box, Monsieur?" she stammered.

"Yes, my box." Erik gestured toward the door. "Someone is in Box Five and Box Five is to be kept empty. At all times. I thought myself clear, Madame."

"Even if you are dead?"

That statement hit Erik directly between the eyes. He wagged his head and rapped his fingers against his temple. "Ah, yes. Erik is dead. Forgive me for momentarily forgetting." Sarcasm curdled at his feet like day-old milk.

"Faking your death and printing your obituary will do that to a man, Monsieur. I didn't think it would be wise to leave the box empty."

Erik made a wide arc with one arm and let it slap against his thigh. He conceded to the old woman's wisdom.

"Death at birth would have been easier." He chuckled morosely, employing his ventriloquism and projecting his voice. It bounced from wall to wall like an invisible acrobat. It entertained him, but obviously didn't amuse Madame Giry. She rushed to the door and scanned the hall before shutting it.

"Do you fear Death, Madame, or just Erik? Even at our birth, Death does but stand aside a little." He hopped to the side. "And every day he looks toward us and muses somewhat to himself whether that day or the next he will draw nigh." He bowed with a grand flourish upon completing a favored quote of Bacon.

"I do not like to speak of such things, Monsieur."

She twisted the skeleton key and locked the door. She may not fear Death, but she feared him. He had a habit of frightening her—one difficult to break.

Fanning his cloak out of the way, he took a seat on the divan. With a flick of his finger, he motioned for her to sit in the chair across from him.

"Speaking of death is nothing compared to being imprisoned by it." His slender hand waved over his face.

He was a hostage, trapped beneath a mask, which shielded the world from the revulsion of his deformity. The ebony prison with its fake nose and perpetual lack of expression kept him caged beneath a false sense of dignity. His thin lips were the only part of his inhuman ugliness vulnerable to the leering eyes of man.

"Why are you here, Monsieur?"

"I am everywhere, and Death is always nigh, Madame. And I am tired of having only Death when I could have so much more."

Erik suppressed a sigh at her furrowed brow. Blessed with a voice more angelic than the heavens themselves, he lived a contradictory life. Like Death—whose mere presence could ruin the purest maidens—Erik was painfully, passionately, and erotically seductive. What the good Lord lacked in judgment by giving him such a face and condemning him to such a frustrating and ironic fate, He compensated with the genius He birthed into Erik. Shame the Lord didn't realize man would judge man by appearance alone. Leaning back in his chair, he pressed his fingertips together to study the way he unnerved Madame Giry. Though his heart was capable of expressing the most ardent emotion, her nerves proved why he never bothered to permit the man in him to surface.

"I am not certain what you expect of me, Monsieur. Did you come here because of your box? What is it you wish?"

"To live like anybody else."

"You cannot do so, Monsieur. You are supposed to be *dead*."

Erik gnashed his teeth and stuck a finger in his ear. The pitches the old woman could achieve at times bested him. He didn't like being reminded of such things and Madame Giry's enthusiasm irked him. Her knees bounced as she sat.

"It would be bad, very bad for you to return. You are a wanted criminal."

"You do not need to remind me of such, Madame. Though I did nothing more than merely love her."

Erik refused to say her name. It perturbed him Madame Giry had no problem doing so.

"You kidnapped Christine Daaé. You tried to kill her fiancé, the

Vicomte de Chagny."

"I let her go, and I spared his life," Erik rumbled.

He knew the crux of his melancholy and his desire for company tonight. It didn't lay in reprimanding Mother Giry. The conscience that made him spare Anna pounded in his head like a kettle drum. Thinking of her made him wallow in pity over the memory of his lost love.

"Please, Monsieur. I don't know what it is you wish of me tonight, but I beg you. Don't live like anybody else. You simply cannot. What is the point in pining for love unrequited?"

Madame Giry's simple frock and overly robust frame contrasted the wisdom he found behind her words. Erik made a note to give her more credit. Who was he to judge outward appearances?

"There is no point. However, 'clarity of mind means clarity of passion, too; this is why a great and clear mind loves ardently and sees distinctly what it loves': Pasquale." Gloom crept into his voice. "That wretched vicomte with all his aristocratic glory could never love as wholly or as ardently as I."

"The past is done, Monsieur. You've been forgotten. Please don't change that."

"And what makes you think I am trying to change that?" A flick of his wrist indicated the world beyond her cluttered office. "I hate men and the world they walk so freely in." He cut himself short. "No, not hate—envy."

"In that there is such irony," Madame Giry muttered.

Erik coiled a fist to his mouth, unappreciative of her reply. Certainly irony, given there was nothing he couldn't achieve, not a man he couldn't overpower, nothing in this world outside his realm of comprehension or mastery. Men should envy *him*, but they never would. So long as the human race refused to look beyond his face, all the genius and beauty buried in his soul would never matter.

"I never should have told you about those packages," she lamented. "I knew it would stir something in you."

Erik lowered his fist and snapped his head in her direction. "You have no need to worry over my actions, Madame. That meddling child is very much alive. But, be forewarned. I will do what I need to do. I do not require counsel, nor do I need your pity. I have far too much of that already." He hastened to the door and nimbly twisted the key. "Nor will I be imprisoned by sentence not of my doing." He whirled angrily toward her before disappearing. "My box is to remain empty. And rest assured I will take up no more of your company. Erik is, and always will be, dead."

He stared at the notes until they blurred. The same stanza stayed trapped in his head, the same word pounding with every beat.

"Pity, pity, pity!" A violent thrust sent papers flying from the organ. The ink bottle shattered against the stone floor, making a small pool before it seeped away into a crack.

The word pity tangoed with shame. He wallowed in it for so long he wore it like a shadow. Erik tired of their unrelenting duet. He knew what he wanted.

"To live like anybody else." He poked and pulled a stop knob making it pop with a satisfying rhythmic snap, in and out then in again.

"Why is it I cannot have that?" he demanded irritably, aware he spoke to an inanimate object adding to the mark he was irrefutably insane.

How had he allowed his genius to be buried beneath his madness? Remorse consumed his life like a spider glutting on a meal. He didn't even know how to take the simple company of an old woman without getting angry.

Plunking his hand on the keys, he drew a moan from the organ.

Such lack of social skills was not his fault. He'd dismissed humankind long ago. Interaction with man he found unendurable and preferred to stay as far away from others as possible. Or so he tried to convince himself. His genius and solitude, matched with a lifetime of emotional and physical scars from a realm reacting to his face alone, had made him a miserable and unpredictable fellow.

He kicked his organ bench aside and rose, then paced his well-appointed living room. Folding his hands behind his back, he tried not to dwell on the past. The soft nap of the Persian rug beneath his bare feet reminded him of his physical comforts.

There were plenty of luxuries for him to share, excellent wines and teas, not to mention his musical genius. Erik could be gentlemanly. If he could just figure out a way to do so without being so damn morose...

He rubbed his temples. "It would be nice to have occasional companionship." Movement from the corner of his eye caught his attention. "But I do have company!" Clapping his hands together, he folded himself formally before his charge. "What is it you would like? Ribbons, bows, a day at the Tuleries or perhaps a row upon the Seine?" He knelt. "Name what you wish of Erik and any trimming you desire will be yours. I will make you a queen for a day—or a king?" He raised an eyebrow.

The rat didn't respond with its gender or to Erik's offer.

Pacing did nothing to help him forget his indiscretions and

speaking to a rat made him seem ridiculous, so he rose and returned to his organ.

Before he took a seat, he ran his fingers across his bookcase. They poised over a sketch lying on the shelf.

A sad smile lifted his lips. He adored the picture. A simple drawing of a Sunday spent in the park where people of all classes met and mingled; where men locked arms with the women who loved them and their children frolicked at their feet. He caressed each figure, tracing the lines over and over again. Loneliness had worn away the charcoal.

Erik only wanted a taste of that world—to be accepted for himself.

He wanted such love.

Instead he was a faceless man, living by an artificial lake in the lowest cellar of an opera house. Forget about bringing his genius to the world. No one would ever be able to accept him. Music was his only friend. It would never betray him, pity him, or shame him.

It would never fault him his madness.

The spilled ink had all but disappeared. He mindlessly kicked at the broken glass, careful not to shred his bare feet. Until the arrival of these packages, he never questioned his existence. One that just was and had been since investigations into The Phantom of the Opera ended, ever since he published his own death. Yet...he stared into the shards looking for something.

The package, aside from the abhorred figs, was so specific to his music. This Anna had to know of his music, but how? When he sang, he gazed upon no one except his shadow cast upon walls by the flickering candlelight. The music belonged to him alone. It reflected his haunted memories, his profound loneliness, his heartfelt sorrow and his most ardent desires. No one had been near his inner sanctum, of that he made certain.

Erik mastered the art of solitude, forcing a comfort in loneliness, only making human contact when absolutely necessary. Then what drew him to these packages? What aching pecked at him? Why had he spared the girl?

He stooped and picked up the shattered vial, remnants of ink coating his hand. Man wasn't designed to live in solitude and despite what men had made him to be, he remained one of them.

A stranger is reaching out, thinking of you in kindness. It is a random act. Leave it be. Madame Giry's wisdom echoed in his head.

"I will not leave it be," he spoke to the shard.

Someone knew. Someone heard. Someone saw, and didn't run.

Energy surged through him in a strange new way, making his fingers pulse greedily with an unexplored need. He rose and walked to the table by the organ. Taking the brown package into his hands, he ripped the paper off.

It seemed he would need that ink after all.

Chapter Two

If she stared long enough into the flickering flame and relaxed her eyes, it appeared to divide and hover in mid air. Blinking abruptly, Anna pulled the oil lamp closer and attempted to focus on the task at hand.

Polishing opera glasses proved more daunting than anticipated. Such tasks were thrown in her lap so the management could keep her occupied in every way imaginable. The previous night, Anna had scrubbed the already immaculate floor of the Escalier, a task about which she couldn't complain—afterward she'd engaged in a rather lively late night conversation with the rat catcher. Tonight she polished glasses; tomorrow she was to tackle bird excrement on the front steps. Anna leaned forward until her forehead rested against the desk. She thumped her head several times. Even thinking of such a task was hard to endure.

Enough of this.

Anna scooped the opera glasses into a basket, not caring if she chipped the lenses. Why bother polishing them if they were rarely used? One thing the management excelled at was running the theater into the ground. Why would anyone patronize the Opera Garnier? The music was awful and the acting abysmal. Anna turned the key on the lamp, gradually fading the room into black. She shrugged, what did she know of opera anyway?

She glanced at the clock on her way out. The hands pushed past midnight. No wonder she hardly had any friends. Keeping such hours, how could she?

Loneliness compelled her to wander the darkened house. The theater halls were a silent friend when sleep betrayed her. During the day the theater was unfamiliar, filled with wealth and talent. But at night it was a mysterious friend: dark, foreboding—magical.

In her dream-like fog, she roamed the empty stage. How huge it was without the players; how vast when empty of patrons. She marveled at the catwalks above and the maze of ropes that suspended them from the darkened heights. She stared until her vision swam then turned to focus her attention on the trapdoors under her feet.

Engineering genius.

Opera could be intriguing after all.

Erik slumped in his usual seat in Box Five, one finger perched across his lips, the finger of his other hand picking at a brass stud in the velvet arm of the chair. Anna roamed his stage. Her curiosity about the trapdoors amused him. Leaning out of the shadows, he studied her as she crouched to examine the orchestra pit.

How close she'd come in her innocent meddling to meeting his madness at an intimate level. The thought seized his gut. He hated the reproachable necessity that forced him to safeguard his life at the expense of others.

Besides, it seemed improper to kill a woman: The concierge he'd dispatched years ago was more than enough.

He rubbed the mask, trying hard not to allow his thoughts to visit the memory again. How many nights was he going to be tortured? Kidnapping his young music student for companionship was entirely different. Erik had long ago released his feelings for Christine Daaé and her lover. He had no desire to be entwined with the young lovers. But still, the echo of Christine's angelic voice was the tip of a needle pushing the monstrous memories deeper into his mind.

Erik yanked a brass stud free and flicked it toward the stage. He glared at Anna. The girl was humming.

"*Pour l'amour de Dieu*, kill me now." He should have just dispatched her—her voice was awful. Nonetheless, her innocent curiosity fascinated him. He had a nagging urge to know more. Perhaps she enjoyed music?

His finger thumped across his lips. Intriguing idea... The girl's humming was excruciatingly painful. He'd rip his ears off before he ever finished the process of polishing her voice. "No!" Erik's rage that the preposterous idea even seeped into his mind sent the woman below jumping.

"Who's there?" she shouted.

"Damn it all."

Quickly slouching, he watched Anna cross his stage. Shouting was probably not a good idea. Her curiosity turned into a cautious examination of every shadow. The girl looked out of place. The stage belonged to the realm of beauty and elegance, and she was ordinary and curious. The dress she wore, probably at one point a vibrant blue, had long ago faded to a washed-out gray. It resembled the familiar color of the mist that swirled on his lake. She wore no adornments except a kerchief around her neck and an inquisitive expression on her face.

He smiled at the way her long, auburn braid slithered around her back. Quite exotic. That braid was nearly as long as Anna was tall, which wasn't saying much. She was tiny in comparison to most that graced his stage. He huffed. Based on her hair, the shape of her face, and the style of dress, he figured he would claim her as Germanic. Just his luck.

He hated Germans.

Erik summed her up like any healthy man would; surprising himself he was even capable of such thoughts. He may live like an eccentric within the foundation of an opera house and have an inexcusable face, but he was at least in acceptable physical condition. He had his theater to thank.

He contended with six thousand steps, a lake, traps, and a network of ropes and flies on which he was used to twirling himself around. Thinner than most would deem comfortable, Erik was of impressive height, agile and quite surprised his mind still functioned in those more virile ways.

Anna climbed off the stage and lowered herself into the pit. Erik lifted an eyebrow. Wriggling off the end of the stage like a fish on a line caused her dress to inch up. He shot his attention elsewhere lest he see parts of a lady a man should not. The music stands clanged together as she hit the floor, making him wince.

The minx would destroy his blasted theater if left to her own devices.

Abandoning his box, he was in his auditorium in a matter of seconds walking the center aisle. His clothing made barely a ripple of sound. Completely oblivious to him, his target fought to upright the mess she'd made of the music stands. Anna thoroughly enraged him, yet he couldn't help but be entertained. She had the stealth and agility of a cat, but the nerves of the mouse it chased.

Casually maneuvering around the carelessly reorganized pit, she stopped every now and then to fondle a discarded sheet of music. Eventually, she climbed the steps to the Maestro's stand. Erik kept his patience in check as she stood facing the stage. He glared at her in the pit. She seemed quite unaware of her audience.

He indulged in his voyeurism, a smile growing across the face she couldn't see. He was having a delightful time.

Caution was unnecessary. Disrupting the music stands hadn't sent anyone rushing into the theater, so Anna determined she was quite alone. Convinced she was safe from reprimand, she scanned the seats and boxes, before resting on a positively supernatural sight. Something stood in the aisle—a large shadow. But shadows couldn't be cast without light. She squinted. Was it moving? Anna peered at it sideways. It turned.

Two exquisite golden eyes locked on her.

"Holy Mother!"

Anna reeled off the back of the Maestro's stand and tumbled into the pit. She cursed as her elbow collided with the arm of a chair. Stands went clanging in every direction again, sending sheets of music raining around her.

Scrambling to her feet and clutching her bruised elbow, she anxiously searched the theater. Thinking she must be daft, Anna squeezed her eyes tightly closed, then opened them slowly. Two yellow eyes stared back at her.

"Light and shadows. I'm seeing light and shadows and hearing echoes." Anna rubbed her arm and moved out of the pit. She searched the theater for what she swore was a man, but her eyes surely betrayed her. It was late. She needed sleep. "Mere light and shadows."

"Make for excellent illusions, do they not?"

Anna spun so sharply her braid lashed around her waist like a whip. Struck stupid she faced the man who addressed her. Man? With such eyes? Slow knots of apprehension crept around her body, and tied her to her spot.

"Are you hurt?"

She fought against her paralyzed tongue to respond. Manners thrown to the wind, for it was very rude to stare, she looked him over. Anna felt tiny, and not because the tip of her head barely reached his mid chest. The man's physique, his dress, the black, foreboding mask and his eyes all held such power. A mysteriously compelling air swirled around him, yet caution crept up her spine.

"Are you hurt?" he questioned again.

Anna's lips slipped open. The voice carried an alluring seduction that made her bones soften, but at the same time its tonality squeezed her stomach.

She didn't answer and mirrored his circling. By doing so, she engaged him in a bizarre and eloquent dance. Their eyes remained locked. Anna skipped a step as he boldly moved closer, altering the choreography. He lifted a gaunt hand toward her face.

That hand! Him! That lunatic in the cellars was her masked stranger? She followed unusually long fingers beyond his wrist and arm to stare at his smile.

He reached out and snatched a strand of her hair untamed by her braid. Its length slid across his palm.

"Amusing," he observed. "Do I frighten you?"

A silky intoxication poured off that whisper. Warm, gentle pulses seduced every part of her body. Anna wanted to drift away on the lilt of his voice. It held a power and magnitude she couldn't attempt to describe, perched somewhere between all the astonishing beauty of heaven and all the power of hell. Its range and intense timbre made it a perfect instrument and betrayed his elegantly bizarre appearance.

Her breath rushed into her mouth. He stalked her again as if sizing up a most unusual competitor. Keeping her eyes locked on his black kid mask, she answered his question with a quick shake of her head.

"Good." His heady voice drifted directly into her ear sending shivers marching across her body. "There are packages to deliver."

The last sentence knocked any composure Anna had right out of her.

Before she could react, he had evaporated into the darkness. Her blood quickened when the disembodied voice of a master ventriloquist echoed across the vast auditorium.

"Red ink—Anna."

Her name floated on a lonesome beauty, yet she was certain she heard sinister laughter following the mention of it. Sinking into a seat, her mind mimicked the blanket of spring fog that cursed the streets of Paris. She touched her temple.

All she knew was he needed *red* ink—and he knew her name.

Thin streams of afternoon light diminished as Erik moved from the archway toward the depths of the sewer. He found it pathetic to be waiting like a cat expecting to be scratched. Once again the package was not in its usual spot. Erik had checked on multiple occasions over a span of several days, and each time met disappointment. He'd become accustomed to their arrival. He didn't expect his emotions to be so disorganized. Did he just expect that poor girl to go scampering off, gathering provision like she was invited to a Sunday picnic at the Bois?

You pitiful fool. Rejection had become a reliable emotion.

Exhaling loudly, he pulled on his gloves. He moved deeper into the labyrinth, desperate to distance himself from the hustling sounds of the Paris streets above. Waving his hand over a random stone, he set off a chain reaction among the gas torches on the wall. Row after row of torches obeyed his whim and ignited the passageways ahead of him, bathing the corridors in soft, warm light. Darkness disappeared like an invisible lover running from the idea of his embrace.

He stopped. Something was off. The scuffling he heard couldn't be attributed to a rat. How had his labyrinth been penetrated? His mood escalated to a feral rage. Erik quickened his pace, the silk rope he was rarely without already coiled in his hand. In a matter of seconds, he could strangle the interloper.

Rounding the corner slammed him right into the girl.

He swallowed a cry as her face contacted with the wall of his chest. She yelped. Anna stumbled back, her head volleying as she scanned the corridor. He played through his sudden burst of adrenaline, brushing past her and tucking the silk rope out of sight.

Damn fool girl. I could have killed you.

Striding forward until he was several paces away, he finally gained enough presence to face her. He spun so sharply his cloak split the air, the sound ricocheting against the endless amount of stone. He pierced her with his glare.

Now what? Instinct told him to defend his territory, but his mind beat against him. This curious thing actually came down into this Godforsaken pit? She either had to be a fool or one audacious little hoyden.

Who the blazes was she?

It would be unwise to leave her standing in his sewer like a startled deer. Annoyed, Erik shook a finger at her ramrod straight posture.

"If you are just going to stand there, then I suggest you give me my package so I can be on my way." She squared her shoulders and filled her lungs, but didn't relinquish her parcel. "Fine," he said, continuing down the corridor. "You have two choices, Mademoiselle: follow or remain as you are."

Upon hearing her cautious footfalls break into a jog, he pondered whether she'd made the correct decision.

Erik glanced behind. He expected to be met with a cowering, mess of a woman, but each time he turned his eyes locked with Anna's. Her intense stare seemed to record every move he made.

They didn't stop until they came to the shores of his lake. Her jaw dropped like a rock upon seeing the water and swirling mist. Folding his arms across his chest, he watched as she explored with circumspect caution. Not many knew a tributary of the Seine was discovered when the Opera Garnier was built, forcing the creation of the bizarre lake. Anna glanced from whence they came, then to her right and left. Lifting her chin to the ceiling, her mouth puckered into a tiny 'o'.

Erik sneered at her startled revelation as it dawned upon her where her bold arrogance had led. They were meters below ground—not merely in a cellar. He turned away to untie a small boat, jerking the rope so sharply small droplets of water fell at his feet. The girl came a bit too close in her shy approach. Erik shot her a threatening glance, warning her to keep her distance.

There was no going back. He initiated this contact. Now he must plan his next move.

This is irrational. How desperate must he be to risk bringing another into his realm?

"Get in," he snapped.

He didn't move out of her way or assist her into the boat. Within minutes they were rowing across the lake. The plunging oars echoed louder than anything Erik had ever heard.

The farther they rowed from the banks and torches, the deeper they became engulfed in an inky gloom. He chanced a glance at his passenger. She cocked her head at an awkward angle and pulled that intense stare open wider. Erik rowed with powerful strokes, forcing the boat deeper into the embrace of ear-numbing silence. Pushing farther into darkness he stared at Anna's slowly moving lips, pondering if she were cursing herself or him.

Either that or she was muttering a prayer.

When the boat hit the opposite shore, Erik leapt from it, eager for distance. He made his way through the entry of his home, removed his cloak and gloves, and gradually turned to face her.

She climbed out of the boat and stood knee deep in water. They'd moored at a small dock, leading into a drawing room. Baskets upon baskets of flowers gave the place a bit of life. The room overflowed with bouquets, like the ones sold on the Paris streets. Their silk ribbons dangled stupidly from their stems. Erik surveyed it along with her. It actually looked quite ridiculous, for nothing truly alive could thrive in such a place. He lifted a brow at her slack-jawed study of his home. She swayed like a misplaced water lily in an attempt to peer beyond the drawing room. Aggravated, Erik approached. He sloshed into the water and gestured toward his parcel.

"My package, if you please."

Anna looked at the crumpled brown packet and pressed it into his hands. She scowled when he snatched it. Erik held her gaze a bit longer than comfortable. He rushed toward his inner sanctum, noting his guest hastened to follow.

She stopped in her tracks in the middle of his living room. Anna craned her neck to see beyond him. He glanced toward his bedchamber and suppressed a rumble in his throat. The keyboard of his pipe organ, which lined the wall between his chambers and the rest of his home, had her undivided attention. Ignoring her curious expression, he stopped to unwrap her parcel. He first removed the paper, carefully pressed out the creases, and placed it on the stack with the others.

Next, he found the ink. He raised the vial to the candlelight and rolled the liquid around. Carefully, he arranged it into a neat row among countless vials of black ink.

He addressed the figs by flipping the pouch into a pile of similar looking bags.

"This is my home," he abruptly announced. "You are not a prisoner here. You may come and go as you please, provided you can continue to find your way. The routes down here are many and the labyrinths appear to shift. An unfortunate and rather deadly adjustment I made years ago." Ridges plowed across his brow. He darted his head up, down and left to right, mirroring Anna's search for those adjustments. "The lake is the easiest route but rest assured you will not find it again. You may explore what you like, but you will touch nothing. Do you understand?"

She nodded.

"Good. You may ask what questions of me you like within reason, and I will determine if they are worth answering. One final rule. You will speak of this to no one. Is that understood?"

His voice cracked like thunder. He watched her take a deep breath and nod again. Turning from her, he took a seat at his organ. Resting his chin in his hand, he silently brooded over the situation. Anna's voice broke the silence.

"I have a question."

"And what might that be?" His hand muffled his voice. He didn't bother to turn and address her like a proper gentleman should.

"What is your name?"

Erik gasped. When was he last asked that? He scanned the worn manuals, hunching deeply over them before lifting his head to study the ceiling.

"Erik," he quietly replied, his name sticking like a knife in his throat.

Their eyes met. A few moments of judgment passed between them before Anna turned her back and headed down the closest corridor.

It would figure she dare not stay. Though he pondered following her, the thought disappeared as quickly as it came. She chose wisely and would find her way back to the theater. With dozens of ways into his underworld, he had to trust she was clever enough to figure them out and smart enough not to breathe a word about them to anyone. His concern lay not in if Anna would want to find her way back to the theater, but if she would find her way back to him.

What would he do if she did?

Chapter Three

The interior of his home glowed in a warm bath of candlelight, its essence tranquil and inviting. Erik perched cross-legged on a small divan, re-stringing a violin. He swayed, leaning in and out of invisible notes as if they passed through his body with an exquisite possession. Moving to the music in his mind served to calm his unsettled thoughts.

It had been days since he gave that girl the key to his kingdom. Nightly he waited to see if she'd return, but was always met with detestable silence. The music he composed served as the only barrier keeping him from total insanity. He moved with passion to a partnerless dance. Everything in his mind orchestrated precisely to the solos he was destined to perform. Everything, except for the tiny footfalls that brought his music to a screeching halt.

He whipped his head to where Anna had entered. His sharp movement pinned his intruder to her spot. Their eyes locked—predator and prey engaging in a final congress.

Erik laid the violin down. Stroking its veneered surface as though it were a precious child, he rose. So she had returned? On her own, coming to him without any provocation, a willing participant to whatever composition would be written.

He suspected Anna would not be all that eager. The fact she returned amused him and sent an odd quiver through his stomach. *This* sensation confounded him and overwhelming unease drilled those shivers into his core.

"Why did you return?" he barked.

Anna didn't reply with words. Reaching into the folds of her dress, she produced a tiny bundle. She held it out to him. Sneering in disgust, he snatched it.

Figs.

A sweeter odor seeped from the package. Erik held the bag to his mask, drinking in the aroma. He peered at her sideways. Anna remained silent. Curious, he opened the parcel. The rich scent of strawberry spiraled out of the bag and filled the air. He grabbed one of the ruby gems like a greedy child plucking a toy from its box.

"You don't like figs." Anna pointed toward the discarded bundles of fruit near the table.

Erik nodded—struck silent. He marveled at her defensive posture: arms folded smugly across her chest, chin jutting up, and her head tipped as far back as possible. The girl glowered. Erik circled. Looming over her petite frame, he was utterly baffled by her seemingly unflappable demeanor. Anna stared up at his mask and scowled deeply. He stopped his inspection. A proper gentleman would have thanked her by now.

Erik was, however, not exactly proper.

He unfurled his fingers, and extended one hand to her, the other gesturing with his prize toward his home. Bowing, he bid her welcome in a voice as rich as warm honey.

"Mademoiselle, *Vous êtes bienvenu.*"

How was it that a glimmer of companionship—however obscure—could give life new direction? Anna seemed comfortable in the labyrinth, and content with the hesitant bonds of friendship building between them.

Erik was not content. Anna had been arriving nightly for weeks, serving as a source of inquisitive entertainment. She usually did nothing more than quietly sit on his divan sewing or knitting something for the world above. When they spoke, it mostly focused on common subjects—rarely about music. Never had she questioned his existence beneath the opera house, and not once had she mentioned the mask. This stupefied him. All his life he'd been pursued by unrelenting inquiries as to who he was, where he'd come from, and why such a creature was allowed to live.

Erik swirled the Tokay around his glass, watching the reddish-brown tide ebb and roll. A connoisseur of fine wines, he rarely drank. It was bad for his vocal chords and he found drink tended to make men stupid. Erik didn't take kindly to stupidity. This particular evening he felt the need to indulge. Slumping in his chair, he studied Anna. The way her hand wove in and out of her stitching was hypnotic.

Or was it the wine?

Erik took another sip and gestured broadly about his cavernous home.

"Why do you not run, Anna?"

He caught her completely off guard. Her sewing fell into her lap and she lifted an eyebrow.

"That is an odd subject for the evening, Erik."

He jabbed an accusing finger at her. "You come here night by night asking nothing of me. Why?"

"You invited me. You said I could come and go as I pleased. Are you now rescinding that invitation?"

She seemed insulted. *What reason did she have to be offended?* He was aghast at the way Anna assumed she could make herself comfortable. To make matters worse, that blasted flutter in his core kept him awake at night.

He stared at her through the wine. The glass distorted her face making it look discolored and deformed. He found wry humor in that.

"You should be afraid," he mumbled sullenly.

"Of you?" Her head snapped back as if slapped. "Surely, you've had too much to drink. Erik, you may be peculiar, even eccentric, but I rather enjoy that about you. You always seem perched on the edge of some sort of thought or emotion." She resumed her stitching.

Erik stood, knocking his chair aside. The glass soared angrily through the air. Shattered crystal echoed like an explosion, raining shards and wine in every direction. The wall bled red.

"Yes!" he shouted, a dangerous undercurrent in his clipped tones. "You should be afraid, yet you do not run. You keep coming back! You know nothing of me. Why, Anna? Why do you keep returning? Why do you not run?"

He lunged across the room, driven by the questions pounding in his head and the aftereffects of too much wine. Erik reached the divan and fell awkwardly onto the seat beside her.

"You sit next to a demon, Anna. Erik has burned in hell so many times he no longer feels the pain. Why are you here?"

Anna leaned away. "*Erik* has burned in hell? That is a rather bizarre and detached means of referring to one's person."

"Answer me!"

"I like it down here. I thought *we* enjoyed the companionship."

He pounded his fists into the divan like a frustrated child. "No! That is not the answer."

She leapt to her feet. He watched with smoldering impatience, then possessive greed, as Anna approached his organ. She purposefully placed herself at the bench. The instrument was forbidden to her, yet there she sat in outright defiance. He took a deep breath and let it hiss out through clenched teeth, but didn't protest. Erik regained his composure, and although drunk and angered at Anna's chosen perch, the melodic timbre returned to his voice.

"You are unlike the others I have dared call friend."

He drew out the last word with supreme caution and gestured impatiently when Anna reeled back. Was he not allowed to use such terms, sarcastic tones or not? Her reaction pulled him back to that vat of pooling bitterness he held toward the human race.

"You do not need to know about me, child, but I need to know something about you." He leaned across the divan and pointed at her, emphasizing each word with a stab of his finger. "Why...are...you...at... my...opera...house?"

Anna looked around his home, obviously uncomfortable, but not intimidated. "Everyone has a story, Erik. Why are you asking for mine now, in this state?"

He stared at her insubordination, his face heated by drink. He ignored the quiver to her voice.

"You want to know? Then you shall know and judge as you may. I'm a pawn, Erik, a human piece in my father's twisted games of manipulation and deceit. I've spent my life being shuffled from place to place as payment for my family's indiscretions." Her voice turned to ice. "I wasn't a wanted child, rather a drunken mistake. My parents were forced to marry into a loveless relationship because of me, and I became the object of their bitterness and resentment. My mother tried to be kind; she at least acknowledged my existence wasn't my fault. But my father saw in me everything wrong in his life. He's a liar, a thief, a compulsive gambler, a con artist, and a drunk."

The words hung on Erik given his current state. He dismissed them with a thrust of his hands.

She continued: "Any living my family made was gambled away by him. If a con went bad, or the debt exceeded what money we had—he used me. Men, he learned, viewed me as an acceptable form of payment. Collectors would readily accept a young girl in exchange for a purse. My mother died when I was young. I wish I had."

"You know nothing of wishing for death," Erik rumbled with angry despair. Such dismissal of her emotions lit her temper.

"I learned many trades in my years of servitude to his debts—a blacksmith, a cobbler, a seamstress, a thief, a liar, and a whore."

Erik slumped back in the divan and wiped his lips with the back of his hand. He looked away in revulsion, unwilling to meet her eyes.

"When I was sixteen, I ran as far away as I could get. I found myself in Paris at the faubourg Saint-Antoine. It seems I'm the perfect fit with the vagabonds and thieves of the Cours de Miracles. It may be the filthiest and poorest of neighborhoods, but there I saw many others whose lives were far worse than mine. They took me in. I repaid those who cared enough to look beyond thieving and begging by teaching them the trades I knew. Two years ago, my father found me. He was in debt deeper than he'd ever been—to Laroque and Wischard, this opera's management. My father tried to control me, but I was too old for his whip and too wise for his manipulations."

"Then why are you here?" Erik said flatly. He sat straighter now that the full impact of her story had sunk in.

"In my absence, he remarried and had a little girl. He threatened if I didn't do as he demanded, he'd force that little girl to do so. He'd impose upon her the horrors he did me. I do this to save her. I thought about leaving many times, but the managers are always threatening to contact him if I act out, using the fate of a sister I have never even met to keep me chained." Anna's voice trailed off. "Sometimes I wonder if those chains are even real. But it's not worth scarring the innocence of a child to find out. I can carry on. This is a burden I know how to bear."

"Where is this man now?"

Anna shrugged. "When we made the exchange I told him I never wanted to see him again. My family lies in the streets of Paris. My obligations are to them. I only worry for the child." Anna rushed to the divan and snatched her things. "You ask why I don't fear you, and why I don't run. I see nothing in you to fear. If you have a story you feel will do so, then tell it, but I'll not ask you for it. I have nothing to fear of the past, yours or mine. What's done is done. I'm through running. I too have burned in the far reaches of hell. You're an ignorant man to think you hold that distinction on your own."

Anna started toward the corridor that would lead her to the dormitories. However, even in his drunken state, his reflexes were swifter than hers. He blocked her path. Harshly slapping a hand on her shoulder, he forced her back onto the organ bench.

"Sit."

A storm brewed that would be too swift for either of them to stop.

Despite knowing the wine had made him unrecognizable to her, Erik found a fresh glass and continued to pour himself a drink. He chuckled morosely and tilted his mask to the ceiling. Exhaustion leached into his voice.

"My story? I am a murderer. A murderer and a Maestro, a magician and a mastermind. There is nothing in this world I have not mastered, nothing unattainable beyond my grasp. I am a wealthy, powerful genius, with the voice of an angel and the soul of a madman..."

Chapter Four

Anna awoke with a sudden jolt of her arms and legs, not fully knowing her whereabouts. She blinked the blurriness out of her eyes. It took a few minutes to recognize the house on the lake. Groaning, Anna wrestled with her stiff limbs. The wool blanket entangling her legs pooled on the floor. She stared dully at it.

Erik.

Memories of the previous night spun in her mind. He'd told her everything. The kind token of a warm blanket and the respect he paid her through the night sharply contrasted the stories he wove for her.

Now, he was nowhere to be found. She set aside her apprehensions—for she thought it foolish to be so judgmental—and draping the blanket over her arm, she cautiously walked past the organ to the chamber beyond.

She never dared previously to approach the room. By the way Erik fiercely guarded it, she'd learned to never cross the threshold. If she were a cat, she would be dead already from her insatiable curiosity. Having it amplified by the stories he wove, spurred her on. She hesitated before poking in her head.

When she did, she dropped the blanket and with it her composure.

Erik's bedchamber was morbidly dark. Black cloth hung from the walls, and an unfamiliar stave of music repeated across them. The coffin centered in the room was her undoing. She was helpless in preventing her mouth from unhinging and fell victim to the goose bumps that made the hair on her neck stand on end. It took a few moments for the image to sink in before Anna found herself staring at Erik.

He sat below a canopy of red brocade fabric on the edge of a small platform, his back to the offending box. Barefooted, his cravat discarded and his collar unbuttoned, he leaned forward with his elbows on his knees and his head in his hands, shielding his face from her view.

Erik nursed a hangover.

The mask lay on the bedside table. She tore her gaze away from him and his coffin and stared intently at it. It had been casually tossed aside as if it were a perfectly normal piece of clothing.

"Erik?" she softly called.

He stiffened and swung his back to her, his hands crushing into his face. Anna regretted her sudden intrusion upon his privacy and hung her head. Judging his idiosyncrasies was wrong of her. He was a product of his past, just as she was hers.

Refusing to turn around, he snatched his mask from the table. When it replaced his dignity, the transformation was both majestic and alarming.

"Mademoiselle." He flicked her toward the other room, refastening his collar and fumbling with the crumpled silk of his cravat. "I do not wish you to be in here."

Shaking her head, Anna stabbed the air pointing at the coffin. "What...who...why?"

Erik sighed and pinched the bridge of the false nose on his mask. "Yes, I sleep in a coffin." He gave the offending box a dismissive flip of his hand, ignoring her quizzical stance, and brushed past her to the main chamber. He flatly pointed backward to the stave of the Dies Irae. "One must prepare for eternity."

His current state made him unable to utter a protest when Anna picked up the blanket and rushed in the opposite direction into his bedchamber. She glanced warily at his face. Erik squeezed his temple and mask as she laid the blanket on a far divan. She recalled he made a point of omitting what lay beneath his mask, and she dared not ask. Giving wide berth to his coffin, she returned to the other room with him.

"Come. I will make tea before I go."

Barely nodding his thanks, he rubbed at his temple. Anna lifted her eyes every so often to study him. He'd folded his arms across his chest and leaned against the wall watching as she lit a small samovar. Fishing around a small basket of pinecones set near the urn, she added a few to the charcoal then lit it with one of the scraps of birch bark rolled in a tin nearby.

"Are you wondering if I will rummage around your life like I do your tea tray?" Anna grinned, mocking the tension she saw coiled around him. "The fact I even know the proper way to brew tea in a samovar should prove to you many of your assumptions of me are wrong."

He jerked off the wall, flinching as if stung. If she could see his face, Anna would have been certain his brow furrowed.

"The past is the past Erik," she announced, wiping clean a cup and handing it to him. "I did not know the man you spoke of last night, so I cannot condemn him. I would like to continue to know you if you would help me understand the man now." She nodded toward his room and her abrupt discovery of his morbid side.

Erik took the cup. He looked at it first before inching his gold eyes from the china to her face. Anna smiled as he turned his head away.

She gathered her things and scampered off to begin her day, leaving Erik to finish brewing his tea. Anna looked back to see him push off the wall and head to his black bedchamber. The teacup shattered against the floor as he tossed it aside. She pushed the air from her mouth in protest, when Erik abruptly stopped. Not acknowledging whether he knew she was still there, he slowly knelt. Taking a piece of the broken cup between two long fingers, he twisted it in the wedge of candlelight. The corner of her eyes pinched as she covertly studied him. Rising to his full height, the omniscient air he left behind him feathered against her skin as he palmed the china into his hand and walked into the open arms of darkness.

Wet spring faded into summer. Life in the opera house mimicked life on the Paris streets. The halls buzzed with activities and the dormitories filled to capacity with talent, old and new. Rehearsals were loud and lively events, an energetic rivalry of sound between the orchestra and the chorus. The opera preened and prepped for the upcoming season in a flurry of activity.

Erik made certain the opera wove its spell across Anna. He enlightened her to the music and allowed the magic to work its charms.

Months had passed since their confrontation. After that night, he entirely opened his realm to her. He broke down the walls of his guarded demeanor to enjoy her presence. They took company together for minutes to hours. One moment her fiery attitude made her an excited little bee around him, but the next had her wearing caution.

He leaned against the strings. Alone in his thoughts, playing his tiny lady, his body wove in and out of the images in his mind. He coaxed an intoxicating, beautiful voice from his violin. He paused mid-sway when he saw Anna arrive and slump against the far wall. She was late. Erik resumed playing, sending rich notes to wrap around her. Rocking slightly, she kept in time with the rising and falling song of an unseen bird.

She slid a strand of hair from her face. Her fingers crossed the ridges in her brow when she did. Usually, Erik stopped playing when she arrived and often scolded her for sneaking up on him. This time he didn't fiercely guard his music, but greeted her with a smile and played on.

Anna's wrinkles deepened. So it would be caution she would wear tonight?

Erik leaned into his music, painting a vivid picture on the air. The sounds he created were sheer seduction.

Her brow had smoothed, and her back arched as if each note and chord embraced her in warmth. Every move Erik made was hypnotic poetry. He allowed her to discover the two sides of him: a mysterious, dark man with an unsettled, deeply disturbed mind and a sensual, inquisitive gentleman hidden just below the surface of closely guarded emotions.

The music seemingly lured her into a trancelike calm.

He didn't mind the silence. The notes lulled his demons asleep. He lowered his violin and paused to weigh his options. Music only calmed the noise in his mind. Anna silenced it altogether.

Like a flash of lightning, he made his decision.

In a move dripping with well-practiced allure, he curled one finger at a time into his palm, inviting Anna to join him. His lips parted at the sight of the color across her face. She lifted her hands to her cheeks. *Why did she hide that blush?*

Anna began to speak, but he placed a finger upon her lips. She stiffened at his unexpected contact.

"Erik?"

"Shh."

Setting the bow and violin aside, he placed a hand under her chin, lifting it.

"What are you doing?" she asked.

"Shh," he commanded again, walking behind her. Determination focused his movements. Lightly, he moved fingers back and forth across her shoulders then down her arms. His primary objective was to place her in the perfect position. His hands progressed down below her ribs pushing a gasp of surprise from her lips. Before she could dart away, he pressed slightly on her lower back causing her spine to straighten. The inappropriate contact made her jolt, but Erik's resolve didn't waver. A glance to her face confirmed the pink on her cheeks had bloomed to an all-out crimson. Easing his hands slowly up her bodice to her arms, he reached and readjusted the chin she kept moving. His focus was absolute.

Sliding her braid from the drape over her shoulder, he smoothed it down her back. He moved to stand closely behind her, hesitantly pressing his body against hers. He'd never come so near her at such an intimate level. Her shudder rippled against his chest. The schoolgirl nerves made him smile. Turning her head, she gave him a quizzical look, one eyebrow raised, her bottom lip jutting out in a pout he found rather appealing. Nevertheless, he once more forced her chin back into position.

He reached for his violin and bow, then around her waist. With the violin in front of her, its back to her chest, he lifted her left arm. The dress sleeve slipped aside, allowing his fingers to slide up her exposed flesh. He pressed the violin into her arms, forcing her to hug it tightly. In his eyes, there was no more intimate way to know the instrument than to feel its every curve pressed firmly against the body. Leisurely, he removed his violin from her embrace and tucked it under her chin. Anna tried to step aside, but he caged her in his grip.

"No, Erik, this is daft."

"Shh," he softly said into her ear, waiting patiently for her to stop fidgeting.

Placing the bow in her other hand and positioning her fingers correctly, Erik wove his hand around hers. He guided her fingers in harmony with his along the delicate neck of the instrument. He lifted her hand, touching the bow to the bridge, and coaxed music from the strings.

Shallow breaths fell from her lips, while his stayed calm and focused. The flush on her cheeks warmed her face. Erik felt the heat, though his mask remained cold and artificial against her forehead.

When her breath caught in a sigh, a smile grew across his face. He tossed his head back as they played. For the first time, the noise in his tormented mind faded. He heard nothing but music.

Blissful, intoxicating music.

Erik swayed as notes floated across the labyrinth. An unearthly beauty embraced them as he whispered the words he knew Anna had been waiting to hear.

And the words he never imagined any moment would demand.

"To understand me, is to understand music..."

Cloaking himself in his finest eveningwear and blackest garb, Erik accompanied Anna on her rounds. She learned to ignore the way he tugged on the brim of his hat in order to fade his mask deeper into shadow. They rarely chanced a walk in the Tuileries together, let alone the streets beyond, but when they did, it was with the utmost caution.

It annoyed her.

"The people you help do not even notice me, Anna. How can they ignore the mask?"

She let her breath out on a heavy sigh as she reminded him. "The desolate pay no mind to difference, Erik, only indifference."

Their evening walk ended at a silent opera house. They calmly fell in step together, moving like the air itself. Each absorbed in their own world.

"Anna?"

She turned to Madame Giry. Erik immediately vanished into a shadow.

"It's very late, have you been out?"

Anna groaned in Erik's direction, wishing for the thousandth time he would not hide. "Good evening, Madame Giry," she greeted. "I hope I didn't startle you."

"Not at all, but you should not be out at this hour."

"With all due respect, Madame Giry," she indignantly replied. "I'm not a student of this opera. I may do as I please."

"I understand, Anna, but I have sound reason for being protective of those beneath the Garnier's roof." The plump concierge folded her arms in a comical attempt to make her look as formidable as possible. Her stance increased Anna's impatience. "Though I may be just an old concierge, I see all the employees in my opera as my responsibility."

"Your opera, Madame?" Erik artfully twirled into view to stand beside Anna. "I assure you Mother Giry, the Mademoiselle is perfectly capable of tending to her own needs."

Mother Giry? Erik knew her? Anna's face puckered in confusion.

"Monsieur, what have you done?" Madame Giry asked.

Madame Giry knew him? Erik clearly hadn't told her everything.

"Done? Why I have done nothing. Please, you act like a frightened rabbit. It is not becoming on a woman your age."

Anna stammered nonsensically. How dare he treat her that way. Anna refused to budge when Erik took her elbow in an attempt to lead her away.

"I'll not have this Monsieur, not again," Madame Giry begged. "Please."

Indignation seemed the music that charmed a viper from its basket. Erik released Anna and spun in disgust toward Madame Giry.

"You will not have this?" He took one well-placed stride in her direction. "You are a feeble-minded box keeper, Madame. Need I remind you, it is not your place to tell me what I can and cannot have?" Erik snatched Anna's elbow again. "Come, Anna, we must be going."

She clawed at his fingers and wrestled for her arm. Prying free, she straightened her sleeve and glared at him.

"What's going on? Erik, do you know this woman?" Turning toward Madame Giry, she bid with a thrust of her arm toward him. "You know of him, how?"

"You will tell her nothing," he snarled. Madame Giry snatched at her ears. Erik's voice had shifted like an angry wind. It had taken on a fantastic quality—a godlike resonance delivered on a gentle whisper. "Anna, come to me."

"No!" Madame Giry rubbed furiously at her lobes. "This will not begin again, please." She reached for Anna's hand and held on tightly.

"Child, now!" Erik's tone dripped with authority.

Anna touched her hand to her ear to silence the odd echo of Erik's voice. Her fingers slid down her cheeks. Whatever tricks he played with his voice, they wouldn't work on her.

"No," Anna said severely, breaking free from Madame Giry's grasp. She marched up to Erik, planted herself head to chest with him, and tilted her neck back to look him directly in the eye.

"You lied to me Erik. You know how I despise that. You told me no one knew you lived below this theater. *You lied*!"

Erik's hands flexed and curled, his thin lips twitched. "We will not discuss this here. You are mine and you will come with me now."

Anna looked at him in utter disgust. "I am *yours*? Spare me your anger, Erik, it's *my* turn." Fury snaked off her tongue with one word of contempt. "Leave."

She stood her ground as Erik's stare darted between the two women. Her stance directly contrasted Madame Giry's shrinking form. He pointed at the old woman, directing his annoyance where it had obvious impact.

"You will tell her nothing." He punctuated the warning with a swirl of his cloak and evaporated into the shadows.

Neither woman spoke. When Anna had calmed enough, she approached Madame Giry.

"Whatever trance he has cast over you, you must break it. He's a very dangerous man," the box keeper blurted.

"Dangerous?" Anna scoffed at the ridiculous accusation. "Please, Madame Giry. Erik is not dangerous." What nonsense. She rubbed at her throbbing temples.

"Anna, listen to me. Please understand. I've spent years serving that man. You don't know with whom you are dealing."

Anna thrust her hands up in the air in a gesture of indignation. "In all the years I've been at this opera house, you've never sent such concern my way. Spare me it now."

"You don't understand him. You don't know who he is. You don't know his past. This is my fault." She wrung her stubby hands together. "I told him about you and after all these years, he's still a madman."

"His past?" Anna said flatly. "What of his past, Madame? That he's a fugitive? A murderer?" Madame Giry's face plastered with a wide-eyed look of horror. Anna gestured angrily toward whatever random shadow Erik had disappeared into. "I know all about his past."

"Anna, please! I will not have this happen again."

"Have *what* happen again?"

"I don't want to tell you for I dread what might happen for betraying the Opera Ghost's trust. But I can keep silent no longer. Not if he is going to entrap another in his twisted web."

Anna barely knew this woman, but she had an uneasy feeling their lives were about to be irreversibly entwined. Her heart raced to the floor as Madame Giry took a breath, and asked, "What has he told you of The Phantom of the Opera?"

Was it morning? Did he even care?

In the past such fury would have easily transpired into murder, but Erik made a point of staying deep underground. Every pound of his feet against the stone, each splash his boots made in the puddles matched a savage rhythm in his mind. He hadn't wanted Anna to learn of the secrets Madame Giry kept. Punching the air, Erik shouted nonsensically. How arrogant he was to step from that shadow.

What a damn fool.

His fist pounded against his thigh. Madame Giry only thought about *her* needs. Like everyone else. People like that exposed his fragile scar tissue to the world—and clamped the manacles that came with his prison tighter around his wrists.

Attempting to convince himself he didn't need companionship, be it Anna or the vagrants he stepped over in the streets, was useless. Something inside twisted with longing when he thought of her. His gut flipped, making him skip a step. His fists tightened until they drained of blood.

Rounding the corner into his drawing room, he stopped short. His fists sprung open upon seeing her. He straightened his hunched posture and tugged on the sleeves of his jacket. Folding his hands in front of him, he met Anna's smoldering gaze.

Her chest heaved. The corners of her eyes were lit with small, angry lines. Her hands strangled the fabric of her dress. Leaping from his organ bench, she toppled it with enough force to send it skidding across the room.

"How dare you!" she shouted.

The bench slid to a stop, coming precariously close to slamming into the far wall. Erik removed his cloak and gloves and laid them neatly over a chair, arrogantly ignoring the formidable opponent in his living room. He walked to his bench, dusted it with his hand and righted it.

"I have nothing to say to you, Mademoiselle, so you might as well leave."

Anna stomped over, her face alive with distrust.

"You lied!" She reeled her hand backward.

Before her slap contacted with his leather encased cheek, Erik dodged, catching her fist. The wrist bent backward with one fluid snap of his hand. Twisting Anna to kneel before him, he felt her bone crumble under his grip. His eyes narrowed with his coursing adrenaline.

Anna's knees collided with the cold stone. Her lips opened in a silent wail. The pain arched her back.

Erik felt her tremble.

Horrified, he released her wrist like dropping a handful of fire. He stumbled backward, watching in sickened disconcert as she hid her head in her knees. The move seemed far too habitual. He lifted his hands to his mouth. They shook against his lips. Her back curved and her forehead met the stone beneath his feet. The world collapsed around him.

"*Mon Dieu.*" His knees slammed to the floor, but he did not feel the pain. Like water to a boil, the horror of his action swelled to the surface. "Anna, look at me." She did, cradling her wrist as her eyes glistened with tears. A cry of remorse strangled in his throat.

"*Le fantôme*?" Her question pierced the armor around his heart.

Erik rolled off his knees and sat before her, hanging his head and entwining his hands around his neck. "No, Mademoiselle, no! Forgive me. Please forgive me. I am not that man." He blanketed his face with his hands, thankful for a change he had a mask to hide behind. "I did not want you to know. Not this way."

Trembling fingers parted enough to see her wipe her eyes with the back of her mobile hand. Her other wrist hung limply in her lap.

"I don't care about that man, Erik. I cannot judge you or anyone by their past. Who am I to do that?" Erik shrunk as her reprimand flogged him repeatedly. "I know the man *now*. I accepted *him*. Why did you lie to me?"

He stood to avoid her piercing look. Frantic circles carved around Anna as he tried to compose himself, but it was of no avail. Noise and music were clashing in his mind to create a cacophony of discord.

"Because of this!" He shoved a finger in his face. "To protect you from this!" Falling before her, he clawed at his mask. His knees ground against the stone as he crawled toward her. A great cry of grief escaped his lips. "What did she tell you, Anna? Did she tell you I am made up of Death? That my wretched mother would not allow me to kiss or touch her? That my father never saw me, and my mother made me the present of my first mask so not to look on me? Did she tell you my cursed ugliness has condemned me to wallow in madness?" He clutched his face "Every waking minute I exist, I fight him." He ground out the words. "*Le fantôme.*"

Erik's agonizing laughter made her jump. He reached for her when she started, but let his hands fall against the stone floor. He tried to grip it instead. It was cold, hard—unfeeling, like man made him.

"I try! Oh yes, I try to be like other men! All I want is to be a normal man. When I did try to have what other men have, I was left behind. I was condemned. I was forgotten!" He erased the memory by swiping the ground between them. "I could have hurt an unheard of number of the human race when she refused me." Erik's breath left his lungs. He stiffened when the impact of his actions slammed against his chest. His face twisted at the sickened look upon Anna's. "You are surprised Erik could have a woman? I did you know—Christine belonged to me." Taking hold of the pinky of his left hand, he caressed the small gold band that circled it. "She was to be my bride. She once wore my ring. But no! She lied!"

Maniacal laughter tore from his lips.

"A simple request, you see. All she had to do was accept my proposal, and I would not blow a quarter of Paris sky high. I would not kill that blasted vicomte lover of hers. Are you looking at me, Mademoiselle? Are you looking? Consent to be wed and no one would be dead."

"You would be wed?" Anna stammered.

"Wed or dead."

Anna jerked backward as Erik leaned into her. He laughed and teetered in his spot, overcome with dementia. "Do you have any idea how close my madness came to destroying an ungodly number of people?" When she didn't respond, Erik came eerily in command of all his senses. "You grow pale? Why? I could have made all of Paris hop like a grasshopper by lighting the powder kegs stored beneath this opera house. Remnants of the war, you know. But I did not. I did not hurt any more people. I wanted her to marry that boy. I wanted her to be happy—in the end. But such noble intentions do not matter in a life such as mine. I am thrust into an abyss of loathsome hatred and denial when all I want is to love and taste life like a normal man." He angrily clawed at his temples. "Madness—in here—madness condemns me to Don Giovanni's fate. Yet unlike he, I repent...yes, Erik can repent. But the Commendatore still sentences me to burn with Hades!" The heat of that inferno panted out his lips. "Is that warranted? Can my lusts make me like anybody? Does that make me normal?"

He searched the cooling blue depths of Anna's eyes for some sign he wasn't completely insane.

"Can a man like me ever be normal? Behind this there is no beauty." Erik gestured to his face.

Maddening silence closed around him like a lid on a coffin.

Anna struggled to her feet. She looked directly into his mask—the one subject never discussed. She leaned sideways, gripping her wrist and curling into the pain he'd caused. Erik winced as remorse folded him in two. Her tongue stumbled over her teeth.

"Beauty? Normal? Do normal men carry their height like you? Move with such authority? Do you hear what I do? Your voice—your indescribably seraphic voice? Do you even know your pure and utter genius?"

"What do they matter? Madame Giry told you what lies beneath the mask. I can see in your eyes you had to search for those words."

She stared at his mask. The raw intensity of her gaze made him pray to retain his one small scrap of self-esteem. He lowered his head and buried his face in the crook of his arm.

"Please," he said in quiet agony, "do not rape my dignity. Do not ask me to remove it."

When Anna spoke, his shoulders lifted as if Atlas were relieved of his burden.

"The mask does not make the man, Erik. You are not sentenced to be the Phantom because of it."

He remained caged by his arm as his breath left his lungs. The sigh only warmed his flesh for a moment before the cold sensation returned to his skin.

"Are they not one and the same?" He stared at his bent and warped reflection in the distant organ pipes.

"Madame Giry mentioned the investigations closed long ago. The authorities were unable to prove any man existed. You are the one chasing a Phantom."

"Am I?" he challenged, lifting a heavy arm and gesturing around him. "Tell me then, why does she fear this ghost so deeply if his life is nothing more than myth?"

Her brow crinkled. "She fears you because she has known no other man. We know two very different Eriks."

His lids lowered. He'd been battling the monster and the man for too long. "I cannot keep up with their duet."

"Then choose one and play it out."

He looked at her for a long moment before turning away. "And the others who know? Are you so sure they will ignore the past and accept it as you do? My crimes cannot be denied."

"Christine?" she consoled, her sympathy contorting Erik's body. Knots tied in his stomach, his neck tightened with the memory of her rejection. He nodded, sadly moaning her name.

"Christine Daaé, Anna. The Vicomtess de Chagny..."

The name tasted bitter. Not wanting to continue, he carried the bench back to the organ and sat. Erik stared sadly at the worn manuals and the dull stops—testimony to many nights pounding out his supreme loneliness through music. Anna followed and sat beside him. The heat of her body hovered over the organ, cloaking it with warmth. Erik lightly touched a key. It was cold beneath his fingers.

"Do you still love her?" she asked quietly.

"No." His voice lifted in pitch, betraying him.

"I am your friend, Erik. Do not lie to me."

He chose not to answer. Silence settled between them before he hesitantly reached to take her hand. Anna winced and he pulled away. The action crippled him and his eyes dipped shut for a brief moment. Never hearing a drop of music again, being sentenced to the worst hell on earth...would be better than bearing the agony of what he'd done to her.

"Forgive me, Anna."

Her eyes showed kindness, reflecting that one terrible act was already in the past. Reading between the lines of emotion on her face, Erik recalled her stories of abuse that made her injury seem inconsequential. Carefully, Erik reached for her again, grimacing when Anna bit her lip.

"Oh, Anna," he grieved, "I broke it."

"I am aware." Anna laughed and sniffed away her tears.

"I fail to see the humor in this."

He would have to hurt her further in order to set the bone. He closed his eyes and took a long shuddering breath. The injury could have been much worse than a broken wrist.

Studying her hand, he hid his unease in his downtrodden stare. Erik yanked his head away when Anna reached for him. She caught his chin. The sensation of a strange pair of hands on his mask made him rigid with unexplored emotions. His eyes widened from the contact, but relaxed as the warmth of her hand seeped through.

"Will I play again, Monsieur?" A playful glint returned to her eyes.

His breath leapt from his mouth. Despite his anguish he laughed—a sound that was pure music.

"Anna," he gently insulted, "you are a terrible violinist."

Chapter Five

The brougham clipped along at a steady pace, the horses' hooves drumming a cheerful rhythm matching Raoul's mood.

On many levels it was good to be back in France. Native soil beckoned to a noble son. Shaking his head the vicomte scolded himself for leaving. Though he enjoyed simpler delights of his Norwegian estate, a nobleman's place was with his fatherland. Staring at the invitation in his hand he pondered if it had become habitual of him to stay away.

They didn't have much to do with the city he'd adored as a boy. He hid his disapproval by rubbing a finger across his small, blond moustache. Christine had stopped performing for the Garnier after her abduction by the Phantom of the Opera. Whisking her away from all her troubles, Raoul divided their time between their stately home in Norway and their estate in France. Judging by Christine's pout, he could tell she wished they hadn't cut their northern visit so short.

Quietly laughing, he dismissed the thought.

He admired the lean muscle of the champion stallion trotting alongside his brougham. What jealous rumblings would spring from the lips of his peers when he partook in a hunt astride that beast! The mounted groom gave a tip of his hat, seeking approval to break from the caravan and head to the stables. Raoul granted it with a curt wave of his hand.

His gaze went from the horse to the building beyond. He no longer laughed. As the brougham whisked past the theater, he could have sworn people stopped and pointed at the crest adorning his carriage. He hoped it was his imagination.

Raoul, Vicomte de Chagny gazed out the window toward the Acadèmie Nationale, still as majestic as when he'd left it as a stoic keeper of many secrets.

He glanced at his pocket watch. Nine o'clock. They would have plenty of time to relax at the hôtél de Chagny in the faubourg Saint-Germain before their afternoon meeting with the managers.

Tucking his watch away, he looked at the woman seated across from him. Just the sight of her made his heart squeeze and his body react to her beauty. Raoul swallowed a smile and shifted uncomfortably.

Christine's fair Scandinavian heritage gave her an angelic air. Raoul enjoyed the rolling hint of Swedish still present in her French. Her eyes usually sparkled like the sapphires encircling her neck, but now seemed dim.

Raoul reached to her. His fingers tangled in the golden waves of hair and her locks cascaded over his knuckles. He rotated his fingers for a second pass, enjoying the cool silk of her tresses against his flesh.

"I know what you are thinking. It was a foolish idea to come." He settled back in his seat.

It took some time for her to pull her gaze away from the carriage window. "Do not be ridiculous. This was our home."

"Then why the tears?" Raoul indicated the kerchief she drew from her sleeve.

"I am happy." The short flip of her shoulder spoke otherwise. Raoul raised an eyebrow. "It is nerves, but nothing more. I assure you."

"You have nothing about which to be nervous. If you are thinking of *him,* you need not. He is gone. Dead. The Phantom is nothing more than a closed chapter in your life."

The crack in her voice sent a crushing ache to his chest.

"I cannot help but think of him. My life has moved on—to a blessed one, but I cannot help but wonder about Erik and the past."

Raoul's nostrils flared at how casually Christine mentioned that demon's name. "He was a madman, Christine. You should not connect your life with his." He shifted, forcing a smile. "You need not trouble yourself with these concerns. Did I not promise to keep you safe?" When she nodded his grin broadened. "Did I not promise to give you the world and more? We can return to Norway this fall, sooner should you wish."

"Chagny is your home, Raoul. You are the Vicomte de Chagny. We should remain here. The viscounties need your attention and while Philippe is away you are to act in his stead."

Reaching across the carriage he stroked his fingers against the back of her palm. He admired her strength and devotion to his duties. "My brother will return from Spain soon enough. There is no need for us to rush to attend Chagny." She opened her mouth to protest, but a well-practiced raise of his brow felled her silent. "Let us just enjoy the reason we were asked to return to the Garnier." He raised the letter in his hand. "Promise you will tell me if you ever feel uncomfortable doing this?"

He relaxed when Christine reached for his hand and squeezed it. "Yes, I promise."

"People are stupid."

"Good morning to you too, Edward," Jacob Wischard greeted, entering their shared office.

Twirling around in his chair, Edward Laroque lifted his glass in a toast, laughing aloud at some good fortune. Jacob groaned. Edward considered himself quite brilliant in comparison to the rest of the human race. A view not shared by Jacob. Edward was the senior-larger partner. Far be it for Jacob to voice an opinion to the contrary. "You're in an uncommonly chipper mood," he observed.

Edward's laugh shook the walls.

Jacob scowled and stuck a finger in his ear. He removed his hat and shrugged off the waistcoat swallowing his frame. Laying his outerwear across his desk and tossing his walking stick aside, he took a seat on its corner and poured himself a drink. He paid no mind to time of day when a fresh carafe of scotch was present. Jacob scrutinized the devilish gleam to Edward's eyes, the scotch glistening on his lips and the rosy color to the tip of his nose. When his partner was this gleeful it usually meant he had something up his sleeve.

"To what do I owe this occasion?" he cautiously asked.

Edward clapped his swollen hands. "Because, my dear friend, we are about to become extraordinarily wealthy."

Now what? "We are already extraordinarily wealthy."

Edward laughed and leaned across the desk to clink his glass in cheers. Jacob winced against his laughter.

"What is it this time, Edward? You haven't cut the company's salary again have you? If you have, there will be mutiny on our hands."

For years they'd been milking the opera. They were masters at skimming the books and stealing money with bogus reasons for cutting the staff's salary. They overcharged patrons, underpaid players, and no one was the wiser. Three years ago they'd stumbled upon a starving opera and saw a gold mine.

"You underestimate me, Jacob."

Jacob lifted a brow as Edward's eyes shifted greedily back and forth. Edward reached into a drawer and threw an old playbill across the desk.

Jacob held it at arm's length. He was blind without his reading glasses. "Gounod's *Faust*. What's this?"

"Our ticket to greatness."

Jacob tossed the playbill aside. "It's *Faust*. That's hardly a ticket to greatness." Edward's cheeks were inching upward by the second. Before Edward exploded with delight, Jacob conceded defeat. "Will you get to the point? I have a pressing engagement with a rather attractive chorus girl."

Edward rose and strutted like a peacock. He gestured wildly, the scotch splashing over the rim of his glass. "Do you know who performed that opera?"

Jacob scanned the program. "Margarita was Christine Daaé. So?"

"So? So?" Edward croaked, scotch flying from his mouth. Jacob wiped spittle from his cheek. "Do you know who Christine Daaé is?" Spreading his hands, Jacob stressed his annoyance. "Christine Daaé is now the Vicomtess de Chagny."

"Ah," Jacob's mouth opened and closed. "Chagny, the former patron?"

"*Oui*!" Edward gave a skip of excitement. The floorboards groaned in pain.

"So?" Jacob replied, yanking on his fob to look impatiently at his watch.

"Forget about your tryst, Jacob. Today we plan the con of a lifetime."

Edward's enthusiasm was contagious and Jacob's curiosity grew. He caressed the rim of his scotch and looked sideways at Edward.

"Go on," he encouraged.

"Picture this: *Faust* the original opera which brought down this opera house was sung by Christine Daaé. Now, who better to return in honor of this opera's upcoming anniversary than the diva herself? She left Paris shortly after the performance ended, fleeing from a Phantom of the Opera." Edward launched into theatrics of his own as he waved his hands moaning like a ghost.

Jacob's brows rushed up then down. "I beg your pardon?"

"He is some sort of legend that was never explained. This Phantom apparently stole her off the stage before a theater full of people on the night she was to elope with the Vicomte de Chagny. It was a scandal Paris spoke of for years. If you ask me, the woman was slightly ill in the head." Edward shook his glass in emphasis, making scotch splash over the rim.

"Edward, I think you are slightly ill in the head." Jacob looked at the carafe. How much scotch had his partner consumed?

"She had all of Paris searching for some horrific Opera Ghost, a man legend says was nothing short of Satan himself. People love mystery and gossip." Edward touched his glass with Jacob's again. "Scandals bring in patrons, patrons bring in money—"

Jacob's hollow cheeks grew in bulk with his smile. "And we pad our pockets. Brilliant Edward! You are the master. One small problem. You may have the Diva, but there's no Phantom of the Opera."

When Edward threw his hands up in the air, Jacob shrugged.

"Don't be so simple minded. It's a minor detail old chap. We shall find out what the legend holds and rebuild him."

"Re-create a man who never existed and a scandal between a nobleman and his wife?" He slurped the scotch. "Edward, you are devilishly insane. What makes you so sure anyone will play into the notion this Phantom ever existed?"

"Something clearly happened at this opera house. Something made them all run. Murders happened, making people believe the ghost was real."

Jacob spit his drink into his glass and rubbed the scotch off his vest. He looked up, his eyes flying open in shock. The plan was dangerous. Edward didn't think so, for his face plastered with an ever-widening smile.

"A chandelier crashed, Jacob. There was even an investigation for Lord's-sake! The authorities crawled all over this theater for months. They found nothing, but the foundation was laid. It became Parisian legend. People are afraid of ghosts and men have a morbid fascination with fear." Poising his hands behind his head, Edward sat in his chair. It complained just as loudly as the floorboards.

"What's the first step? We haunt the opera house?"

"No, for Christ's sake, don't be daft! We aren't actually going to re-create this. We simply build her trust. The vicomtess believes she's here for the anniversary celebration, which she legitimately is. We announce her surprise arrival during a masquerade ball—an event I specifically chose because of how it plays into the history of the Garnier. The players will lead the way. We just sit back and watch the show."

Jacob marveled at his comrade. "And exactly how did you manage to persuade her?"

"Didn't have to. The vicomte's letter included something about revisiting old friends, reliving past triumphs, love of the Paris Opera, and putting to bed old wounds. Bah... I told him the opera had been suffering in the past years, and it deserved a moment of grandeur. Damn fool."

Jacob stood, first adjusting his hat which fell close around his eyes then reaching for his coat and stick. "Edward, you may not know a damn thing about opera, but when it comes to running a con, you are a genius."

"I know," he gloated, seeing Jacob out.

They paused in the doorway, leering at the girl who walked past. Anna shot them a look that had them dodging the daggers flying from her eyes.

Edward flashed a wet and toothy grin. "I learned from a master."

The afternoon bored him.

Figures below moved like puppets on a string he didn't control. Perched high above the stage, Erik nestled like a spider in the web of ropes and catwalks. He left the sanctuary of his cellar home, choosing instead to keep a silent presence in and around the empire he'd built. Content for the moment to only observe, he hadn't made his presence known. Content—but bored. Breathing deeply, he filled himself with the earthy fiber of the ropes, the dusty folds of rolled scenery, and the alcohol lingering from the breath of fly men. It was good to be back in his realm.

The stage teemed with activity. His opera had come alive in the last few weeks. A group of ballet students stood straight and proper before their teacher, leaning on her instruction and copying her every movement. He groaned. Skinny legs wobbled under their costumes and their arms were sloppy. They were as coordinated as drunken foals. He glared at the *Maîtresse du corps de ballet*. She could do much better.

Bored with them, he pondered the orchestra. He shouldn't be too hard on the ballet mistress, for the ballet could only dance as well as the music commanded. He cringed. The rats in his cellar sounded better than the musicians warming up. Not a single one had a sense of pitch. The orchestra's display was just as terrible. Erik drummed his fingers against his cheek. Should he introduce the concertmaster to the meaning of the word bow-mark? He huffed. What good would that do? The concertmaster could only follow as well as he was led.

Folding his arms and anchoring himself by his feet, he looked at the current Maestro. The man was practically tone deaf and had no concept that an audience not only watched the stage but the pit as well. As he studied the scurrying stagehands, he critiqued the chorus lining up. The opera had moved on and had done so poorly. Erik blamed the two blithering idiots directly below him—Laroque and Wischard.

Everything about them was detestable. They gestured wildly, quite like the drunken foals. What had them so excited? Leaning out of his nest, he strained to listen. The managers were buzzing about something, that much was certain.

"We will spare no expense in this, Maestro. Your every focus must be on making this event a success." The fat one strutted about the stage like an overly pompous stock dove.

Laroque and Wischard seemed pleased at how everyone leapt at their every command. The ballerina's appeared eager to impress. Stagehands hurried to organize scenery and the orchestra tuned their instruments loudly. Everyone seemed starved for the limelight.

Almost everyone.

A satchel soared through the air and hit the floor between the managers with an ungraceful thump. Their eyes narrowed as Anna walked toward them. She gestured to the sack. "They're done."

Perhaps his afternoon would not be dull after all. Erik artfully twirled himself to a lower fly. He hadn't laid eyes on her in weeks. His lips fell open slightly, watching her braid sway with every angry stomp she took. He'd swallowed his approving laugh when she tore the satchel from her shoulder and launched it artfully through the air. She did have a little spirit of shrew in her.

The unusual quiver in his gut made him scowl. Anna's nightly visits to his labyrinth had waned over the last several weeks. Did he actually miss her companionship? She was a curious toy to him, a tiny puzzle he had yet to figure out and one which made emotions stir in him that he thought he'd dismissed long ago. He dared not seek her out for worry his emotions might cause him to become clumsy and—even worse—be seen. The managers were keeping her busy on whatever project they were so enthused about. How Anna must hate it. Erik's fingers drummed against his cheek again. He pondered teaching them a lesson for interrupting the current status quo of his life.

That would be entertaining.

He heard Wischard growl, "Have you no manners girl?"

Erik bridled.

"Pardon, Monsieur," Anna said apologetically to the Maestro.

Laroque gestured to the invitations overflowing at his feet. "They're doing us no good sitting here. Get them to the post."

Anna rubbed her hands harshly up and down her dress, bending to retrieve the invitations. Erik's eyes tapered. Blast that girl! His gut seized the instant he noted her un-splinted wrist and the ripple of pain on her face. Despite the time since their encounter, there was no way that wrist could have healed enough for her to remove it. A seething glare landed on the managers. He made her swear for the sake of her comfort and his guilt to tend to her needs first. He suspected her reluctance to wear it had something to do with the buffoons below him.

"See to it this gets to the post as well." Laroque pulled a letter from his waistcoat and let it flutter to the ground. Anna stared at the envelope then lifted her eyes to the overweight slob leering at her. "And I will know if it doesn't get delivered. Jacob, shall we?"

He indicated his partner and stepped over her.

Anna spit on the envelope before shoving it in the bag. Erik almost laughed out loud. Slinging the satchel across her shoulder she stood, its weight pulling her to one side and into Wischard's chest.

He cupped her chin. "Come now, Anna, where's your pretty smile?" He leaned in for a kiss, but she turned away.

Wischard laughed.

Erik moved.

A fierce jealousy burned at the sight of those hands on her face, a dangerous heat rose off the back of his icy neck. What would be entertaining at this moment was out-right murder. If he watched any longer, he'd have had a lasso around that man's neck quicker than he could compose. He couldn't decipher why he felt so possessive of Anna, he just did. Having seen enough, he left...determined to meet with her one way or another.

"Madame, a word please." Madame Giry caught the wave of her managers rushing toward her. She paused and shifted the stacks of playbills to her opposite arm. "We beg your pardon for the interruption, but we have some rather exciting news we're certain you'd like to hear."

She scowled, thinking it rather unusual for the managers to pay her special attention.

"Messieurs?"

Edward raised his eyebrows, rubbed his hands together, and looked at Jacob. She darted her gaze from the skinny manager to the portly one.

"As you know, we're planning a much needed overhaul of this opera for its upcoming anniversary," Edward explained. "We're staging a grand masquerade, and we've put out a call for new composers to showcase their work during a fantastic concert series."

Madame Giry slowly nodded.

"We'll need you to be involved," Jacob added.

"Involved, Monsieur?" She drew out her question. The programs wrinkled under her twitching. She looked behind, toward the box to which Edward gestured.

"You are aware whose box that was?"

"Is," she corrected sharply, puffing out her chest with pride. "That box belongs to the house of de Chagny."

"We've taken the liberty to make this a truly splendid event by inviting a certain diva to attend." Edward leaned in toward her, stressing the word diva.

She drew back. “Diva?”

“The Vicomtess de Chagny. I’ve been informed you know of her.”

The playbills slapped to the stage. With trembling hands, she bent and retrieved them. She brushed hair from her face and straightened her tiny hat, acting as if the news hadn’t fazed her.

“Yes, I know her.”

“Excellent,” Edward said pleasantly. “She and the vicomte will be here shortly. I trust you’ll see to their comfort. Now please don’t let us keep you from your duties.”

Madame Giry shot a glance over the manager’s shoulder to the Chagny box and the equally empty Box Five on the grand tier. Before she could utter a protest the two headed off stage.

Shocked, she pushed and poked at her hat. Raoul and Christine were coming to Paris. The thought of them arriving in the opera house filled her with dread. She pressed a hand against the sickness in her stomach.

The vicomte and vicomtess had no idea of Erik’s location. All assumed he’d died. None knew of her continued servitude to him. She brushed a hand across her forehead and bounced nervously in one spot. If Erik discovered Christine was returning, no telling what he would do. She’d already seen him begin to lure another into his lair. What would he do if he saw Christine again?

She spun in place, whimpering senselessly. This was madness. Gulping down her panic she made a choice. If the past had to be confronted, then she would warn them. She would only keep Erik’s secret until then.

The box keeper’s blood ran cold as Anna rushed down the center aisle. History was repeating in the girl, but this time something was different. Bit by bit, Madame Giry’s neck pulled back like being tugged by the invisible string of a marionette. She searched the catwalks.

They swayed above her.

Chapter Six

Madame Giry shuffled around her tiny office. A raging headache throbbed at her temples and she cleaned in a frantic effort to distract herself. Picked up a program here, stacked it there, and moved a pile of opera glasses from one side of the room to the other. Nothing helped. Her head echoed their names: Raoul and Christine, Erik and Christine, Erik and Raoul.

Erik.

No tonic relieved the pounding. Madame Giry's chin sagged wearily against her chest when a knock mocked the sounds in her head. With her hand on the doorknob, she thought seriously on the benefits of retirement. The old woman squeaked in surprise the instant she opened the door.

"Good day, Madame Giry," greeted a handsome gentleman.

Self-consciously she placed her hands before her mouth to hide her toothless grin. "Monsieur le Vicomte," she declared, curtseying so quickly she felt the feathers in her hat flutter.

He bowed slightly before removing his hat and gloves and setting them aside. "I have known you since I was a boy. You have leave to use my Christian name."

Her cheeks heated at the thought. He smiled and indicated his wife.

"Mademoiselle," Madame Giry said. Giving a flustered wave of her hands to erase her lack of respect, she corrected, "Forgive me, I mean Vicomtess. Welcome back."

She smiled as Christine reddened. Clearly such a title still took her by surprise.

"It is good to be back and to see you are still an institution at this opera."

Ushering them to sit, Madame Giry began busying herself with a pot of tea.

"Are you well, Madame?" Raoul asked.

She studied herself in the polish of the teakettle. Did she look old? Tired? "I am fine, fine. Everything is fine. Your box especially."

"The opera is just bustling with energy," Christine observed.

Madame Giry set the tea tray on the table between them. "A good deal of work is going into this opera house."

"No doubt," Raoul agreed. "We were eager to be a part of the upcoming celebrations."

"Eager, Monsieur le Vicomte?" She handed the vicomtess a teacup and addressed him, but kept her attention on her.

"Quite. Messieurs Laroque and Wischard mentioned the opera's financial difficulty. We had to come to do what we could. We know how much this place means to the citizens of Paris, to you, and the effort you have put into it over the—"

"Raoul, please," Christine said quietly. "We came to see you and the friends we have here, not out of concern for his opera."

Madame Giry stopped fussing as the air in the room stilled.

His opera?

The past hung like a lead curtain threatening to crash down, silencing each of them.

Finally, Madame Giry said, "The opera has been quiet, I assure you. Your concerns are unfounded." She held her apprehension behind carefully chosen words.

Erik had been damn quiet—too quiet. She'd never known him to be so resigned. Comfort was found in the familiar and change a frightening force. Now he was changing in ways unknown to her. Guiltily, she forced herself to accept the changes. In all the years of ministering to Erik's whims and genius while cowering before his madness and authority, she'd barely known the man. Comprehending change in someone she saw as one-sided seemed unfathomable.

Guilt was a powerful emotion and history threatened to repeat itself. With the vicomtess here, guilt made her wish she'd never been a part of the past.

Exhaustion pitched Anna into another chorus member. A grunt burst past her lips. Dragging her feet, she mumbled an apology.

Laroque and Wischard had been particularly demanding, and she'd grown weary of the Opera Garnier. Many times she thought of leaving, but couldn't bring herself to do it.

"Watch it," a stagehand warned, rumbling past with a cart bogged down with decorations.

With a limp wrist, Anna waved him off indifferently. The stage was being set for the masquerade. The invitations were written and now delivered thanks to her aching hands and neck. With that monumental task behind her, Anna hoped to find a little respite in the secrecy of the cellars. Who was she kidding? Whatever scheme

Laroque and Wischard were planning didn't involve pause for her. Apathetically moving through the hallways, standing clear of passing dancers and demanding divas, Anna wished she could simply disappear.

A troupe of young ballerinas pranced like overly excited ponies. Heaving a great puff of air through her nose, Anna gave them an exhausted, contemptuous glare. She'd give anything for their boundless enthusiasm. Resigned that such frivolity was not her course, Anna stepped out of their way and directly into the hand that snaked from behind her. One by one, long fingers covered her mouth. She didn't have a chance to scream.

More artfully than a ballerina, Anna pirouetted clear of the hall and tumbled into an empty classroom. The force of the attack spun her to the ground. Her wrists and forearms took the brunt of her weight. The door shut with an ear-splitting bang. A surge of adrenaline forced her to her feet as instinct kicked in. She stopped in her tracks at the reflection of the man on the mirrored wall.

"Holy Mother of God!" Whirling, she tore the satchel from her shoulders and heaved it at her assailant.

Erik wasn't quite fast enough to miss its collision. It smacked against his chest and tumbled to the floor

"You scared me half to death!" Anna shouted.

Folding his arms, he grinned. He gestured to himself, first indicating his head and then with a flourish, he ended pointing at his toes.

"Forgive me, Mademoiselle, Death is to seduce a maiden. I did not mean to frighten."

Anna rolled her eyes. His humor was often macabre, seldom arrogant. "Then change your tactic." She winced and clutched her wrist. Landing as she had made the barely knit break throb.

He sheepishly approached with his head lowered. "Are you all right? Erik did not hurt you again—did he?"

Anna shook her head and pursed her lips.

"That should still be treated." He reached for her hand. "Why have you undone my splint?"

"How would I explain it? It's best the managers don't even know I was hurt." The incredulous look on her face should have been enough words. "They know I have no funds for a physician. If they saw me with an injury, any injury that was tended that is, it would arouse suspicions. They would think I was skimming the books." A wave of her wrist insisted he put his concern and remorse aside. A newly healed wrist was merely an annoyance to her. The slump to his shoulders hurt her more. "I am fine. What are you doing here?" Anna gently asked.

He shrugged like a bored child. "Watching, listening, looking for you."

"Well, I'm found." She regarded him as he strolled past. He tilted his head back in innocent study of the ceiling. Realization struck that she'd missed his companionship. She glanced at their reflection in a mirror and smiled. They were an odd couple, but Anna liked being accepted by a gentleman such as Erik. He didn't mind her history.

"Wischard touched you."

Her breath hitched. Obviously, he'd watched that display on stage. She was in no mood to deal with his possessive streak. He'd become fiercely defensive of her honor like some sort of demented round table knight, sheltering her from leering eyes on her rounds, or crossly questioning bums if they were brazen to ask her attention. She ground her thumb and forefinger against her eyes.

"Wischard always touches me. Can we not discuss such matters?"

"Killing that lying gambler would be so easy." Erik rummaged through the bag. He spun out of Anna's reach when she snatched for it.

His meddling was rewarded by an envelope. Anna stomped toward him, wagging her fingers impatiently.

He shook his head. "I am not about to be challenged on my sources of entertainment, *mon petit*." The envelope ripped open. "I am curious to see what is so precious to my managers that you have to remain indisposed and away from my cellars."

La Fête d'Anniversaire pour l'Opera Garnier.

He covered the length of the rehearsal room with a few strides as he read, pivoting sharply on his heel each time he reached the end. The mirrors mimicked his angry movements.

Erik yelled and spit as he paced, driving each word into her like a nail: a masquerade ball, an open call for composers and a final concert to showcase the world's finest Maestros. Every time he looked at Anna, she cringed and looked away.

"If you do not wish your neck to meet the end of silk rope, I suggest you speak."

"I was going to tell you weeks ago when I had the chance, but you've been getting difficult to find."

He crumpled the invitation tightly in his hand. "Some of the finest music in the world will be played under the acoustics of *my* roof, and I can have no hand in the composition."

"You are still very much a part of this opera house."

Erik stared at the paper in his fist and laughed bitterly.

"This theater would not exist without you," Anna reminded.

"Nor would it have fallen," he snapped.

"You can still partake. Come with me to the masquerade."

"No. I will have no part in this." His shoulders deflated as did the corners of his mouth.

"You might as well because you already do."

His lip twitched. "What did you do, child?"

Anna lifted a shoulder. Absently she bit her thumbnail. He closed the distance she attempted to put between her defiance and his temper.

"The violin concerto," she stammered. "I submitted it."

Erik's head cocked as if her confession stuck in an awkward spot in his ear. Taking advantage of the alarming difference in their heights, he hunched over her, forcing her to splutter quickly in her defense.

"Some of the finest musicians in the world will be here. Your music deserves to be heard."

"You went through my music?"

She mumbled her guilt. The concerto, only second to his magnum opus opera, *Don Juan Triumphant,* was the accumulation of years of his work. It sang of his love of beauty, his heartbreak, shame, anger and his revelations on love.

"You meddling, infuriating little minx, you had no right!"

"I know," she replied.

"There are times, child, when you are chipping away at your own epitaph."

Anna kept the attitude of triumph she wore and ignored his sarcastic wrath.

His tone changed. "Anna, there is no musician in this world with the talent capable of giving voice to that concerto but me."

She sauntered toward him much like a rat catcher proudly parading his tailed minions. When she reached for him, she felt his discomfort at being touched tighten his forearm.

Standing on the tips of her toes to reach his ear she whispered, "I know."

Madame Giry spent the better half of her time trying to convince the vicomte and his wife their concerns were unfounded. After all, she'd almost convinced herself. She toured them through the theater reliving the better days, speaking of changes and introducing them to eager and star-struck young pupils.

Weary, she was glad to see them safely off. The quiet isolation of the concierge office beckoned and she locked the door with a relieved click.

Her peace was short-lived.

In total exasperation, her head fell forward, knocking against the wood with a light thud. She didn't have to turn to know he was there.

"Madame, what do you know of this?"

"Monsieur," she moaned into the woodwork, turning to lean against the door for support. Erik tossed the crumpled invitation on her cluttered desk. "I have nothing for you. Why do you keep pressing me?"

Erik tapped impatiently on the top of the invitation.

"Yes! All right! A masquerade, a concert. All to benefit the opera's anniversary. Surely, you were aware this day would come."

"To whom were they sent?"

"The affluent, anyone who could pull this opera out of its disrepair. Laroque and Wischard are doing what they can to save the opera house, hardly enough to give it the respect it once had. But they are at least trying, which is more than I can say about you." She folded her lips into her mouth. Her tongue would get her in trouble.

"Those are the patrons. What of the players?"

"There was an open call for composers. Our diva and the opera company will perform what music our Maestro deems appropriate."

"Our diva and the opera company," Erik echoed. "What pitiful choices for redemption. Only I could restore grandeur to this house."

The underlying tone of remorse in his voice rubbed against her like sandpaper. She hadn't expected it. "The management assures us they have a way of filling the theater, Monsieur."

"And what way is that?"

"I really have no idea." Not a complete fib... Her skin pebbled under the intensity of his gaze. She rubbed her upper arms and shrunk from the chill that wrapped around her.

"Why do you so fear me, Mother Giry?"

Minutes dragged before she had the presence to speak. Their moment of confrontation was at its apex. A considerable look of challenge unfolded in his eyes. He knew...somehow, he knew. She glanced at the invitation with weary resignation and met his stare. "Did you come here looking for her?"

"Of course."

"Why are you doing this?"

"Your affright is groundless; however, not without validity. I admit that."

She didn't trust his calm frankness. Erik retrieved the invitation and slid uncomfortably close to her, unlocking the door as he did. He momentarily caged her against it. Her breath caught in the back of her throat. She moved her head enough to avoid his yellow stare. His whisper tickled her ear as warm breath touched her cheek.

"I will no more harm her than I would you."

The door slipped open and he moved like a liquid shadow, bleeding into the walls of his opera house and out of sight.

She clutched at the pressure in her chest. He sought Christine! Lifting her hands in an attitude of prayer, she begged to God to understand Erik's motives and sought strength to act when it was her moment to take the stage.

Winding his way from the concierge office through his secret passages, Erik moved lower and lower into his labyrinth. No matter how hard he tried, he couldn't convince Madame Giry of the changes he felt. He tossed his head back and laughed. Why should it matter what the world thought? He knew what he wanted out of his miserable existence. His servant would never come to terms with the fact that the woman she feared him seeing was the one reason he had for living. It was useless to try to make her understand. Useless to try to make any of them understand.

Quickening his pace, a new and exciting emotion blossomed untamed to tear through the earth that covered his existence. One person understood and one person was all he needed. With her he could be a monster or Phantom. Erik could live with his madness and his genius and be accepted. It sent a white hot energy through him. He knew what he had to face. Although it terrified him, it was such a welcomed emotion for what he viewed himself to be—a man.

No longer would he be ruled by an opera house and imprisoned by his heart. He'd navigated the waters of *Pyriphlegethon* and Anna had doused its flames.

Chapter Seven

Ghosts and ghouls, clowns and fools were all in equal standing.

The fantastic took control of the Escalier of the Académie Nationale, filling it with fantastic costumes. Politely, Anna stood away from the center floor, so not to interfere with the revelry of the invited guests. Her emotions were jumbled in a knot. Clueless as she found them to be, it surprised her that the management had pulled something like this off. The invitation thrust in her hands at the last minute came as quite a shock. A rare, small token of gratitude on their behalf.

Spinning in a circle, she delighted in the costumes and the air of make-believe. People stared. One elegant lady walked past and Anna couldn't resist reaching out to caress the silk of her gown, quickly snatching her hand back before she was caught. She rubbed her fingers together, recalling the sensation of the cool, soft fabric. The scratchy wool of her own skirts made her scowl. Not often did she feel shame, but her plain and faded dress stood out among the fancy ball gowns and paled in comparison to the elaborate costumes of the more daring guests. It pleased her that she managed to make her own mask for the occasion. Running her hands over her face, she smoothed the feathers around her eyes. Anna likened her face to that of a lark.

She stumbled to the side as a troupe of ballet students crowded in next to her. The girls giggled and flirted with the throngs of handsome single patrons. Anna self-consciously straightened her dress and mimicked their movements. She batted her eyes, looked coyly over her shoulder, and laughed.

Tucking a stray wave of hair behind her ear, she tossed her tresses. Rarely did she wear her hair unbraided, but fancying it her finest attribute she did this evening. Perhaps it may turn a head? Anna rumbled under her breath when the last girl was whisked onto the dance floor.

She shook the gentlemen's dismissals off with a toss of her shoulders. No matter. She found herself moving to the music anyway. How could someone not get caught up in a masquerade? Watching several couples, she focused her attention to one pair. They were a perfect match of grace and elegance. The previous flare of jealousy sparked into outright fire.

The woman's face had the perfection of ivory dusted with rose powder, her eyes brighter than sun on an ocean. Anna's lips pursed into a small bow as she craned her neck to watch the gown sparkle as the woman twirled. Anna touched her own hair, taking a clump of the roughened edges into her hand while admiring the smooth blonde tresses that waved behind the dancing woman. Twisting a lock between her fingers, she admired the lady's partner. Strong and tall, yet somehow gently effeminate, he seemed a handsome balance between man and gentleman. She swallowed a sigh, acknowledging she wouldn't mind taking a turn around the floor with him.

Watching them with a dreamy smile, she stayed neatly tucked away like an afterthought as the whirlpool of revelers enjoyed the festivities around her.

Erik watched the ball with lips drawn into a tight line. The shadows dressed his shoulders in a cloak of black. He hadn't bothered to find a mirror to judge his costume. His hands pulsed at his sides. Mirrors were implements of pleasure for the vain, instruments of pain for the degraded. He didn't take kindly to gazing upon himself. He suffered enough knowing what he was. Seeing himself reflected in all his repugnant glory was to stab his eyes with the well-worn poniard of suffering.

He hadn't been out in a public spectacle such as this since the Bal Masque before Shrovetide some years ago. This time was different. He hadn't attended this affair to stalk sniveling little vicomtes. His lips curled into a snarl. How dare that boy trespass upon his kingdom and steal the woman he loved.

A deep breath governed his emotions. The Vicomte de Chagny was out of his life as was Christine Daaé. Erik hadn't donned his costume and ventured out in public to restate a claim on the past.

He lurked in the background, watching the upper crust of society flirt and flit about the Escalier. Everyone in Paris put on a mask or a phony air of some sort it seemed. How many of these players were here to flaunt on stage? How many were genuine in their intent to be a part of the production?

A couple raced into his dark corridor. The youths fell together, hands and lips groping for any possible reward of flesh, forcing Erik from the comfort of his spot. The voyeur in him took control. He studied the sway of their bodies as they pressed against their kiss. Watched their hands roam with amorous intent. Did they really understand love and carnal pleasure or were they caught in the air of drink and merriment?

He tore his gaze from them to scrutinize the ball. He'd come to this affair to understand exactly what love and pleasure could be. With a devilish smile toward the couple in the throes of passion, he joined the stage.

The music changed and a new dance began. The tune sent images of secret rendezvous and heated embraces racing through Anna's mind. She swayed with its seduction. A ripple raced across her lower back and her scalp tickled when her hair was caressed. An arm encircled her waist. Arching her back and taking a sharp breath, Anna stiffened as another arm stretched across her shoulder.

"Shh," the sound shivered in her ear. The rich, tenor voice made that single sound remarkably pure and warm. Her mouth slipped open and her eyes closed to the velvet notes.

"Erik?" she inquired.

Sliding his arm from around her waist, he stepped in front of her. She muffled her delight by covering her mouth as her gaze shifted from his feet to his head. His costume accented his elegant form. The short coat of scarlet and long cape slung over one shoulder only punctuated his extraordinary height. Her mouth slipped open and closed beneath her hand, mimicking her eyes. His vest and ascot boasted embroidery that rivaled her skilled stitching. Gold thread gleamed in the light. She laughed at the black felt hat perched rakishly on his head and the long plume draping from it. Accustomed to seeing him in funereal clothing, she couldn't tear her gaze away from the color draped on his frame. She covered her heated cheeks. When was the last time she'd actually blushed?

Erik's cold fingers trickled down the length of her face as he claimed her hand. Without a word, he coaxed her to the center of the floor.

At first he barely held her in his grasp, leading her delicately by the tips of her fingers. With heat only experienced in fever, she felt her flush deepen. She tried to back away, but he reacted quickly, firming his grip. Their fingers tangled together in a union of fire and ice.

When he walked backward, she held his gaze. His look radiated such possessive intensity she felt heat crawl from her cheeks down her chest. Around her, the space exploded in sound the closer she came to the center of the Escalier. Her head raced as fast as the couples twirling around them. Her blush spread in panic while muscles between her shoulders clenched into a knot. She was not worthy of this. Her free hand frantically clawed at her dress. Although clothed, she felt exposed.

Fanning his cloak out of the way and catching it in the crook of his arm, he raised her hand to the level of his chest and bowed. Anna's head whipped over her shoulder. Was he bowing to *her*? *Here*? If she didn't know the absurdity of it, she would have burst into flame like a Phoenix. Why was he looking at her like she was some sort of prize? With a quick and expert movement, he lifted her hand, took her fully in his arms, and danced.

Erik was music personified, his body an extension of the Maestro's baton, conducting her across the floor with ease, agility and beauty. Unmatched, their movements were seductive, playful, and exquisite.

Anna, too shy to look her partner in the eye, noticed the dance floor had cleared. Guests, hovering in tight circles muttered and pointed. Could it be *they* envied *her*? Marveling at the sea of masks that swirled past her, she praised her years dancing around the communal campfires of fellow wanderers. At least she knew she didn't look like a complete fool. Her face must have matched the color of Erik's jacket for she even felt her eyes grow warm. The regard he paid her and the contrast in his attitude was unfathomable.

Erik cared not for the crowds or the peers. He took notice of no one but Anna. At long last nothing else held control of his mind. The freedom was liberating and addicting.

To him, nothing existed but music, his opera house, and Anna.

The music stopped, but his heart danced on its own. He stared at her trying to regain his breath. He felt as if he shook all over with emotions he couldn't identify.

"I must go," he said abruptly. Far too many eyes drilled into him. He hastened away, leaving Anna no choice but to follow. The lights of the Escalier dimmed and the sounds faded as he escaped down the vestibule toward the street.

"Erik, wait!"

Stopping mid-stride, he stared at the doors. It would be easy for him to continue and slip out of sight. Pass through the doors and rescue himself from all his emotions and the pomp, but instead...he turned. He looked beyond Anna, to the crowds that gathered around the marble steps in the Escalier.

"Don't go," Anna said breathlessly.

Feathers fluttered against the rosy hue of her cheeks. Such a face should not be masked. Stepping up to him, she took his hand and squeezed it slightly. A human glove of warmth wrapped his wrist.

"Thank you for the dance. It was kind of you to pay me notice."

He caressed her with his gaze. The last several months of debating his emotion and torment came forward in his mind.

"Ladies and Gentlemen..." The sounds of the ball drifted around them.

Around her he was a man and a Maestro, part of a human race that had both compassion and dignity.

"May we have your attention, please..."

He'd partaken in this charade for one purpose alone. His heart slammed against his ribcage.

"Our esteemed and honored guests of this evening..."

Her fingers remained entwined in his, and he watched her reaction as he covered her hand with his free one.

"...will now lead us in the grand tradition..."

She shook her head and opened her mouth several times, but spoke nothing. Didn't she know what to make of the moment, or his silence? No matter. He stepped toward her causing her to tilt her head back to meet his eyes. How could someone so small fit so perfectly? The noise in his head—his warning of madness faded. Not even the din of the crowd beyond could replace the music.

"...of the Midnight Reveal."

Unsure of himself and his inexperience, he brushed a finger across Anna's forehead with the inquisitiveness of a child. He'd only kissed a woman once...on her forehead. In this instance Christine's name disappeared from his mind.

His hand trailed down Anna's face, tracing the wrinkle to her brow, the small creases on the side of her eye, her mouth plumped in a slight pout. One finger came to rest against her lips, finding them as fascinating as any sculpture he'd ever seen. Breathing deeply, he closed his eyes. He couldn't resist the pull of having a woman's lips against his nor could he deny the powerful urges such a thought sent racing through his body.

"Let the countdown begin."

Twisting his hand, he tipped her chin. Lifting the purse of her mouth higher and higher, he bent deeply to meet their ruby lushness. For the first time in his life his cold lips brushed against the warm allure of a woman's. Nerves reached out and squeezed him with invisible hands. His body tightened like a knot of wet leather at the thought of her pulling away. But he felt her shoulders melt into his grip. He hadn't expected such a reaction and acted upon it.

Tangling a hand in the waves of her hair, Erik fell into the emotion. He kissed her with all the power and passion he found in their friendship. Though that ardor played in his grip, holding her tightly and crushing her small frame, he kissed her lightly. When he pulled back, he watched as she covered her lips with her fingers and looked away.

He looked beyond her again, toward the rotunda.

"Ten...nine...eight..."

Desires that before were only ever present in his fantasies blossomed into vivid reality. His chest tightened. The earthy scent of her hair centered on a deeper need. His tingling lips recalled her sweet taste. And the passion. It surged from the depths of his soul—foreign, urgent and welcomed. Treasuring their friendship he discovered he loved the woman, and if she were to love the man—

"...seven... six..."

She had to know all of him. Staring intently at the rotunda, he forced the shallow demand from his mouth.

"Anna, take off the mask."

Trembling, she pulled the feathered costume from her face.

"...five ... four..."

"No," Erik's voice pulsed. "Take off the *mask*."

The urgency in his tone made Anna drop her costume. Her hands shook. Erik crushed a fist to his mouth. He would not cry out.

"Erik, I..."

"...three...two..."

"Do it," he demanded. Grabbing her shoulders, he braced himself for her inevitable reaction.

Erik's eyes never left the scene over her shoulder. It had to be done. He couldn't bear to look directly into her eyes. He heard her crying. He hadn't meant to frighten her, but he had no choice. She teetered on the tips of her toes before lifting her hands to his mask. Hitching a breath, he jerked his head backward. He could feel the heat of her hands as they reached for his most intimate part. They trembled as the mask slipped away.

"One!" The rotunda exploded in jubilation.

The deed was done. The distant light from the ball beyond cast odd, contorted, shapes across his deformity. Anna didn't move; she didn't take her gaze off Erik for a second. She closed her eyes and then slowly opened them; hearing his raspy breathing and feeling his hands shake on her shoulders. She knew what lay beneath the mask. She'd always known.

But nothing prepared her for Erik's face.

The blood rushed from her face and down her body. She fretted she would find scarlet pooling at her feet. Swallowing against the pulse beating in her throat, the pain she saw twisting Erik's visage made the awesome unjustness of his curse more bewildering to behold. Taking a deep breath, she closed her eyes. She'd allow herself one minute to stand paralyzed by the cruel irony of his face before reaching out to embrace the exquisite image she'd created of him instead.

When next she opened her eyes, she'd never seen a face that could hold more emotion than Erik's. He looked at her. Dejected, his chin met his chest.

The mask he wore—was shame.

The sounds of the ball continued to taunt them.

"And now ladies and gentlemen..."

Anna searched his face. She expected it to be hard and harsh, knowing what loathing toward the world he kept caged beneath the leather prison. She assumed it would be devoid of emotion. But the smallest of wrinkles decorated his brow. They deepened when he frowned. Anna stared at the unmistakable anguish of rejection etched like a permanent mask upon his visage.

She cried as the revelry of the ball behind her mocked the tension dressing Erik.

"Paris is truly honored..."

His back rounded, pulling his face deeper toward the pit of his stomach. He searched as if looking for a means of escape. He backed away. Caging his face beneath his hands he staggered, the agony in those steps made Anna weep more. Her tears strangled her ability to speak. She felt his anguish. The ball moved forward as time stood still.

"... and the Opera Garnier is deeply blessed...."

His hands slid to the back of his skull and his elbows shielded his cruel deformity. Anna tried to control the tears he attempted to drown out. A gargled word clawed past his lips, catching on the moisture of his sob. Monster...

"Let me see your eyes." The demand tore from her throat.

Erik shrunk away like a reprimanded child, but lowered his hands enough to look at her. Her sigh floated like the lingering notes of an aria to dance with the continuing announcement.

"...to have here with us tonight..."

The beauty of the ball paled to what she looked upon. Anna could see Erik's emotional eyes clearly now that they were uninhibited by his mask. She'd met their frighteningly inhuman hue by night before. Witnessed them in anger, in pain, in madness, and now in shame. But without the mask they were paler than she ever thought, like the shard of glass she'd once found that had been softened by the waters of the Seine. Mistrust, insecurity, and suffering shone at her from his deeply set eyes. Unless extremely close, they could barely be seen at all. They were by the dim light around them, so pale a yellow they were almost empty of color.

Anna gasped when he moved deeper into the sanctuary of the shadows. She didn't understand what odd twist of fate the Lord intended when He gave Erik's eyes that ability to intensify in hue.

Those eyes held so many stories, lessons, and feelings; all completely visible to her. He could never fully understand their seductive beauty. Her heart tugged with joy as if birds beat in her chest. She bit her lip, swallowing a sob.

"I can see your eyes." Laughing through her tears, she let them run down her cheeks, paying no thought to wiping them away. The only masks between them existed in a masquerade.

"...a woman unmatched in talent and grace..."

Erik slowly lowered his hands, staring at them intently before looking at her. Snatching her cheeks with his hands he roughly pulled her to him, setting his jaw as though expecting a fight. She didn't yell or turn away under the intensity of his grasp. If he sought rejection, he would not find it.

"...the pride of the Paris Opera..."

Her mouth slipped open as he relaxed his grip. Raising her chin to his face, he sought her lips again. Anna closed her eyes anticipating, for the first time, a kiss of pure desire. Curling into the crook of his embrace, she lost herself in his lips. Taking the lead, she moaned as Erik followed her, moving against her lips, tasting her with long, deep pulls.

Her breath floated away when he gently broke the kiss. His fingers raked through her hair, pulling a gasp from her lips before he spread his hand against her cheek and wept. Anna reached up, laying her hands on his forearms. She smiled. He found his voice and in it she found his beauty.

"Anna, I love—"

"*...the Vicomtess de Chagny*!" The rotunda exploded in applause.

An icy wind churned around them, lifting that name and spinning it through the air. Erik's hands dropped numbly to her shoulders as he lifted his gaze to the figures on the rotunda. Anna stiffened.

She followed where he stared. His eyes had locked on the woman being led down the steps by the arm of a dashing vicomte. His grip tightened. Her small hands beat against his forearms, but he ignored her attempts to gain his attention. The tension she felt in the back of his hands could cause them to split in two. Veins pulsed with a grotesque rhythm against his temple.

"Erik?" She hammered at his hands.

His grip tightened more, digging into her shoulders. She buckled under the force.

"Erik!"

An awesome transformation took place before her eyes. Malevolence poured from his gaze, locking away the gentleman that seconds ago held her transfixed. Now he gazed on her with savage intensity.

"Did you know about this?" The heat of his passion burned away the cold wind. They were in brilliant contrast to the lyrical sounds that had made her wish to meld her body against his.

"No," she gasped, uncertain if he'd heard.

He focused on the rotunda and the nobility that held the opera in the palm of their hands. Lip twitching and eyes flaring open in a sinister manner, he shoved her away.

"Damn you," he spat viciously.

Anna's head moved in staccato jerks as she glanced over her shoulder to the woman in the Escalier. "Who? Damn who?"

He didn't reply. Her face rearranged in silent shock as she clutched Erik's mask to her breast.

He ripped it from her grip.

His whole body, absorbed by a perverse insensitivity, made no move to comfort as Anna covered her face with her hands and cried. A hollow indifference had replaced his heart.

Leaving her, he stormed from the corridor, his livid strides forcing the cloak to sway behind him.

Chapter Eight

Anna stepped with caution.

Tables were overturned and chairs strewn at odd, broken angles. Reams of music coated the floor. Not a single fragile item was left unsmashed. Red stains dripped down the far wall, further emphasis of a blind rage. Pools of scarlet liquid formed among bits of broken glass. The pungent aroma of well-aged wine mixed with the oil-puddles from shattered lamps. She should have known he would turn to the drink again. It explained the havoc he'd unleashed.

With a tight throat, she wove her way through the debris of the place she thought of as a second home. Never would she have imagined Erik would allow himself to drink to such oblivion.

He sat in a heap on the platform, leaning against his coffin, obscured by its shadow.

"Leave." His voice poured past his lips, that one syllable overly annunciated.

"No."

"Do not test me, child, you are not welcome here."

"You are drunk and not thinking straight."

He stepped from his dismal perch. One boot hit the floor then the other, both grinding against a remnant of a destroyed token. He turned to the light. With the exception of removing his blood red jacket, he hadn't changed from the night before.

Mist beaded his brow. His cravat, marred by small sweat stains, lay limp around his neck. Shamefully, she turned away. Why did she not think such a masculine trait could apply to him? Looking once more, she noticed small lines carved around his eyes. Caution rocked her. She searched for his mask, noticing it lying on a satin pillow in his coffin.

Turning, he cradled his violin beneath one arm, the bow a mess of snapped hairs.

He was not drunk.

Never would he insult his music by playing with a drunken mind. He'd torn apart his home in poisonous fury before escaping in the antidote of his music. Gently, he laid the instrument in his coffin. His eyes darkened when he turned to her.

"Can we speak?" she persisted.

"Leave."

"Erik, we need to speak."

"Leave, me!" he shouted furiously.

Anna flinched, a sharp cramp racing across the muscles of her neck. "No."

He grabbed the sides of the coffin and shook it violently. Best he does that, she figured, than crush his hands against anything more fragile.

"You will not disrespect me!" He whirled toward her. His coffin rocked when he released it. "Now leave!"

"No. We must speak. You're confused."

"I am not confused," he said tersely. "Since the day I sprung forth from my mother's womb, I have never been *confused.*" Striding past, he knocked her aside with his shoulder.

Although staggering, she wasn't deterred by his temper or the menace in his voice. "Fine then," she spit at his back, "denial."

He threw his hands in the air to deflect that word. "I deny nothing."

"You're denying everything. You're denying me now."

Erik twisted his way through the house, knocking objects out of his path. It seemed his entire life was in his way. She followed, stumbling over the aftermath, gesturing broadly around his destroyed home.

"Look at this place. Do you mean to tell me that you deny this is because you saw her? The Vicomtess de Chagny is here, Erik. You cannot deny that."

He stopped in his tracks, lifting his face to the ceiling, then turning to look at her. With an arrogant roll of his shoulders, he indicated the remnants of his wrath.

"Why would I ever deny Christine?"

His fingers dug against his breast. Was he trying to keep his heart from leaping away? That name made his body contort in what seemed like pain. Yet, those lines etched around his eyes, softened as he spoke of her. Who was this woman whose name rang like music from his lips yet tore apart his soul? What power did she have over him?

What power did she have over Anna that caused her heart to sink?

"Why would all this be a result of Christine?" he asked, pacing circles around the organ.

Anna rocked from one foot to the other. Wasn't this because of Christine? She grabbed at her upper arm, hugging it close against her body. She felt exposed. Responsible.

"I do not want you here. I curse the moment you arrived." Erik's finger sliced the air around him. "I curse every last sensation you ever aroused in me."

She kept the cage of the organ pipes between them. Never had she seen him wear such controlled fury. His finger cut the air and with it the hope in her heart.

"I curse your very existence!" His scream echoed against the stone walls.

Grabbing her dress and twisting the wool, the wrinkled fabric matched her brow. How could he say such things? All those awkward nights when they contemplated each other and when he wove her fantastic stories of his past, were they meaningless? She'd shown him compassion and that even he—murderer, madman—was allowed the feelings he denied.

"You think you've betrayed her?" she blurted. "Because of me?"

Moving faster than an uncontrolled tide, he shot out from behind the organ and pointed an accusatory finger in her face.

"Leave, now. You will not put voice to what is in *my* mind. How dare you think you can understand a mind as complex as Erik's." Everything in his stance shouted she was no longer welcome in his home, his mind or his life. "Leave my theater!"

"No."

His inhuman voice reached levels she didn't think possible.

"God Damn you—you maddening little Pandora! *Do you have a death wish*? Leave!"

With a violent thrust he cleared the top of his organ of vials and papers. Throwing her hands over her head, she ducked his ire. Glass and nibs raced past her head. A bottle slammed against her forearm, coating her sleeve with blood red ink.

"Erik, I can never be Christine. She was your world, but she made her choice, she doesn't love you like you wish her to. You didn't betray her. You've been afraid of letting go because you were fearful of betraying what you felt for her. You're not a prisoner. Christine will always be a tangible part of you, but why stay faithful to an affection she never truly expressed? Infatuation is a fool's love." When she took a bold step toward him, he backed away. "Come to terms with this, Erik. You've suffered long enough. Allowing yourself to love isn't betraying her, it's empowering you."

Anna touched her fingers to her lips, ignoring the ink dripping down her arm. Her eyes heated as they filled.

"I want you to leave this opera house," he demanded sharply.

Her hands trembled and tears spilled over the rim. He'd made her cry in pain. He'd made her cry in what she thought was love. But why did he make her cry now?

"Why? So you can try to win her back? So you can be her Angel again? So you can become a Phantom?" That word passed her lips in a loud cry. "I am just as worthy as she—despite who I am. Erik, last night–"

"Was a mistake."

Anna's hand slapped lifelessly against her thigh, his actions cutting her off and slamming a blade between them. So this was his decision? He wished to deny her along with the rest of the world? She closed her eyes and tilted her chin to the ceiling. He couldn't allow himself the ability to live like a man; he didn't know how. If he did, he wouldn't have soiled the shy gentleman she saw in him. The man she so desired to have upon her arm.

Those words stung like salt in a raw wound. She'd spent her life being a mistake, wandering day in and day out, vividly awake in a living nightmare because of her family's transgressions.

"Last night was not a mistake," Anna insisted softly.

Erik closed his eyes. His chin pulled against his chest. "It was. Leave my theater."

Anna backed away, tripping over his rejection. "You know that I cannot!"

She turned, dodging broken glass and leaping over splintered furniture. She didn't look back.

Erik watched her leave. He knew what Anna was trying to tell him, but her words fell as useless as desert rain. It was too soon for him to come to terms with a love not grounded in infatuation or desperation.

"Christine," he softly moaned.

Curled hands moved against his chest. He withered into the pain of an old obsession as he stared at Anna's back.

Out of sight, the only sounds he heard were her distancing footsteps, the rising noise in his mind, and the pounding of his impenetrable heart.

Chapter Nine

Jacob breezed into the office. Last night's affair had put a spring in his step and brought a lively air to the opera around him. He enjoyed a good party when it involved throngs of feeble-minded members of the upper crust. Edward already sat at his desk, his fingers peaked in front of him.

"Edward, brilliant affair last night." Jacob tossed his hat and stick onto a chair. "I feel a renewed interest in the opera coming. That diva of yours really turned them out. We may not need your scandal."

Laroque leaned back in his chair, the springs squealing in protest. "Jacob, don't be so simple-minded. A bigger purse is at stake. A mere diva will not bring it in."

Jacob glared at him. Arrogant bloke. Always thinking *he* over-simplified things while Edward's pompous ass was the brain behind their schemes. The chair groaned as Edward shifted. *Overweight son-of-a-bitch.* Repulsed, Jacob leaned against his desk and thumbed through the morning's post.

"Edward, drawing people in to see a pretty face is one thing, pulling off your scheme is quite another." A note landed in the wastebasket. "I honestly don't think you have it in you." Holding another to the lamp he discarded it as well. "You tend to think these Parisians are stupid. They're not going to fall for your scam. I say we let your diva sing and skim the books like usual. The crowds will be large enough to satisfy our wallets."

Hearing Edward clear his throat, Jacob looked up in time for Edward's curt nod to draw his attention to the windowsill. Jacob's wrist went slack. The mail floated to the floor.

"God in heaven..."

The man on the windowsill pursed his lips and narrowed his eyes. His boots were polished with the utmost care and he dressed in the finest clothing: black and ominous. His jacket and vest were precisely tailored and molded perfectly to his extraordinary frame. Across the back of a chair lay a satin-lined cloak. Thin fingers fondled a black mask.

"Son-of-a-Bitch!" Jacob chanced a look at Edward.

"Jacob, may I introduce you to The Phantom of the Opera."

The figure moved to stand behind Edward, mask still resting in one hand. Edward didn't move a muscle or so much as take a breath.

"Son-of-a-Bitch," Jacob gasped, wiping at the sweat upon his brow.

The man skulked from behind Edward to stalk him. Jacob shakily looked up at him. His mere presence demanded fearful supplication, and Jacob provided it.

"Edward," he cried, backing away. He slipped over the bills littering the floor.

Edward spread his hands and linked them behind his head, his grin reaching from ear-to-ear. Seeing no help in his partner, Jacob's attention shot to address the man hovering before him. He backed against his desk and leaned as far away from him as he could. Summoning his courage he bellowed, "Son-of-a-bitch! Where's my money?"

The man broke out in a hearty laugh and took a seat on the desk's corner. Tossing his mask aside, he entwined his fingers.

"You have my daughter. What more to you want?"

"Gentlemen, please," Edward intervened. He rose and pulled three glasses and a carafe from the cabinet. "We must be civil."

Jacob leaned against the opposite corner of the desk and snapped his neck from side to side making it crack.

"Richard Barret, so you're what that letter was about." He glanced at Edward who extended him a glass. Jacob grabbed it, sending scotch splashing over his wrist. "Look at you. Christ. I hardly recognized you."

"Impressive isn't it? Edward said it would be the role of a lifetime."

Richard Barret could never resist roles. A master of manipulation and deceit, he lived for the thrill of a con and the promise of money and drink. He was a true criminal mastermind. Jacob hated admitting it, seeing as it only added to Richard's arrogance. The man raised his glass to Edward in toast and he eagerly accepted. With well-respected caution, Jacob followed suit.

"Edward, how did you pull this off?" Jacob circled, marveling at the transformation. Richard Barret was an imposing, rather crude man who barely could carry off the look of refinery. Yet, to his credit, he managed to wear this illusion with a modicum of grace and dignity.

Edward shrugged. "I heard tales, snuck a peek at some police sketches, used a bit of creative genius, and violà!"

Richard snatched for the mask, holding it to his face. He shouted a loud *boo*. He extended a hand and Jacob shook it, putting aside the definite reservations he had for Richard Barret.

"Ah…like old times, eh?" Edward raised his glass. "A toast to that."

"What's the next step?" Jacob took a greedy slurp of scotch. Nothing would be the same now that Richard was involved.

Edward stared at his cuticles. "We take our cues from our diva. You've seen the poor thing's nerves. She's bound to let something slip." He slapped his Phantom on the knee. "Do you wish to see your seed?"

Jacob looked in anticipation as Richard studied the scotch. He watched Richard's gaze harden. "Keep her away from me."

Jacob snorted. He figured as much. That girl embodied everything that went wrong with Richard Barret's life. She'd ruined one too many cons as he'd dragged her across Europe. Richard's own stupid conscience prevented him from dispatching her years ago. The lesser of the partners were not about to soil their hands with the deed. Richard was the murderer in the trio.

"I trust she is serving you well?" Richard asked.

"She is defiant," Edward spit, causing Jacob to roll his eyes.

"Lower your standards and shag her every once in a while and she won't be." He lifted his glass toward Richard. "Her attitude is a bit annoying, but she's been a worthy purse. However, my bloody money is much preferred. Are you certain you don't wish to see her? She is at our beck and call."

"Not unless her *head* is on a spit." Twirling the remaining scotch, Richard tipped his head back and downed it with one swift gulp.

"Ladies and Gentlemen, Father of the Year!" Edward toasted.

Richard threw his empty glass at him.

"Really, Richard," Jacob remarked. "You should be castrated."

The excited atmosphere of the night before hadn't worn off. Christine could feel the air hum with anticipation of the upcoming events. She and Raoul arrived that morning amidst the whispers. Young aspiring divas took to shadowing her every move, hoping to bask in her glory, steal glances at the unsurpassed looks of her vicomte and wishing for a tale of The Phantom of the Opera.

She worried her reputation would precede her. The past linked around her ankle like a chain, following her wherever she went, no matter how much the actual events had faded into fable. Christine was resigned and polite; assuring her young troupe such stories weren't true. She might be able to convince the naive, but never herself.

Erik's presence traveled like an unbidden ghost through her memories. She buried the images of him deep in its recesses, willing him never to surface. But he would. Too many times when she slept, his skeletal face would appear, taunting her, harming Raoul and threatening to tear apart the life she'd made. But when she sang, her soul was tormented because the face that floated before her was that of her masked angel: patient, protective, and loving. She loathed Erik's deranged face and deeply respected the illusion that had given it life.

"I will take leave of you here, Christine, and meet with you later."

Raoul drew her thoughts back to the present. "Where are you going?" she asked.

He kissed the wrinkle of worry upon her forehead. "You do not need me to select the music for the series. Maestro Fontaine and Laroque are expecting you."

She swallowed her protest when Raoul held his hands before her.

"Christine, I just wish to have a look around, nothing more." He ran his hand through her hair. "For your peace of mind..."

How could his resolve be so solid? He seemed certain the past no longer existed. His self-assured strides bespoke a man who wouldn't allow the Paris Opera House to put him on edge. He knew the Phantom couldn't be trusted. And Christine knew his alleged death had never sat well with her husband either. What little they spoke of the past told her the darkest parts of Raoul's mind wouldn't battle with a Phantom and an angel like she, but instead dueled against a madman. Raoul would stop at nothing to protect her.

With that thought close to her breast, she turned to face the day.

"This one is lovely." Christine slid a sheet of music across the table.

"Yes, indeed." The Maestro looked the aria over carefully. "But it perhaps is better suited to the range of our reigning diva?" He handed the sheet to Edward.

Christine tipped her head in encouragement. Edward scrubbed his chin in what appeared feigned interest. Swallowing a knowing chuckle, she politely removed the music from his hand. Managers, it seemed, viewed opera as nothing more than a musical purse.

She continued to sift through the compositions, selecting pieces for herself and the rest of the company. A leather bound work set off to one side caught her eye. Sliding it toward her, she untied its satin ribbon.

"An amazing violin concerto, Madame," the Maestro remarked, removing the tip of his baton from his lips and jabbing it at the portfolio. "I have never seen an instrumental of its quality."

The notes fell and climbed on the stanzas at a frenzied pace, and then slowed, hovered and repeated. If paper were given voice, this work would have all the angels in Heaven weeping on bended knee. She shifted one page behind the other as the concerto wore on, growing in beauty and drama with each sheet. In all her life she'd never seen such a curiously eloquent combination of maddening and delicate notes. Her fingertips stroked her lips and she bit sharply on a finger.

Red ink.

Black to red, red to black, the colors shifted with the music. As she flipped the pages, her panic crescendoed with every bloody note.

"Who submitted this?" Her throat ran dry.

"I wish I knew, Madame," Maestro Fontaine lamented. "We want to showcase the piece, however, we are finding it difficult to locate a violinist capable of giving it a voice."

Christine stared at the dizzying notes. It was his. It had to be. No one could put form to expression with such exquisite beauty.

"When was this written? There's no date. Is this an older piece?"

"I am unaware of the date. It just appeared mysteriously in my office."

She fanned the heat around her neck. The room dimmed to black.

"He is here." The announcement of her shock floated from her lips against her will.

The Maestro tore his gaze from the aria he scrutinized. "Who is here, Madame? Do you know who wrote it?"

Maestro Fontaine leaned forward rapt with interest, as was Laroque. The pages slipped from her grip and slid across the table. Feeling the blood drain from her face, she bid herself not to swoon.

"*Le Fantôme de l'Opéra,*" she barely mouthed the words, biting her lip when she realized she had. Taking a deep breath, she forced herself to her feet. "I'm sorry, Maestro. I thought it looked familiar, but I'm afraid I'm mistaken. I cannot imagine who wrote this work. If you'll excuse me?"

With a hand upon her stomach, Christine made haste to the door. She flung it open and took a deep breath once in the hallway. Her morning meal threatened to reappear. Pushing off the wall, she rushed down the corridor. She'd almost set the whole Phantom of the Opera fiasco in motion with her words. She sent praise to God they hadn't sprung fully from her lips.

Chapter Ten

Richard Barret wore an air of self-righteousness like the scotch on his breath. The Opera Garnier was his realm and he its reigning king. After all, he was The Phantom of the Opera.

He snorted and wiped the spittle off his lips. This really was the role of a lifetime. Already a criminal, Richard took great delight in playing the role of an allegedly insane Phantom.

He laughed in earnest, leaning over the rope railing of the fly.

Criminally insane. He liked the sound. Richard haunted the opera house wholeheartedly; just enough to make certain the impressionable minds of the younger ballerinas believed something could be present. He did the usual things—noises in the night, stealing objects, fleeting glances of a swirling cloak. It was child's play and the opera was eating it up.

When not portraying the Phantom, the master con artist took to the Paris streets telling tall tales about a diva and her ghost, encouraging all he could impress not to miss out on the concert event of a lifetime. Laroque was right, people had a morbid fascination with gossip and ghosts, and their curiosity filled their pockets.

Currently he took large swigs from his flask and leered at the pretty heads of the ballerinas. He smiled broadly at the tales while pulling in discomfort at the neck of his costume.

The ballerinas gathered in tight circles of ribbon and tulle as they headed across the stage.

"Madame said it has been years since the theater has been booked so tightly."

"I heard the music is going to be fantastic and it is all because of La Christine. If only I could sing like her."

"I heard it is because of the Phantom." A wave of giggles burst from their lips.

Their high pitch made Richard twitch with vile arousal.

"Do you believe the stories?"

"Eloise saw him."

"She did not?"

"She did. She saw a man in a swirling cloak just outside the dormitories!" The ballerinas giggled again.

"He's killed people you know," one said, causing gasps of disbelief. "With a dagger he hides up his sleeve." The ballerina finished in a hushed tone, making the sign of the evil eye to ward off spirits lest she invite an unwanted guest.

"Not a dagger you dolt, he kills with a lasso, the Punjab lasso."

"What's a Punjab lasso?"

"I've heard his violin," one girl bragged as the rest stood enraptured.

Richard took another big slurp. Their stupidity centered on his groin, making him hard. He shrugged though, having to agree with them. Edward's suggestion that he learn the instrument was brilliant. He was getting quite good with that violin, if he did say so himself.

"He uses it to cast spells. I heard if you listen to the violin for more than a minute it will seduce you, then the Phantom will sweep you away to his dungeon lair and take favors with you."

A few girls broke out in frenzied hormone-induced laughter and covered their ears. Richard settled back in his perch, enjoying the scotch rolling down his throat and the tightness in his pants. He closed his eyes to rest for a spell, thinking briefly on sweeping away the fair, untouched womanhood of a ballerina.

Take favors indeed.

"Enough," Christine commanded.

The snap stopped the ballerinas mid giggle. It halted Anna as well. Christine stared at the cluster of girls and judging from the pout on her lips, the vicomtess' feelings had been viciously offended.

The girls scampered off, issuing embarrassed apologies between their laughter.

"Do not be too hard on them, Madame," Anna urged, pushing aside manners and not waiting for the vicomtess to address her first. "Children will tell tales."

Her frank address and bold manners caused the woman before her to go wide-eyed in shock. Anna's curiosity rose as she regarded the woman who commanded Erik's heart. It didn't take much observation to understand why so many envied her. Anna found she stared, and upon realizing her impoliteness, she looked away.

"Have we met?" Christine asked.

"No, Vicomtess." Anna felt like an ugly stone in the presence of such beauty. Her heart sank. No wonder Erik called her a simple child. Standing before this woman, it was obvious why he would cast her aside.

"Yes," Christine must have realized. "You danced at the

masquerade with that remarkable gentleman. You are Messieurs Laroque and Wischard's assistant. Mademoiselle...?"

Anna was not about to provide her surname. It was a deplorable part of her character.

"I am their assistant, yes." Her lips puckered from the disgusting taste in her mouth. She forced herself to curtsey. Damn aristocracy. She regretted having stopped. Thankfully another group of students hurried past, this bunch swirling pieces of fabric behind them like waving opera cloaks. Anna noticed the wrinkles creeping onto the vicomtess' perfect skin.

"Pay them no mind, Madame. They embellish what stories they hear. There's always another side."

Christine clasped her delicate hands together and pulled herself a bit straighter. Anna scowled under her examination. She knew judgment when she saw it.

"I beg your pardon. Exactly what other side have you heard?" she asked politely.

Anna studied the floor, chewing on her inner lip. Dare she answer? If Christine took offense to the silliness of little girls, how would she react to what Anna knew? Longing panged her gut, nearly doubling her over. She needed this confrontation. Perhaps it would soothe the sting of the unexpected love she'd discovered and lost in Erik.

"I heard you had a great tutor. An unsurpassed vocal coach who trained your voice into the instrument it is today. It was said he loved you deeply, and his passion for you clouded his judgment. When his love was unrequited, he hid from the entire world never to be seen again." She found smug satisfaction in rendering Christine speechless. "You see, children tell ghost stories. His was a love story. Ignore the tales you hear. There is no Phantom of the Opera."

Anna thought passionately of the curious gentleman that would occasionally sneak out from behind Erik's dour and cynical exterior. She missed that gentleman. But standing before Christine and knowing Erik as she did, it was best to set her needs aside. Erik's heart mattered. It was his happiness she wanted to thrive. Excusing herself, she searched Box Five expecting to see a glimpse of him, believing with a heavy heart exactly what he wanted her to.

He would be looking for Christine.

That voice was unmistakable. The attitude behind it his curse. Richard bolted upright. His eyes flew open, his lewd daydream irreversibly ruined.

That little wench. He tucked the flask in his vest pocket so violently, he sent the fly swaying. *So the Opera Garnier is not so big that our paths wouldn't cross.* He looked in contempt at his daughter. Not much of his precious little girl had changed. She was still a meddling, defiant, little strumpet.

There is no Phantom of the Opera. That girl was once again going to ruin his life, his con, and his chances at fame and fortune. The mere sight of her made him either want to drink to a black oblivion or make her life as miserable as possible. He chose the latter. It would be more fun. He rushed out of the flies.

Time to play this game—his way.

Erik lurked in Box Five. Like a fragile leaf clinging to a branch, knowing if it fell it would have no set path, anticipation trembled within him. He stared down at the horseshoe auditorium, locking his sights on Christine. His mind hadn't quieted since the moment he'd seen her. He disregarded the madness he knew was on the rise. The bliss of years ago called to him like opium to an addict and he chose to ride on a wave of false euphoria.

How should he make his presence known? He didn't want to frighten her. It must have been shocking enough for Christine to discover her Angel of Music was nothing more than mere man. He could only imagine what it would be like for her to discover he wasn't dead.

His thumb stroked the fingertips on one hand. How he longed to hold her again. He could almost feel her.

"Mademoiselle, wait," Christine called. "Where did you hear such a story?"

Anna's shoulders lifted. "It is just a part of the mystique that lurks around this theater. Why? Is the story true?"

The delicate feeling on Erik's fingertips evaporated. He balled his hand into a fist. The distance between him and Christine was closing in, and now Anna had entered into his act uninvited.

I told you to leave my theater and yet you do not obey. Why, when I need you to leave my mind, do you continue to cling?

Anna had purposely goaded a response. His glare could have melted iron.

"Yes, it is true," Christine replied. "The Angel of Music was a great teacher and he did love me. He inspired my voice. He all but gave me this opera house."

Erik's blood coursed so hard the pulse pounded in his throat. He caught himself before he leaned too far out of his shadow. Caressing the velvet of the armchair, he imagined stroking her sensuous form, whispering his adoration into her ear, and proclaiming his love for her in ways he only dreamed.

Yes, I gave you it all, Christine. I would have lassoed the moon for you.

"And you gave nothing in return?" Anna said. "He loved you."

The memory of how he'd shunned Anna wrapped around his heart like a rope of thorns. The raw passion he felt for her tightened those binds until he swore his heart would puncture. He forced such passion away. He didn't want it. Not now. He clamped his teeth in an attempt to govern the thoughts tumbling drunkenly in his mind. The velvet shredded beneath his fingers.

Damn it, you little minx. Stay out of my mind.

Christine wandered the empty stage staring out across the seats. "There was nothing I could give. Least of all love."

Ridges plowed into Anna's brow. "Why?"

"He was horrifically deformed. He frightened me. I was put through so much horror."

"Then why did you continue with the lessons?" Anna demanded sharply. "If you knew he loved you and you couldn't give that in return, why torment him?"

"I wanted to know the music for I had never experienced anything like it. I deeply respected the Angel of Music and cared for him, but I could never truly *love* him. Not in the way he wanted. His affections were so powerful—they frightened me." Christine shook her head. "A woman such as you could never comprehend the situation. He was a distorted soul, a madman. I couldn't be expected to look on *that* with love. No one could."

No one could? That? Respected? Rejected!

Erik tensed as he shook from head to toe. His hands crushed to his mask. He cursed his ugliness. Looking at the two women, he recognized the confusion Anna had mentioned. With all his being, he tried to control his demons. His inability to do so was not *his* fault. Man made him this way.

He turned his attention to the woman beside her. Erik leaned forward avoiding the urge to fold himself over the velvet railing and scream to the women below.

Anna, make her understand me.

"Did you even know his soul?" Anna attacked. She shook her head so forcefully her braid snaked against her back. "Perhaps you were too scared of him and fright made you *believe* you cared? You had so much invested in the Angel of Music you didn't want to see if you could love the *man*. Of course he would react with violence. What other life did he know? No one offered him compassion. Regardless if you felt threatened, you took his love—which was just as genuine as all you feared in him—and used that with your belief you could never escape and *pretended* to understand him for the sake of your liberty."

"I beg your pardon."

Anna's voice rose. "Taking what he wanted was the only way he knew how to love. Outcasts are easy to fear. They're often misunderstood because no one gave them a chance to *be* understood. When he professed his love, could it be you were ashamed to think your admiration could eventually win, because of his outward appearance? Could it be you were too crippled by his command over you to discover the limits of your heart? He was a deviant and you a woman of society. What would that do to your status, to your vicomte? Perhaps you were not up to that challenge because you were too immature to explore it." A sharp stomp of her foot ricocheted across the stage while her words shot like darts. "Maybe you were too afraid to look to see if he was a human being."

"You know nothing!" Christine indignantly shouted. "Nothing of that man or what he put me through. Why am I even speaking to you? A complete stranger and a common peasant? You don't understand the roles of which I am a part. How dare you speak of them!"

"A common peasant, Madame? Were you not a peasant before the Académie Nationale?"

"You hold your tongue," Christine insisted, leaning into Anna with one well-placed step. Unimpressed, Anna didn't budge.

Erik watched as she calmly recalled every last detail of Christine's life as told to her by him.

"You could never separate man from father or Angel from Phantom so long as you refused to first know yourself."

Lifting a shaking hand, Christine batted her lips with her fingers. "How could you speak of such things?"

Anna lowered her face. "Because I never had a father. Guardian Angels do not exist for me, and I have stared phantoms of many kinds in the eye. I respectfully ask you accept my apology. The world represses what it does not understand. I suppose I simply don't know the life you lead. It's difficult, you see, to be cast aside in indifference when all you wish is to give unconditional love."

"Unconditional love? That man manipulated me. He deceived and used me. Why I ever returned to this opera house is beyond comprehension. Don't speak of such matters, Mademoiselle. You know nothing but the opinion you have constructed from ruthless rumors. Don't tell me what I do and do not understand. It is *you* who doesn't understand."

Christine hastened past her. Stepping aside, Anna lifted her face toward Box Five. Erik rose, moving enough to make his presence known. Their eyes locked. An omniscient air pulsed between them, forcing her from her spot. She looked over her shoulders only once before rushing out of his theater.

He sank to the seat, indifferent to being spotted. He gazed at Anna's back until she was out of sight.

How could he have never seen how frightened Christine had been all those years ago? She was young, impressionable and her mind too easy to bend to the whims of his voice. She could never have seen beyond the spell his music had cast over her, he had never allowed his guard down enough. His chest tightened like a drowning man. No matter how he fought he couldn't break the surface for air. He recognized the profound panic as the difference between Anna and Christine. Chancing vulnerability, he wore no emotional masks around Anna.

He'd given her a glimpse at the man.

Back then he'd tried so hard to give Christine the world, filling her nights with intricate dreams through his music. Never had he attempted to awaken the woman within and present her an opportunity to meet the man. It wouldn't have mattered. Did he even know the man in him then? Anyway, he never would have been able to pay her such regard.

Then he'd never known how, because until one is looked upon in love, the soul remains in slumber.

Chapter Eleven

Three taps stopped her dead in her tracks.

She paused in her efforts to close down the boxes. Over the years, and with due cause, Madame Giry had developed a mistrust of the Opera Garnier when it was as silent as the dead.

The dead after all, did walk and talk.

Certain she'd heard three taps, she glanced in front of her and then behind before hesitantly pushing the door to Box Five open. The Opera Ghost would always tap three times if he needed her, but why would Erik be in Box Five with an empty theater? She stuck her head in before entering.

Cautiously she leaned her plump frame against one of the pillars in the box and pressed an ear against it. Knowing the hollow pillar to be one of Erik's hiding spots; she strained to hear any evidence of its retired occupant. She breathed a sigh of relief, tittering over her paranoia. Waving her hands in front of her, she shook off her silly notions and turned toward the hall, dragging the door closed. She stopped as the loveliest male voice prevented her escape.

"Where are you going?"

That voice tickled the back of her neck like a spider dangling from a web. The shiver that followed had been trickling down her spine for years.

"I didn't realize you were here, Monsieur."

"I am everywhere and nowhere, Madame, of that you are quite aware."

"You've not requested my services for a while. What is it you need?"

His exhaustion floated like a feather caught on a breeze. "Letters...deliver my letters."

Madame Giry snapped to attention. Nonsensical stammers bubbled past her lips. She wouldn't be a part of his charade again. She flirted with Erik's unpredictability, but she couldn't and wouldn't hold her tongue.

"No!" she barked with an indignant stomp of a fat foot and wag of her head that sent the feathers of her hat swaying. "I will not. I will not cater—"

"One letter will be given to my managers in the usual manner. The other is addressed to you and your two most honored guests."

Somewhere a shadow spit those final two words. It sent the hair on her arms standing on edge. "I'll not be a part of your attempts to—"

"See to it you read the letter in their presence."

"I refuse to—"

"Madame Giry!" Erik's voice boomed like cannon fire. He must have heard her small shriek, for he softened his voice. "Forgive my tone, Madame. I am weary. I mean no ill will. I only wish a brief audience with the vicomtess to put to rest her concerns."

Madame Giry sat. She'd never taken the company of the Opera Ghost in his box. Was he in the seat next to her? Behind her? Was he simply in the air? Erik indeed seemed everywhere and nowhere. It made the invisible spider creep again.

"Don't you think discovering you're alive will add to her apprehension instead of calming it? Why do you wish to meddle with her emotions?"

She cringed when she heard the sound of fabric sliding across velvet. A dark silhouette rose in front of her. He slowly turned. Madame Giry wrung her hands together. Would she be reprimanded for inviting herself into his territory? He draped the cloak across the crook of his arm and lightly touched a finger to his temple as if trying to repress a thought. He seemed tired.

He seemed...human.

"She dwells on the past, Madame, and with it me. If I am meddling with anyone's emotions, it is my own fool heart."

"Monsieur, you cannot win her love."

"I do not need to win it, Madame."

A cold rush of air poured across her skin as Erik brushed past her and out of sight. She absently bit her thumbnail, trying to rotate herself out of the puzzle. She cursed herself for caving to Erik's whims.

Resigned that he was a man never meant for her to understand, she rose. Placing a hand on the small shelf in the box, she searched for Erik's notes. Tears pulled at the corner of her eyes when she touched the parcel. A smile inched its way across her lips. She placed the notes in the pocket of her dress, hugged the tiny package of English sweets to her chest and closed the door.

She had letters to deliver.

Gentlemen,

Fondest greetings. Welcome to my opera house. You have my regrets for not greeting you earlier but I have been unavoidably detained. I admire your Herculean efforts to take over the reins from your predecessors. They left my theater in a state of disarray and I am most certain did not leave you with any expressed knowledge of my existence. You need not worry about the state of current affairs. Nonetheless, now that I appear to have my affairs in order, I do have a few simple instructions.

It has come to my attention you have acquired diva Christine Daaé, the Vicomtess de Chagny, to perform during the anniversary events. My congratulations on arranging such a feat. I respectfully command you put a stop to the ridiculous rumors regarding her and a certain 'Phantom of the Opera.' What is past is done.

I expect you to treat the diva with dignity. Mark my words, I will expose you as liars and frauds if these rumors continue. If need be, I will take back control of my theater. Make no attempt to contact the vicomtess regarding my demands. I will see to it she is contacted personally. I strongly urge you to follow my orders. I am watching.

Your most humble and obedient servant,

Ph. of the O.

P.T.O: Monsieur Wischard, if you lay your hands on Anna one more time, I will be forced to react.

"What in bloody hell are you trying to pull?" Edward burst into his office, the force of his entry causing the door to smash against the wall.

Richard and Jacob looked up from their drinks in bewilderment.

"Good morning to you, too, Edward, what the devil—"

Edward cut Jacob short with a thrust of his hand, roughly shoving a letter into his chest. The scrawny manager stumbled as Edward made his way toward the man reclining behind the desk.

"You son-of-a-bitch, I run my cons my way."

Without ceremony, he grabbed Richard's feet and flung them to the side, sending him toppling to the ground. No easy achievement for a man of Edward's unhealthy physique. Richard reacted to the insult in a split second's time. Springing to his feet, he slammed the portly manager backward and pinned his throat against the wall with his forearm.

"Gentlemen," Jacob shouted. "Richard, let him go for Christ's sake."

Edward regained his composure; straightening his collar as he took the letter Jacob had perused.

"Richard, what is the meaning of this?" Jacob interrogated.

"What is the meaning of what?" he growled.

Edward flung the letter in Richard's face. "No one tells me how to run my cons."

"Calm down. There must be an explanation," Jacob reasoned. He indicated the letter Richard held. "Unique choice of red ink, Richard. And nice touch with the P.T.O. Very effective."

Richard read, his nostrils flaring open. "That bitch. That meddling little blower! I didn't write this you idiots."

"You didn't write it?" Edward controlled his shout by pounding his fists in the air.

"Anna," Richard snarled, tossing the letter on the desk.

"Oh, dear God, you're paranoid. Jacob, I need a drink," Edward bellowed. "Screw the hour."

"Richard, what are you talking about?" Jacob asked.

"Not what. Who. Anna. It wouldn't be the first time that bloody girl has tried to ruin a con." Richard stalked to Edward and snatched the carafe from his hand. "I saw her yesterday speaking with your diva trying to convince her there is no Phantom of the Opera. She's not an idiot. Anna has to know the money this petty rumor is pulling in. She's out to cheat you, and if you've been anything like the others with whom I've put her in service, I can promise she despises you." Richard greedily swigged directly from the carafe.

"Anna knows nothing of this. She's as clueless as the day she was born."

"You think so, Edward?" Richard challenged. "I've seen that girl's intuition ruin far too many of my games. Why do you think I got rid of her?"

Jacob intervened. "Richard, I side with Edward. The girl is mindless. Anna is absolutely under our thumb. You are obsessing."

Richard sank on the couch and spoke over the rim of the carafe. "You only say that because without her, all you would ever be is piss proud and frustrated."

"You son-of-a-bitch!" Jacob shouted over Richard's snickering. "I dab it up with plenty of women. Your bloody daughter is just convenient." He reconsidered. "Did she see you?"

"Of course not." Richard's knuckles turned white. Vile distaste for Anna writhed from behind his teeth. "Believe what you will, I don't trust her."

Edward raised his hands in defeat. "Fine then, what do you propose we do?"

He scowled at the two men and at the empty carafe. "I'll figure something out. I always have."

Mesdames et Monsieur,

I recognize the profound shock you must be experiencing upon reading a letter from me, but I thought it best to address this matter with the utmost haste. I dislike scandal and realize what may arise from this. While I may appear to have risen from the dead, I have yet to die.

You have my heartfelt apology for the state of the opera house. My neglect of the facility has been most reprehensible.

Please accept this note as a token of my esteemed appreciation on your return to Paris. I hope your stay has been comfortable. Since you have been so kind as to patronize my theater, I would like to address you each in turn and in regret for the time past since our last contact. This letter is long overdue.

To the noblest Vicomte de Chagny I say this: Well done. You have proven a worthy opponent. I trust you have treated her well and with the admiration she deserves. Do not scorn her. If I had understood, as I do now, you would be in a very different place.

To Madame Jules Giry: You have my deepest and most respectful thanks. You have been a faithful and obedient servant through the years. I owe you a formidable debt of gratitude. I will see you are not held in contempt for your years of servitude; most I find do not understand the circumstances.

As for the Vicomtess de Chagny, I will address her in person. See to it she meets with me tomorrow evening. Madame Giry will know of the appointed spot. I ask Christine to bring a certain violin concerto. It has come to my attention this work has been submitted for the anniversary celebrations without my expressed consent. I would like it returned. No harm will come to her. I only wish the briefest of audiences.

I remain in your kindest regard,

Ph. of the O.

P.T.O: Madame Giry, deliver my humblest and most heartfelt apologies. Tell her it was no mistake.

Raoul solemnly folded the letter. A remarkable calm draped over him as he ran a finger over his lips. Madame Giry's fingers beat a shaky rhythm against her teacup. Her toes bounced her knees. Raoul couldn't fault her nerves. He addressed his wife.

"Are you well?"

Christine sat stiffly in an overstuffed armchair, staring blankly into the morning fire. Just a short hour ago, they'd finished a lovely meal. She'd commented on the delightful morning and had looked forward to the day, but now their world had come to a standstill. Raoul knelt in front of her and reached to stroke her cheek.

"Christine, you need to share your thoughts."

Her body shook in unison with the dancing flames. A sickly hue colored her normally flawless skin.

"He is dead," she muttered. "He is supposed to be dead."

Raoul sighed and let his chin fall against his chest. Rising, he turned to Madame Giry.

"We were informed he was just that, Madame—dead. His former lackey, known as the Persian, told us himself—"

"It took weeks for the information to reach us," Christine interrupted breathlessly. "Erik made me swear I return to put him to rest. When...when...I did...who...what did I—"

Madame Giry rubbed her neck several times. The teacup rattled as she set it down. "You buried remains of *les carrières de Paris*. The Opera Ghost is well aware of numerous souls who rest below Paris. The obituary was written; a skeleton exhumed from the catacombs and placed where it could be found." Pity crept into her voice. "Who would know the difference between what he was in life and any other poor soul in death? He knew the length of time that would have passed until you returned. Combine that with the conditions in the vaults...faking his death was simple."

The pools of Christine's tears magnified her blue eyes into a sea of emotion. Raoul's heart tore in two seeing her in pain. "This is sick and maddening." He shook the page in his hand. "This is some sort of cheap jest focused on making a mockery of the torment my family went through."

Madame Giry hung her head. "Monsieur, I may be many things, but I'm not a liar. He is alive. He has caged himself away in those vaults as if he were entombed."

Raoul turned his back to the old woman and braced himself against the mantel.

The Phantom lurked at the Opera Garnier. All these years Erik had dodged the authorities and ignored the debt he owed society for the murders, for Christine's abduction, for the chandelier. Regret shook his head. He gripped the marble until his fingertips turned white, crushing the paper still in his hand.

"Years of servitude?" he repeated. "Madame Giry, *why?*" Raoul pounded a fist against the mantel. A candlestick wobbled in its spot. "With all the patronage my family name has given to the Garnier...why would you do this to us?"

"You don't understand, Monsieur, you cannot possibly understand." She slapped her hands against her thighs. "I should have torn that letter to pieces and gone against his whim. I tried to go to the authorities many times, but my life and his are so intertwined—more than you could ever know."

"Madame Giry, he is a demon," Christine cried. "He tried to kill Raoul! How could you?"

"Please forgive me. You of all people should know the power of the Opera Ghost. But you must understand they were crimes of passion. Despicable, heinous crimes, but deep inside he meant no harm. You have to believe me. He would never harm you. Especially now, he's different."

Raoul pushed off from the mantel. He studied Madame Giry's face. If Erik had changed, then why did she look so guilty? "Different? You speak of him as a long lost friend. It does not appear to me he has changed, Madame."

Clasping her hands, she shook them in her lap, pleading for him to understand. "I didn't tell because I was frightened. You and the vicomtess fled, but my life is here. No matter how much I try to deny it, he is a part of that. I'm a simple woman, and he has a way of involving one in his life."

Raoul turned away, not willing to allow her to see the flicker of recognition pass across his face.

"I learned, just like the other box keepers before me, that if we allowed him his venue, he was harmless."

"Harmless?" Outrage jutted his body backward. A hand rested on his hip while his other arm waved wildly, gesturing with disgust toward Paris. "Is that how you view him? His blatant disrespect for life is harmless? What he unleashed on the opera house, harmless? His madness, harmless? Attempting to blow up a quarter of Paris, harmless?" The letter snapped in the air as he waved it in her face. "Is this letter to be considered harmless? Are we to believe what happened in the cellars will not happen again?"

"Why are you placing blame on me? When you ran, you knew he still lived. When you learned of his obituary, you knew that skeleton was not solid proof. You knew he was a trickster. Why did *you* not pursue him?"

His stiff posture diminished as he sat next to her. "You are right. Forgive me, Madame Giry. We must not divide ourselves. We all own a burden of responsibility, but we end this now. I will not have my family chased by him any longer. Where is he?"

Christine's head shot up. "Raoul, what—"

He calmed her by laying a finger to his lips and turning a stern gaze on the older woman.

Madame Giry shifted uncomfortably. "I don't know. He comes to me very rarely, if at all anymore. Something is very different about him. I cannot quite understand."

"The difference is Christine is within his grasp. He is most assuredly in the labyrinths and cellars."

"I don't truly know. They were sealed off after the investigations. You know as well as I, the efforts of Prefect of Police and his investigators. The passages lead to dead ends."

Raoul detected an air of uncertainty in her voice. Something about the tilt of her head and the way she fiddled with her fingers made him question her sincerity.

"Then what do we do?" Christine asked.

Her plea made him dismiss the box keeper's suspicious posture. Raoul contemplated the letter again. "*Tell her it was no mistake*," he read aloud. "What is he talking about? What was no mistake?"

"That he let me go." Christine's voice trailed to a whisper. "No mistake he gave me my liberty so he could always be there, haunting me, possessing me." Christine lifted a hand kerchief to her lips and attempted to stifle her tears.

Raoul buried his fingers in the cool silkiness of her hair with one hand and wiped a stray tear from her chin with the other.

"Abide by his wishes, Madame. Meet with him and deliver his concerto." A note appeared from Madame Giry's sleeve. Raoul fought to keep his revulsion in check lest his fingers tangle Christine's hair. "He asks that the vicomtess meet him in her former dressing room tomorrow evening. He will keep his word. He has calmed."

"No." Hate crawled from Raoul's voice. "I will not allow her to fall prey to his traps again. I will contact Inspector Legard. I am certain he will be willing to work with us."

"Work with us?" Christine gasped.

"I am not going to let this lie, Christine. If Erik is alive, this ends here. I cannot have him tormenting you. He needs to be found." She opened her mouth, but he silenced her with a press of his hand to her lips. "He is a killer. I cannot believe he means you no harm. There are crimes he has committed for which he has not answered. He was a fool to ever let it be known he was alive. This is his undoing. Now Erik will play by my rules, and this time I will be waiting."

Chapter Twelve

The mantel clock chimed thirty past one.

Christine delicately slipped out of bed. She glanced around the elegantly appointed room Raoul insisted upon sharing with her, before resting her eyes on him. He wouldn't hear of separate chambers. The thought of how he wanted her near warmed her at night. She sat on the bed's edge, her gaze moving in rhythm with the rise and fall of his bare chest. He was such a beautiful man in body, mind and soul. How had she captured his heart?

Christine brushed her lips against his. She dressed, making certain Raoul still slept before sneaking out of the bedchamber. Her feet padded softly through dimly lit halls. Swinging on a cloak, she took one last look at the hour and escaped through the front door.

Nerves swirled inside of her like the mist coating the fog-filled streets. The brutal force of regret crushed against her, and she laid a hand against the pain in her chest. The brougham approached on time, the driver having done as instructed by covering the Chagny coat of arms on either side of the doors. Rumor was richer than an emperor's coffers in Paris. She didn't need prying eyes staring at their crest. Christine looked over her shoulder toward the window where Raoul slept. She didn't wish to deceive him, but an irresistible longing pulled at her.

A weary footman opened the door and helped her inside. He gave her a tired, but polite smile.

"To the opera," Christine directed.

Erik stared unblinking into the bleak emptiness of Christine's former dressing room. How many mornings had he stood behind this mirror waiting to coach her? How often had his heart stopped as she brushed her flaxen hair, read a script, or daydreamed like a silly child? How completely had it filled his life?

Silence beyond the mirror taunted him. The solemn stillness of the room reflected his mood. He thought she'd come—he needed her to come. Spreading his hands against the mirror, his mind argued against his heart.

Damn this fate!

"Christine, why?" A fist pounded the mirror. Tiny cracks spread like a spider's web across its glassed surface. Erik mindlessly traced the progress with his finger. "Why did you come back? Why now?"

She should have never returned after burying that body. His forehead fell forward to meet the unfeeling glass.

Torment in his heart exploded with intensity and drove the memories of her raw rejection through him. His body joined his forehead, pressing his weight against the glass. How many nights had he embraced the mirror trying to fill his arms? Erik yanked his face from the glass and braced his hands against the frame. He felt his heartbeat in his fingertips.

Raoul de Chagny, how he despised that man. He had everything: freedom, unsurpassed charm, respect, and Christine's love. Curling his fingers together, Erik took a deep breath, controlling his need to smash the mirror. The boy was the reason Christine hadn't come, why he was unable to speak with her. Erik had allowed Christine the freedom to choose whom she would love. Should he not be afforded that same scrap of respect? He had spared the vicomte's wretched life. Should he not be spared his own pitiful existence?

Lifting two fingers to his forehead, Erik tipped his neck back and gave in to the sounds in his mind. Noise rolled savagely with music. The name of one woman battled against the next. He had to profess to Christine how deep his love ran and no matter what came to pass part of his heart would remain hers—for eternity. In the past he'd lived for Christine's happiness. Now, he wanted his.

Loveless Hell was not where he wanted to be imprisoned. Long ago he'd wished for a wife to take out on Sundays. He thought he'd purged all need to live like a normal man, but as he stared into a broken mirror in a damp and narrow hallway, he found buried beneath his bitterness he still longed for those Sunday walks.

Staring into an empty room did nothing but make him feel pitiful. He had a message for Christine and he was being ignored like a common mongrel. He traced the cracked mirror again. Forget the Vicomte de Chagny. The Phantom's voice would be heard. This was his kingdom. The vicomte should beware how he walked through it. Even mongrels had rights and he'd get his message to her in the only other way he knew how.

Erik backed away from the mirror and turned to slink into the inky blackness of his labyrinth thinking not on how he was built of the macabre, but wondering what it felt like to have sun upon his skin and to see the shimmer of the Seine by day instead of the mist of his lake by darkness. Picturing what joys would come from wrapping her feminine frame in the warmth of his cloak.

His eyes slipped shut. She stowed into his dreams like an unfinished strain of music begging to be finished. Completely alone in his maze of catacombs, he felt her invisible hand curl around his offered arm. He touched the unseen weave of her braid, swearing when next they met he would stab fate with the same dagger it had placed in his back and wander freely with a woman to love dressing his arm.

Through his scorned resentment one sound calmed the rising noise in his mind. The shroud of his madness frayed when he whispered his affections.

"Mon petit."

Paris stilled this time of night with the exception of the farmers wearily pushing their carts through the streets to market. Occasionally a turgotine whizzed past on its way out of the city. The clip of the horses' hooves lulled her into a trance as they mockingly beat, why, why, why...

Why was she compelled to bend to Erik's whims? Trying to ignore his request would be like ignoring the beat of her heart. She must not keep the Angel of Music waiting.

Without warning, disbelieving relief surged upon her mixed with apprehension.

Erik lived. What would she do when she saw him and heard his exquisite voice again? Should she yell out years of frustration? Blame him for the secret anguish she kept locked in her heart? He couldn't take total culpability for what came between them. She owned the responsibility for blindly accepting his illusions as truth.

Glancing at her hand, Christine wondered if she shook out of relief or a more sinister emotion.

The confrontation on stage with that girl kept her awake at night and made her mind spin with conflicting emotions. The fear of Erik could be outgrown. It must. How often does one get a second chance to redress their choices? The need to do such without being influenced by propriety sent her heart fluttering in her chest. As much as she loved Raoul, part of her still slavishly wished to be chosen by the Angel of Music.

And she was no longer too immature to address it.

She pressed a hand against her belly to stop the trembling. What would it mean to be truly chosen by the Angel? Erik loved with such fierce intensity. How could anyone handle all the ways it might manifest? She swallowed the memory of first seeing his face. If Erik was alive, then so was the madness. *What might he do to her husband? What would redressing foolhardy choices do the life she had now?*

Christine's apprehension rose as she watched the opera house grow in the distance. Raoul had no idea of her whereabouts. Guilt turned the anxiety to a rock in her stomach. The opera house loomed before her.

Raoul loved her. He was the safe choice. The easy choice...

Christine banged on the roof to catch the driver's attention. "No. Return!"

The carriage swung around in a weary circle before heading in the direction it had come. Christine closed her eyes in an attempt to make Paris disappear. The walls of a maze closed in around her and she was caught in the middle between the love of the devoted, handsome man sharing the bed she'd abandoned and the mysterious adoration of a dark, sensual angel roaming the deserted halls of the opera house.

She would not choose between the two tonight.

"I cannot," she whispered.

Anna recognized most of this was her fault.

With a frustrated jig, she attempted to shake manure off her boot. As expected, her insubordination to the Vicomtess de Chagny hadn't gone unnoticed by Laroque and Wischard. She paid the price by an added workload in the stables. The dance made no progress, so Anna used a point of the pitchfork to dig out a clump of the offensive matter.

Remorse was probably called for. The disrespect she'd shown had been blatant and one thing Anna held in the highest esteem was respect. She laughed softly, quite satisfied with the confrontation. What she'd found was enlightening. She'd needed to see for herself what the mystique was behind the famous diva. As the pitchfork stabbed into the muck, she winced. A dull pain raced from her wrist to her forearm. Yet another reminder of Erik...

The prongs hauled a steamy mess of hay over her shoulder. Anna completely understood how he could have fallen in love with Christine. On a heavy sigh, she realized he still was. She poked at the hay, trying to pick through her thoughts. Erik seemed to horde every emotion with such deep passion, and every need with wanton abandon. She found it melancholy that Christine never returned those sentiments. How could the woman not want to know Erik as she had come to understand him—a dark and intriguing, inexcusably insane yet erotic, mysterious, childlike and utterly insatiable *man*?

She tossed her feelings aside like the hay she flung around. Above all else, she wanted Erik to be happy, and if he wished to pursue

Christine's affection, then she'd not deter him. Love would find her someday. It would be ignorant to think otherwise and selfish to stand in the way of anyone's quest for it. Still, she thought she'd found a hand to fill hers. She'd never been in love and despite Erik's unpredictability, she found he flamed her emotions with passions she never knew possible. Her heart fell to her feet when she realized she would never explore them.

Anna twisted her back to the right, then left. Every muscle ached, but the work kept her from being found by Erik, not that she thought he'd be looking for her. It was best to leave him be. Perhaps it was being stubborn, but she didn't quite know what to make of their confrontation after the masquerade. The sound of his betrayal still pulsed in her head. *She was a mistake.*

Leaning the pitchfork against the stall, she rubbed the sting of manure out of her eyes. A horse whinnied softly.

"I know how you feel," she muttered to the stallion, reaching out to draw a finger across the Chagny coat of arms decorating the horse's blanket. She swallowed the jealousy bubbling inside of her. The vicomtess already had the heart of a respectable man, why did she need Erik's as well?

"Anna?"

She spun. The lanterns around her did nothing to penetrate the dark.

"Who's there? Who addresses?" She stepped from the stall. The voice had an unmistakable and familiar pitch. "I can't see very well," she cautioned, eyes still watering from her rubbing. The horse nickered nervously.

"Anna?"

The lantern swung through the air. It crashed against the side of her face. Anna screamed. She threw her hands to her head as the hot metal and glass seared her temple. Losing her footing, she hit the floor. She clawed and grasped at the hay.

A shake of her head tried to rid the ringing in her ears. She attempted to clear her clouding vision, when a boot slammed into her back. A stabbing pain roared across her lower back. She fought to obey the adrenaline coursing the command through her body.

Flee!

It came too late. Prone on the ground, she stared at black boots and the edge of a long cloak. A man stooped next to her. Savagely, he grabbed her hair and twisted her head around. She cried as her world dimmed. What she couldn't see, she could hear and feel. His breath pulsed against her cheek and his voice poured into her ears.

"Stay out of my way."

The far reaches of Anna's mind registered a glimpse of her assailant. The image plunged her into the grip of unimaginable terror. Her head thudded against the floor as he shoved her aside. The man rose, the hem of his cloak caressing her body as he stepped over her and into the shadows.

Mercifully, Anna disappeared into a shadow of her own.

Chapter Thirteen

"To what do I owe this audience, Madame Giry? Are you not busy entertaining your precious guests?" Irritability rumbled out his mouth. Two fingers flicked the door closed. "I believe your bothersome need to summon me is because the vicomte is ill-pleased with my note? It is after all quite unusual for *you* to come looking for *me*."

Erik strolled through the room, less than thrilled to have his time devoured by trivial requests. Madame Giry's trademark twitching didn't help his already perturbed mood.

"I imagine he does not rejoice that I live," Erik casually said. "And I am certain Christine is a bit disenchanted." He clicked his tongue. "I only need to speak with her for a moment. Pity, the boy has not learned to mind my demands."

If Madame Giry patrolled the room with any more resolve, she would shred the already worn carpet. It was as annoying as the rats constantly scurrying under his feet. A single thrust of his arm in her path stopped her short.

"Mother Giry, why did you summon me?"

"There's been an accident involving the theater." She ducked his arm and backed against the far wall.

"An accident?" Erik feigned shock. "How unfortunate in its timing with your old patron and his wife visiting." He leaned against the door and gestured around the room in condescending concern. "Shall I ask what kind of accident?"

"It was horrible, simply horrible."

A bored roll of his shoulder added to his performance. "And why should this concern me? I no longer manage this facility. This opera has been faltering for years. Unfortunate events seem attracted to it."

Erik projected his laughter. Madame Giry spun in her spot to stare horrified at the snickering tea kettle. She spoke to it, the news spluttering from her mouth.

"Anna's been assaulted!"

The carefully constructed indifference he dressed himself in evaporated with the weight of her words. Their meaning fell around him like shattered glass. Erik jerked off the door and proceeded mechanically toward a chair, carefully stepping around the implication. He gripped the edge of the desk for support as he sat. "Assaulted?"

The word stung his tongue and rendered speech impossible. Around him the room pulsed and swelled in cadence with his mounting tension. Erik's hands curled around the edge of the table, his calm fraying like a strand of silk.

"Was she...violated?" Erik contorted his neck. Disgusting imagery coated his mind. The edge of the table cracked under the savage intensity of his control.

"I don't think so, Monsieur."

The news did little to comfort. Splinters dug into his fingers.

"She's resting now, but is battered and bruised. The theater doctor tended her earlier."

Erik relaxed his hands and breathed deeply to cleanse his mind. He honed the technique through the years when the urge to give in to the noise was far too great.

"Why did you not summon me immediately?" he asked testily.

The pressure in the room fractured like ice upon a frozen lake. A puff of air broke through her lips as her small bubbling steps turned into long strides.

"Suspicion is running wild. The Phantom's name has already been uttered since the vicomtess arrived. And you add to the fire with your letters. Judgment has been made and the tales are already woven of your resurrection."

Venom shot from Erik's gaze. How dare she say such things. She moved a chair and sat in front of him. He leaned away. How dare she be so bold.

"No one knew you were still here or for how long. It has been peaceful. *You* have been peaceful. I knew if I told, you'd immediately jeopardize that. I agonized over what this may have stirred in you. I didn't want to see anyone hurt."

Silence stretched the delicate strand of tension between them before Erik found his tongue. "What this stirs in me is of no concern to you, Madame Giry. If you also dread the presence of the Opera Ghost, then so be it. He has been buried so *I* can live. I was under the impression there were perhaps two who believed that, but apparently there is only one. You will take me to her now."

His fist slammed the splintered edge of the desk cracking the last thread of wood under his rage. The chair beneath him toppled as he rose. He stood aside to allow her to pass, noting she dared not meet his eyes.

"You must not be seen," she urged.

Madame Giry opened the door to the concierge office where Anna lay sleeping on the divan. Erik paused. A foreign sensation had a stranglehold on him, making it difficult to breathe.

Fear.

"No one has any idea how this happened." Madame Giry turned up the lamp by Anna's side. "The stable master found her early this morning."

He breathed deeply, unaccustomed to the emotion swirling in his pit. Anna's breathing was shallow, one temple swollen and bruised from the brunt of her assault. A jagged cut ran from the corner of her eye and across a large burn.

Cocking his head, like a curious child looking upon a wounded bird, he pulled a chair close to her side. He lifted one finger to her temple. Her clammy skin prompted Erik to remove his cloak. Fingers tangled and tripped over the clasp. He never knew he could tremble.

"I will keep vigil with her. You may leave." His eyes never moved from Anna's face. As he draped his cloak around her, a treacherous sigh of grief escaped his lips. This was not how he envisioned his cloak wrapping her small frame.

"Monsieur, you must not get involved. The vicomte will arrive and with him half of Paris. Look at the circumstances. There will be suspicions."

"Damn, the circumstances! Damn their suspicions!"

One arch of his arm cleared the contents of a table. A lamp shattered against the floor. Opera glasses and programs flew across the room. The next thrust of his arm directed her toward the door. Tension colored his voice an awful shade of black. "Just leave us be."

He turned his back to Madame Giry.

Anna's hair spilled around the divan in long waves. He reached out and ran his fingers down the length of it. With his hands hovering over her, he paused, not entirely sure of himself.

Madame Giry held her breath as she watched Erik gather as much of Anna's tresses as he dared. Shyly, she thought, he twisted her hair into a long braid. When finished, he laid the braid aside, laced his fingers and sat back, silent and watchful.

The simplicity of the gesture shed light on everything she'd tried to understand. A man lay beyond the madman. Her mouth gaped and she covered her revelation with her hand. She turned to bustle out of the room, her heart beating heavily with the humanity of Erik's emotion—but stopped.

Her head dipped to her shoulder as she became entranced by a mesmerizing melody. He sang to his charge—a thick drape of hauntingly beautiful notes. No splendor outside of heaven matched what she heard. Standing in servant-like respect, the tendrils of his voice wrapped around her like a poignant embrace. She hastened to leave before her own confounded emotions disturbed the moment. After dragging the door closed behind her she paused, listening to his voice drift through the wood.

For what days she had left on the earth, she'd never forget the image of him braiding Anna's hair or the sound of his indescribable song. Madame Giry pondered how many times in Erik's life he'd wished to have someone simply listen...

For its intended recipient, the song would fall on deaf ears. It would do nothing but fill the silence. Madame Giry made her choice. *She* would listen. If it was the last thing she ever did, she would listen and understand.

Pushing off the door she rushed away, her head filled with revelations she never dreamed possible. Around her, droplets of sound rained through Erik's stirring lament.

It was as if Death himself chased her down the hall, weeping nothing but pure music.

Jolting awake, it took Erik a moment to register his whereabouts and the understanding of it rushed over him in sickening waves. He rubbed a kink in his neck. He laid his hand on Anna's cheek. She had pinked, her flesh now warm.

"Anna?"

"She still sleeps, Monsieur."

Madame Giry emerged from a far corner of the room. She approached, extending a cup of hot tea. He stared quizzically at the cup before accepting it. Nimble fingers wound around the knot at his neck until the silk of his cravat loosened.

"Why should you look so uncomfortable, Madame Giry?" Bitterness fell around him like an unraveled bow. "Have you not seen a man undo his neckwear before?" She flushed. He was too weary to inquire as to why she looked at him so oddly. "How long did I rest?"

"Not long enough. You look worn."

"I assure you, Madame, I could look worse." Erik gestured toward his face, permitting his off-sense humor to give Madame Giry a glimpse of the man he kept hidden.

"Anna looks better," she encouraged. "Rest and time will do her well. You had best be gone. The authorities will speak with her when the laudanum wears off. You should not be seen here."

Erik kept silent. Placing the untouched cup on the side table, he tenderly brushed a lock of hair from Anna's swollen eye.

"Why do you stare so, Madame Giry? I find it most disagreeable."

"Monsieur, what are you looking to gain from this?" She stomped her feet against the floorboards. "What is it you expect of her?"

Erik's brows pinched beneath his mask. "You have the serpent's tongue. I find I do not like your line of questioning."

"And I find I do not like your stubbornness."

Erik rocked back in surprise. "It seems you have found a backbone."

Madame Giry's lips tightened. Giving an indignant bob of her head, she gestured toward Anna. "You can say I take my cues from her."

"You should not," Erik snapped. "Her tenacious spirit is not becoming on you. Do not play such dangerous hands with me. I am in no mood."

"What is this friendship you have forged with her?"

The box keeper's sudden audacity was sword severing their well-constructed roles. Erik rose. He yanked loose the bow with an angry twitch.

"A stare decorates your face again, Madame Giry." Erik tossed the cravat aside with a contemptuous flick of his wrist. "Does such an action seem too normal for you? Of course it would. Anything normal when applied to me is instantly regarded as repugnant, even by friends. You are shocked I use that word? I suppose that term could be applied toward us. You have been a faithful minister." He wandered the room, fondling objects he came in contact with. "Faithful and fearful."

He picked up a likeness of her only child, and stroked the glass. When he lifted his eyes he caught the heavy lidded look to hers.

"Did you give me a choice?" she said with soft authority.

He lifted a brow she couldn't see. She was growing bold in her old age.

"I have given you much over the years, have I not?" he replied. "My manipulation of the management advanced your child to the front of the ballet line. Your daughter's dancing was much improved. Shall we discuss the marriage I arranged for her? Is she happy as a baroness?"

The square to her shoulders had dropped and with it her attitude.

"Meg is fortunate and quite content," she replied gratefully.

"Would you have served me had you not received something in return?" Erik nudged the picture back in its spot, making certain it was exactly as he found it. "You did me a great service years ago ministering to the Opera Ghost's needs, but it ceased there. Where your compassion ended your ill-ease began. You see, our arrangement did not evolve. I bribed you for it. You received what you desired and I the same. I did not have to do that with Anna."

Erik sat on the divan observing the slow rise and fall of Anna's breathing. "The years that have passed have seen some of my darkest moments. I was a pathetic shell of a man who thought faking my death would silence the madness that every waking moment punished me for my deeds. I was too cowardly to give in to death when He appeared at my doorstep. I tricked myself into thinking I was worthy of love.

"I deserved nothing other than death. Even in that I could not find peace until it found me. I am not deserving of her friendship." He stared intently at Anna. "I did not trick her into coming to me by masquerading as a man for whom she yearned, bleating like lost sheep for love and adoration. I did not weave some spell across her." He looked sharply at Madame Giry. "That is what you believe, is it not? That she is another Christine Daaé and I the dog that would lie at her feet?"

Madame Giry made no sound, but the subtle shift in her posture screamed her reply.

"As I thought. You can be certain, Madame, she is no Christine Daaé. I am no longer a fool."

"Fool? Your love for the vicomtess brought the opera house to its state today."

"Yes, an arrogant, unspeakable fool. I want to love Christine. I have always wanted to love only her. But, as Anna told me, infatuation is not love. I do not know how to love a woman such as Christine. She wanted the illusions of the Angel of Music—not the man. She would never have accepted my past, my fate, and my *face*." His expressionless mask met the confusion twisting Madame Giry's countenance. He clutched a fistful of the fabric on his shirt, desperately trying to reach his heart.

"I know what I am. How this mind works." Maniacal laughter ripped through the room. He followed it with a wild gesture. "Tell me, could Christine ever accept the man that lies beneath? Would I ever have allowed that monster to shatter her soul? I could not make her look on me in love no matter how much I wished."

He turned from Madame Giry to resume his silent vigil, thankful she was completely unaware of the revelations crumbling his world to ruin around him.

"But Anna has accepted that man? I was at the ball. During the midnight reveal—I saw."

Tension drew across the room tighter than a bowstring. His hands twisted the fabric of his trousers. Madame Giry stared at his mask with such scrutiny; he nearly drew blood on his thighs.

"What did you see?" Even the perfection in his voice was capable of cracking.

"You kissed her. It frightened me. I fled."

The room sighed when he sank back into the chair. Profound sadness edged into his voice. "My humanity made you flee? I try to taste life on the lips of a woman and even that is feared? Every part of me is to be repulsed then? I repent of my transgressions. I know to pay my debt for them means I will be put to death. I do not have much time to be a man before my past catches up to me." Erik's eyes heated beneath his mask. He refused to remove it and wipe them free of emotion. "I exist, Madame Giry. Will no one let me live?"

"Does she love you?"

"Can anyone look on me in love? Anna gave more to me than a lifetime on this earth. She never passed judgment and never questioned my reasons. She did nothing but accept me. One who has been judged dares not judge, you see. Yet I did that with her. My obsession for Christine destroyed my chances for love and with it any belief Anna had in me. I am left with only the resonance of her kiss."

Exhaustion edged across him like a dull knife. A clock chimed the lateness of the morning, cutting the tension in the room. Madame Giry leapt to her feet.

"The authorities will be here soon. You must heed my warnings and head back to your labyrinth. Time is the only thing that will help Anna now. You can do no more."

She swept her hands toward the door. Erik rose. He understood the gravity of the situation and was too weary to pose argument. Staring at Anna, he memorized how she looked sleeping under his cloak. He closed his eyes, savoring the image.

"I understand what you say." Madame Giry reached out. "Go now, I will find you when she wakes."

She followed him to the door while sounds of the approaching police filled the halls. He veered off to one of his many secret passages. Turning to glance at her, he caught the saddened pinch in the corner of her eyes.

The look abraded him like glass.

Chapter Fourteen

The flame burned, innocently serving its duty. Pain sliced into the back of her head as its blinding light seeped through her injured eye. She groped for the lamp's key but stopped, the pain too intense to move. The steady rain snapping against the windowpane drummed an unrelenting beat in her head.

Anna reached up and touched the gash across her temple. Her fingers prodded protruding flesh.

Lying still, she watched the rain slither its way down the window. She had no idea where she was and the ache in her head made her care not. Thoughts and memories were fuzzy images. She recalled nothing other than a brilliant flash of light followed by blackness. In a stubborn effort to collect her thoughts, she struggled upright. She fought the nausea and took a few deep breaths before swinging her feet to the floor.

"Anna, be still. You must not try to move so soon."

A moan slipped out her lips. "Madame Giry?" She swallowed a bitter taste in her mouth.

"Anna, rest." A glass of water found its way into her hand. "Drink this, I will be back to explain as soon as I can."

Before Anna could blink, Madame Giry disappeared. Her abrupt departure made Anna question if she'd fallen down a rabbit-hole like the wayward Alice. She stared at her cup, evidence she wasn't dreaming for she couldn't recall filling it. The idea of anything in her stomach made it lurch again. Not wanting to toss her accounts, she placed the container on the table. She forced herself to her feet as the door swung open.

"Good Heavens, Mademoiselle, no!"

Anna teetered before falling forward. The man's reaction was swift as he rushed to catch her. As he eased her onto the divan, swirls of color ebbed and flowed in and out of her vision. She noticed the diamond stick pin in his cravat first and felt the fine linen of his clothing as he settled her down. He smelled of expensive soap and her hands remained locked on a set of firm forearms. A kind, masculine voice hushed her silent. She blinked to clear her vision and to get a good look at the stranger. His smile was warm like a summer day.

"Who are you?" she asked in a raspy voice, mesmerized by his dashing good looks. Perhaps she dreamt after all.

"My name, Mademoiselle, is Raoul. I am the Vicomte de Chagny."

"de Chagny?" Anna echoed. Why was that name familiar? Her eyes focused enough to see the graceful creature floating through the door behind him. Was that an angel? The vision glided forward and sat next to her.

Anna peered at her in hesitant recognition. "Vicomtess de Chagny?"

Why, of all people, were these two seated before her?

"We came as soon as the authorities sent us word. Are you well?" the vicomtess asked, delicate notes of pity to her voice.

Anna jolted to her senses. Bits and pieces of the previous night tumbled before her eyes. She touched her temple. Ripples of confusion pinched her face making her wince in pain. She looked in question to the vicomte.

"You were assaulted last night," he said pointedly.

"Raoul, some compassion!"

The vicomte pulled up a chair to sit across from her and his wife. He leaned in toward Anna with a certain gentleness reflecting behind his eyes that contradicted his curt words.

"Christine, we need to know what she remembers so we can help the authorities."

"Authorities?" Anna demanded, artfully beating back the panic that word instilled in her.

"For Mercy's sake, the girl has been though enough."

The tone of Christine's voice split Anna's already aching head in two. She raised a hand to silence them.

"I remember nothing." Her eyes chased the fragmented images flashing before her.

"Mademoiselle, anything you can remember will help the authorities. Your assailant's size, his shape, anything at all."

Anna twisted the drape warming her lap in an effort to grip something tangible. "Vicomte, I cannot." Confusion had her tightly wrapped with no way to loosen the binds. Remarkably drowsy, she didn't notice the door had opened admitting Madame Giry.

"Vicomte, vicomtess," Madame Giry said, quickly glancing over her shoulder.

Anna looked to see who else she should expect to come through that door.

"Are you safe?" Raoul asked. "I was informed of this assault shortly after breakfast and told my meeting with Inspector Legard would need to be here. We were worried about you."

Anna's fear deepened. Those binds constricted around her. What concern should he have for Madame Giry? What meeting?

"I am fine, Monsieur, your worry should be for Anna."

The fabric Anna grasped wrinkled and unwrinkled in fluid motions.

"Relax, Mademoiselle," the vicomtess calmed. "We will see you safe from this injustice."

Questions plagued Anna, but she couldn't find her tongue. Her glance wandered toward the vicomte.

"I am concerned for her I assure you, Madame Giry." He leaned toward her ear. "However, a note mysteriously appeared in my drawing room this morning. It was rather terse, its author making it clear he despised the fact that certain arrangements were not met last night. He said he had a message for Christine he was forced to deliver by—other means. I intend to help the authorities locate the Mademoiselle's assailant, but she does not know what implications this holds."

What implications? What notes? Anna's hands clung to her makeshift blanket and attempted to draw its warmth closer around her body. The vicomtess stood, removing it from her lap. A puzzled frown decorated her face as her fingers slid across the fabric. Anna reached for it, but the vicomtess backed away.

"Where did this come from?" she blurted in horror. Her eyes widened unexpectedly. "Did he wear this cloak?"

"Mademoiselle, do you recognize this?" Raoul asked.

A flicker of recognition made Anna wince. Fluid waves of black rolled elegantly against the air as she watched the cloak perform as an extension of his body. Anna grimaced. Why could she not put a name to its owner?

"You do know!" Christine shouted. "He wore this cloak and a black mask. Didn't he?" Christine swung around toward her husband, outright fright replacing concern. "Raoul, it is him. This was his message. He meant this for me."

The assault came flooding back: the swirl of a cape, the flash of a mask, the impact of the lantern. Silent screams unhinged her mouth. Anna grasped frantically at the air around her. He wore a mask. Leaping to her feet, she snatched the cloak from Christine's hand.

"The Phantom," Raoul spat. "I have heard enough."

Anna looked from the vicomte to the vicomtess. Her gaze fell on Madame Giry, begging to be rescued from this waking nightmare.

Madame Giry froze in shock. "I cannot fathom that he would—that he could—"

Anna didn't allow her to finish. Her mind replayed what she'd seen; the pain of it clubbing her emotions. She couldn't take the sudden betrayal. She bolted for the door.

"Mademoiselle, no," Raoul grabbed for her.

The final thing Anna saw before a cocoon of darkness enveloped her was the handsome face of the vicomte as he swept her into his arms.

Chapter Fifteen

Raoul found him, cheek to floorboards staring intently at oil slicked hay. The man rose with great deliberateness as if no other could feel the weight of what he was charged. He moved with caution pausing every now and then to kneel, look around, measure something or mutter.

"Inspector?" Raoul called out.

Inspector Jules Legard stood quickly at the sound of his rank, brushing hay from his meticulously groomed uniform. He kept his focus locked on the task at hand and replied without bothering to see who addressed. He raised one finger toward the sound of the voice.

"Move no further lest you destroy my evidence." He stabbed at his notebook with a lead before jamming it into his jacket pocket. "Why I must tolerate interruptions when in the middle of an investigation is beyond me."

Raoul folded his hands behind his back and respectfully waited for him to realize who he addressed. Legard turned. A well-placed cough behind Raoul's fist served to hide his laughter at the embarrassment he saw flash across Legard's face.

"Vicomte de Chagny." Raoul filled Legard's extended hand with his own. "Forgive my impropriety. The Prefect mentioned your return. He advised you wanted to speak with me, but didn't say why." Legard indicated the burned hay. "I regret this has fallen in the path of our contact. What brings you to the middle of my crime scene?"

"Did you find anything?" Raoul gestured to the broken glass and fire scarred floor.

"No. We're fortunate the whole building didn't burn. I haven't questioned the poor girl yet. I'm still gathering evidence here." He resumed his pacing of the scene. "The doors weren't locked. I've told the management to do so at night. The city has been riddled with crime of late—muggings, rape. I blame it on absinthe and loose attitudes. I only hope the girl wasn't violated in such a vulgar manner. I have no evidence as to her assailant here."

Inspector Legard was a tall, proud man, several years Raoul's senior. He was the best in his field, working tirelessly until a crime was solved, taking personal blame if it wasn't.

Raoul reached into his jacket pocket, produced the note, and handed it to Legard. "I have all the evidence you need."

The Inspector's lips pursed. "Perhaps I don't want to know why you're back in Paris and wanted to meet with me after all, especially while being armed." He lifted a disapproving eyebrow.

Raoul hastened to cover the pistol previously concealed by his coattails. Legard unfolded the note. As he read, Raoul placed a hand on a hip and stared at the charred hay.

"Christ, Raoul!" Legard shouted. "*Merde*! Why didn't you tell me you were coming to Paris? Is this for certain?"

"I am afraid it is, Jules."

Legard stopped in his tracks. "The man is dead." Raoul's expression spoke all the truth Legard needed. "Where's your wife?"

Raoul nodded toward the far end of the stable where Christine fed his stallion.

"So this assault?" Legard gestured to the hay with the note.

"Him."

"Christ!" Legard plowed his hand through his hair.

Raoul filled him in on the details they'd discovered when speaking with Anna. Without warning the Inspector spun, releasing his disbelief by kicking a hole in the nearest stall door. Raoul started with the noise, but could cast no blame for the Inspector's actions. If it were within his breeding, Raoul would have done much more than merely abuse a stall door.

"He's alive? That son-of-a-bitch is still here? I breathed that investigation night and day, uncovering nothing. I ate, drank, and slept that case and got nowhere. We couldn't even prove he existed, and now you're telling me he's alive? *And still in my city*?"

"Jules, lower your voice please."

"Vicomte, I'll have every last one of my men in this opera house. I'll tear it apart until I find him. I—"

Raoul held a hand up, knowing his authority wouldn't be argued against. "I want this kept quiet, Inspector. I do not need any vendettas. Christine endured enough with the last incident of the Phantom. I do not want this tormenting her again."

"Then what are you proposing?" Legard asked restlessly. He stood like a matador ready to wave red. "I want this man's head mounted on my wall."

"'Tis a trophy we shall fight over. Walk with me, Jules."

"A Phantom of the Opera?"

Edward snorted. He leaned back in his chair making the leather upholstery squeak as he shifted the substantial girth of his thighs. As he stroked his chin, he pondered the pretty youth before him. The news of a Phantom rippled the vicomte's countenance. The Vicomte de Chagny appeared the type more comfortable with a sword upon his hip than trying to make heads and tails out of the con Edward had created. He just confirmed nobles were indeed a dim-witted bunch of ninnies.

"A Phantom of the Opera?" Edward repeated for good measure. "My dear sir, I assure you this assault was random. I have no specters in my opera house."

The meeting grated against Edward's nerves, and he did his best to keep that from his voice. While he expected the rumors to bring the vicomte groveling into his office, Edward hadn't anticipated any assaults. This turn of events was most annoying. Jacob's pacing wasn't helping matters.

"Gentlemen, I know this is difficult to comprehend, but the Phantom is very much a man. You have most likely heard about the stigma marring my name. I am telling you truthfully, there is a man in this theater who will stop at nothing to claim my wife."

Raoul leaned forward in his seat. Edward cleared his throat to keep from laughing. The vicomte's forearms were upon his knees, his head bowed in servant like respect. The idiot.

Edward folded his arms to strike a defensive pose. "Vicomte, I'm well aware of the rumors, but you're describing the unbelievable. The attack on that poor child was a message meant for you and the vicomtess because you shafted a Phantom?" Laughter burst from his lips.

Whoever was responsible, and he had a fairly good idea who it was, it complicated matters while at the same time added to the illusion Edward had built. It was infuriatingly brilliant.

"It runs much deeper than that, Monsieur," Raoul cautioned.

Edward rose and walked the room with Jacob. "Find Richard," he growled into his ear before addressing the vicomte again. "Vicomte, forgive me, but what more is it you want me to do? The authorities were notified." Edward choked on that word. Damn inspectors. Luckily, France had no clue about their rather disagreeable life across Europe. "They'll be treating this as the heinous crime it is, but to ask me to pursue a Phantom?"

Raoul stood. "Gentlemen, I am not asking you to get involved in any pursuits, you clearly underestimate what I am telling you. I merely ask you to do everything you can to make certain this opera house is secure. I will spare no expense in keeping Christine safe."

Edward's ears pricked up like a hungry dog. He thought on his feet, feigning concern. "Vicomte, perhaps it's best we cancel the celebration and you take your wife home where it's safe."

The suggestion brought Jacob to a standstill. Edward made a discreet gesture assuring him he'd baited the hook.

"Monsieur, that is precisely what we do not wish." Raoul reached for Christine's hand. "The opera needs this event. Too much ill air is associated with this place. We will not allow this man to drive us away. I want this manhunt kept quiet. I do not want this stigma to follow Christine wherever she goes. Worry not about the finances gentlemen, name your price and you have my purse."

Edward could hear the vicomte's coins rattle into his greedy hands.

"I have arranged security for my wife. It is imperative she be kept safe," Raoul added.

The purse strings snapped shut. Security? Edward covered his grimace by smiling at Jacob. He wouldn't have to deal with security or police if that bloody thorn in his side named Anna hadn't had her face rearranged.

"Very well, Vicomte, we'll do our best," Edward assured.

"Thank you, Monsieur. We will stay in contact, and please take care."

Edward and Jacob nodded emphatically as they saw Raoul and Christine to the door. Edward didn't waste any time in dispatching Jacob.

"Find Richard."

Anna sat in the windowsill tracing a writhing line of water wandering the length of the glass. What would it be like to shatter? Glass, like happiness, was easily destroyed. She'd had one moment of bliss at a ball, but even that had been a carefully orchestrated lie. A well-constructed con—like her life.

The years of abuse closed in around her, pushing her deeper into a claustrophobic world of her own, slowly shredding her spirit. She leaned hard against the pane; trying to splinter the image of the one man she trusted assaulting her.

Beyond her reflection, Madame Giry poked her head in and out of the door. Focusing on the sound of the rain, Anna all but drowned out the stunted conversation going on behind her.

"Please, Monsieur, you must go."

"You summoned me. Let me see her, Madame Giry."

"Monsieur, no!"

A blurry figure joined Madame Giry's reflection, but Anna looked beyond it. She studied the rain, wishing she could drown in the drops.

"They are all here, Monsieur—the vicomte, the authorities, Christine. You must leave until this is figured out."

"This is my opera house, Madame. I will deal with their suspicions later. Anna?"

She lifted her head from the window. Had someone called her? She stared deeply at her reflection and that of Madame Giry's, watching the rain warp their images.

"Anna?" Erik tried again.

The mirror image grew in size, the distorted black mask taking shape in the pane. Like a raven coming in to perch on her shoulder, it grew larger and larger. A distant memory swam in her mind. When it broke the surface, she screamed.

Leaping from her seat, Anna slammed her back against the wall. She scrambled from Erik, hugging the perimeter of the room.

"Anna, it is me!"

"No!" she cried, desperately trying to make her way toward the door. "He wore a mask! He hit me. He wore *that* mask." Anna stabbed the air with her finger.

Erik's head snapped like the crack of a whip in Madame Giry's direction.

"Monsieur; I tried to tell you!" she wailed as Anna inched closer to the door.

Erik blocked her path. He grabbed her shoulders without regard to her obvious fright. "Anna, it is me, Erik."

Anna shrieked. Digging her nails into the flesh beneath his shirt, she gouged ridges down his arms. He cried out. It afforded her a second chance to rush for the door. Hooking her arm, he spun her harshly against his chest, preventing her escape.

"Anna!"

The power of his voice rattled her so violently she froze in terrified silence. "He wore a mask."

Like the strike of a match, she blazed to life. With every ounce of strength she had, Anna rounded herself against him and broke free. She flung the door open. The haste of her retreat caused her to trip over the threshold and tumble to the floor.

Erik leapt for Anna's prostrate frame, action that prompted from her a panic driven grapple.

She propelled herself backward with frantic swimming motions of arms and legs. With a feral growl he lunged. Catching her by the ankle, he dragged her, kicking and whimpering across the floor. A dark mask of dread covered her face as her skirts shuffled up in the scuffle.

"Anna, stop." Erik dodged her fist. "Please, listen to me!"

A primal need to fight replaced any sort of reason. She kicked at him with fury and repetition. Had he any sort of sense of how to handle himself like a gentleman under such circumstances, the situation wouldn't have been nearly as traumatic for her or as confounding to him.

"Stop!" he snapped again, artfully deflecting the small foot that flailed at his chest as it made several vicious passes at his mask. Finally, he succeeded in pinning Anna's arms. "Listen to me!" he growled, subduing her with all his weight.

She turned her head. Her breath came in shallow pants. "Be done with it," she mumbled, defeat smothering her will to fight. "Just do what you need and be done with it."

"*Anna, mon Dieu, no*!" he shouted, aghast.

"Monsieur, they're coming," Madame Giry harshly whispered. "You must go. Leave her care to me."

He balled his hands into fists and slammed the floorboards on either side of her splintering them in his rage. She cringed, closing her eyes.

"I will not leave, Madame Giry. This is a hoax, some cruel mockery of my existence and she is paying the price. She is not thinking straight. I will not have her believing I would ever touch—"

A voice interrupted his confessions.

"Madame Giry? Anna?"

In tandem with the box keeper, Erik's head spun toward the far end of the hall and the approaching vicomte. For a fleeting moment his eyes locked with Raoul's. The sniveling boy went pale while Erik's face heated beneath the mask. He struggled to his feet. Legs straddling the woman beneath him, he loomed to his full height.

The stance spurred Raoul into action.

"No!" he shouted, spinning Christine away from the sight. When the vicomte shoved her aside and began to race down the hall, Erik threw the challenge at his feet.

"Pass no judgment."

Racing against Raoul's approach, Erik charged down at Anna. Her eyes flew open. He gripped her face. Turning her, he forced her to look upon the plea in his eyes. He manipulated his voice, hoping for once it would penetrate her strong will.

"Listen to me, Anna."

She rolled her head against the floor. "Don't hurt me again, please..."

Anna went slack. Erik's grip tightened; he was losing his command of her! Raoul's shouts were louder and his approach quickening. Erik caught a glimpse of the pistol in his hand.

"Anna?" Erik bent in close and pressed his lips to her ear, whispering with a light and daring pressure against its lobe, his plea that she hear him and listen to *his* voice. He quickly glanced at the vicomte and looked into Anna's eyes, frantically searching for a glimmer of recognition.

Anna's eyes focused. "Erik?"

"*Se soviner ma voix. Je ne susi pas un fantôme.*"

With one quick leap he vanished, disappearing into the walls of his opera house.

Chapter Sixteen

Raoul spewed curses around them.

Madame Giry reached behind her, one arm groping for the door-frame, the other clutching her chest. She didn't start breathing again until Raoul shoved the pistol out of sight. He immediately apologized for his vulgarity. Though he buttoned his waistcoat to conceal the weapon, he made no effort to act contrite.

"Are you both unharmed?" He extended a hand to Anna.

"Yes, Monsieur," Anna replied, though her voice quaked enough to warrant additional inquiry.

"Are you certain? Did he harm you further? Did he put his hands on you in any manner?"

Madame Giry softly called his name. The subtle shake of her head respectfully asked for silence. Anna seemed shocked enough; the box keeper didn't want to add to her confusion. She kept Anna close as Raoul frantically conducted a search of the shadows.

"How did he get near you? Was the door locked as I instructed?"

"Yes, Monsieur," Madame Giry replied, curling the blatant fib into her mouth. A perplexed squint squeezed the corners of Anna's eyes. Before she could flap her tongue to contradict her, Madame Giry hooked Anna with one arm slapping a tight grip around her shoulders.

"Mademoiselle, is there someplace you can go?" Raoul asked. "That man, your assailant, he will be looking to harm you again."

Madame Giry bit her tongue at the confusion distorting Anna's face. She tightened her grip.

"That couldn't be the man," Anna stammered.

"That *was* he—the Phantom," Christine said. "Forgive my impoliteness the other day. I never would have wished this on you."

A fierce urge to protect Erik struck Madame Giry in the chest. Phantom? How dare her. Erik was a man, a mere man. As Christine lowered her head and empathy filled her stance, and Anna's bewilderment deepened, Madame Giry's resolve tightened like a cobra constricting the last ounce of life from its meal. The need to usher Anna away was imperative. Madame Giry didn't know what was going on, but she knew she had to get Anna safely away from any assumptions the vicomte and his wife had regarding Erik.

They, after all, didn't know the same man.

"Vicomte, Vicomtess, she should rest. Anna can return to the dormitories. She won't be alone for a moment. You can station what security you wish, but speak of this no more." She hustled Anna away. "For Anna's sake."

Madame Giry followed her charge's lead as she turned to look behind her, watching Raoul grip Christine as tightly as she gripped Anna.

"Madame Giry," Anna asked softly, notes of profound sadness painting her voice. "Did Erik do this to me?"

"Hush, he will tell you himself."

Richard Barret sauntered into the room, followed by Jacob Wischard. He kicked the door shut as Edward wasted no words.

"Richard, are you insane?"

"Of course I am Edward; it's one of my more endearing traits."

Richard casually took a seat on the couch and crossed his legs. He straightened his vest and brushed nonexistent lint off his costume. Satisfied he was primped as a gentleman should be, he bit at a loose piece of flesh on his thumb. Edward turned various shades of purple.

"You beat the bloody hell out of your daughter? What were you thinking?"

Winking, Richard slung his arm over the back of the couch. "I didn't do it. Rumor has it was a Phantom."

"This is doing nothing for my constitution, Edward." Jacob bemoaned.

Richard waved around the room. "Oh please your nerves. If you were there, you would've gladly taken advantage of her position." He swallowed a lewd laugh. "She's lucky I was only in the mood to knock her senseless. It's been awhile since I had a bit of her. I told you I'd take care of her meddling. This is no different from when she was a child."

"Richard, the authorities were here. I have a vicomte who wants a bloody private security force running around this damn opera house. We are wanted men, you Goddamn fool! This was a simple con, what the devil were you thinking?"

"There are no simple cons, Edward. Have I taught you nothing? Jacob tells me the vicomte will spare no expense to keep his wife safely out of the clutches of this Phantom." Edward shrugged as Richard rolled his head against the back of the couch. Seriously, how stupid could his partners be? "How much will he pay if she were *in* the clutches of a Phantom?" He stunned Edward and Jacob into silence, raising the level of his arrogance. "I've done you a favor gentlemen. The stakes just got higher. This is *my* con now."

The reins of control were firmly in his grip. The hierarchy had been reestablished and Edward and Jacob could do nothing other than stoop to his whims. Richard headed for the door, roughly smacking Edward and Jacob on their backs. They stumbled out of his way. It wasn't a bow, but would suffice.

"If you'll excuse me, gentlemen, I need to play the violin." Richard bowed his imaginary instrument and slammed the door behind him.

Two snifters clinked together in an apathetic attempt at cheers, though Raoul didn't feel like indulging in the finesse of an Armagnac. One elbow atop the mantel, he watched Legard stare across the Chagny library, seemingly uninterested in the volumes of books he inspected.

"You can rest assured, I'll see she is protected," Legard said. "Tomorrow, I'll ask that some of the finest gendarmes work with the theater and Paris police. We'll keep this silent until we find him."

Raoul nodded his appreciation. "What of Anna?"

"A watchful eye will be on her as well."

The vicomte studied his friend who'd begun to pace, a clear indication he was sorting through his evidence.

"He has to be in those vaults," Legard said decidedly. "Where else could he have been hiding?"

"You know, as well as I, that all the entrances are sealed. At least the ones of which we knew. Madame Giry assured me she knows of no way into them."

"What of the gate on the Rue Scribe side?"

"I never found that entrance to the underground lake. You know that, I know that, the Prefect of Police knows that. It is useless."

Legard's pacing became more agitated. He flicked his fingers together, splashing his drink around the glass. Raoul wondered if that was greed or just a nervous habit. Either way, he'd allow neither to get in the way of this investigation.

"I want this kept silent and without causing the upheaval of innocent people. I want nobody involved but my family and those in service to you. Do I make myself clear?"

At Raoul's reproof, Legard nodded, staring uncomfortably at his drink.

The tension snapped when a servant arrived with a note on a silver platter. Dismissing him immediately, Raoul took one look at the scarlet writing, and handed it off to Legard. He rose and walked to the window, bracing himself against the sill as Legard read aloud.

Monsieur le Vicomte:

I recognize your concerns given the act you witnessed and such suspicions disgust me. I assure you, I am the most convivial of gentlemen. While I acknowledge your need to increase security about my facility, I implore you; your concerns involving me are unfounded. I will personally be looking into this assault and suggest you do not make it difficult for me to move about my theater. I would like to attend to my affairs unhindered.

In addition, I beseech you again for a moment of Christine's time. Fret not her safety. My fondest greetings to Inspector Legard. I trust he is well.

I remain your most humble and obedient servant,

Ph. of the O.

P.T.O. Nevertheless, Monsieur le Vicomte, you stand warned. If you pull your pistol on me one more time, you will truly make me angry.

Raoul laughed in horrified unease at Legard being bid welcome personally in the letter; the blasted Phantom really did know everything.

"You pulled a pistol on him?" Legard asked, clearly incredulous at such a show of stupidity and bravado.

"Yes. Next time I will fire."

Richard's fame had spread by the following morning. Or rather the Phantom's fame had. Richard strode through the opera house as if he owned the place, listening with glee to the gossip regarding the innocent young girl that had fallen prey to the monster. The feeble-minded were eating out of his hand. He grinned lewdly. Anna could still come in handy.

He throbbed with the excitement of the havoc he was to unleash, or perhaps the arousal was caused by the woman he stalked. Christine walked a few paces ahead of him, as ignorant as the rest of the opera company. He folded his hands behind his back and called to her.

"Vicomtess de Chagny?"

It took a few seconds for her to turn. *Meek little thing*. He cleared his throat and straightened the cuffs of his latest costume. Free from Phantom attire, he was dressed in a well-tailored suit. The mention of a needed escort to accompany the vicomtess hadn't slipped past the keen eyes and ears of Richard Barret.

"Beg pardon, Vicomtess, my tardiness is most inexcusable."

"You are to be my escort?"

Richard tipped his head and moved his coat aside to expose the pistol on his hip. He watched her reaction intently. She nearly melted in a pool of relief.

This was going to be a savage delight.

"My name is Richard, Madame. I will see to your safety."

The vicomtess smiled. He returned the gesture. Meek, dependent, stunning *and* rich. He resisted the urge to tug on his trousers. He gestured for her to continue walking.

"Thank you for agreeing to my husband's wishes. It isn't our intent to put you in danger."

"Put your concerns to rest. I have years of experience. The vicomte can breathe easy when you're with me." Richard hid his chuckle by looking around as if exhibiting that experience.

Christine smiled and stopped before a classroom. "I need to warm my voice before rehearsals." She indicated the door.

"I understand, Madame, by all means." Richard affected a graceful bow toward the door. "Please allow me to look first?"

He stuck his head into the room, giving her a nod that all seemed well. "I'll remain just outside the door." He nearly burst through his trousers when she laid a hand on his arm.

"I feel safer already. I'll do whatever you wish of me."

"Oh, I have no doubt you will."

Anna's day started uneasily. Against the doctor's wishes, she immersed herself in her usual tasks, hoping it would make the last few hours of her life disappear.

Reminders lurked everywhere like peasants with outstretched hands. People stared at her face as she walked by and the burn near her eye stung with every blink. The vicomte had reopened the investigations into the Phantom of the Opera and Inspector Jules Legard had security at every spot. The gendarmes wore plain clothes so as not to arouse suspicion. Anna saw through their façade. Although safe in France from her former life, their presence put her on edge.

Erik invaded every thought. Had he meant to harm or protect? His final admission haunted her. *Souvenez ma voix. Je ne suis pas un fantôme.* "Remember *my* voice. I am no Phantom."

If only she could believe those words.

Her answer came in the form of a note delivered by Madame Giry. The box keeper hustled Anna to the security of her tiny office. She handed Anna the letter once the skeleton key twisted in the lock assuring their privacy.

Anna turned it over. The unfamiliar seal in deep black wax and the scarlet ink addressing it to her attention caused her heart to pound. A childish scrawl of shaky and misconnected letters hovered haphazardly across the page. She looked in horror at Madame Giry.

"Go on," she coaxed.

Anna broke the seal. She squinted as she read:

My dearest Anna:

My deepest and most heartfelt apologies for this tangled web in which you have become involved. I write this letter with the humblest of hearts in the hopes you will understand.

I will do everything in my power to find the individual responsible for the crimes committed against you. This assault was not at my hand. Do not believe anything told to you by the vicomte or his wife. Their judgment of the situation is clouded. Believe only that I meant to meet with Christine to speak with her in person. I assure you I mean her no harm. I only wish to deliver the message that you were right.

Christine was my world. She was the essence of my art and the voice of my soul. But I built the most triumphant illusions and could not see beyond my pitiful existence to embrace reality. But you saw and you were right. She could not and she will not ever wholly love the man behind the mask.

If there is a way for a scarred and darkened heart to beat again, I have found it. There was no mistake, mon petit. Your compassion, dignity, and friendship ignited a passion in my soul that lies far beyond my realm of mastery.

While Christine was once my world, you have become the air I breathe. If you will have me, I remain yours, in love...

E.

Anna pressed her trembling fingers to her lips. Such eloquence exuded from the pages, bringing back to her the image of that shy and refined gentleman she knew in Erik. The tears running down her face stung the corner of her eye.

"Forgive me, Anna, for not understanding him as you do."

Anna controlled her tears and looked up. "Madame Giry," she inquired, choosing for the first time to view her as an ally, "can I trust you?"

"Implicitly."

"I need to find him, but the guards—"

"We will find a way," Madame Giry said with a toss of her shoulders, a shake of her head and the determination of an army of thousands.

Chapter Seventeen

Anna's fingers glided along the hedgerow, coaxing awake the heady aroma of the roses. They rambled along the garden wall drinking in the last moments of the afternoon. Twilight would soon fall and night would tuck them safely into bed. Anna envied the roses.

The paths she roamed led away from the street and iron gates that exposed her to the stares of the citizens on the opposite side. Anna cocked her head and dragged her feet along the soft soil beneath her boot. She wondered on the kings who'd meditated on these paths and the traitors who'd plotted on them. But it was the lovers who'd strolled on their evening trysts that she dwelled upon.

The massive cypress trees guarded her as she waited. The gnarled trunks contrasted the flat and pristine paths they decorated while large branches divided the isolated part of the Tuileries into a garden of light and shadow.

Anna sat on a stone bench and pulled the note from her pocket. She stared at the scarlet writing, willing it to replace the awful images in her mind. Anna puzzled through all she felt over the days since she'd last had any intimate contact with Erik.

The idea that she'd someday find love seemed ridiculous. She'd never received a letter before, let alone one professing affection. Perhaps she'd been wrong to dismiss the idea that her someone could be Erik. Neatly creasing the note, she tucked it into the folds of her dress.

Anna was assured it would be safer for Erik to find her outside of the opera house than for her to attempt to slip unnoticed into his labyrinth. It was a fitting rendezvous, knowing he often chanced wandering these gardens, spying on young couples and pondering his fate. Here, among the falling twilight and shelter of the trees, she waited for the unlikely man she may call a lover.

Movement caught her eye. Erik appeared in the distance, cautiously rounding a massive trunk. She rose, feeling like a nervous violet, fearing if plucked she'd wither away and disappear. Erik's impeccable dress was gone. Beneath the jacket his shirt was smudged with dirt and he neglected a cravat. His sleeves were rolled to his elbows exposing pale forearms, and his boots and pants were wet. When last she'd seen him, he'd looked very much like a Phantom, now he simply looked like a man.

Anna watched him edge around the garden. Was he apprehensive of closing the distance between them, or of being seen? Her belly shivered. His eyes turned a terrifying gold as he passed from shadow to shadow. Perhaps he moved in such a way to be wary of the bounty on his head, or like she, his guarded steps echoed a circumspectly mindful heart.

Keeping his chin tucked to his chest and the collar of his jacket around his mask, his gaze rested on the ground between them until he looked upon her face.

Step by step, Anna closed the distance between them. Her heart beat so severely she swore it would leap from her chest. If she were going to speak, she figured it best to do so quickly before her nerves caused her to hare away.

"Erik, while I know what I saw and what I heard and while I have been led to believe it was your hand using me to get at the vicomtess—my heart does not obey." She walked closer to him, shame dipping her head. "I know no part of you capable of doing that to me or to her. Forgive me for even thinking it." She reached out and placed a hand on his arm.

Her eyes followed Erik's as his gaze rested on her hand. She saw him stiffen as if being touched by another was a forbidden desire.

"You have nothing for which to apologize, Anna."

The mellifluous tones of his voice soothed her. She tipped her head to peer into his lowered gaze. "Erik, your note..." her voice cracked, forcing his stare from the ground to her eyes. Anna chastised her weakness and gathering all her emotions, she took a deep breath. "I will...have you."

Erik turned his face to the sky and spoke to the changing afternoon colors.

"Do not say such things, child, unless you understand where my mind can lead you." Although he wanted to cherish the words she'd just uttered, he realized the wicked deception of his madness could tarnish them in an instant. "By having me, you belong to me and all that I am. And I am not a normal man. This world you have lived in exists for me as a different plane of reality. I do not fit into the world's ideals. I am the very embodiment of all that men fear and hate."

"Erik, I know—"

"Oh, but you do not know. I can strive to live and taste of your world, but you can never live in mine." He stared at her like a chasm had split between them and he didn't know if she had the strength to take the leap across. "Unless you dare to trust me."

"Trust you?"

"Trust I know and understand my mind, and that I can control the battles being waged beneath the beauty and music I constantly hear."

"What battles, Erik?"

He reached to help her across, but his hand brushed the air instead of her cheek. He spun away. "The battles between my dementia and genius, the past and the present, anger and joy, right from wrong...good from evil." He circled, gesturing sternly at his chest and stressing his words as if they physically hurt his tongue. "Between my passion to live like a normal man and my want to feel all the desires and sensations normal men have, and the stark reality that so long as I live there will be life denied me. So do not say you will have me unless you understand the precipice upon which you stand... unless you recognize the prison to which you sentence yourself... unless you truly understand *me*."

Dreadful silence stood between them like an invisible sentry.

"To understand you, is to understand music," she recited. "To view the world in layers with all its harmony and counterpoint, understanding that one gives birth to the other. They are two sides of the same thing. They look at things differently, each sound barren and meaningless if played separately. One can exalt and support while the other can equalize yet create discord. But somehow they entwine in richness and join music. The harmonist in you moves from chord to chord with each being finished in its beauty. While the contrapuntist is never at peace, unpredictable, and achieves nothing until the music is made totally complete."

Blue eyes locked an intense stare on him. Erik slowed in the circle he carved around her. His lips parted, giving her the only indication of his disbelief.

"Music can be soothing and full of beauty." Eyes still pinned, she rotated with him. "Yet it can switch in a heartbeat's time to be painful and full of dissonance. You are made of madness and Death just as you are full of passion and life. It is my choice to run or listen. And if you are giving me the choice that you denied the vicomtess, then I choose to listen."

His chest expanded and collapsed as the weight of his breaths filled the air between them.

"I know your demons," she continued, "but I can feel the need of a most ardent and willing gentleman repressed for too long by judgment. I understand your music and I will have you—but more than that—I wish you."

Her words lingered in the air before trailing away like a puff of smoke. Erik closed his eyes as they moved from her lips to his ears. Anna spoke the ones he'd waited a lifetime to hear.

"I love you."

He rocked backward, not caring if he fell into an invisible abyss and never felt solid ground again. The impact was the most powerful thing he'd ever felt. Not a composition in his soul could match them. He approached, intoxicated by three words easily taken for granted by those who heard it from birth. He dared not speak lest anything chase away their sound.

Air trapped in his lungs as she stood on the tips of her toes and reached to his face. She teetered as she entwined her hands around his neck. With gentle pressure to the base of his skull and an amazing strength that belied her petite size, she pulled him toward her. Her lips closed over his.

His entire body deflated the moment she stole his control. Like a sailor drawn to drown by the beauty of a Siren, he stood bewitched by her affection and transfixed by her seduction. His mouth fell open to greet hers, and he slipped away into the gentleness of her kiss. He could do nothing other than be a pupil as Anna taught him to be a man. She parted her lips and invited him in, this kiss more daring than the one before. He hesitantly followed her lead, exploring her with his tongue—seeking, learning and understanding.

The crescendo of sensations rose and rocked him with waves of deeper and more urgent needs. Her scent, her taste, their union in such a simple gesture he would not live without again. The instant she confessed her love and offered her lips, his murky existence faded and he swam toward music.

He curled his arms around her tiny waist, lifting her level with him. At what point in his life had he ever imagined such a moment would come true? He knew not, nor did he care, for the first time nothing seemed to exist but the present. He drove his kiss deeper seeking to make it match the profound pulsing of his heart.

When she gently broke the kiss, his bottom lip imperceptibly trembled. He lowered her and grabbed her hands to lay them against his mask wanting to feel the warmth of her flesh flow through it. In her hands it was beauty. Gazing on her for a long time, his mind searched for the words to reply—words for the moment he knew only how to express in music. Instead, silence said all he needed. The only things he wanted to hear echoing in his mind were the three words she'd just said. With a heart shaking in awe of what he was about to do, he wrapped her hand around the crook of his arm, and walked.

"You are wet," Anna noticed, wiping her hand on her dress.

"I had to make some adjustments to the labyrinth for the second time."

Anna stared remorsefully at her feet. "Erik, I'll fix this. I'll go to the vicomte and tell him it wasn't you. I'll get him to end the investigation. He'll have to understand. They're hunting you for no reason. This is unjust and my fault."

He smiled weakly, sternly laying a finger on her lips. "Your naivety is most endearing. What is just does not matter. In this case, only the past does. Do not worry about the vicomte; he is the least of my concerns. You are to bear no burden in this. None of this is your fault, nor is it without cause. They have their reasons for suspecting me."

Anna couldn't meet his gaze. "As much as I accept your past, it has become evident how hunted you truly are. Yet they're looking for a Phantom, not you."

"I told you before, in many eyes they are one and the same. I am not about to ignore my past; it has defined who I am." His defensive tone carried with it an edge of warning. "Nor will I allow it to catch up with me. Let them hunt. They will not be able to hold me. My only concern is to find the man who did this to you." He turned her chin to look at her face in the fading light. "That may scar," he said with painful familiarity.

"Should that matter?"

"Anna, do not let this investigation weigh on you. I want you to be safe. My only concern is for you."

"And what it will do to the vicomtess?"

That name was a hot iron to his heart. He nodded. The truth had no place hiding from Anna. She was like the violin he prized, in tune with his every emotion.

"Oh, Anna, I love her." Erik turned his head to peer at her from the corner of his eye. "Is that wrong of me now? Is that still possible?"

She spoke to her feet. "I do not know. I, unlike you, have never loved before—until now. I suppose you always will love her. If I must, I can live in her shadow."

He filled his thoughts with the image of her hand wrapped so contentedly around his arm. "I love her, Anna, and you must understand Erik always will. But my mind wrestles with disorganized notes when I think of her. I want my mind to be still." He slid his arm to untangle their embrace and turned her to face him. "You make it so. You complete the counterpoint." He lifted her hand to his lips and kissed her palm. His fingers caressed where his lips had been. "I cannot live like anybody else without speaking with her, without seeing her one more time. I must let Christine know I meant her no harm."

"What will you do?"

The answer came without warning as his hand dug into the back of her neck, the other clamping over her mouth. He gave a quick nod toward the direction of the garden's center and the approaching footsteps.

"Are you seriously just going to let him get away with this, Edward? I'm telling you the man is insane."

"The man's a genius, Jacob. If he wants to run this con, let him run it."

"Edward, you saw what he did to the girl. This is madness."

Erik twirled Anna against the trunk of a tree, rounding them out of sight. He leaned on their every word, watching Anna intently.

"Jacob, since when are you so concerned about Anna? Do you think with all the police about you won't be able to force her into your bed at night? You're as bad as him."

A soft cry escaped her lips. Erik reached for her arm, but she cringed, sending his anger toward the two men raging. Lava coursed through his veins. No man would touch her again.

"I'm concerned about his intent toward the diva. We have no idea what his con is going to involve."

"*We* have no idea, Jacob? Perhaps *you* don't know his intent because of your bloody nerves."

"We need to take back our control!"

"When have we ever been able to take back control from Richard Barret?"

Anna bolted like a bullet speeding from a pistol. Grabbing the hem of her dress, Erik tackled her to the ground. They landed roughly as a tangled mess of arms and legs. She struggled beneath him for a moment, but his stern look silenced her tongue as forcefully as he held her down. The voices drifted into the distance and disappeared. He rolled off her. Crimson bloomed across her face and she shook with a savage anger he'd only witnessed in himself.

Erik gripped her shoulder. "Anna?"

"Richard Barret...my father."

Chapter Eighteen

Music relaxed her. Once she cleared her mind and let the music take over, she felt as if she'd drifted away to heaven and fell back to earth refreshed. Calm and confident, Christine could greet the remainder of the day's rehearsals with her best foot forward. She'd ignore the guards and rumors and focus on the music. That's why she returned to begin with. Opening the door, she smiled politely at her escort.

"Finished, Madame?"

She nodded. He had a kind and genuine smile.

"Might I be so forward as to say you sing like an angel?" Taking her elbow, he led her down the hallway.

Such flattery never failed to bring warmth to her face. "Thank you, Monsieur," she said, adding sadly, "I had a great teacher."

They weaved through the hustle of the hallways. If Christine didn't know any better, she'd never have thought anything was amiss at the Opera Garnier. With the exception of the plainclothes police, who nodded their acknowledgements to her and Richard as they passed, the opera continued as it always had. It saddened her to know that behind the excited exterior beat the heart of a man she was forced to consider a Phantom. She turned down the corridor leading backstage, but a sharp tug on her arm prevented her.

"Do you always travel backstage this way, Madame?"

Christine nodded.

"Might I suggest a different way? If the man pursuing you is as crafty as I'm told, he'll know your habits."

Her warm blush rose to a nervous heat as she hastened down long hallways, twisting more times than a mouse in a maze. She glanced up at her escort, whose sudden stoic exterior built in her a predisposed apprehension. They sped through progressively darker corners of the opera house, winding farther and farther from the upper levels. Instinct told her something was amiss, but her heart reminded her Raoul hired this man for her safety. Cool air swirled and chilled her with an impending sense of dread. It reminded her of cellars.

She didn't like cellars.

"Are such tactics necessary? The vicomte has this opera house well-secured. I'm sure it would be safe for us to use a less involved route."

"Of course it's necessary, Madame. You wouldn't want to cross your Phantom."

His hand slid possessively around her waist. He yanked her close and smiled eerily.

"Unhand me!" That instinct kicked her heart into a wild rhythm. She twisted to pry herself free.

The cold metal of a pistol rammed into her side so harshly the flesh bruised beneath her corset. "Who are you? What do you want?" she stammered.

He opened a door. "Inside," he growled.

A jarring pain traveled up her wrists as he threw her to the floor. The stench of rancid mildew and rot filled her nose. The door slammed shut with an earsplitting crack.

Her eyes adjusted to the dim light. Staring down at her were twisted horse's heads, birds thrust back in silent calls, and distorted masks of every shape and size, forever frozen in assorted emotions. Discarded and gruesome objects from long forgotten operas crammed every available space in the waste prop room. This was as far away from the theater as one could get before venturing into the cellars that led to the lake.

To the Phantom.

Shivers, like millions of invisible fingers, raced up and down her body. No one came down to this room. The amount of dust and rat feces stinging her nose was testimony. Her hands slipped on the dust coated floor. Her legs tangled in her petticoats as she scrambled away from the man looming over her.

Richard knelt before her, tucking his pistol into his waistband. "Let us—"

"Release me!" she shrieked, swinging her hand toward his face.

He caught her wrist. The room filled with a cackle that made Christine's blood run cold. His laughter stopped as quickly as it began when he dragged her toward him, giving her no room to resist.

Although the blow of his hand against the side of her head was not enough to bruise, it was enough to make her freeze in terror.

"Now," he yanked Christine to her knees, "let us have a little talk. You can scream all you want—no one will hear you. I made certain to keep you as far away from them as I could. I apologize for the state of your room." He laughed as he looked around. "It was either here or the communard dungeon and I figure that would be the first place they'd look, here the last." He gave a quick click of his tongue. "People are stupid."

Moving his waistcoat aside, he produced a rope from an inner pocket. Its length flowed over his fingers. Richard snatched her hands and tied them tightly behind her back. With her arms bound, her position provided him with a view of her décolletage and the heaving bosom caged within.

A second rope secured to the first tethered her to an exposed beam against a dark corner barely giving her enough slack to sit comfortably.

"Forgive me for binding you, but I cannot have you running. You are going to be safely tucked away for a while."

A scream pierced the room. One crack of a backhand silenced her into submission.

"You would make a lovely little mollisher now wouldn't you?" He usually forced Anna to serve as mistress to him and his various partners in crime. It would be a sweet change of pace to have a beauty do so instead.

Hot pants of horror fell from Christine's mouth. "You vile man, get away from me!"

"Come now, dear. You cannot possibly find pleasure night after night dallying away your ladycocks in the bed of a pretty, rich boy?"

Richard rose in front of her. One by one he sprung free the buttons on his trousers for the sheer delight of hearing her whimper. He laughed at her struggles to back away from his fully exposed excitement. He was painfully stiff. As tempting as relief of such arousal might be—since the moment was perfect for leisurely violation—he decided against it. He fondled himself as he took his time buttoning his trousers. He sneered when she slammed her eyes shut.

"Now," he directed, electing to stroke his pistol instead, "if your husband is wise, he will abide by our demands and deliver the ransom we desire. Or rather the ransom the *Phantom* desires."

He smiled with menacing deliberation as her eyes flew open.

"What?" she croaked.

"You really are a lovely woman," Richard complimented, brushing his lips lightly against hers. He laughed as she yanked her head away. "Sit tight, Madame, we shall return."

Without further regard Richard slipped out, locking the door behind him. He sniffed loudly and grinned at the man waiting in the hall.

"Is she settled and comfortable?" Edward asked.

Richard chuckled, as if any woman was comfortable when he was in control. "Like Anna is in a brothel."

"Jacob is questioning your motives."

"Jacob is a fool." He shoved Edward down the corridor. "Stick to your job of keeping him in the dark and all will be fine. Trust me."

Trusting Richard Barret was like relying on a coiled cobra not to strike. He smiled as cordially as possible when Edward turned to meet the stare penetrating into his back. Richard raised an eyebrow, challenging Edward's next move. His look had the desired effect as the man swallowed loudly, stepping aside to allow Richard to pass.

It was Edward's place to follow.

Christine had never experienced such helplessness. She shrieked as the bony tail of a rat whipped across her ankle. Her voice echoed in the room before being swallowed by silence.

This cannot be real. He would not do this to me. He is an Angel. *He loves me.* The ropes chafed her skin raw as she jerked to free herself. Pain bit at her wrists when they tightened. *He is not doing this to me. He gave me my liberty! This is not happening!*

She cried again and kicked violently at another rat. "Erik!" she yelled.

The Phantom's name bounced off the walls as if taunting her. It did nothing but fall lifelessly at her feet. Fear of the uncertain gripped her mind, body, and soul. History was repeating itself and she was once again its limelight.

"Lord, forgive me. Raoul!" She forced the correct name from her lips. "Raoul!"

"Monsieur?"

Jacob glanced sideways to the clock and the empty carafe in front of him. Resigned he could do nothing about the hour and his lack of scotch. He removed his reading glasses and tore himself away from scrutinizing the books.

Anna stood in his doorway, her head cocked in the defiant little way that always got under his skin. She was going to be difficult, he could feel it. As if he didn't have enough to deal with. Jacob shrugged and sank back in his chair determined to at least get some pleasure out of her arrival.

"What do you want? I didn't summon you." Aggravated, he tossed his glasses on his desk.

"A word, Monsieur."

"A word." He snorted. "Anna, you never have just a word."

He laced his fingers and tilted his head, mocking her posture. She stared at him with a tiny, insolent air about her—her bottom lip out, wrinkles in the corners of her eyes as she glowered.

"Have your say then and get out of my office." He wasn't prepared for the words that tumbled from her mouth.

"What con are you running with Richard Barret? What does he want with the Vicomtess de Chagny?"

Squinting as if blindsided, Jacob pursed his lips. This was an interesting development.

"That was a mouthful." He rose, moving to the corner of his desk.

"I know he's here running a con."

"Running a con?" Jacob parroted, giving an overly theatrical sigh. "Anna, we're respectable and retired gentlemen. If you think Richard Barret is here, it has nothing to do with any cons. If he's here, it's probably your fault."

"It bloody isn't and you know it!"

Jacob fanned the phony heat on his neck. "My, what vulgar language from a lady."

Anna's face scrunched and he knew it was best not to entice her. She'd only launch into a tantrum and what was the point? Richard was clearly insane. He was running a con under the noses of the police.

"Do all Barret's have such audacity?" His lip jutted out to match her face. "Yes, Anna, Papa is here. Did you come running to Jacob to protect you?" A scuffle behind her cut him off. He studied the room but saw nothing.

"The rumors around Paris, the ghost sightings, the haunting—it is all him, isn't it?"

"Your father was right. You are an intuitive little wench. Papa is the mythical Phantom of the Opera. He's rather good at it don't you think?" Jacob winked and touched the corner of his eye indicating her scarring flesh. "Edward's idea this time. Re-create the scandal to bring in the patrons." He slid the leather bound book across the desk toward her. "Works rather well, too."

Anna shoved the ledger away. "I heard you in the garden. What does he want with the vicomtess?"

"Even if I knew, I wouldn't tell you. Your father has turned a harmless little con into an opera."

Taking one step forward, she slapped her hands across the desk. Jacob smiled as his trousers bulged. He liked her feisty.

"Don't think for a minute I won't expose him. I have before."

He shook his head. "Look where that got you. What do you plan on doing? Are you going to run to the vicomte and tell him a phony Phantom is playing him the fool? That some petty country con artist has turned them into the laughing stock of Paris? Please, they hardly had cause to notice you until your Papa made you cry."

She snapped. He knew she would. Anna wheeled her fist back to strike. One hand was all it took to block her blow. Grabbing Anna's fist, he wrestled her onto his lap. She growled a string of rather inappropriate expletives, arms and legs flailing in protest. He gripped her tightly and laughed. Finding an exposed spot on her neck, he nipped, prompting more thrashing and louder cursing. His lips bit her earlobe while one hand dove between her legs, hiking the lengths of her skirts.

"Really, Anna," he crooned, crushing her against his arousal, "this sudden bravado is quite alluring."

A shadow erupted and was on Jacob with savage force.

Murderous vengeance roared to the surface as control slipped from Erik's grasp. Knocking Anna roughly out of his way, he sent her toppling to the floor. Lustful vengeance began to eddy around any sense of reason.

With a feral growl, he pinned Jacob against the desk. The incomprehensible ferocity of his possessiveness unleashed itself against Jacob's miserable little throat.

"Two rules," Erik spat, knocking Jacob's head roughly into the wood. "You do not molest her and you do not mock me."

The swell of Jacob's cowardly eyes and his stammering tongue only fed Erik's disgust. He raked gouges down the back of Erik's hands. Erik dug his thumbs deeper into Jacob's windpipe, his lips curling into a menacing smile.

"Who...who...are you?" Jacob sputtered between breaths.

"The Phantom of the Opera. Now answer the lady's question!"

His neck purple, his throat raw, Jacob Wischard tore apart his office at a frenzied pace, gathering what items he could and shoving them into his briefcase. No con was worth being hunted by the actual Phantom.

The authorities would be onto them soon anyway. But that was the least of his worries. He only cared about that black masked madman who poured terror down his throat. Jacob jumped when the door blew open. He didn't acknowledge Richard except by packing more frantically.

"Going somewhere, Jacob?"

"To the devil with you, Richard. I'm leaving."

He'd barely moved his fingers out of the way before Richard shoved his briefcase closed.

"Leaving?" he asked, leaning on the case. "You can't *leave* in the middle of a con."

He yanked the briefcase from Richard's grip. "Blast your con. A madman is running loose in this opera and I will have no part of it."

Richard's question tumbled around his laughter. "What kind of madman?"

"A bloody masked maniac! He was here with your damn daughter. She was ranting about cons and divas and *you*. Then *he* came from bloody nowhere. The man is a living shadow, and I will not be caught in its path again."

He grabbed his coat and walking stick and started for the door. Richard blocked his path.

"What did you tell Anna?"

"Everything, Richard. I would have told them about your intent toward the diva, but thankfully I've been kept in the dark on that." Jacob stabbed his walking stick against Richard's chest and pressed him backward. "You would have told as well if you found your throat on the wrong side of that demon."

Richard stalked him with a hunch to his posture that made Jacob stumble backward. "You betraying son-of-a-bitch. Let's see how you fear the wrong side of me."

Erik fled through the opera house, passing from shadow to shadow like a man possessed. His need for vengeance had Anna breaking into a jog to keep pace. She didn't know what to make of the situation, but she knew as she followed him through the winding passages that he could have killed Jacob Wischard. The restraint it took for him not to do so was terrifying to witness.

As he rounded a corner, he pulled up short, causing Anna to jump back in surprise. He shifted his weight and tripped a door below him. The floor swallowed him whole and Anna made haste to jump through it.

Pain shot up her ankles when she hit the floor. She caught her breath and squinted in the darkness. What corner did he command now? In a split second's time the answer rounded on her.

An arm hooked her throat. The hall spun as she was twisted against a man's body. His angry breath throbbed along her temple.

"Erik, please!" she shouted. The room pitched again as she was whipped around to face him. Grabbing his forearms, she locked eyes with him. "You ran from the office so suddenly. It is only me following you."

Eerie silence pulsed between them. "*Mon petit*?" he asked apprehensively.

Anna nodded. The breath slipped out his lips. A rising furor began to lift his voice.

"You will be wise to note how close you came to meeting a man you do not want to know. Not much can restrain Erik when he does not wish restraint. You will learn not to follow Erik when you are not invited." His roar bounced from wall to wall.

Given a moment, the disastrous degree of his anger would fade and she would see a calmer man before her. She was not about to back down and bend to his requests. He paced like a jungle predator searching for the scent of its prey.

"Where would Barret take Christine? What does he want with her? What will he do to her? Of what is he capable? Answer me, Anna!"

"I don't know. He's capable of anything. I've seen him do it all. He's clever and calculating, and a man you don't want to cross."

Maniacal laughter rolled around her.

"It is me he does not want to cross. I will not have Christine harmed, do you understand me? Erik will not allow harm to come to her. Not now, not ever."

"You don't have to tell me that, Erik." Anna pointed angrily to the ceiling. "But you cannot fly around this opera house like some raving lunatic."

His head snapped in her direction. "Forgive me, Mademoiselle, but I *am* a raving lunatic and you and your defiance are inches away from meeting the end of a silk rope."

"Blast my defiance and deal with it." She stood back as her entire body wound into her anger. They stared at each other as if a line had been drawn in the sand. "If the vicomtess is missing, you can be damn certain the person they think took her is you. And you can be positive they'll be looking for you tenfold now."

"They should be looking for Christine," he bit, shaking his head rapidly. "Erik must find her himself." He pivoted and headed down the hallway, his fists balled against his sides.

Anna stomped her foot and ground the heels of her palms against her eyes. Trying to get through to him was like trying to squeeze water in her palm—a fruitless effort. Erik charged back and forth on the lines of a dangerous battleground, and she had no idea which side of the man she attempted to love would win. Sinking into dismay, she called his name.

He stopped, relaxed his hands, and turned. Without looking, he extended one long arm to her. She entwined the tips of her fingers in his. He guided her to him.

"I warned you, Anna. You stand on a precipice and face life imprisonment to attempt so boldly to understand this mind. I know control, but I will not rest while Christine is in harm's way. She needs me."

"I am not asking you to rest. I know you could never do that."

He pointed down the hallway, showing Anna a passage that would lead her from the cellar, issuing one gentle warning. "Do not involve yourself in this. You were not a part of my past."

Erik teetered imperceptibly. Anna winced, understanding the signs of his madness when it reared its ugly head. He turned to leave. She flung herself into his embrace, keeping a firm, possessive grip around him. The tension she felt threatening to crack his spine relaxed as she squeezed his waist and laid her head against his chest. Snuggling against him, she heard his deep breath and felt the tip of his mask bend to her hair.

"I was not a part of your past, but I think you want me in your future. Do not deny me my choice."

"Go," he replied, backing away as if she were a force he couldn't reckon. "I cannot be near you now. I need to think."

In a flash, he evaporated very much like the Phantom he was.

Chapter Nineteen

Seven hundred and fifty people, three acres, seventeen stories, seven of them underground.

Sitting behind the desk in the concierge office, Raoul stared in dismay at the dusty copy of the Garnier architectural plans. No wonder no one ever knew the Phantom lived in the bowels of the opera house, save a select few. His lair could stretch in endless directions. How could anyone find it?

Raoul took a break, rubbed his bleary eyes and swiped his stray locks back into a neater queue. Madame Giry was correct; all the ways to penetrate the lower cellars that Raoul knew existed were sealed off to prevent anyone from going in or coming out.

A great puff of breath broke through his lips as he leaned over the designs. His palms wrinkled the paper. If he had to, he'd tear the place apart brick by brick in order to keep Christine safe. A knock reluctantly pulled his eyes away from the blueprints.

"Enter." Instantly, he sensed Inspector Legard's tension. "What is it, Jules?"

"Vicomte, there has been an incident."

Raoul heard the controlled caution that made Legard's words slow and deliberate. He matched the tone. "Christine?"

"She is fine. I saw her with a member of the theater police." The Inspector delivered the blow. "Jacob Wischard is dead. A maid found him in his office about an hour ago. His neck was broken. I have no doubt he was murdered."

Raoul lifted his dusty hands to his mouth before running them through his hair. He waved his hands about in front of him as if trying to erase what such a deed could implicate. He stammered to the blueprints.

"This is a coincidence, Jules, merely a coincidence. This cannot be connected to the Phantom."

He watched, horrified as the Inspector produced a note. "This was found with the body."

The letter snapped as Raoul snatched it. It was formally addressed to the Vicomte de Chagny and written in scarlet ink. He tore the envelope open, painfully conscious of how his chest heaved. Fury or fear? A numbing silence filled the room until the vicomte had the presence to speak.

"Inspector, locate my wife. I want her by my side. Then find Laroque and bring Madame Giry and the Mademoiselle to me." Raoul stared in loathing as the note ignited years of hatred.

Vicomte, abide by my demands or I spill more blood.

With a shout of boiling rage Raoul upended the desk vowing to do the same to the Opera Garnier.

Erik's explosion with Jacob was not a good sign. His temper was shortening as the entire affair wore on. If she concentrated, Anna could still feel Erik's arm hooked around her throat as clearly as she could feel the intimate way he laced his fingers in hers.

He'd lost control of the opera house he'd taken steps to regain, losing it to unfounded rumors and mockery. He was on a warpath to locate her father before he laid his hands on Christine and Anna's best judgment told her none of it was good. She might not have been a part of his past, for which she found herself more and more thankful, but she was tangled in the present and hoped Erik knew what he was getting himself into.

The hem of her dress blurred as she stared at her boots. Shaking her thoughts and vision clear, she quizzically glanced at the man she walked beside. It came as no surprise the theater police were looking for her. Anna figured it had something to do with her confrontation with Jacob. Stupid snitch.

Maybe the old weasel had a heart attack. Choking on a laugh, she recalled the look on his face when Erik unleashed on him. Her laughter stopped as Inspector Legard took her gently by the arm and opened the door before them. He indicated for Anna to enter; Madame Giry and Raoul were already present.

"Where is Christine?" Raoul asked as Anna was escorted in.

"Officers are en route to fetch her," the inspector responded.

"Find them," he snapped, dismissing Legard.

Confusion inched across her brow. A reprimand by theater police or gendarmes she could handle, but to be scolded by a nobleman was insulting. A long and calming breath helped silence her while he spoke.

"Are you all right, Mademoiselle?"

The vicomte emphasized his concern by laying a hand upon her upper arm. Anna glanced at his hand and then looked him directly in the eye. She may not be viewed as a proper lady, but she still had her boundaries, especially with noblemen. Rolling her shoulder away from his touch, Anna swore she heard the walls of the room hiss in response to his touching her.

"I'm fine, Monsieur le Vicomte." She scanned the room for hidden serpents. Certain it was only in her mind, she took a step out of the vicomte's reach nonetheless and glanced to Madame Giry who stood still as marble in her spot.

Raoul turned to comfort the box keeper. "The situation here has escalated. I worry for your safety as well as Christine's." To Anna he said, "You as well, Mademoiselle, as you have already been the Phantom's target. Jacob Wischard has been murdered."

Anna covered her mouth to hide her shock, mirroring the alarm Madame Giry displayed by withering into a chair, a wrinkled hand clutching at her chest.

"He was found with this." The note landed on a nearby table. "Another little warning from our friend."

"That's impossible!" Anna grabbed it. She turned it over, recognizing the neat hand was unlike Erik's matchstick scrawl. Clearly the vicomte's judgment was shrouded with previously drawn conclusions.

"Vicomte, this is a mistake. You don't know with whom you're dealing."

"Mademoiselle, I am certain I know with whom I am dealing. You and Madame Giry are to leave with the vicomtess. I have made arrangements to take you to our chateau in Chagny."

Anna's temples throbbed. This entire farce grew more complicated by the minute. Leaving the opera house to sit around pampered in some nobleman's estate she wouldn't tolerate. Not with her father running one of his notorious schemes. Innocent people were in danger and she wasn't about to back down. Madame Giry was another matter, Anna noted, seeing the pallor upon her face.

"I am sorry, Madame Giry," Raoul apologized. "I know how much this theater means to you, but I will not have your life endangered. Like Christine, you need to recognize the Phantom for what he is. I will not allow him to hold you captive any longer. Until arrangements have been made, I want a gendarme with you at all times."

Of all the ridiculous demands! The blinders upon the nobleman were unbelievable.

"Monsieur, I am begging you to listen to me," Anna said. "I know far more than you think and I'm telling you the man you call a Phantom has nothing to do with this."

She obviously had overstepped her bounds, or the vicomte wasn't used to being addressed in such a manner. As he rose, Anna followed the path of his eyes to the tip of the scarlet note peeking out from the corner of her dress pocket.

The vicomte snatched the letter, his passion manifesting in the quivering of his fingers.

"Exactly what is it you claim so ardently to know?"

Anna pressed a hand to her belly. "Vicomte, please." She stared at the paper as if it were the one precious gift she'd ever received. "Give it back."

The vicomte looked at Anna, his visage darkening. "What is this?"

His eyes shot to Madame Giry, but she averted her gaze. Taking a step closer to Anna, he waved the letter in her face.

"What kind of sick joke are you playing? How do you know the Phantom by name?"

"Vicomte?"

Anna's breath hitched as they swung toward the door. Her letter fluttered in the air as Raoul waved Legard in.

"I am afraid we have another situation on our hands," Legard informed. "This Lieutenant was to be assigned as the vicomtess' personal guard."

Raoul addressed him sharply. "Was to be assigned?"

"Yes, Monsieur le Vicomte," the lieutenant replied. "We are unable to locate the vicomtess."

"You told me she was with her guard!" he shouted at Legard.

He nodded. "She was seen with a member of the theater police."

Anna rolled her eyes. Another signature move by the great Richard Barret—murder *and* kidnapping. She tried to contain her disgust. Judging by the color on the vicomte's face and the twist to his upper lip, any suggestions she'd make at the moment wouldn't be well-received.

"What did he look like?" he barked to Legard.

"His face was not seen, but he was tall, thin and incredibly well-dressed."

Raoul covered his mouth with a fist and turned his head to the side as though trying to swallow the emotion clogging his throat.

"That is all the information needed. I should have been by her side protecting her." His remorse weighed him down like a heavy unseen presence. "Inspector, find the vicomtess. Lock this opera house if you must. Lieutenant, escort Madame Giry wherever she needs to be until the arrangements are made at Chagny. See to it she remains safe."

Raoul smiled at Madame Giry's kind nod of comfort as she left with Legard and the lieutenant, but when Anna tried to follow Raoul put a hand up to stop her.

"You are going nowhere." That curtain of remorse lifted. He

waved the letter again.

Anna caught the subtle nod Madame Giry made before disappearing through the door. It was toward a shadow which in an instant explained the old woman's silence and the hissing room.

What Anna would not give to be a snake charmer...

"How do you know of Erik, and why does he speak of Christine in this letter?"

Anna dodged the question. "The man you're looking for is Richard Barret. The man who attacked me is Richard Barret. And the man masquerading as the Phantom you chase is Richard Barret. Find him and you find your wife."

"Answer my question," Raoul said sternly. He stood too close judging by the low growl that vibrated the room.

Lion taming would be good as well...

"How do you know Erik and why does he write of Christine?"

"Vicomte."

An icy silence penetrated the heated room. A shape took form in the doorway. It blocked the light and cast long, dark shadows across the room. Raoul turned toward the address, startled out of his tirade, and faced the Phantom.

Erik moved with strong, deliberate steps and with unfathomable calm. "I am rather disillusioned I was not invited to your little meeting." He reached out with one finger and shoved Raoul away from Anna.

Raoul stumbled to the side. Anna watched the vicomte's lips move subtly. No doubt he was praying for strength. His eyes darted back and forth as if he'd played out the scene a thousand times and had suddenly lost his cue. The vicomte moved with caution, once again taking up the position he had and placing himself between the Phantom and her.

Erik paused, studying Raoul like a hunter pondering if such a meager prize was worth his appetite. He smiled at Raoul's paltry show of bravado.

"Ever the gentleman, Vicomte."

Raoul swallowed hard. "You live."

"So it would appear." He passed a hand over his mask. "Looks can be deceiving you know." He leaned against the desk and folded his arms comfortably, waiting for the vicomte to make his next move. He stood as king while the vicomte was merely pawn.

Erik chuckled. "You have not changed. Somehow I suspected you to be different. You are still dashingly handsome—albeit a bit feminine in feature."

Erik's smile grew as wide as Anna knew her eyes to be. He was baiting the vicomte and judging by the way he struggled to maintain calm, Anna thought it not a good idea. Erik shrugged, ignoring the incredulous glare she presented him.

"So the sniveling, spoiled boy has nothing to say in my presence? Perchance he has been replaced by a man? Impressive. How long did it take for you to grow a spine?"

Raoul didn't react to Erik's taunts, except to reach out and gently put a hand on the small of Anna's back. He pulled her against him. At the sight of Raoul's body against hers, Erik leaned off the desk. Even if the vicomte's gesture was a feeble means to protect her, Anna knew Erik's possessive streak would not view it as such. The force of some unknown emotion started to rally around Erik. He tipped his head as one side of a lip began to twitch. A faint tremor shook his shoulders. A rumble came from deep in his throat.

"Do. Not. Touch. Her."

Raoul's grip tightened. Reaching beneath his coat, he drew his pistol and swiftly aimed the barrel at Erik's face.

"Do not think I will allow her to fall prey to you as well."

Erik fleetingly glanced at the pistol before he leaned back against the desk. "Put down your weapon, Vicomte. I am unarmed."

"You are never unarmed."

"Where are you manners? Would you strike me down in front of a woman?"

Raoul backed her toward the door never allowing the weapon's aim to leave Erik's face.

"Anna, run," he insisted, but she stood her ground.

"What a wonderfully outrageous display of valor." Erik laughed. "She has a bit of a defiant streak in her. A feisty little mongoose that one. I dare say she tends not to obey."

Erik lowered his arms which only served to make Raoul hold the pistol higher. A delicate balance for control surfaced between the two.

"Vicomte, you are beginning to make me angry, and I do not have the time to be angry." Erik took a step forward spreading his arms. The posture made him appear larger than life. "I suggest you listen to what the girl has to say if you intend to find Christine."

Raoul's shoulders stiffened. In a flash, he lowered his weapon. With a sudden burst of energy, Raoul lunged. He knocked Erik off balance and pressed the pistol against his mask. Raoul pinned him against the wall with strength that leached years of anger.

"Where is she?"

The pistol shook. The air flowed like an untamed river, poisoned with disgust. The scales balanced in the vicomte's favor for only a moment.

"Vicomte," Erik spat, "you are trying my patience. If you wish to find Christine—"

"Her name will not come from your foul mouth!"

The trigger cocked.

Anna dove toward the vicomte too shocked to scream. Raoul pivoted as she flew at him, giving Erik the opening he needed. With an enraged shout he backhanded Raoul, reeling him into the opposite wall, crumpling him to a heap. The pistol flew into the air and crashed against the floor.

Anna rushed to Erik's side. But instead of reaching for him, she reached for Raoul.

"Christ! This has turned to madness!" She shook the vicomte, desperate to bring him around.

"You never would have made him understand." Erik panted, the heat of his passion coming out in great puffs. "I tried reason, Anna. For your sake I tried. But sometimes the past simply cannot be ignored." Erik cackled as Anna shook Raoul harder. "My madness seeps to your mind now. He has already had my trial and cast my sentence. You may shake all you wish, but you will never make him understand. Help me find Christine my way."

His tone snapped Anna's head up. He stared at her in silent awe as if she possessed some invisible crutch he desired to lean on. Never in what she knew of Erik's history had he ever needed to rely on another. Christine was his one weakness in life. The desperation dressing him tore at her heart.

"That is the second time I have had that murderous soul within my grasp and the second time he has slipped away."

Anna reluctantly turned her attention toward the murmuring vicomte. No doubt he had a headache judging by the way he slumped on the couch. He rubbed lightly at his bruised jaw. It would most assuredly make his face shades of purple within the next few hours.

Anna couldn't blame Raoul for his defeated posture or the ill look upon his face. If the vicomte felt he was failing his wife, she understood, for she felt she'd betrayed Erik by staying behind. The look of rejection in Erik's eyes held more misery than she ever believed possible.

Convinced the vicomte's mind functioned with the same stubborn inability to listen to reason as before, Anna headed for the door.

"Where are you going?" he asked

"To find Edward Laroque. You were perhaps hoping I'd say to find the Phantom? One thing I'm not, Vicomte, is stupid. You'll never understand him as I do. He slips from your grasp because it invigorates him. If you weren't so obsessed by the past, perhaps you would realize Edward Laroque is nowhere to be found. Did you not summon him as well?"

He nodded.

"And did he come?" She took satisfaction in the hesitant shake of his head. "Richard Barret is here for a reason—because Edward Laroque asked him to be. It is Barret about whom you should be concerned."

A tense silence floated between them before Raoul spoke.

"I do not trust anything you say. Your mind has been seduced by the charms and illusions of a madman as Christine's once was until she saw him for the monster he is."

Anna wheeled on him. "Monster, Monsieur? I see nothing but a man."

"Monsieur le Vicomte," Inspector Legard shouted as he burst into the room.

Raoul leapt instantly to his feet. "Did you find Christine?"

"No, but you must come quickly. A man is in the theater asking to speak with you urgently."

Chapter Twenty

The rehearsal came to a standstill. Below him, clusters of frightened chorus girls gathered in tulle circles, hovering close to the safety they found in their ballet mistress. Richard laughed as stagehands and fly men emerged from every angle possible and the Maestro and his orchestra stood, baton and instruments frozen in shocked silence.

Richard leaned back in a lush velvet seat to watch a plump old lady bubble like water in a teakettle. She wrung pudgy hands together and darted her eyes around as if searching for impending doom.

Impending doom. Richard posed with his hands behind his neck and complimented himself on his choice of words.

He basked in the limelight. All eyes shifted to Legard, Raoul, and Anna as they rushed on stage.

"Ah, Vicomte, glad you could make it," Richard bellowed, moving to lean over the railing. He sniffed loudly and cleared his throat. "Now we can conduct business."

Like puppets on strings the small crowd swung their attention, looking in anticipation at the Vicomte de Chagny then back to him. This con was entirely too easy, judging by the stance of the nobleman. The man stood so stiff it seemed a pole replaced his spine. Pity, only one piece of anatomy should ever be so rigid.

"What business? Who are you?" Raoul demanded.

"Begging you pardon, Monsieur, I forgot not everyone knows who I am."

Richard pounced upon the railing like an agile alley cat. The crowd gasped nervously. An unmistakable voice lifted through the din.

"That bastard," Anna spat.

Richard laughed. He would have fun toying with her. He caught the puzzled look the vicomte gave her. Was the vicomte wary of his seed? A most excellent development. Anna's hands twisted the fabric of her dress. Her discomfort made him positively gleeful. Life was a delight when hers was miserable. Richard folded his arms across his chest and crossed one foot casually over the other. He leaned against a column. "My name is Richard Barret. And I believe I have something you want."

"Christine?" Raoul shouted, signaling to Inspector Legard. Instantly pistols were drawn.

"Vicomte! I suggest they lower their weapons if you want me to continue." Richard smiled smugly as he watched Raoul unwillingly bend to his whim.

The guards complied.

"Good," he said. "Your wife is fine, currently unharmed." He padded along the rail like a tightrope walker and gave a mock teeter to elicit gasps from below. "Quite the lovely lady I might add." He reached between his legs. "She makes me delightfully hard."

"You bastard!" Raoul shouted.

"She'll remain unharmed so long as you meet our demands." He leaned back into position.

Raoul shared a glance with Legard. "*Our* demands?"

"Oh, yes, did I not mention it? Do forgive me. I'm merely the messenger you know, my associate is somewhat of a Phantom."

"You lying snake!"

His head snapped toward Anna's outcry and he sent her a sarcastic and obvious wink. She would have climbed to Box Five and ripped his throat out if not for the nagging dread in the pit of her stomach he was certain she had. He turned his attention back to the vicomte.

"Your Phantom fellow is not one to be crossed. I know it. You know it. And certainly by now Christine knows it." He leaned his head back and gave a deep pleasurable moan. "Oh, but the way it seems he can make her tremble. The things he does to her are sinful."

The vicomte's face turned redder, and Richard wouldn't be at all surprised if that scowl upon his face caused the veins in his temple to rupture.

Raoul roared, "If that creature so much as touches her…*where is he*?"

"He couldn't make this particular meeting." Obviously, he couldn't be two people at once. He jumped back into Box Five. "The Phantom will be in further contact with the conditions of his demands. His first is that you call off your private army. It makes moving about rather difficult. I strongly suggest you follow his instructions if you want your wife to remain unharmed. You wouldn't want her to end up like Wischard or Laroque."

Raoul strode across the stage. "If you lay one hand on Christine…"

Richard leaned over the railing shaking his head. "You're not listening. Not *me* Monsieur, *the Phantom*. Why the Phantom would never share her. He prefers to bury his wick at a leisurely and more intimate pace. Good day, gentlemen. We'll be in touch. Oh, and Anna," he called, giving her a gentlemanly bow, folding himself far over the railing, "nice to see you again."

Erik paced the flies, a slow, majestic anger rising within. Glad, at least for the moment, of the physical distance placed between him and Barret. If not for his concern over finding Christine, Erik surely would have killed again.

The urge mushroomed inside, building and roiling like a black plague. Hatred conducted toward Richard like lightning to a rod. Erik wanted to kill for the abuse he'd perpetrated upon Anna. He would make Richard suffer for laying his filthy hands on Christine. And now—most fervently—he wanted to kill for the ridicule. For a phony Phantom to be abusing the power Erik had carefully crafted disgusted him. The respectable life he'd tried to build was crumbling before his eyes.

The letters he'd sent upon Raoul and Christine's arrival were written in the utmost respect. Shouldn't that have been testimony to his gentlemanly air? He'd tried to project his intent as an honorable man, not a Phantom, but clearly the expectations of him lay elsewhere, thanks to disgraceful gossip. He couldn't separate himself from the past now, not with another investigation, not with another *Phantom*.

Erik twirled himself from rope to rope, up and down the flies as he worked out his thoughts. He wouldn't have Christine within such a contemptible man's grasp. The thought of Richard Barret being near her turned everything before his eyes crimson. Barret couldn't have what was not his...

If those below so vehemently believed the Phantom had been instilling terror, let them have their ghost. No one in the theater, save Madame Giry and Anna, cared that a man lay behind the mask.

Erik swung himself around one final rope before taking a moment to catch his breath. He wanted to feel his renewed power course through him. He surveyed those on stage like a puppeteer, deciding which string to yank next.

He listened as excited whispers floated upward.

"*Mesdames et Messieurs*, Maestro Fontaine, I urge calm," Raoul addressed. "As you all undoubtedly know, there is a situation at hand. As of this moment, Jacob Wischard and Edward Laroque have been removed from their positions and no longer manage the Opera Garnier. I will be acting in their stead until suitable replacements can be found."

Erik's gaze pointed like a bow on a target. His madness was pulled to a dangerous level. He'd already set his sights, so if Raoul de Chagny wanted to become a marked man, this was the way to do it.

"This matter will be addressed quickly and with swift justice. I implore you to continue with your usual routines." Raoul nodded at Maestro Fontaine, urging him to continue and took Anna securely by the arm. "You, Mademoiselle, will stay with me. A bargaining chip if you will."

"You are being played a fool, Vicomte," Anna snapped.

Erik had reached his boiling point. He damned the fate that sucked on his veins, pulling blood and madness through him. With his gaze locked on Anna, he leapt to his decision. His choice to relive the past plummeted his heart into a bleak misery faster than gravity to the stage.

The girls of the corps de ballet shrieked. Their pitch sent Raoul's and Anna's heads whipping in their direction. Erik landed on his feet with a crack that shook the stage, his cloak briefly engulfing him. With a magnificent swirl, he fanned it out of his way and surveyed the crowd cowering before his grand entrance. He laughed arrogantly as police started toward him. It only took him one well-practiced glare toward Raoul and the Inspector to get them to stand down.

"Bonjour, Messieurs," Erik said cordially. "Were you not expecting me? Perhaps you thought I was myth?" He tossed his head back and sighed. "Ah yes, I recall now—Erik is dead."

His voice amplified like he leaned on an invisible sustaining pedal and pulled screams from the mouth of the youngest ballerinas.

"Erik is alive!" he exploded. "I have a message for my new manager. It is regrettable our reunions could not have been more civil. I truly did not wish for our paths to cross in such a manner." He circled Raoul and Anna. "Heed my warning. Do whatever is asked of you without question or pause."

He sensed Raoul's tension for it left finger marks upon Anna's arm. If he acted on his impulses, he would have wrenched Anna free from the vicomte's haughty grip. But he knew the self-important little aristocrat didn't have the presence of mind to help Christine. Erik relied on his belief that Anna's ever-defiant spirit would be able to deal with the vicomte and would prompt her to believe none of what she was about to see.

"Do not underestimate the situation if you intend for Christine to remain unharmed," he said with indisputable demand. "You will never understand me, Vicomte, so do not even try. It will only lead you down the path of madness. There are those around you who know dimensions of me you could never possibly comprehend."

As he passed behind Anna, he grazed the small of her back with his hand. Did fear of him or something else cause her to tremble? Erik's lips didn't move as he slipped by her, yet the whisper of his apology floated to her ear.

He backed from Raoul, holding his gaze steady. "Obey the demands for Christine's sake." With a sudden earsplitting noise he disappeared, swallowed by a trap door.

Chapter Twenty-one

The stagnant props surrounding Christine poisoned her memories from her years at the opera. Silent horses, circus clowns, and mythological beasts stared at her in frozen mockery.

She'd stopped struggling to free herself hours ago. Her writhing gave her bracelets of red skin and every time she swallowed, her throat scratched, worn raw from screaming. It was no use. No one could hear her.

The Phantom had her captive.

She was a prisoner to his needs yet her heart beat wildly against her mind. Her memories were egging her apprehension, but her heart refused to believe Erik would live only to treat her so cruelly. Nothing made sense, not even her memories of times past. Not even her choices or her heart. Horror and love remained locked together in an endless spinning cyclone. The harder she tried to separate herself from Erik, the farther she was dragged away from the peaceful eye of the storm.

Tears dripped freely. "I cannot."

Blinded when the door opened and the light of the lantern flooded the room, she squinted sharply, and crawled farther into her corner.

"Let me go!" she yelled, as Richard's frame filled the doorway.

"You really should stop screaming. A pretty voice such as yours should not sound so hoarse."

"What do you want with me?"

"Oh, Madame, that is a question a woman of your beauty shouldn't ask a man like me. Beyond the purse your vicomte will pay, you are of no use."

She bit the quiver on her lower lip as Richard knelt in front of her. He tipped her chin up to gaze into her eyes.

"Do you mean for such a pout to seduce me? You should know I think you're an excellent temptress. I do enjoy when women tremble for me." Her head jerked as she tried to wrestle her chin from his grip. "Come now, I'm giving you a choice. Usually I don't ask." He leaned in for a kiss, but she sharply turned her head.

"What does the Phantom want with me?" she asked breathlessly.

"Well, little lady, the Phantom wants you. I get the money; he gets you. That was our arrangement." He slapped his hands on his knees and stood. "Ah well, I suppose I should save you for him."

"I don't believe you."

"You think I jest? It would be best, my dear, that you do believe me. The Phantom does not take well to folks who think him a fool."

Christine followed the thin beam of light arching across the room as Richard gestured with the lantern to the doorway beyond. Her mouth gaped then closed, as the lifeless body of Edward Laroque was illuminated.

"Poor old chap got in his way," Richard explained. He cleared his throat. "The *Phantom* regretted having to kill him, but he prefers to work alone and Edward would've just become difficult to deal with once he found out about Jacob Wischard."

Richard laughed into his fist. The sight of the dead man launched an uncontrolled horror in her and she screamed, hoping against hope itself that some angel would hear her and deliver her from hell.

Erik thought it best not to ignore or suppress his anger.

He found his display on the stage invigorating and wanted to feel power course through him like it once had. Too long he'd kept his emotions in check while battling his inner demons. Not this time. Not with someone holding Christine in the balance and playing with Anna's mind. Erik used this power to drive him forward with renewed determination to put an end to this abomination.

Night fell quickly. He moved uninhibited through the opera house, driven by the stories he replayed in his head. He was a genius, not a mind reader, so in order to find Christine he had to think like Richard Barret.

Unfortunately, he knew enough of the man to do just that. Richard acted on his threats, with no regard to woman or child. Too much was at risk to take this opponent lightly. The man was a drunk; Anna had suffered great misfortunes as a result. Erik used logic and the plentiful supply of drink in the opera's wine stores to corner his prey. It would only be a matter of time before Richard came here. Sometimes their train of thought was not that different.

A figure, arms laden with wine, shuffled out of the stores, prompting Erik to sink into his hiding spot. He breathed deeply, a familiar sensation awakening his body. The feeling was a great relief of energy, a surging tension of mind and body, building before releasing in one long and glorified explosion. He'd always equated such ecstasy to what it must feel like to bed a woman.

Erik waited for his prey to pass, forcing himself to prolong his agony and wait until just the right moment. Holding back, coiling his need, focusing his desire.

He rounded.

The thin, silk rope snaked from his hand and hit its mark around Richard's neck. He clawed at the rope. The bottles crashed to the floor spraying alcohol everywhere.

Erik snapped back on the silk. He held it taut, quite satisfied the vermin on the other end could do nothing defensive. Moving from behind his victim, he smiled when he saw the look on Richard's face. He twitched as the elegant lasso bit into his neck. Erik enjoyed that expression. It was one of the glories of killing by silk. There was no need to soil the hands and no blood was spilt. The Punjab provided a detached method of dispatching those Erik deemed not worthy of further efforts.

Holding the silk in one hand, he released the tension with his other. He indifferently fingered its remains as he moved into what light the wall lamps emitted. Controlling his prize like a dog on a leash, Erik cast an evil look deep into the eyes of Richard Barret.

"Bonsoir, Monsieur. I believe you wanted to meet me."

Richard blinked hard. Erik blinked as well, deliberately knowing the eerie quality of his eyes would drive those not used to it near mad. Richard tried desperately to loosen the cord around his neck. Erik took pity and gave him enough slack to allow him to respond.

"Holy Mother! You are real!" Richard cracked.

"Quite."

"What do you want with me?"

What arrogance. Erik reeled his captive in by the neck, closing the breadth between them. Richard stumbled and flopped like a fish.

"I want Christine. Where is she?"

Richard stopped struggling as his breath came out in rasping, shallow pants. "I won't tell you." He fought to smile which incited from Erik another violent tug. "And you can't kill me because then you'd never find her."

That was the wrong answer.

Erik yanked the Punjab and pulled Richard into his grasp. Swinging him, Erik slammed Richard against a wine rack. The bottles crashed, sending glass and wine everywhere. Erik kept him pinned against broken bottles, suppressing his taste to murder him right then.

Richard winced. "I see you get my point."

"What do you want with her?"

"Why would I tell you? If you so desperately want her, you can have her when I'm through," Richard countered, getting enough bravado and strength back to shove Erik away.

Erik jumped toward him, but Richard regained his authority. He dodged Erik's oncoming attack, rolled out of the way, and grabbed the shattered remains of a broken bottle. Erik twirled out of reach as Richard waved his makeshift dagger. Eyes narrowed on slender steel as Richard slid his jacket aside to expose his pistol.

"You are a worthy opponent." Richard tugged the rope around his neck free. "An unusual choice of weapon, but quite effective."

Erik caught the silk he threw and coiled it between his hands. "What are your demands?"

"I only have demands with the vicomte. I'm under the impression he doesn't like you very much."

Erik held the silk strand tighter. His flesh colored to crimson around the rope.

"You could actually be of use to me," Richard mused. "I might get more out of this con by running it with an actual Phantom."

Erik weighed the options. He had no idea of Christine's whereabouts and there was no time to conduct a search of his opera house or the streets of Paris. Being a wanted criminal would make doing so difficult.

The only hope to find Christine lay in working with this despicable man and not against him. If there were going to be any Phantoms running around his opera house, Erik would rather it be himself anyway. The fluttering in his stomach became increasingly persistent.

"Go on," Erik urged.

"Excellent. You help me get what I seek, do whatever it is you Phantoms do, and I'll give you the girl." Richard raised the glass shard higher. "The game is played my way, however, lest you want me to kill her."

Erik hated playing second fiddle. He would play Richard's game only until he had a chance to turn the tables and come out first chair.

"Very well," he rumbled irritably.

"Perfect. I need you to pen a letter. I understand that is an area in which you excel; beyond that, when I need you I'll contact you." He scowled and admitted defeat. "How exactly does one contact a Phantom?"

"*You* do not."

"Fine." He shrugged. "I dare say you are better at being a ghost than I am anyway." He gestured toward the door. "*Après vous*."

Erik knocked him aside as he passed, twitching with rage.

"So, you have a soft spot for the diva? Does she love you?" his nemesis jeered.

Erik quickened his stride. If he stayed, he might change his mind and kill Richard now.

"I've heard the tales you know," Richard called after him. "Scorned and rejected by the beauty because you're a monstrous beast. You don't think the diva ever loved you? You don't honestly think there's a woman alive who could, do you?"

Erik's loathing churned like a ravening hunger. It mingled with a passionate longing he dare not tame. Centering his thoughts on that sensation willed away the dark need to give in to his madness. He glanced at the rope in his hands with a perverse need for the relief it would bring and a grim recollection of a past he was trying to forget.

Focus on her and the need to end this ridiculous cheat.

How many times had Richard Barret's life been spared by his daughter?

"Actually, there is," Erik called back.

"I dare say I would like to meet her!"

Erik turned from his laughter, for the first time feeling fortunate he was condemned to vaults of the theater. For if anyone had crossed him at that particular moment they would have witnessed Richard Barret meeting a violent and unforgivable end.

Chapter Twenty-two

Every minute ticking by seemed like an eternity. Anna's silent contemplation of everything around her was maddening. Raoul sat in the dimly lit manager's office as he rolled the nightmare around in his mind.

Abiding by the first demand and ridding the opera house of its security was a decision Raoul hadn't taken lightly. Without Legard, having been forced to dismiss him as well, he was a one-man army of which he was not in command.

Damn fool.

Raoul tried to ignore Anna, but he sensed her eyes on him. He squeezed his shut, cursing the entire situation. Alone, unchaperoned with a young lady—everything about this blasted affair was *not* good. In the presence of a lady, he would have carried himself with more dignity. But at the moment, he damned propriety and permitted his stance to reflect how deeply worried and profoundly in love he was with his wife.

"How do you know Richard Barret?" he asked softly, for his throat had gone dry.

Such a question she apparently was not willing to answer, for she responded with silence.

"And the Phantom?" he prodded. "Do you still expect me to believe what this letter implies?" He pulled her note from his jacket pocket and waved it before her. A flush rushed across her cheeks.

"Believe what you want," she murmured.

"I hope what you witnessed on that stage proves the man who penned your letter is incapable of mercy, let alone love."

"What I witnessed, Monsieur, is the desperation of a man deeply devoted to a woman who was once the light of his world and whose shadow I will always be in."

"What *I* believe is that you play into this somehow and will be most useful in helping me find Christine."

"So I am to be a pawn? How unique." Her sarcasm fogged the air. "I tried to reason with you. I told you about Richard Barret, but did you believe me?"

Raoul clamped on his tongue to school his impatience. "What do they want with Christine? What are the Phantom's demands going to be?"

"Mother of God. I should have known a man of your pedigree would wear the badge of prejudice with pride."

Convinced he stared in the eyes of an accomplice, he stroked his mustache. The girl was compliant and silent one minute, defiant and crass the next. "Just an answer if you please, Mademoiselle."

"Erik has nothing to do with this. He wished to speak with Christine with the most respectable intent. He has told you that countless times, but you choose not to listen."

Raoul let his forearms drop against the desk before he slid back, seeking comfort in the chair. "I really wish you would not call him that."

"Erik? Why not? It's his name. Does it make *Erik* too human to you?"

"No, because it only draws you deeper into the spell he has cast over you." He looked at her, finding it hard to admit his weakness. "Mademoiselle, I am not keeping you as a pawn. I wish to protect you from him. Clearly I was unable do so for Christine, and I will not have another woman fall victim to his twisted mind. It pains me to know you already have suffered."

"While I admire such respect, Monsieur, I'm quite capable of taking care of myself. I don't need to be protected from Erik, nor do I—" The door clicked open.

"Vicomte?"

"Madame Giry," Raoul said, shocked. He glanced at the desk clock. "Why are you here? My *maître d' hôtel* should have sent someone for you. I shall call for a carriage to bring you to my estate. And this time, you are to leave."

"No, Monsieur," she pleaded. "I have been a part of this longer than you. I will not leave this opera house. I was resting in my office." She extended a note. "I found this on my desk."

Raoul sighed at the sight of it; he was growing weary of notes. "What does it say?"

"Box Five."

Anna leapt to her feet, Raoul close behind.

The newly installed electric globes on the stage were lit and a few were left to illuminate Box Five. The rest of the theater remained shrouded and emotionless as a tomb. Erik kept himself tucked out of sight while Richard reclined in his usual pose as their company took the stage.

"My apologies for the lateness of the hour," Richard shouted. "But we'd rather not have an audience."

"Get to the point," Raoul demanded.

"As you wish." Richard reached into his jacket and produced a second note. It fluttered to the seats below. "Those are some additional demands and conditions if you will."

Erik moved from the shadow and glanced at the letter drifting to the theater seats. Madame Giry instinctively went to retrieve it. Erik stabbed a contemptuous look upon Richard. He didn't like being double-crossed.

"What did you send in that note?" he demanded in a tone that floated directly into Richard's ear.

Richard jumped. "Just our demands."

"What demands?"

He smiled sarcastically instead of replying. Turning from Richard, Erik found Raoul had leveled his eyes upon him.

The boy refused to look away. He remained fixed in his spot with an impressive resolve. Raoul's hand stroked the sides of his legs. Erik noted the imperceptible tremor to his fingers. Their eyes locked. Erik's gaze dared Raoul to draw that pistol he kept hidden and aim. Aim right between his golden eyes and extinguish them forever, if he be so bold.

Erik stared at the vicomte with calm indifference before focusing his attention on Anna. His attitude changed imperceptibly to soften at the sight of her. His eyes shifted to meet Richard's raised eyebrow. Erik followed as he turned to study Anna's stance and her quizzical expression.

"It's not polite to stare, Anna," Richard snipped.

"This is a con you won't win," she warned.

Richard laughed and clapped. "The strumpet finds her voice! I always win, Anna. Haven't you learned that yet? How is that sister of yours?"

His laughter pinned Anna to her spot. Her gaze fixed on her feet.

"Poor little strumpet," her father pitied, "you never had one did you?"

Erik's eyes burned with incomprehensible vehemence. He spun toward Richard. He swore in the time it took to complete that sentence he'd seen the spirit he'd grown to admire in Anna shatter, yet could do nothing to help her pick up those pieces so long as Christine was held in the balance.

Erik clenched and unclenched his fists as he watched Anna struggle for composure. He suppressed his reaction as Anna choked back a cry and crushed her hands to her ears unable to do anything to force out the sounds of her father's laughter. That laughter combined with her quiet tears made Erik snap.

"Some respect in my theater!" He grabbed Richard's feet and shoved them off the balcony railing. It did little to satisfy him.

Richard glowered. "You really do have a temper."

"And a wise man knows not to tempt it," Erik warned in a hauntingly furious whisper.

He stared intently at the Vicomte de Chagny when Madame Giry returned with the note. Raoul looked up to Box Five, horror struck.

"What kind of deviant are you?" he shouted at Erik.

"We expect you to obey the demands, Vicomte," Richard replied, staring at his cuticles.

"This is unjust." Raoul looked from the note to Anna and back at the note.

"You know the options. Do not scorn the Phantom for Christine's sake."

Erik took a step toward Richard, but spun sharply at the last second. He wouldn't be seen crushing his fist to his mouth. Every minute he permitted Richard to have control was a minute longer than he could stand. He could lift Richard Barret and throw him to his death right now, but Erik forced himself to think of Christine.

"I want to see her," Raoul shouted. "I will do none of this until I see her—until I know she is safe.

Erik glanced over his shoulder and commanded Raoul to be silent with one piercing look. He needed to think.

"You will see her, Monsieur," Richard interjected again, this time biting around his thumb.

Erik vulgarly looked at the nail Richard spit on the fine velvet of a seat. Richard started to stand, but Erik shoved him back down for spite, his mind racing faster than the notes he composed. He had to find a way to get Christine out of the reach of Richard Barret and safely into his hands.

"She will sing in the series tomorrow as her public expects," Richard said. "I'll see she takes the stage. You'd dare not risk her life by doing anything rash in front of hundreds of people. Be forewarned, I'm an excellent shot. One false move and we kill her."

Erik leveled a look of perverse antipathy on Richard who was tapping his forehead precisely between the eyes. His heart drove a furious need for control throughout his body. Richard would die before he'd ever dare speak of her in such context again.

"Agreed," Raoul conceded. "Allow me to see her, allow her to sing, and I will meet all these demands." He glanced at Anna, a sick color crossing his face. Raoul waved the note at Erik. "When do I deliver this? When will you bring me Christine?"

Erik's thoughts raced and his eyes tapered at the vicomte's nerves. What was in that note? He had to think quickly—and like the Phantom. "When retribution is paid."

"Erik!" Anna's appalled shout made his stomach writhe like a nest of snakes.

He stood like stone, while the man beside him turned his attention toward Anna. Erik's hands convulsed at his side. He didn't take kindly to the lewd and curious way Richard leered at her. And though he'd ordinarily address such a condescending and vulgar look, the deadly silence that had descended upon him after Anna's shout was awesome.

Richard scrutinized Erik before he turned his attention back on his daughter. He shrugged his eyebrows as a grin spread across his face. It was all Erik could do not to unleash his loathing upon him.

"I will accept the delivery, Monsieur," Richard chimed in. "When we're certain everything is in order we'll deal with your wife. Follow through with the demands as—"

"She will sing the Madrigal." Erik's voice reverberated with vehemence never before heard. He locked eyes with Madame Giry. "See to it all demands are adhered to exactly as written. Make no mistakes as to how it is carried out."

The authority behind Erik's voice made Madame Giry bob her head emphatically. She took Anna's hand and gave it a light squeeze.

Anna's jaw unhinged. "Madrigal?" she mouthed to Erik.

Erik locked his stare on her, his face hardened like granite beneath its leather prison and his mind taunted him with his inadequacies for command. He ground his teeth and a loud, frustrated growl escaped his lips. He clenched the hem of his cloak in a tight fist and spun sharply from Box Five. He moved with such swiftness the air cracked through his cloak and boomed throughout the theater.

The Madrigal was the only composition Erik had taught her on his violin. The first intimate gift he'd given a woman. He hadn't made her aware of its mournful lyrics. A sentimental piece to him—the key he handed Anna to unlock his mind the instant she grasped his violin. A tune that had Erik's heart and mind arguing against each other and questioning exactly whom she had freed with that key—man or Phantom?

Richard sauntered out of Box Five. He skipped down the Grand Escalier humming a merry tune about fame and riches. His spring lost some of its step.

Erik waited for him at the base of the stairs where—in full

Phantom glory—he paced, glancing sharply up the Escalier. Richard was forced to go on the defensive.

"I don't like being interrupted." He stopped a few steps higher than Erik. "My con, my way. Remember?"

Erik's fist split the air. One swift crack flattened Richard to the floor. He tumbled clumsily down the remaining stairs. Erik gave him no time to throw a punch before he had him by the collar.

Richard's back nearly snapped in two as he hit the marble banister. He grunted, but covered his pain with a laugh. "I didn't think you were the type of man to resort to such demeaning means of control."

"I prefer techniques that use a bit more finesse and calculated thought, but flesh contacting flesh just feels good." The room lurched as Erik yanked him forward. "What was in that note?"

Swiping his lip, Richard spit blood onto Erik's mask. The hall filled with echoing curses. Richard rounded his shoulder into Erik's chest, forcing him backward. "Don't do that again for your diva's sake."

"The note," Erik snarled.

"Ransom. And don't think you're getting any of it. The vicomte delivers the money to Box Five and once everything's in order, you can have your way with the diva."

Richard brushed past Erik and jogged down the remaining steps.

"You are lying." Erik's voice thundered across the Escalier, reverberating through Vestibule de Contrôle.

"Am I now? That's the mystery that makes Richard Barret, Richard Barret. It's a simple con." He swaggered toward the Grand Vestibule. "You're the one trying to complicate it." Turning, attitude dripped off his shoulders. "You really want to kill me, don't you? Or perhaps hunt me down, find the girl and whisk her away like a knight on a white stallion? You see that's the beauty of it all. Your reputation precedes you, mine doesn't. Ultimately, they want you, not me. I'm merely the messenger. Do you want to play games with me? I'm quite good at them. Or perhaps you already know that—*Erik*."

Man didn't need to see a face to understand the body. Richard sneered when Erik wavered. He moved his jacket aside, his pistol adding power to his warning. "Come now, follow me. Let's see how good a shot I am. I have certain suspicions. Try anything to stop me and you won't like the results. I believe you know I'm a man of my word. We're much alike, you and I, except you may indeed have the brawn, but I, the brains."

Erik was ravenous in his approach, like a tiger stalking his prey. His boots clicked angrily against the marble, forcing Richard to think quickly. "And the girl..."

Erik stopped.

Richard smiled greedily. "You really are lovesick aren't you? Tell me, does your sweetheart know?" He backed away and spread his arms triumphantly. "Now, who could that be I wonder: the diva, the strumpet, or perhaps both? Oh the irony that a man such as you would have two women!"

Richard stopped before the mirrored wall in the huge main foyer, watching Erik's reflection pitch and tremble with rage. He walked farther, keeping his hand above his pistol and gesturing around him at Erik's reflections.

"But do you have them? Or does he?" He pointed first to one reflection and then across the hall to the next. "Or he?" Richard clutched a hand to his heart. "I'll tell you something, Monsieur, since I pity you so deeply." He ran his hands up and down his chest in a manner that made the man before him clench his hands into fists. "Taking command of a woman's body, thrusting unrelentingly into her core is sheer power, sheer delight."

Richard's imagery severed Erik's angry impatience. He raced down the vestibule. It was quite possible that Erik would kill him right there, so Richard made certain to bring the monster to a standstill.

"I've already tasted of one in that manner multiple times. Now who could that lucky lady be? The diva?" He ran his tongue across his lips. "Or the daughter?"

Erik stopped short. For a moment he stiffened, his eyes darting as if trying to erase such imagery.

The maddening notes of Erik's voice played through the vestibule. "Christine will sing the Madrigal," he demanded. "You will bring what it requires to her."

Richard tossed his head back and laughed at that. His throat cinched and his glee gargled when a thin hand encased his throat. Eye to eye with a black mask, he felt Erik's fury vibrate on his flesh.

"Do not parry me when the well of my hatred is deepest, Monsieur. My music, my way."

Getting Barret to agree to bring Christine what she needed for the Madrigal was no simple task. It was evident neither man trusted the other, but Erik had come out the victor, though he felt the fool.

He stood in the silence of the Grand Foyer, a space big enough to hold two hundred people. Yet tonight, all it greeted was the intense emotion rolling deep inside him. The ten chandeliers that lit its length had been dimmed long ago, so barely a glimmer of light illuminated the space and the murderous look caged beneath his mask.

He walked the center of the foyer, a huge raven of death watched by the stone eyes of Maestro's past. He wanted to kill the Vicomte de Chagny for caving to the whims of Barret and standing down the theater police. This foyer might not be empty if Raoul wasn't such a child. More people might be looking for Christine if Raoul wasn't so weak.

Erik blamed the boy for this.

If he'd been allowed the freedom to speak with Christine when he'd asked, perhaps this grim farce wouldn't have been created and she wouldn't be locked away somewhere, cowering in terror. And, he assumed, terror of him. Richard Barret had indeed succeeded in resurrecting a Phantom.

But the Phantom would not be played the fool.

Erik stopped in the middle of the foyer his head tilting to the unorganized notes in his mind. He could lie and cheat himself, but Christine loved the boy and misunderstood him.

The reason stared at him out of the corner of his eye.

Erik whirled. Shouting vehemently, he sent his fist and forearm colliding into his reflection. A great relief of pressure kicked him in the chest when the mirror crumbled around him. If only he too could shatter.

He stared at the hall he'd fled down days ago when he tried to outrun the heart he'd discovered still beating in the man he was. In the past he'd forced Christine to choose her love. He'd threatened her with violence, holding Raoul's life in his hands. Now Barret was threatening him by holding Christine's life and honor in one hand while his malicious mind toyed with Anna. Barret didn't know it, but he was forcing Erik to choose.

He chose Christine.

He'd see to it she was found safe. Erik would tell her what he needed, kill Richard Barret and then deliver Christine to the arms of her vicomte. *Wretched boy. Let her love him. It matters not.* He would not relive the past. Erik only wanted the life he was yet to have.

A new and unfamiliar emotion shook him like a fragile bloom in the breeze: insecurity. He chose to aid Christine, but he loved another and was uncertain he was ready to face that. The part of leading man was a role the Opera Ghost was hesitant to play.

He paused before retreating to the bleak shade of his underworld. Kneeling, he fanned his cloak out of his way and picked up a piece of the shattered mirror. Its sharp edges bit into his flesh and a small trickle of blood coated his fingers.

The present only echoed the past, urging the company to take the stage in unchallenged performances.

"I will not leave it be."

Chapter Twenty-three

Christine faded in and out of restless sleep. Her dreams were a combination of the gentle affections of her husband and the dark, alluring mystery of her masked Angel of Music. Her cheeks were stiff with dried tears, her shoulders ached, her wrists were raw, and her spirit was breaking. She only wanted someone to rescue her—anyone.

She gasped when the door swung inward and in sauntered Richard.

"Hello, diva dear. It's dreadfully late. Were you waiting up for me?"

Christine shook her head trying her best to put on a mask of bravery. She watched as Richard dragged several small bundles into the already cluttered cellar.

"Now," he began, "I'm going to untie you and you're going to listen to me. Understand?"

Christine cautiously nodded. She stiffened as he crawled uncomfortably close and reached around her waist to fumble at the knot tethering her to the wall. She swallowed the lump of fear as her wrists were freed. Raw, angry flesh marred her hands. She thought to flee, but exhaustion had command of her legs.

Richard carried a basket to her. A fresh facille poked out the basket and the pungent odor of a maroilles wafted around the warm loaf. Her stomach rumbled and her mouth watered. She tried not to look eager for such a small kindness.

"The Phantom," he said with marked aggravation, "insists you eat. He claims you will need your strength." He shoved the basket toward her and held out a large flask. "You're instructed to drink this. Something about your voice..."

The heat from the flask made her fingers tingle.

"From him as well." A large box landed at her feet. "Apparently he prefers his divas in pretty things."

Christine reached out and lightly touched the dress box, all the tokens giving her a glimmer of a teacher she knew long ago.

"And this." Richard produced his final parcel, throwing it on top of the box.

Her eyes welled with tears. A leather folder held the pages of an unfamiliar score. The beautiful silver hair comb and the freshly plucked rose woven between its teeth sent her tears falling over their brim.

"Your sentiment is pathetic. Learn it," he snapped, gesturing at the score. He kicked his lantern toward her. "It is nearly dawn and you sing tonight." Before she had time to react Richard swung out the door, locking it behind him.

Christine looked at the semicircle of gifts, dazed at what they could possibly mean. She caressed the box. Opening the lid, she peeled away the tissue that protected its contents, and sighed deeply. The most exquisite dress she'd ever beheld lay before her. The fit would be perfect. In the past Erik had sworn on bended knee that he'd pay attention to her every need and fancy. Christine didn't doubt his tokens reflected the bizarre love he still held. As she fingered the pearl beading, frightened nerves tickled the back of her neck.

Setting the dress aside, she hesitantly reached for the score. She undid the ribbon that clasped the binder shut, careful not to damage the comb and rose. With a final tug on the ribbon, she lifted the comb to her nose and took a deep breath of the rose's fragrance. The next gift she examined with the utmost care and regard.

Across the top of the score in Erik's oddly elegant hand was written: *Madrigal du Rossignol.*

A sad melody, perfectly matched to her range, poured off the pages. The notes rose and fell like the song of the bird itself. Christine could almost hear the nightingale mournfully singing into her ear.

"When Nightingale falls scorned from favor of heart and flock; Seeks his trial and alone bleeds against a thorn; He sings to deaf heaven a final dirge as he commits his sins against nature's swift sword, " she read aloud.

The pain of the lyrics struck her deeply. She read on, pitying the bird. A simpler tune followed and Christine's heart slowed with every stanza until it nearly stopped beating. She stared at the message being conveyed to her in a combination of notes and words. The uncertain nerves in her belly churned into a small, but tiny fire of altogether different emotions. As she read, the emotions she'd been trying to refute surfaced with ferocious force. The realization of it pinched her stomach and curled her forward. She could deny the lie she'd been living no longer...

"I cannot, but I do."

Christine rocked, fearing for her husband, his name, and his life, yet thinking on the future of hers.

She couldn't be in love with Erik.

As she read and reread the lyrics, the message screamed at her like a siren. She refused to believe them. That tiny fire in her pit blazed out of control.

Confusion and longing heated her eyes. Christine clutched the sheets to her chest and gave in to her tears.

Chapter Twenty-four

Anna reluctantly accepted the vicomte's hand. Raoul helped her from the carriage onto the grounds of the Opera Garnier. The crepuscular light barely glowed as they turned through the doors and into the near-deserted building. She didn't agree with the vicomte's decision to leave the grounds the previous night. Inspector Legard's last request, before his services were severed, was to leave the opera house lest the vicomte become a victim of the Phantom as well. It was nothing short of ridiculous. The entire charade was as preposterous as her being paraded at a nobleman's side.

When he laid his hand lightly upon her forearm she shot him a seething glare.

"You seem weary," he said. "Did you not sleep in comfort last night? I should have insisted upon you staying in the guest chambers instead of that chair you chose in my drawing room."

She smiled with tight lips. An overly plush chair by a warm fire was far superior to a muddy street or mildewed stack of rope. The damn aristocrat had no idea in what he was tangled. "I didn't sleep, knowing your vicomtess was in the arms of Richard Barret. I doubt you can tell me any different."

He took a deep breath. "I did not rest, knowing my wife is in the arms of the Phantom."

"I'm telling you, Monsieur, Erik means her no harm. That person we saw on the stage was not who Erik truly is."

Raoul twisted the knob on the office door and shoved it inward. His gesture bid her enter before him. He shut the door and shrugged off his waistcoat, recklessly tossing it on the divan. It exposed the pistol strapped close to his hip. Raoul turned the key on several lamps. "You speak as if you intimately know the Phantom."

"I know Erik."

"You know nothing." Raoul slapped his hands on the desk. He pointed at her, a rude gesture on his behalf, but Anna had seen worse. "I will not be convinced otherwise. That beast tried to kill me. He trapped me in a room of mirrors, Mademoiselle, a torture chamber of his own creation which blazed with heat and then tried to drown me while the woman I loved watched his every move. He then drugged and chained me in the Communard's dungeon." Raoul slammed a fist on the desk so hard he sent the blotter teetering. "Fate allowed me to avoid that degrading place only to be imprisoned there by a deviant madman. My screams could not be heard, my wrists bled from the chains and my abhorrence of him hit levels I never knew possible. But worse—I could not reach Christine. I had to rely on others to act as the man I could not be."

He knocked a knuckle against his forehead.

"The Phantom plays disgusting mind games. My wife tried to kill herself because of them. She spent a fortnight locked away with him while he terrorized her and forced his filthy mind on her. He tried to manipulate her into loving him. That will never be so, even now if he tries it again. The monster is obsessed. The man's mind is like an endless wheel churning up filth and there is no way he can or will ever love. I will see to it his games end now."

"Erik can love," she said with quiet sadness once he finished his ranting. "I know because he loves the vicomtess more than anything.

"Please, Mademoiselle, I am in no mood."

A band of tension rounded Raoul's shoulders when Anna forced her point of view.

"Erik wants the chance he gave you and the choice he gave her. He released you from that dungeon and presented you to your bride unharmed."

His brow contorted.

"Yes, that look upon your face is correct, Monsieur le Vicomte. I know more than you think. Erik wants to live like someone of no consequence. You lived without the past before you knew Erik lived. Why live with it now? Have you no mercy for second chances?"

Anna returned his blank stare. A wave of his hand bade her to sit behind the other desk. He replied by asking her to balance the evening's queue—a clear attempt to keep her silent and occupied.

She did so, but turned to him after a time. Timidly, she rotated her pencil in her hand. "Monsieur, may I ask for the return of my letter?"

The thought of such made her neck heat with the insecurity of her newly desired love for Erik. But Raoul's laughter added resentment to the flame.

"Why, Anna? Are words on a page enough to persuade you Erik is the man you so want him to be? That his scrawl is enough testimony he loves? Anyone can write flowery poems that woo and seduce. The Phantom is a master. Death is the ultimate seducer of young maidens, is He not?" Raoul laughed despairingly. "To think of the irony that a man such as me has a rival such as him." Raoul erased the air between him and Anna away as if he intended the action to cleanse the room. "That note is another manipulative trick. Spare yourself the pain. The man has nothing but evil in his soul and Death upon his countenance."

Such injustice burned into her heart. "You do not know his soul," she replied. "I felt no evil when he reached for me. Only relief, passion, gentleness and want. I felt only what we all want from love. I felt no evil when he pulled me against him. When he took me in his arms and lifted me so to kiss—"

"Enough!" Raoul's lips pursed and his face colored to a sickly green.

"It is as I suspected," Anna observed. "You only want to believe what past dictates for you. Is that the only way a man should be judged?"

"You are naïve, Mademoiselle. I am right in my duty to protect you. I will not have your innocence scarred or ruined."

The pencil slammed down on the desk along with her palm, splintering it in two. Gone was the apprehensive and timid tone to her voice.

"Naïve? Innocent?" She rose, leaning across the desk toward him. "How *dare you* assume anything about me! I spent the better half of my more formidable years wandering the countryside of France whilst you pranced about pretty upon your pony. I partook in acts no woman should be privy to as you and your vicomtess danced and dined and lived the comfortable life your precious noble indicator allows. I wore all the masks of virtue while condemned to live in a world forbidden to most. The last thing to prevail in this, Monsieur, is my naivety or innocence. I can take care of myself, which is more than I can say about your seemingly meek and spoiled wife. The only reason I'm permitting you to keep me as some bloody adornment on your arm is because I know and understand the man you should be in fear of—Richard Barret!"

Wiping the passion of her words from her lips, she peered in disgust at Raoul's rush to judge her so simply.

Wide-eyed, he leaned back in his chair. "Is that so? You are positive Barret is the man to fear more than the Phantom? There is your naivety. I am going to ask you one more time and I expect an answer. How do you know Richard Barret?"

The question shot tiny darts of hatred through her. The steadfast devotion she saw behind the vicomte's eye was admirable, but did nothing to sway her dislike. Leaning on her arms harder, brought her closer to the supercilious noble. She jerked her head to the side. "He killed my mother."

The rapping at the door curbed her low-bred and formidable temper and permitted a bit of color to return to the vicomte's face. Anna shoved off the desk, disgusted.

"Come in," he snapped. His eyes and Anna's remained locked in a blue battle.

"Monsieur?" Madame Giry's arrival forced Raoul to lose the stare down. He rose upon seeing her. "Pardon the interruption but—"

"But what, Madame?"

"The concert series is this evening and—"

"And?"

"We are without managers, and you said you would be acting in their place. Maestro Fontaine needs to speak with you. He is hopping mad."

"Madame Giry, please deal with him. I have bigger problems to handle."

"I warned you not to take on this opera," the box keeper said, puffing out her chest. "The manager deals with the Maestro. I deal with boxes. I suggest you speak with him. This concert must go smoothly for the vicomtess' sake." Anna smiled smugly at Madame Giry. Raoul nodded and conceded his defeat. "And then you must deal with the reporters of *Le Époque*, *Le Matin* and even *L'Echo*. And Inspector Legard is on the grounds as well."

Anna admired the fact Madame Giry clearly had the upper hand, judging by the way the vicomte's head snapped up.

"*L'Echo*?" Raoul jutted a hip. The last thing the Vicomte de Chagny needed, or any of them needed, was to tango with a reporter from Paris' primary gossip rag.

"Word of murder travels quickly in the streets of Paris, Monsieur," Madame Giry replied.

Raoul grabbed his waistcoat and swung it on. "I will deal with your Maestro first. Have Inspector Legard handle the reporters. I do not want a word of this affair leaking out. Do not let the mademoiselle out of your sight."

Anna stumbled out of the way as Raoul rushed past her and into the hall. Once she had her opening, she bolted for the door, intent on finding Erik. Madame Giry blocked her path.

"Let me pass, you bloated old ninny, lest I knock you senseless."

She didn't have to act on her threat. Erik's entry nearly flattened Anna to the floor. He kicked the door shut behind him and shoved a bundle of scores into Madame Giry's arms. "The vicomte will be busy for a while. Keep these safe."

Snapping his head to the side, his smoldering gaze leveled on Anna. In three strides, he backed her against the far wall. Pinning her to it with one finger digging into the soft spot beneath her chin, he gestured back to the music he reclaimed.

"That was not easy. *Never touch my music again*!"

Anna glanced at the sheets in Madame Giry's hands. His violin concerto was being crushed by the box keeper's trademark twitching. The concert tonight was without its final act. Laughter burst past Anna's lips. She curled her delight into her mouth and swallowed hard. Erik's shoulders hunched and his lip twitched. She turned her chin upward as far as she could to stare unblinking into his eyes. Let him reprimand or punish her for mocking him as he saw fit. She wouldn't waver under his attempt to intimidate.

The anger abated as Erik shifted the finger that pressed into her to cup her chin gently. The slight caress of his thumb against her cheek contrasted the tension Anna saw curved around him. His touch made her mouth slip open and his intense stare struck her mute. She scowled, thrusting her bottom lip forward. He leaned close to her ear. Anna swore her knees were going to buckle when his voice shivered against her cheek.

"While I find it incredibly tempting to investigate the very seductive nature of a woman's pout, you would be wise not to light fires in me I cannot address at the moment."

Heat raced across every inch of her skin as her belly warmed.

He shoved her face aside and rumbled in frustration, then anxiously paced the room.

"Erik, what is going on in that head of yours?" she asked.

He sneered.

"Being held under the constant scrutiny of the vicomte, I have no idea what to expect of you. What was that ridiculous display on the stage? You're like two different men and I don't know to which I speak. Would you prefer I call you Phantom?"

"Do not call me that."

"Then tell me what the bloody hell is going on! Seeing you keep company with my father isn't what I anticipated."

Erik leapt out of the way as sheet music slid across the floor.

"Your father?" Madame Giry's jaw dropped open.

"Not now, Madame Giry!" Erik and Anna yelled.

Anna took a cleansing breath. "I'm sorry, Erik, I didn't mean that. It's not easy for me to see you with him. This investigation is..."

Anna's posture finished her statement. She sank into a chair as if the reality of the entire situation forced her down.

"I have to do this for Christine." He hovered above her with his arms folded across his chest, looking elegantly commanding. He spoke with chilling resolve. "Parents are disagreeable creatures. I can only speak for the monstrous woman that bore me. I cannot say I know what that despicable gentleman you continue to refer to as a father put you through, but I know enough to believe the sooner Christine is safe, the better."

Anna couldn't argue. "Do you know where the vicomtess is?" she asked.

Erik shook his head.

"But you have a way of getting her?"

"I will be able to get Christine off the stage when she completes the Madrigal. She will not be thrilled to see me. I will need you to take her and assure her I mean no harm." He looked toward Madame Giry. "Once you have her, bring Christine to Madame Giry and keep her safe until I can tell the vicomte where she is."

When Madame Giry grinned and her twitching turned to a small jig, Erik smiled. Anna frowned. The old woman couldn't contain her excitement at being actively involved in one of the Phantom's notorious schemes, and he clearly liked it. Their exchange was disturbingly twisted.

"Wait beneath the stage when the Madrigal ends," Erik instructed Anna.

"The vicomte won't let me out of his sight. How will I manage that? Why not bring the vicomtess to him yourself? Show him you're doing this to save her. Prove them all wrong."

Erik tossed his head back and chuckled morosely. "Such the shrew in you. I can see the image—the Phantom escorting the vicomte's wife to him with an apology and polite bow. Anna, stop this madness," he insisted. "I cannot change the past. You will have to get away from the vicomte somehow. Just do as I ask and keep Christine safe."

The warmth that had settled around her at the sight of Erik had shifted. An uninvited shiver made her grab an arm. The bitter undercurrent to his voice carried the undeniable threat of a man who was dangerously close to embracing madness. Only a suicidal fool would ignore the folly of challenging him.

"Once I have Christine, Paris will truly meet the Phantom."

Chapter Twenty-five

The day waned into a typical evening. Couples wandered arm-in-arm in the fading light, decorating the streets with an air of frivolity. Hooves rapped on cobbles as carriages rolled past, and the clang of plates and chairs scraping rang as nearby cafés set up for what they expected to be a bustling evening.

Paris was costumed in finery, as was the Opera Garnier. The marquee proudly announced the concert series and its star. The banners made Raoul wonder if the star was his wife or the Phantom.

The vicomte's temper burned on a very short fuse. Raoul prided himself on being level-headed, but the longer this affair wore on, the more frayed his nerves became.

The opera was ready for this evening's performance thanks to Raoul's insistence that Maestro Fontaine find something to replace the second act. Raoul didn't bemoan the loss of the violin concerto. He knew who took it. Yet another way the Phantom thumbed his nose in Raoul's face, an image the vicomte found condescending.

Pacing the courtyard of the Cour de l'Administration, Raoul tugged at his jacket and pulled at his cravat. He made a point of keeping out of sight of the reporters Legard expertly addressed. Gossip traded like gold in Paris, and the nobleman provided quite a bit of the currency for it.

He waited while Legard thanked the reporters and turned them away.

Once safely out of prying eyes and ears, Raoul approached. Inspector Legard removed his hat and shook Raoul's extended hand.

"I cannot thank you enough for this, Jules."

"My stories will satiate them for now. This evening is another matter. I'm glad you came to your senses and summoned me."

Raoul smiled weakly. "As much as I think with my heart, at present I need to think with my head." He extended the ransom note. "We had another late night meeting with the Phantom after I dismissed you. He delivered this. Christine is to take the stage tonight as scheduled. Barret assures me the Phantom will be watching and taking aim if we try anything. I am to carry out those demands,"—

Raoul jabbed a finger against the note—"as Christine sings."

Raoul stroked his clean-shaven chin as Inspector Legard rubbed the darker shadow upon his.

"Anna is the girl that was assaulted. Why would they want both her and Christine?"

Raoul's hand slapped limply against his thigh. "Is it not every man's fantasy to be with two women?"

"Vicomte!"

Raoul pinched his lips closed. "Jules, forgive my lack of decorum, I have not slept. The Mademoiselle professes the Phantom loves her. Then why take Christine? Revenge against me? Why demand Anna be delivered to Richard Barret if he is such a demon? Spite? Lust? Madness?"

Inspector Legard laid his hand on his shoulder. "Do you think he will act on his threats if we do not bring him the Mademoiselle?"

"They are connected somehow. I have every reason to believe Christine will suffer if I do not."

"This is a substantial sum of money, Vicomte."

Crossing his arms against his chest, he replied to the ground. "I have the funds, but I do not make it a habit of traveling as a walking bank. I can only give him what I have in the accounts here in Paris. I only hope he will not notice."

"When is the opening curtain?"

Raoul fished for his pocket watch. His stomach clenched. "Six o'clock."

The Inspector read the note closely. "And Barret is to meet you in Box Five to gather all this before Madrigal's end?" Raoul's nod made the Inspector shrug. "I will have my men there at the ready. We will grab him then."

Raoul tossed his hands in the air. As if it could be so simple. He shook his hands on either side of his face. "And the Phantom, have you forgotten? Think, Jules. We are working against a man and demon. You must recognize he knows everything, he sees everything. The Phantom is everywhere. You make one move against Barret and he will know. He will harm Christine."

"So we let him take the girl?"

Hearing Legard's voice crack, emphasized for Raoul that what he was about to suggest was nothing short of incredulous.

"When the Madrigal ends, disperse your men and get them backstage. Let Barret and the Phantom think I have done their will, let them have the Mademoiselle. As soon as Christine comes off that stage, may the Lord forgive me if you do not get her." Raoul covered his barely trembling lips with his fist. He spoke around his hand.

"Barret will not be able to get far with Anna, not with these crowds. We can get her back."

His knuckles went white and his fist ground his lips against his teeth. Legard was not reassuring.

"I certainly hope so, Raoul."

"The crowds are gathering, diva dear," Richard proclaimed. Leaning against the doorframe he leered at Christine as she frantically struggled to clasp the final few buttons on her gown.

"Come here," Richard commanded, waving her forward eagerly. She moved like an automaton, clutching the silk of her dress close against her body. Her fingers shook against the bodice.

"Magnificent," Richard exclaimed. "Your Phantom has fine taste in women's clothing."

Dragging an arm across her shoulder, he admired his prize. He stopped behind her, his rough hands fondling the buttons she couldn't reach. Christine arched from his touch.

"Why do you stiffen? Have you been so pampered you've become used to a dresser to help you don your clothing?"

Hot breath caressed her cheek. One by one he purposefully undid the buttons. His coarse fingers ran down the exposed skin of her back. He tugged at the corset.

"Too bad there is not time to explore such flesh." He pulled her close against him, swaying so she could feel his excitement. "Tell me," he crooned as he continued his vulgar dance. Artfully he twisted each pearl button closed. "Those tears you shed when your Phantom gave you this gown, they were not of fright, were they? I know tears of fright. Those were tears of want." He drew out the last word, his lips against the crook of her neck and shoulder.

Picking up the silver hair comb, he held it in his hands.

"I don't think a woman who so feared a man would shed such tender tears." Gathering the sides of her hair together, he twisted them into a surprisingly elegant knot and secured the tresses with the comb. "You'll look lovely for when you meet your lover." He wrapped his arms around her waist drawing her backward so she wouldn't miss a word. This time he made sure the pistol was hard against her hip. "You must look ravishing when you confess to the Phantom your adoration, longing, and desire. Remember, I know tears of fright when I see them. I command them. Shame on you. You lie with your man and yet fantasize about the arms of another. It's so obvious. What will your Phantom fellow do when you tell him? Or perhaps he has already relieved his filthy lust against the body of another?" Richard's tongue flicked against her cheek.

Christine yanked her head away. Her mouth slipped open. Even the darkness of the cellar couldn't hide her surprise. Richard read the fragile emotions of this tender young thing like an open book. The chaos he was about to release on the Opera Garnier thrilled him beyond belief.

"Come." He laced her dainty hand around the crook of his arm. "We've a concert to give and I've obligations to attend. Worry not, you've done nothing wrong. It's fine to love two men. Why, duels to the death have been fought over a pretty face."

Richard looked at her from the corner of his eye. Her ruby lips stood out rich as blood against her porcelain visage. They trembled two words not meant for him to hear. But Richard read her lips and laughed.

"Oh yes—you can."

The Opera Garnier basked in the glory of the evening. Splendor and majesty reigned again at the great opera as patrons flocked to witness the famous diva take the stage. The salons sparkled with the finery of their guests and hummed with excited chatter. The first act had been met with thunderous applause and set the stage for the anticipation of the diva's grand appearance.

Anna sat next to Raoul in Box Five. She scanned the crowds below, her hands stroking the lush velvet of the seat and railing. The theater's dim light cast eerie shapes across the mouths of the ornately carved muses decorating the columns surrounding her. Whether the faces were forever frozen in a laugh or scream, Anna couldn't tell. She found it fitting that Erik, a man whose expressions couldn't be deciphered, would choose this box as his. Anna decided the muses were mocking any who dared come near. It seemed like Erik was everywhere and even without him near, Anna sensed his commanding presence. Staring down at the finely dressed men and women in the seats below and watching as their heads leaned together in excited prattle, Anna realized Erik ruled them like puppets on strings. For who were they really here to see, the vicomtess or the Phantom?

Anna scowled. How would she get to Erik before the Madrigal ended? She turned her attention to the gentleman at her side. The vicomte blended in perfectly with the majesty of the evening. Elegant in his evening dress, Raoul projected the image of refined taste and well-mannered masculinity. The pose he struck spoke otherwise, for his chin rested upon his hand, a frown decorated his face. Anna felt a spark of pity. Could it be he was just as nervous as she?

Together, they waited for the top of Act Two. While Anna felt pity for the vicomte's plight, she admired his devotion to his wife.

Reaching out she touched his free hand. Raoul jolted, snatching his hand away.

"Monsieur le Vicomte," she gently pleaded, "I am begging you to realize you are battling only with Richard Barret. Erik is doing everything he can to get your wife away from him."

Raoul straightened his white tie and brushed the spot on his sleeve where Anna had touched. She followed his eyes as they studied the patrons below. Anna bit her cheek to keep from cursing. Would there be no end to the prejudices? If he were concerned about the leering eyes of those looking for a bit of gossip regarding the woman he chose for company, he should listen to her and let her go. Anna rose.

"You don't have to worry about the vicomtess or me."

Raoul reached up and grabbed her forearm. She stifled a cuss when he forced her back into the chair. "I will not have any more of your insolence or your delusions. Somewhere in this opera house the man who abducted my wife and who tried to kill me is attempting to haunt my family again. And this time, he has convinced others to do his bidding. Your attempts to persuade me that this man, who you claim loves you, is a man at all are fruitless. It disgusts me to even think about it."

He released her arm, but not before he smoothed down the wrinkles he caused in her sleeve. His fingers hovered above the back of her hand for a moment, almost as if he desired to give it a tender squeeze. Instead, he curled them into his palm and lifted his hand to his mouth.

Christine stared across the stage. In the past an excited ripple would be shaking her to the core. Apprehension coursed through her now. She searched the seats and the flies above, wondering who would be listening—Angel, man or Phantom?

She turned to the man next to her. The pistol in her side was neatly concealed. Performers and stagehands hustled by wishing her good luck. They thanked him as well. She fought down the acid that burned her throat and prayed for Raoul while the man beside her winked.

"All the world's a stage. And all the men and women merely players," he crooned. Christine sharply bit her cheek. She glanced at him, but jerked her head back toward center stage to avoid his lewd stare. "People are stupid, diva dear. Not me. Even a vulgar man can be cultured."

The pistol twisted, making her lean to one side. The scotch on his breath was rank.

"You should take a man like me between your legs, you might be surprised."

She grabbed the silk of her gown and closed her mind to such an image. Her throat tightened.

"Don't do anything you'll regret. Sing your pretty song and all will be well. I've no problems killing you if you attempt anything. I'll be watching as will your Phantom lover. Your public awaits." He shoved her toward the stage.

Stumbling from the wings, she struggled to get her legs and breathing under control. The light stung her eyes and she jumped as the theater exploded with applause.

"Brava! Brava!"

Once securely in the limelight with no means of escape, she looked toward Box Five, fearful of who was seated there.

"Raoul!" Her pulse pounded in her neck, her heart leaping in her chest. With no regard to the thousands of eyes staring at her, she rushed across the stage. She wanted to be near him, she longed for the sense of safety and security he brought to her.

He yelled her name and discreetly held his hands up. He wanted her to slow down. "I love you," he mouthed.

Christine demurely cocked her head and nodded, comforted by his mere presence. Taking a deep breath, she turned to face her adoring public. She lowered her head and dipped her body gracefully into her curtsey—silently cueing the past into present.

Looking across her shoulder, she acknowledged the man approaching. The Madrigal had been written for her voice and a violin. Her accompanist entered the stage in a fantastic cloak and hood in a bird motif, a violin and bow tucked under his arm. The hood of the cloak fanned out around his face, framing it in feathers and shrouding it in darkness.

Christine smiled at him, but frowned upon glancing in the pit. She pursed her lips and shook her head telling the Maestro she didn't understand the meaning of his frantic direction. He jabbed his baton to the spot on his right.

The concertmaster had not left his seat.

Erik approached, stealing a glance across the sea of wealth that churned in his seats before he looked briefly up at Box Five. A tiny spark of resentment simmered at the sight of the vicomte, but dimmed by the presence of the woman sitting next to him. With calm deliberation, Erik allowed his gaze to fall on Christine.

He wasn't prepared for the onslaught of emotion that rocked him. It slapped into his chest nearly making him stumble. Raw heat raced across his skin. He filled his eyes with the cooling ocean of her gaze. Her hair shone in the limelight making her look like a majestic angel. He punished himself for repressing the memories of how regal a creature she was. The vision of grace before his eyes bound him to his spot.

Heart seizing at his memories of her, he remembered the silent lessons and the sound of her voice as he coached it into a near perfect instrument, the plans he'd woven for their future and his lips upon her forehead. He closed his eyes, briefly recalling her smile and her childlike wonder. The longing she had for his music. He forced his feet to move when he remembered all too vividly her betrayal, and rejection. Bewitched by her beauty and crippled by confusion, he stopped a few paces from her.

He watched as she glanced down toward the concertmaster, who looked up at her with a bewildered expression. It would not be his violin leading her in the Madrigal. Erik followed her eyes toward Box Five, his teeth clenching at her need to look at the boy. The confusion vanished as he abruptly bowed, rippling the feathers on his cloak and forcing her attention back to him. When she returned his gesture, the audience applauded loudly.

Rising, his gaze twisted around her body from the hem of her dress, to the small of her waist and up to her swollen breasts. How many nights had he imagined being this close to her again? His blood quickened and he filled himself with her smell: honey and lavender. Why was she not his? Erik tore his eyes away and looked back to Box Five.

The answer stared at him behind the eyes of a woman of intrinsic simplicity in a beauty all her own.

He found the juxtaposition of him and Christine and Raoul and Anna cruelly ironic. Erik divided his glances between the stage and the box. For a fraction of a second, he weighed his options, but raised the violin to his chin and chose to play.

The theater hushed. Intoxicating tones, painful in their beauty stretched from the violin richly seducing all who listened. Erik moved with persuasive majesty as the introduction to the Madrigal wore on. Placing himself with his back to the audience he raised his face.

Christine froze and her eyes grew wide. He leaned into her shock, deeply stroking the violin as she leaned away. The fire and ice that filled his soul were being narrated upon the jarring notes of the violin. A trapped sigh lifted from her lips as her head pulled toward one shoulder. He danced small circles around her as she clutched her chest. A white hand delicately touched her cheek. He laughed softly at her shock, sending those notes directly into her ear. Did she think she'd never see him again? The hand against her chest had turned to a claw that dug against her breast. Was it shock or longing that made her twist her hand against her heart, and paled her color? Did he really want to know? He continued to play, delicately whispering, "Sing, Christine."

"No," she whimpered.

"Your mind disobeys, but your soul demands willing participation. It always did..." his seduction trailed away. She shook her head missing her cue. No one knew. Erik disguised it perfectly. "Sing, Christine," he gently prodded, walking around her nodding his head as she shook hers.

"No, tell me what it means," she begged.

Erik rounded her again, positioning himself in such a way she had no choice but to meet his eyes fully. He shook his head. Her cue approached again and his command hit her ears.

"Sing..."

Erik sighed in ecstasy as Christine, shrouded in obedience and wrapped in a curtain of seduction she couldn't shake off, lifted her voice and sang his Madrigal.

"When Nightingale falls, scorned from favor of heart and flock, seeks his trial and alone bleeds against a thorn; He sings to deaf heaven a final dirge, as he commits his sins against nature's swift sword."

In a blurring whorl of man and cloak, Erik swept in, commanding the violin to wail in sadness. A surreal hand of music reached toward Christine lifting her voice and making it soar throughout the theater. The air pulsed with short stabbing notes until the pain of the music gradually faded. Erik played on, coaxing Christine to continue.

"His final pleas, simply for love: wishing he your heart possessed; to be loved like the One with whom your affection's rest; Looking even in Death to shroud his plumes with that of most men's fortune."

"Christine..." he moaned.

Her voice sent tremors of desire spilling down his back as the violin coated the air with years of profound longing and sadness.

"What music Nightingale once loved—he could love no more; And despising these thoughts he would wish to die; singing plaintive anthems that peal forth his eternal bitter pain, he dead and cold, deems once more upon his rightful grave to die."

Drawing out long, mournful notes, Erik's eyes, in tandem with hers, looked toward Box Five. The drunken desperation in her gaze was all she could control. His voice and violin commanded her every move.

Erik moved closely behind her, so the bird he portrayed

practically perched upon her delicate shoulder. He taunted the man in his box with his motions—pure and sensual like the notes he played, boasting his rule over Christine. Swaying, he lured her into a trance with the music. He leaned in toward her when she laid her head back on his shoulder. It sent a shudder of warmth rippling through him. Her body shivered and arched in protest.

She rolled her head on his shoulder and looked deep into Erik's blackened face. He stepped away, and playing on, ordered her with a shift of his eyes to look to Box Five. Silently, she was bidden to study the woman seated there.

Christine's lip quivered while Erik's drew into a thin tight line. Her eyes welled with tears.

"Sing, Christine," Erik insisted sharply, instead of melting the command past his lips. He spun, and looking to Box Five he released a string of beautiful notes that rolled from his heart across the theater.

"Until by chance the Lark of day alights upon his sword and freedom in the dark didst rise anew! A breath, a song, not written, not heard, not felt before, perched life upon his soul."

The tears glistening down Christine's cheeks didn't deter the passion behind his playing. Erik shot her a threatening glance, urging control. His playing took over the next few stanzas—abandoning Christine. Beneath the hood a deliberate smile decorated his darkened face. Erik knew she could do nothing as the Angel of Music commanded the stage and, unwillingly, her heart.

Chapter Twenty-six

Raoul stiffened as soon as he heard the man take a seat behind Anna. "Lovely night for the opera," Richard commented.

Anna's back lifted from the chair, moving away from the sound of his voice. Raoul clenched his teeth as Richard leaned forward and rested his chin upon her shoulder. Nothing prevented Raoul's stomach from seizing as Richard drew his tongue across his mouth, mocking the small speck of blood glistening on her freshly bitten bottom lip.

"Are you ready, Vicomte?" Richard asked.

Raoul reached into his jacket pocket. A billfold flipped from his hand to land in Anna's lap. Greedily, Richard lunged for it.

Anna's nails sank like daggers into the arm of the chair.

"Just go," Raoul whispered brokenly. "When will you give me Christine?"

Richard stood, sliding a hand beneath Anna's braid and clamping it around her neck. "That's the Phantom's call. He's watching and will be in contact. Enjoy your evening. Come, Anna."

The piercing sound of a single name tore through the box as Anna cried out. The plea for help would not make it to the intended recipient below. Raoul gripped the railing of the box and crushed the velvet upon hearing her call Erik's name. Fear—like a black and unseen sickness—wound around his body. He stared in dread as Christine sang.

"With such thought Lark's song can such blissful succor bring; that Nightingale would perchance lift his song with dawn. Guided by the Lark of day he chances to withdraw the bloody sword; to wipe the breast of Death with love—and sing her ardent chords."

Erik cradled her in his arms as he deftly played.

Christine reached behind her and stroked the feathered hood. Erik moved his head in unison with her caress as she turned in his arms and completed the Madrigal.

It was a seductive tango that, like an earthquake, shook loose the last rock of Raoul's foundation.

"In thought that Lark's song can such happy acceptance bring; if

Nightingale would perchance in daylight sing."

She barely touched the hood when Erik grabbed her and tripped the door beneath them.

Raoul rushed from the box, a river of dread spreading through his soul.

He was beginning to despise opera.

As soon as he hit the floor, Erik heard the chaos above him.

"Jules, Madame Giry." Though muffled, the panic in the vicomte's voice cut through the air. "That was the Phantom."

Throwing off the feathered cloak, Erik scanned the area. He darted in and out of wheels and twirled his lithe body around ropes.

"Madame Giry?" Legard's muted voice floated down from above this time. "All these traps lead to the sub-stage, correct?"

"Amongst the wheels and pulleys," Madame Giry replied.

"Then he is probably still down there," Legard interjected.

Erik rounded on Christine. Her jaw lay slack and her complexion had paled. She glanced rapidly back and forth between him and the ceiling. Erik read the look in her eye and briefly glanced at her swelling bosom. Even a man such as he knew what those signs indicated. "Do not scream."

Christine's mouth dropped even wider as she stared up at him and to the trap above. Her chest filled further. Erik leaned over her, both palms pressing the air between them.

"I am warning you. Do. Not. Scream."

Before her wail had a chance to break the air, Erik lunged. Yanking the cloth from his sleeve, he smothered her nose and mouth. Her arms pushed repeatedly against his chest as she flailed against the Mazenderan scent. The fight left her as she fell lax in his arms. Erik cursed his habits. It didn't surprise him that he'd have to sedate her. History seemed destined to repeat.

"Erik will not harm you, Christine." Her eyes dropped shut and she fell helplessly into the cradle of his arms. He laid her gently at his feet.

"Anna?" No reply. "Anna?"

Christine moaned. Erik wandered around the darkened area again, listening closely as Legard's voice dripped on him.

"I need two groups—one to come with me, one to track Barret. The vicomte will be charged with maintaining calm in this opera house. Fan out, but stay focused. If you shoot—shoot to kill." Erik snarled at the stage above. "I want the vicomtess unharmed. Now go!"

His patience wore thin. Drugging Christine complicated matters. He didn't want to resort to such measures, but he couldn't have her screaming. The scent would wear off quickly. He'd seen Anna leave Box Five, where was she? Now wasn't the time for her to defy him.

"Anna?" he snapped.

Silence.

The voices grew louder. In and out of wheels and pacing circles around Christine, Erik harshly called for her again. Did Anna design for him to take Christine someplace safe himself, like she had insisted he do? With no other choice, he moved.

Damn!

Grabbing his violin and bow, Erik looked down into Christine's listless face. She lay like an injured bird at his feet. Tenderly he reached out and caressed one perfect cheek and ran his hand through her hair, sighing as her tresses spilled over his arm. Why did she have to be so exquisite? So delicate? He cradled her as close as he dared.

"Anna? Damn you!"

Richard wove his way through the sea of silk and waistcoats crowding the Escalier. The gendarmes and police milling around were an annoying deterrence to his escape. Ruining his fun was Anna. With every step she struggled. Richard, used to twenty-three years of dealing with his daughter's attitude, maintained a perfect air of calm. He smiled and nodded at patrons, roughly jerking Anna's arm the first chance he had free from suspicious eyes.

"Make this easy for me, Anna. I'm not in the mood for your attitude right now." He shoved his pistol into the small of her back, careful not to draw attention. He twisted the steel to make certain she winced. "Get me out of this Escalier, away from crowds, and do it without so much as a ripple of attention."

He kept the pistol against her side as she wound them toward the empty arena of ticket offices.

"You impress me, Anna." He paused to check his windfall. "You really know this opera house like the back of your hand. Remind me to buy you something pretty as a reward."

Richard's fingers rippled through the notes faster and faster until he slapped the billfold shut. There was only a fraction of the amount demanded. He shoved it into his waistcoat pocket.

"Stupid move, vicomte."

Snatching Anna by the back of the neck, he yanked her into a secluded corner. Anna cried, but he muzzled her one-handed. Lifting the index finger of his opposite hand, he jabbed it in her face.

"This Phantom fellow of yours—Erik you called him? He was on that stage wasn't he?" She didn't answer. He slammed her head into the wall. "Son-of-a-bitch."

He was not about to be duped by the vicomte, and have his meal ticket stolen away by an insane apparition. His hand slid from her mouth to encase her throat. "Where did he take her?"

"I don't know."

"For a Barret you're a terrible liar." He forced her forward, keeping his hand tightly against the base of her skull. "If I didn't know better, I'd say my suspicions were correct and you were sweet on him." Anna skipped a step. The realization of that excited him. "My little strumpet, you are! I knew it!" He spun her to face him. A sharp tug backward on her braid forced her face to him. "What an interesting little boudoir scene that would be: his pretty little diva astride one hip and you perched on his other."

"Stop it."

"Yes, I can see it now. He pounds out his lust with one and has a spare just in case the first faints dead away in repulsion."

"Please, stop."

Richard jerked down on her braid, catching her by the throat. He savagely pulled her toward him. Strands of hair tore free and slipped to the floor. He wrapped her auburn rope tightly around his wrist. Anna's flesh went taut around her face. Her throat coated with the spittle flying from his mouth.

"Take me to him, so I can reclaim my diva and what is due me. If you don't, mark my words, you'll not live long enough to find out which one of you he chooses to straddle."

Chapter Twenty-seven

His forearms leaned against the ghastly box. How easy it would be to crawl into the coffin and drift on eternity like he intended time and time again. Give in to the comfort of insanity that had caressed him all his life.

Two pieces of glass, one stained by dry ink, the other clear enough to reflect his horrific visage, tumbled in his hand. A third piece of fine china clinked against them. Erik twisted them faster and faster in tune to the music in his mind.

Christine was here. He could touch her, love her...

He thought of Anna and the music shifted. The shards slowed until his mind fell silent. Erik held them in front of his eyes. Each piece had shattered differently, but somehow they fit together. He curled them into his palm as he let his head fall into the cradle of his hands.

Christine was his past and he still deeply loved her.

But Erik wanted a future, and for now, he couldn't have it. Not until the past was put to rest and Christine was safe. He wanted that future so passionately it made his shoulders heave and shake.

That future was with his Anna. He slipped the three shards of glass back between the satin lining his coffin and turned to attend the past.

Delightful warmth wrapped around her. Christine curled deeper under the rich pleasure of the bed. The lushness of a soft pillow surrounded her head, her body caressed by fine linens. The blanket swaddling her begged her to sleep and give in to its comfort. She stirred reluctantly, fluttering her eyes open.

The room blurred and her eyes drooped heavily in protest. She blinked a few times and took a deep breath of moist air. The contrast of such against her luxuriant surroundings shocked her completely awake.

Where was she?

She saw the mahogany desk and the open door to a bath. Oddly, she couldn't see a door to the room itself. Her eyes paused over a chest of drawers and a cluttered whatnot. She rolled over, groggily hugging a pillow. Her gaze trailed across the ceiling. A tiny window in the far wall and the folding set of stairs leaning up against it caught her eye. She frowned. Why would there be a need to see into a window so high?

Christine screamed.

This was a dream!

She bolted upright. The door she couldn't find swung open. She shrunk against the headboard as a tall, black-masked man approached.

She hadn't been dreaming. He was the one on stage and this was his house by the lake. Christine shrieked again as her torpor vanished and her fear took firm control.

"You must not yell, Christine. It will do your voice no service. Worry not, you are in no danger." Erik held out a steaming cup. "Drink this, it will help."

Christine stared at the extended cup and then at Erik. She looked around the room fully realizing who he was, what he'd done, and where he'd brought her—again.

"I do not want any more of your potions!" She knocked his hand aside.

The drink sprayed everywhere and the cup shattered against the far wall. Erik shook his wet hand. "That was tea. In rather fine china."

Christine grabbed at her temples, trying to rub the fog out of her head and the reverberating echo of Erik's seductive voice. He disappeared momentarily and returned extending a second cup.

He gestured to the blanket and encouraged Christine to accept the tea. She obeyed without question. "Wrap yourself again and drink all of that. It will help clear your mind."

She hugged the blanket around her in a vain attempt to comfort herself. Erik sat at the foot of the bed, never once taking his gaze from hers. With a trembling hand, she placed the untouched cup on the bedside table.

"You are truly alive."

"I thought that was quite clear on stage."

"You live? You *live*!" She lashed out.

Erik dodged her swat and swung himself to his feet, leaving her assault to fall harmlessly against the bed.

Christine cowered before his awe-inspiring height. The intimidation lasted only a moment. She leapt to her feet and turned in a panic toward the wall that hid his torture chamber.

"Where's my husband?" Christine ran toward the wall and slammed her fists against it. "Where is he?"

Erik folded his arms and allowed his voice to float across the room in a tone richer than the sheets. "You need to remain calm, Christine. You have been through an ordeal."

She scratched at the wall. "Where...is...my...husband? Is he in here, Erik? Is he in here?" His stony silence launched uncontrollable sobs. "I cannot! I cannot! I will not lock myself in a tomb again with a corpse to love me." She blurted without thinking, "Even if I admit that I so wish. I simply cannot."

Erik released his arms and took a sudden step away from her.

"I will do it this time, Erik. I will kill myself before your eyes, so I do not have to choose who I truly wish. The truth is not what I want to see. Now where is my husband?"

"The boy is fine, Christine. I will bring you to him eventually."

Christine's hands fell to her side as if made of lead. "The boy? *The boy*? You tried to kill him!" Flinging herself at Erik, she pounded out the ferocity of her panic against his chest. "Say his name! He has a name. My husband has a name!"

She beat him as hard as she could, and he stood unwavering though her blows. Christine sank to her knees. She was a prisoner, but this time to her own heart.

"Do not make me choose again." Like an odalisque bowing before unseen, unspoken commands, she sat in supplication at the feet of her master. "I rue my mistakes. I do not wish to hurt him with my lies."

"Raoul," he lifted her to her feet. "His name is Raoul."

Christine's cries stilled as soon as she heard that name slip past his lips. She settled on the bed as Erik lovingly wrapped the blanket across her shoulders.

"Raoul is safe. I will not make you choose, Christine. I will not harm him and now you are safe from danger. I will find your husband, tell him you are well, and bring you to him." Her breathing slowed as his voice lulled her into calm. "Richard Barret will not find you here. This will all be over soon."

Christine stared intently at Erik's lap and his left hand. The gold ring encircled his pinky. She reached out to lightly touch the band. The ring hadn't changed. It still remained a simple token of Erik's love that had once been hers. Christine's chest tightened. She closed her eyes at the memory of returning to bury him. Of slipping that ring back on his finger while tears had filled her eyes...

Her stomach lurched. But it hadn't been *his* finger...

"You are alive," she said.

"I am." Erik boldly grazed a long finger over hers as she caressed his ring.

"Why? Why did you make me think you were dead?"

"I needed peace, Christine. I needed to forget you. Not that I ever could. When you returned upon my alleged death and buried me with my ring, I had my answer. You truly did love the boy. You made your choice. It was not poor, unhappy Erik. You did not wish my love."

How much had changed over the years? Her eyes filled with additional tears. A small cry escaped his lips, causing her to look into his ebony face. She followed his finger as it reached to catch a tear.

Christine recoiled. His hands! That icy presence upon his hands! Erik stopped and rose.

"Do forgive me." He coolly folded his hands out of sight. "Clearly I can never be whole in your eyes. You made your choice and I have now made mine."

He left the bedchamber, leaving her behind to calm her tears. She slid off the bed, wrapped the blanket around her chill and followed. Her eyes never left as she watched him shrug on an overcoat and conceal a slender rope in an inner pocket.

"I apologize for bringing you here. It was not my intent, but the plans were altered. At least you will be safe. There is more tea in the samovar and if you are hungry—I have...figs."

Christine's head cleared of her dementia, and she called out before he had a chance to leave. "Please. Wait."

Through the ever-present mist of his lake just outside his doors and the glow of the candles, Erik truly looked like he *could* be an Angel of Music.

"Do not leave me," she insisted.

The slight tremble to his hands displayed the urge he was fighting to remain. "You will be fine, Christine."

"No. Do not leave again."

The blanket slid off of her and onto the floor. As it caressed her body, Erik snapped his attention elsewhere. She saw in his stance the same ravening desire she saw time and again dressing her husband. Christine's face heated. *Did* he desire her? She couldn't know for certain what he thought, only what his body told her. His mask tilted to one shoulder, his body clenched against some screaming need. He would look anywhere but at her. Could he still be wholly in love with her?

Seeing him fight a need that his mask couldn't contain, the heat on her face grew to spread across her bosom and down her belly. She knew if she had only first obeyed him and never divested him of his mask, she never would have left him. Before that moment, he'd already won her devotion and filled her equally with horror and pity. His voice and adoration of her would have been enough to awaken her love of him, and his genius would have been all she needed to stay by his side.

She stared into his face inquisitively, cursing the leather that made it appear harsh and cold. The silk mask she spitefully burned years ago made him seem gentler, and she flooded with guilt. He stood before her—fighting turmoil like she—and she couldn't help but wonder who it was she gazed upon—Angel or Phantom?

"Why did you bring me here? Why do you continue to do these horrible things?"

He kept his tone low and his temper on an even keel. "I have done none of what you think. You have been a victim in a cruel affair and it is my intent to prevent it from progressing."

"And how do you know what I think?" she sharply demanded.

Erik softly laughed. "Years ago you chose to move on with the man you professed to love along with the world you so naturally command." He gestured around him. "I stayed here, where madness forces me to be. To you I am the Angel of Music, the guardian God cloaked for you in airs of beauty, whilst the truth is so far from your reach. To you I am a grand illusion. Someone, perchance, you could love so long as the truth remained hidden." He gestured up and down the length of his body until his fingertips rested on his mind. "The sides of me you refused to unite are the same sides the world forces me to separate. I am no longer able to walk freely in the dark of night. Solitude," he rapped his temple, "has a way of driving one mad even if you already are. However, when you do not have influences of others perpetuating your memories, it is easy to decipher them, accept the past and move on." He backed away as Christine intently began to walk toward him.

"I am a wanted man, Christine, for many reasons. But because of the past, I am now a living, breathing legend. Do you know what that is like? Existing in body yet questioning if you ever really existed in soul?" Her head dipped sympathetically. "Spare me the look of pity, Christine. Once, perhaps, I needed it, but no longer. I have accepted all that has come to pass and who I am. I am not legend. I am not myth. I am not Angel. I am not Phantom. *I am not your father*." The grim confession which should have been resurrected years past shocked her into a dumbfounded stupor. "I am merely the man you never saw. It took a long time to recognize there was such beneath all I had become. A long time—and a lot of packages. None of what has occurred is my doing. My only intent was to speak with you, which I was denied. Lingering on the past does nothing but deny the present a chance at moving forward. Now rest. You have been through an ordeal."

The soliloquy clung to her like a dark, constricting mist which no means of warmth or light could burn away. The lyrics of the Madrigal ran through her head. Reaching for his hand, Christine braved his touch and tangled their fingers. It pained her how hard Erik tried not to meet her eyes. "Tell the Madrigal's meaning."

Erik pulled his hand away. "Its meaning is clear, Christine."

"No," she reached for his hand again, "no."

If that were the answer, then she was losing him again. Erik came back to her. She loved Raoul but in the dark reaches of her mind and heart, she soulfully took comfort in knowing she would always have poor, unhappy Erik. "You cannot leave me. You love me."

"Christine—"

"No. You love *me*."

Christine searched for a reaction as she stepped into him. Her mind screamed against what her heart beat, and as if not by her own command, she quickly brushed her lips against his.

The kiss only lasted an instant.

Christine took a sharp breath and curled her lips into her mouth. Dear Lord, why had she done that? Her lids fluttered in surprise. How soft his lips were. How sweet they tasted. The horrible curse that lay beyond that mask contradicted the way his kiss—however brief—was full of life. She shook her head against the thought she'd been fighting and reached to kiss him again to confirm it, but he turned away. Her tears came quicker, uncertain as to his rejection.

"Erik?"

She didn't hesitate. Grasping the sides of his face she felt him stiffen. She fanned her fingers across his face to possess his lips—this time urgently. She boldly explored his mouth and slowly let her fingers glide beneath the mask.

To gaze on him again would be her final confirmation.

Erik's hands shot out. Fingers stiffened and clawed at the air. Honey flooded his mouth as he tasted her. Memories exploded around him. An ache crushed his chest. His heart raced as her fingers slid along the mask's edge and grazed his flesh beneath. Her body fitted tightly against his, her breasts pressed against his chest and her smooth, graceful fingers teased the length of his mask, threatening to expose him.

Yes, please, yes.

For a moment he desired her to remove the barrier that stood between their love. He wanted Christine to gaze on him with unconditional adoration. He wanted her to accept his fate, his face, his madness. To cast aside the past and take him body and soul. He needed her to love him and only him. Erik longed for her to make him whole.

Her kiss deepened. He responded—forcing more passion behind it. *Yes, if there is a God, please.* Erik's heart pounded a healthy rhythm, his body responding in kind. Her lips moved like silk against his, her tongue stroked his need for her.

Christine gently inched the mask away.

Yes. Take me! Want me. Look, upon my curse! Heal my devastated soul. I have spent too long with it shattered like—

Glass.

His breath hitched breaking their kiss. Snapping his hands up, he tightly grabbed her wrists and lowered them from his face. His voice haunted him for a change: *Lingering on the past does nothing but deny the present a chance at moving forward.*

"No one looks upon my face but her." Erik watched as the invisible tip of a dagger found its way directly into Christine's heart.

"Who," she gasped. "Who is she?"

He clenched his teeth. He rubbed a finger across the taste of her and turned to flee from his sanctuary. "When I am able, I will bring you to your vicomte. Until then, rest."

"How could you betray me?"

The question slammed into his back like a sword thrust of truth. He forced himself to turn. She'd made her choice and he'd now made his. She stared at him, her face painted red with emotion.

"I do not know you anymore."

"You never truly did." When he saw the sting his admission had slapped upon her face, he softened his position. "That is my fault. I had much to understand. The past is past, Christine; there is nothing in it that can be revived."

He headed through the drawing room chased by her confused cries.

"Who are you? Angel or Phantom?"

Erik stopped, following the echo of her desperate plea. He'd devoted his entire life to constructing identities and illusions that could be razed as easily as they were built. How quickly they crumbled now. He turned toward her as if listening to a tremendous ovation before dismissing the past and moving forward.

"This cannot be. I cannot!" Christine cried. "Who are you? *Angel or Phantom*?"

His home, both tomb and womb, replied without him present. The walls repeated in one long and haunting whisper:

"*I am Erik.*"

Chapter Twenty-eight

Raoul tossed his waistcoat and vest on the couch and with them his holstered weapon. Slumping behind the desk, he let his exhaustion overtake him. Sitting in the darkened office, not giving a care to the music floating faintly in the background, he took a sip of scotch. It did little to take the edge off. The concert continued in quiet oblivion to the demands and deals revolving around the disappearing diva. He listened without interest, silently praying for his wife.

"Raoul?"

He opened his eyes. Had he heard something? No. The office was silent, just as Wischard and Laroque left it before their demise. He rubbed his neck, feeling the chain of his religious medallions roll against his skin. He closed his eyes again.

"Raoul?"

His lids flew open. He scanned the room as a nimble hand reached over his shoulder to pluck the glass from the desk. Startled, he cursed and rocked back in his chair.

"I am disappointed you would choose to drink at a moment such as this." Erik walked around the front of the desk, sniffing the drink before tossing the contents into a nearby plant. Raoul leaned toward him.

"You bastard. You inhuman, subterranean..."

Erik leaned casually against the arm of the couch, crossing his arms. "Is that you addressing or the scotch, because I much prefer Erik."

"Where is Christine?" Anger forced Raoul to his feet. The chair skidded backward.

"Christine is fine. She is safe and none too happy with me at the moment, which should please you immensely."

Raoul inched his way toward him like a man balanced on a thin blade in danger of falling off. He glanced to the pistol on the couch. "I did as you asked, now bring her to me," Raoul tried his best to hide the waver in his voice.

Erik tossed his head from side to side. He bounced a finger on his lips.

"Not with Richard Barret running around. Christine is safe where she is—in the comfort of her room." The sarcasm Raoul heard evaporated from Erik's voice. "Anna—whom you have unwisely chosen to decorate your arm—can take you to her. She is intimate with my ways into the—Oh *Sang de Dieu*!"

Reaching down, he snatched the pistol. "Is this what you want? Your vain attempts at creeping about are most annoying. I dare say it is not befitting a man with such a precious indicator before his name." He heaved it toward Raoul. Loaded steel soared through the air.

Raoul scrambled to catch it before it misfired. "You are insane."

Erik lifted one shoulder. He gestured to the pistol. "A coward's weapon by the way, no art or finesse involved. I did not intend to bring Christine into my house. I do like my privacy and I have had enough of women roaming about my home of late. My aim was to get Christine from Barret. Anna was to meet me and bring her to Madame Giry. I figured since you have spent the last several days arrogantly ignoring my letters and casting my sentence, you would not trust me. I assumed you would trust Anna. Clearly that plan did not happen. However, since Anna knows the labyrinth intimately, she can be your escort to Christine."

"Where is she?" Raoul asked, his voice metallic.

"How much of that scotch did you drink, Vicomte? I just told you."

Raoul raised his weapon. "Anna. Where is she?"

Erik's calm ripped away. "Pardon?"

Raoul cocked the trigger and blinked sweat from his eyes. "I did as you asked. I gathered your money and gave Anna to Barret. You can keep the money, but I will not allow you the flesh needed for your filthy lusts. I will not be responsible for the dishonor of two women." He clutched his chest as if such a thought served him acid and burned his heart. "I do not give a damn about you or me. I only want my wife. And frankly my precious noble indicator and the airs that come with it can go to hell right now—now where is Anna?"

A deadly silence filled the room before Erik lapsed into a fury fierce enough to kill. His hands shot out. He slammed Raoul against the far wall, his unworldly reflexes not allowing him to take comfort in his pistol.

"You gave her to Barret?" The red-hot fire of his voice seared the room.

"I did what I had to do. Forgive me if your good opinion is lost to me and if I do not bother to look for it. I have betrayed my wife by my inability to be a man and I will betray the Mademoiselle no further than I already have. You are correct, I am not about to trust you. What have you ever done that deems you worthy of trust? I will not back down to you this time, Erik. Now where is she?"

Erik curtailed his taste for murder into a crushing blow to Raoul's stomach. He cried out and doubled over. Erik picked him up by the back of his hair and leaned in close to his ear, manipulating his voice so the timbre shattered into his eardrum.

"Pardon my need to act with such ungentlemanly conduct. I usually prefer more sophisticated ways to demonstrate my temper, but I am finding I rather enjoy this more masculine means of display." Erik shoved Raoul into the desk. Blotters, books and the scotch-filled carafe careened across the room. "Do forgive *me* if your good opinion is lost as well. Your bravery amuses. You are less of the puppet you were years ago, but pity, you are the least of my concerns right now. Clearly you will be no help to this charade. I suggest you stay out of my way."

Raoul's temple hit the desk with a sickening thud as Erik forced his face against its edge. With long strides he propelled himself toward the door, never looking back.

It was a mistake that arched Erik through the threshold and sprawled his body to the floor.

Raoul rose from the desk in a daze having had shot from a prone position. He lowered his shooting arm as the air cleared of the pistol's acrid smoke. The breeding of a gentleman was replaced by his training as a naval officer. The indication of shooting a man in the back momentarily startled him with remorse. The pistol hung limply in his hand while his other flexed and pulsed at his side. He cautiously approached the doorway.

Erik coughed and attempted to rise, but his feet slipped out from beneath him, slamming his body to the ground. Rolling to his back, he stared at the ceiling, gasping for breath he couldn't find. His back arched repeatedly off the floor as he tried to find his footing. Tracks of blood spread crimson across his coat and spilled on the floor.

Raoul heard the pain drag breath from Erik's lungs as he struggled to his feet. Erik clutched his shoulder and upper arm. His disjointed steps pitched him back and forth as he met Raoul's empty stare. The blood snaking down Erik's arm dripped to his palm. Raoul thought for a moment on the irony of Erik literally having blood on his hands. Erik reached beneath his overcoat.

"I will consider myself fortunate you are a horrible shot," Erik hoarsely said.

The lasso flew through the air.

The rope was a deadly weapon when wielded by a master assassin. Raoul instinctually moved his arm to the level of his eyes, but the rope hit its mark with exact precision, aimed not for the neck but coiling neatly around Raoul's opposite wrist. Erik yanked back jerking the pistol from his grasp. It skidded against the floor. Raoul jolted forward. The air filled with Erik's cry of pain, but despite being weakened, he had Raoul defenseless and head-locked in a heartbeat's time. Erik jerked on Raoul's wrist to free his lasso.

"Once again, Vicomte, you stand between me and the woman I love," Erik snarled. Raoul bucked, but Erik's lock tightened, his arm crushing against Raoul's throat. "If anything further happens to her as a result of your paranoia of me—I will kill you."

Flinging Raoul aside like a rag doll, he disappeared.

Raoul grunted as he hit the floor. By the time he rolled to his feet not a trace of Erik existed beyond the lingering pain around his throat. He was retrieving the pistol when Legard and his men skidded around the corner.

"I heard a gunshot," Legard shouted.

Raoul dismissed his inspection as Legard's eyes roamed over the pool of blood, then searched up and down his body.

"And it hit its mark," Raoul snapped, disregarding Legard's horrified expression. "Find the Mademoiselle and Barret. I am going after Christine and the Phantom myself."

Inspector Legard blocked him with his hands. "Now is not the time to be *more* irrational. You cannot do this alone. Which way did he go?"

Raoul nodded in the direction Erik had disappeared. "Horrible shot I may be, but I find myself most fortunate that living shadows bleed."

Mindless panic slammed Erik first into one wall and then the next as he staggered down the narrow passages. He moved until the pain made him slump against the labyrinth wall. Every sense was assaulted at once. His vision blurred, the cavity of his nose stung with the damp aroma and the fresh, metallic scent of his blood. Somewhere beyond the walls in which he hid, he heard shouts and pounding feet.

Hot pain throbbed the length of his arm while the remainder of his body was ice cold. Suppressing a cry, he shook off his overcoat and glanced at his scarlet sleeve. Warm, sticky sweat coated the inside of his mask. He laid his cheek against the wall, hoping its cold surface would penetrate and calm the heat burning down his arm. He tried commanding his hand to move, but his fingers scarcely rippled. Forcing his hand into a fist, he screamed as pain shot up his arm.

Erik clenched his teeth and huffed heavily. Fumbling with the silk around his neck, he yanked the cravat off with a sharp twitch. His back lifted from the wall before slapping against it once more. He slammed his head to keep from crying out again. Hissing his breath slowly in and out between clenched teeth, he bound his arm as best he could. Panic gripped him that his world would go dark, making him shove off the wall. Moving would keep him conscious. His heart raced faster than it should, but was nothing compared to the agonizing thoughts screaming through his head.

Left then right, a sharp turn through a trap then left again. Anna ran as fast as she could on the slick stone floors of Erik's underworld. The halls twisted and turned at a blinding pace. That corner was a dead end, this one illusion. Anna spun herself through the dark labyrinth never pausing to look behind her. She knew better than to think twice when fleeing from her father. Losing him in the palatial maze of the opera house had been easy. The trick had been out-smarting him and turning his attention away from his greater plans—Christine.

Sweat dampened her brow by the time she burst into Erik's house. She grabbed the stitch in her side. Taking a breath that made her chest pinch, she jumped when Christine leapt from the divan.

"Anna," Christine cried.

A crushing tremor of trepidation overcame her. Why was she here? Thinking on her feet, Anna lunged at the vicomtess.

"Get to the boat." Pulling on the silk of Christine's sleeve, she dragged her toward the drawing room.

Christine tripped over the layers of her gown. "What is going on?"

Anna shoved her through the doors. The lavish warmth of Erik's home collided with the cold mist of the lake greeting those to his lair. Christine froze like a frightened animal facing the barrel of a rifle.

"How did you get down here?" Christine asked toward the lake. "What other twisted ways are there into this insanity?"

Anna shook her head, her lungs burning too much to go into detail. "I can't explain now. Just get in the boat."

Christine stumbled out of the way as Anna rushed past her and back into Erik's house. She made her way around at a dizzying pace, throwing what items she thought could be of use into a satchel. She took great care with Erik's violin. Christine watched from the drawing room.

"I see you know your way around here intimately, Anna."

Anna started to reply when a crash sent the sound of shattering glass echoing around them. A man's voice filled the house with rolling curses. The violence spurred Anna into action.

"He's figured it out." She leaned all her weight against Christine.

"Get in the boat."

"How dare you put your hands on me. Tell me what is going on."

Anna's temper—drawn taut—broke. "Vicomtess, get in the boat! Get in the boat! *Get in the bloody boat*!"

"I am not going anywhere."

"And I'm not giving you a choice," Anna shouted, grabbing the woman. She shoved an arm back toward the noise. "If you wish to fight with me you will lose. Now you will do as I say and get in that bloody boat, unless you are wise enough to the ways of the world to do this yourself. Richard Barret is on his way here and you have got to get in the boat!"

"Anna?"

Both women spun at the sound of Erik's voice. He emerged slowly like a shadow taking shape in newfound light. Anna didn't give anyone a chance to speak. She flung the satchel in his direction, not noticing how he staggered upon catching it.

"You have got to get out of here. They are tearing the place apart looking for you. I tried to get the vicomte to understand. I tried to get to *you*. He duped Barret, the con went bad, and Barret still wants *her*." Anna gestured wildly toward Christine. "He's figured out we have a connection and he forced me to take him to her. *Bloody holy hell*, I crossed him." She stomped her foot. "I diverted him here. She was supposed to be with Madame Giry. Why of all places did you bring her here?"

Erik swayed in his attempt to answer. Christine cautiously approached.

"You're bleeding. What happened?"

"Nothing of concern. Erik is fine," he said hollowly.

"You're not fine. You've been shot."

He squeezed his eyes tightly shut, unable to control the buckle that brought him to the ground before Christine.

"Mother...of...God." Anna lost all the warm breath in her lungs. She shoved Christine out of the way and grabbed Erik, forcing him from his knees and making him sit. Shaking hands fumbled with his makeshift bandage.

"Who did this?" Anna quietly demanded. She followed Erik's numb stare as he focused an empty gaze on Christine.

"Raoul," he replied.

"You lie," Christine said incredulously.

Anna shot her a deadly look and tumbled to the side as Christine knelt before Erik.

"Do not say such dreadful things." She lifted Erik's hand to her lips, brushing the back of his knuckles against them. "Raoul would never do such a thing. You're mistaken. He knows how much I—"

"Vicomtess, get me the wine."

Christine clutched Erik's hand closer to her breast.

"The wine," Anna hollered, "other side of the room, in the stand next to the divan."

Christine moved only when Erik slipped his hand from hers. Anna dug frantically through the satchel. Erik trailed the back of his hand from her eye to her chin. She stopped, gasping as her skin quivered. She couldn't explain, but the ice of his touch had a way of heating her marrow. His hand shook as he caressed her lips. Anna paused for a second allowing the simplicity of that gesture to completely fill her.

Erik eyed the knife Anna wielded. "Are you versed as a surgeon as well as a blacksmith, cobbler...?" Pain forced an end to his sarcasm.

"Do not wage war with me, Erik." Anna inspected his crimson arm.

The ball entered at a steeply awkward angle. As best she could tell, by means of a miracle it missed bone. The lead slanted through the fleshy outer edge of his shoulder and upper arm leaving a gaping hole of raw and torn flesh in its wake. Her fingers dug against the wound causing him to curl into the pain. He groaned in agony. It was impossible to tell if the bullet went cleanly through or not. She wasn't willing to take chances. Anna had seen plenty in her years to recognize the seriousness of the wound.

"This will hurt," she warned. "I have to make certain the bullet is out. I don't need you poisoned. Do you trust me?"

Anna stood in front of him, level with his eyes. He lifted his gaze at the foolishness of her question. Erik rarely trusted anyone. Silence moved like a thin tendril of smoke between them before he dejectedly lowered his head. His lips barely moved as he mouthed *only you*. Anna accepted the indiscernible nod of his head that she proceed, but rejected how he stared at Christine's approach. She swallowed her ill-timed jealousy.

She twirled to face the vicomtess head on. Not willing to waste any time, she grabbed the bottle, used the knife to dig at the cork and poured the liquid across the blade.

"Anna?" The air growled in her father's voice.

Anna's hands shook as she offered Erik the bottle. He forced her to take some deep breaths for her sake and that of his arm before he drank in great gulps. Christine edged closer to him. She reached for him and, like a bride clutching the just wed hand of her groom to her breast, tossed a possessive gaze toward Anna.

"Where is Barret now?" Erik asked Anna, oblivious to the tension carefully stretched between the women.

"I lost him in the labyrinth. I made sure to lead him into the mirrors."

A shaky grin lifted his mouth. "*Mon petite Fantôme—*"

Erik's next breath was a torturous scream as Anna dug for the bullet.

Chapter Twenty-nine

Bits of cloth, sticky with blood, littered the floor—amid them, a small round lead. Anna wrapped his arm as best she could and packed moist cloth against the wounds. Erik's breathing was haggard. He licked wine from his lips.

"Are you all right?" Anna asked, using the hem of her dress to wipe the blade and her hands clean of blood. "If this gets infected—"

"Erik will be fine." He did his best to ignore the throbbing pain.

He had no place to look to find relief. The imagery of blood upon Anna's small hands made his throat tighten. Christine knelt before him, her porcelain skin wrinkled and her usually watchful eyes filled with childlike apprehension. Her perfect lips thrust into a frown. The look tore at him like brambles. Her innocence was far more impressionable than Anna's. Christine should not have witnessed such.

"Erik?" Christine comforted, stroking his mask. He turned. "You are going to be fine. I will take care of you."

Erik glanced at Anna who awkwardly averted her eyes. He grabbed Christine's hand, lowering it from his face.

"Anna!" Barret cried. When Erik saw Anna's hands grab air at her side, a renewed energy dragged him to his feet. He headed with deadly purpose toward that voice.

"Erik, stop," Anna warned.

"Child, stand aside and let me do this." He'd never wanted to kill with such perverse intensity.

"Erik, you're hurt. You're underestimating him and the vicomtess is what matters now."

Anna stood her ground as usual, infuriating him. His lip twitched with the need winding its command around his mind. Even the desperation in Anna's voice didn't deter him.

"You must get her out of here," she insisted. "You can't go through the passages, the gendarmes are tearing the opera house apart, and the place is thick with crowds. Barret is armed and angry and if he finds her, there's no telling what he'll do. He can't follow you on the water and I don't know my way across the lake."

Her statement knocked down the passion of Erik's need to react. Anna had never crossed the lake alone, and he pondered with slight remorse the adjustments he told her about. He cursed his genius that made his lair impenetrable to anyone but him. It would have helped to have an easy means of escape. Anna's eyes bore into him and no matter how hard he wanted to fight her, he caved to her plea. Growling in frustration, he headed to the boat. Beneath his mask his brow dampened and his face contorted against the pain. The boat had to be untied despite the agony it caused.

"Christine, get in the boat," Erik rumbled, heading for the oars. She stood still as a stone.

"Anna, so help me God," Barret called out.

"Erik, go now," Anna yelled.

As Barret's voice grew closer, Christine stood paralyzed, her eyes wide. Erik stood next to the boat and extended an arm to her.

"Christine, come to me," he commanded with immeasurable softness, rippling his fingers into his palm. Like a trained canary alighting on a perch, she instantly obeyed. Erik looked to the woman still in his drawing room. "Anna, get in the boat, I am not leaving you."

"No. If I go, Barret will know he's been deceived. If I stay I can stall him, divert his attention from her, and cover the direction you went."

"Anna Reneé Barret!" her father screamed.

"For once, will you not defy me?" Erik shouted, stomping the boat and sending the craft rocking. "I am not leaving you with him."

"Erik, I can take care of myself."

"Anna, you will not disobey me."

"Erik," Anna sighed. Closing her eyes caused a tear to drip free. "She's Christine. You love her." Erik lowered his face to the rising mist, hiding the expression in his eyes. "Go. Bring her to Madame Giry—that will be safest. I'll find you later."

Erik thrust off from shore. Anna would not be swayed once she set her will in motion. "Promise me you will run. If he breaks through, swear you will run again. Do not do anything rash."

Anna hung her head. She nodded and turned toward the house.

"Anna—" When he met her eyes he abruptly fell silent. He looked first at Christine, who stared up at him fragile and trusting, and then at the woman fading away in the distance and felt irreproachably tired of his life, his madness, and his heart.

Lake Avernus was aptly named for it was still as dark as the tomb Erik commanded, and like him—eerily silent. One arm dragged heavily back and forth as he rowed, unable to keep a steady rhythm with his uninjured one. Erik dropped the oars.

"Why are we stopping?" Christine asked timidly.

"I need to rest."

"The pain is terrible?"

Erik nodded.

"That does not surprise me. That woman practically tore your arm off."

"The bullet is to blame," Erik corrected, straining to hear sounds behind him. Nothing greeted him, but the dreadful silence he'd often called friend. "When we get to shore I will bring you to Madame Giry. You are to stay with her and lock the door until I can get your vicomte." The name passed his lips with utter disgust. He forced his shoulder to roll and flexed his hand trying to get circulation into his fingertips.

Christine winced. "Here, allow me."

Beneath his mask Erik's face twisted strangely. His body twitched as Christine willingly reached for him. The horror instilled in her in the past seemed to have faded. She gently took his hand trying to massage feeling back into it. Her tender affection shot blinding pain up his arm, but he'd never let on. Merely being touched by her filled him with sensations beyond comprehension.

"Raoul did not mean to shoot, I know it. You are lucky he did not kill you."

"Your husband is a lousy shot, my dear; however, I do wish he had not hit my primary bow arm." He took his hand back, momentarily staring at the places her fingers had been. He reached for the oars.

"Erik, you must rest."

"Christine, there are people looking for you and other matters I need to address. Your liberty is yours. I will not have you revisit your past by waiting out this charade in a tomb."

"Let them look and let them wait," she said with absolute authority. She peered at him curiously. "You are different. All those horrid things that occurred years ago made it seem like you were a man possessed. That monster was different from who I see before me now." She reached for his hand again, choosing this time to gently stroke it. "One cannot forget, but one can forgive."

The boat teetered dangerously as he leapt to his feet. Forgive? What had he done that deemed forgiveness? Did he not tell her he would be a slave to her every need? A man who would worship her soul? He couldn't help who he was or that he'd had to make what rendezvous he could in his life to seek normalcy. He couldn't help the events that caused her to label him monster. He didn't need her forgiveness, for if he had to—if he wanted to—he would do it all again. He glowered at her as the past rolled over him in rapid, undulating waves of confusion.

"Exactly what are you saying?" His demand exploded the silence.

"Seeing you again, hearing you deny me in the Madrigal made me realize much. I will never forget the fortnight I spent locked away with you. One cannot forget your intent to destroy the theater and a quarter of Paris, nor can I forget how you tried to kill my husband." She turned her eyes away from the mesmerizing dance of the blue smoke above the water to give Erik a seething glare. "I can forgive you all that because time can change a person. And I must forgive myself. For I cannot...I cannot love two men, yet I do. I cannot choose one over the other, but I suppose I must. I love Raoul with all my heart, yet I deny him by selfishly giving you my soul. How is that possible?"

Erik found his seat and plunged the oars roughly into the lake. Water splashed around them as waves rocked the boat. With a set jaw, he hauled off with long thrusts and kept his stare straight-ahead.

She rose, moving to sit beside him.

"Return, Christine." He nodded toward the opposite end of the boat. She looked at him like a wounded child, but he wouldn't be swayed. "Who you see before you now is a man who will not settle for being divided. Love Raoul with all your heart and me with all your soul, go ahead. Too long I have wandered without the attention of either."

Her face twisted. He had a stranglehold on the oars as he tried to maintain every emotion surging through his body.

"I love you in every way I know how," he said gently, making her face lighten with her smile. "That is why I am risking everything to keep you from the danger you are in."

Christine reached up to wrap her arms around him.

"Return," his voice boomed, halting her gesture. "I may have just sacrificed everything I have ever sought after for you."

She glanced around in the inky blackness and pulled herself up tall in her defense. "The past says I was everything you sought after."

"Damn the past. Look at this place! Even in my fabled death I was condemned here like a rat in a maze and a mole in a burrow. I am tired of it. Tired, I tell you. Erik no longer wants secrets!"

"I do not understand."

"No!" He huffed, and leapt to his feet not caring how the boat rocked. "It is *I* who does not understand. Erik does not understand any of this!" He thrust a finger in her direction. "Before you arrived I was coming to terms with the idea that there could be life beyond these cursed vaults for me. I began to believe I could live like a normal man despite my despicable actions. That I could have all that without *looking* like a normal man. And have it without locking a woman away and condemning a wretched recluse to love her. I believed I could think freely and act freely whether as man or madman and still have that woman to dote upon. That a *real living bride* could be mine. I thought I had everything arranged, but seeing you again makes me see how much of a cheat my life is." He rocked the boat like an impatient child, sending Christine a ferocious stare and an insane wag of his head. "Where is the fear, Christine? Can you tell Erik? Where is the fear? I frighten you still do I not?"

She held her body stiffly and her head high. "Fear can be survived, Erik. I am not naive anymore. I want the freedom to make my own choices. I know my feelings."

"But do you know Erik or only your Angel of Music? You can love two men, Christine, that much I know is possible because one can love two people. I gave you my world once. I gave you the key to my kingdom, and I have handed it over to you again because *this world,*" he rocked a finger back and forth in the space between them, "no longer matters. Behind us is my life. Standing on the shore of a lake, holding back a man who has done nothing but abuse her, is a woman willing to do anything to prevent my heart from breaking. *My heart* from breaking." He thumped a fist against his chest. "A fate she knows will happen if any harm ever came to you. I love you, Christine. How many ways and how many times must I tell you that? I love you, but I..." Erik collapsed in his seat and leaned onto the top of the oars despite the pain in his arm. The awareness of what he had been trying to deny dawned on him in wild revelations.

"I love you, but I have every intention of being *in love* with her, both my heart and my soul—all of me."

Tears welled in Christine's eyes. "You don't know what you are saying. You know nothing of intentions or need, nothing of fear. How could *you* ever be afraid? You lived your life without love. It is not as clear as you would think. In her you are making a fool's choice. Choosing only what you *think* you want."

"It is my choice to make this time, Christine. Years ago I asked you to choose who you would love, and *you* foolishly chose *me* when you knew it was not what you wished."

"Not what I wished? You terrified me! You were threatening Raoul. I accepted your proposal to save him. Could I not realize now that I accepted it because I love you?"

"No, Christine, you cannot for it is not me you love. Do you not see your recklessness? I knew I inspired you with horror. I knew you could never love Erik for himself. What did I do *for I loved you enough to keep your heart from breaking?* Or have you forgotten?"

"You gave me liberty to marry Raoul, but—"

"But nothing, Christine. You say Erik has made the fool's choice in what he chooses now?" He forced the boat onward, the echo of his feelings surprising even him. "I will always be imprisoned. I have cried to be beseeched at the mouth of the lake too many times only to be borne over and over into *Tartaros*. Erik is what he is and love or no love, he will no longer listen to the judges..."

Chapter Thirty

The water stared blankly back at Anna. The mist stopped its seductive tango, the ripples undulated until a calm washed over the water and the shore fell as still as the dead.

Standing alone, Anna was sixteen again. Breast heaving at the end of a dark alley, facing a crowded Brussels street, not knowing which direction to turn before her father caught up to her. The difference here was there would be no crowd in which to evaporate.

"Didn't anyone ever teach you to come when Papa calls?"

The hair on her neck lifted. She didn't flinch, but merely blinked a few times before presenting herself to her father.

Richard Barret was red in more ways than one. The flare to his nostrils and his tapered eyes told Anna his ruby coloring had nothing to do with drink—but her. One hand dripped blood from a large cut. Anna rushed beyond him and out of the drawing room, forcing him away from the lake.

"I thought you were right behind me. Did you get lost?"

"Lose the sarcasm, Anna. You know how I hate it when you make me angry." He followed her, stopping suddenly to scrutinize the cavernous house. His eyes filled with a devilish gleam. "My, my, my... strumpet's been relaxing in the lap of luxury. Your Phantom fellow certainly has fine taste, present company excluded of course."

He rummaged through items he ought not and wandered into distant rooms. Anna followed, her anxiety rising. Grinning wickedly, he walked around Erik's coffin. He reached into the box and caressed its lining, then contemplated the dark divan in the corner with its piles of pillows and blankets.

"A choice for pleasure, how macabre. Your Phantom has a taste for fine things. Tell me strumpet, is this coffin nice to roll in with him?"

Anna shriveled into her discomfort like a fig left to dry. He swaggered toward her, taking a final long stride to whirl her into his embrace.

"When he lies with you in all his repugnant glory, his pillicock stiff and in obvious want of such a fine ladybird as you, does he keep the mask on or take it off?" Anna stayed stoic and silent. "You can't be serious? Don't tell me you two haven't...with all the men who have had...hah! This just gets better and better. Just as well. No man would ever bed you out of sheer love and desire. You are damaged goods."

He shoved her aside, electing to perch upon the organ bench. He shifted in such a way as to wedge himself in the corner of the semi-circle of manuals and propped up his feet. A long, mournful note sagged though the air as the organ protested the weight.

"So, where are Erik and my diva?"

"I thought he would bring her here, but clearly he did not," she lied.

Shifting his weight, the organ yelped again. "Then where are they?"

"I do not know."

He leapt from his position, snatching Anna's arm. A sharp pain shot up her weakened wrist. The edge of the Persian rug tripped her, slamming her knees into the ground at his feet. Richard stared deep into her eyes and she glared back—just as rebellious as he.

"I suggest you figure that out, Anna. You're testing my patience and if you continue, I'll have no problem teaching you a delightful little lesson in that coffin he has yet to shag you in."

Fury caused her to claw his hand hard enough to color her nails red with his blood.

"Blasted bitch," he snarled, jerking his hand away. He snatched her throat, forcing her to her feet. "If you can't find him and my diva, then we deal with the money due me in a very different way. Take me to the vicomte." Richard caught her arm before she got out of reach. "And no more tricks with mirrors. Is that understood?"

Anna did everything in her power not to make the matter worse by spitting in his face. He roughly kissed her forehead.

"Good girl..."

Inspector Legard had a viselike grip on Raoul's neck. Once in the office he slammed the door and shoved Raoul away.

"Of all the stupid—"

"If you so much as lift a finger to me again in such disrespect, Inspector, I will—"

"—asinine things I have ever embarked upon!" Legard's shout won. He plunked down on the couch. "Living shadows bleed. Christ, Raoul. Bleed they may, but we are not bloodhounds. We are lucky to have found our way out of that maze alive."

Legard tilted his head back, pressing his thumb to the bridge of his nose. Their attempts at following the Phantom were feeble at best, quickly having lost the trail in the dark and winding passages.

"He is there somewhere, Jules."

Legard watched him pace the office.

"This time I will kill him when I find him."

"Wonderful, Raoul. Do that and I'll arrange for an upscale cell for you in my prison. I'm well aware the Phantom is somewhere, but this opera house is probably full of those secret passages. We cannot track him. We'll have to wait him out."

"And I am supposed to settle for that answer? I spent years waiting out the Phantom. Wondering if Erik were truly dead, questioning if I did enough to protect my bride from him. I was young and weak. I freely admit that, but now Christine is *my* responsibility. She has *my* name and *my* nobility, and is *my* life. There will be hell to pay before I allow any form of weakness to come between me and my pursuit of the demon haunting my family."

Legard saw sheer determination light Raoul's eyes. He admired such devotion, but realized the difference between a man trained to protect and a man reared as a gentleman. Calmly, he reached beside him to grab the jacket Raoul discarded earlier. He held it out to him.

"Put that on, straighten your cravat and calm yourself." Inspector Legard pointed out the office to the theater beyond. "This series is winding down and hundreds of people will be anxious to meet this theater's benefactor. I told you to maintain calm, but instead you chose to fire pistols and chase down Phantoms. You're lucky no one heard you. You're the one who said no vendettas and look at you now. Keep your focus on Christine and let me do my job. Right now you need to do yours." Rising, Legard jerked open the door.

Raoul lifted his eyes and Legard saw a stone cold look that he never wanted to see again. He stood with the door open unwilling to back down. Reluctantly, Raoul complied.

"I'll not fail you this time, Raoul."

Raoul paused to tap his arm. "You never did, Jules."

The boat bumped against the opposite shore. Slinging the satchel over his shoulder, Erik stepped from it, first laying the oars aside before tying the boat to its mooring. He took a deep breath of the cold air to clear his head before extending a hand to Christine.

Refusing his offer, she clambered to shore in an awkward motion of rustling skirts. He focused on her hemline as she brushed past.

"Not that way, Christine."

"I know my way, thank you, Monsieur. I have not forgotten how you once led me here. Drugged I may have been, but I remember." She headed up the road before turning on him with a self-assured air.

"We have years of history between us. I am not simply going to dismiss that as you have."

"I have not dismissed it." Erik pointed with the hand of his uninjured arm. "We need to go this way."

"I spent years wondering if you were well, hoping against hope itself you still thought of me."

Erik let her fume. "Christine, please." He gestured toward the corridor again.

"No. Do not toss this aside like some outworn history. I was not the object of your obsession and my husband the object of your jealousy for you to brush me aside. You have seeded yourself in my soul, Erik, and my emotions have fought for space between your roots for too long. This is how you repay all you put me through? Deceiving me and faking your death? To think of all those nights I lay awake, sharing my bed with Raoul whilst still hearing your voice in my mind."

Erik's shock played openly upon the face she didn't have the privilege to see. He backed away, unwilling to take pause to address that comment. Knowing it was best that he move—given the imagery such a statement fed—Erik headed down the path alone.

"I suggest you follow. I am not taking you through your dressing room. I am bringing you to Madame Giry as promised. I am certain you do not know the way."

Her voice rose. Erik squeezed his eyes shut, trying to block out the annoying bee that kept stinging the back of his neck.

"You tire of living down here yet you speak of choosing a life with a woman such as her. She can bring you nothing." Her hand brushed the back of his cloak. "Erik, listen to me. You are a man of exceptional talent and *hidden* beauty and you choose to shamefully waste it. Your place is standing in a society where your genius can shine. She cannot be a part of the dignified world I now know you deserve."

He faltered in his steps. Never had he heard Christine speak with such resolve or passion.

"I can help you transcend your transgressions and stand beside you in that realm. You cannot tell me that she understands you as I do."

That made him stop. "Christine, please, I need to bring you to your vicomte so I can deal with other matters."

"Never mind my vicomte."

Alarmed, he spun to see her cover her mouth. He shook his head in appalled disapproval, presenting his back to her again.

"I believe I can give you so much," she said with calm intensity. "Why can I not have the chance?"

Erik stopped. All he needed to do was turn around, extend his hand, and offer Christine that chance without any doubt she would accept it. He teetered between the unfathomable—the love of not one, but two women. She seemed oblivious to his torment.

"Tell me one thing she has done for you that I did not."

Erik nodded. Yes, his choice had been made. Once again, he turned, making certain the darkness played against his eyes. Even in the dank corridor, Christine's radiant beauty rose from her posture, her scent, her grace... But his mind sought the refuge he found in the beauty of a very different woman. His eyes flew open at the mere thought of her and the flash of gold greeting Christine served its purpose of pinning her to her spot. "She chose me."

Shock plastered across Christine's face. He bowed low before her as she rushed past, not swayed by the tears he saw tracking down her cheeks.

Patrons milled like well-herded sheep. Madame Giry walked along the outskirts of the crowds. She studied Raoul as he wandered toward the Vestibule des Abonnés, accepting praise and congratulations on the Opera Garnier's triumphant return to glory. She stayed closer to her class in the Vestibule de Contrôle, hearing him deny all concern regarding his diva and assuring everyone she was safe. He artfully turned away any questions about the demise of the management. He painted a convincing façade.

Raoul's calm confounded her as she paced between her office and the crowds. Where on earth could Anna be? Madame Giry hoped to God she had Christine and not Erik. Shame on her for thinking that way, but old habits were difficult to change. She cursed under her breath as she wound her way to the solitude of her office.

But solitude is not what she found.

"Madame Giry, we need to speak." The Inspector indicated for her to take a seat, offering her water or tea in the process.

Wary, Madame Giry denied both. Nothing would settle her nerves at this point. She closed the door.

"In the interest of time I will get right to the point. You, like many of us, were involved in the original investigations. I never thanked you. However, I no longer believe thanks are warranted." Inspector Legard crossed his arms.

She had no choice but to give him her undivided attention.

"I'm a friend to the Chagny estate and a highly respected member of the Paris authorities. I take this investigation personally. You know more than you let us believe. You knew more then, and you know more now." He tossed a note on her dressing table. "Your years of servitude end now."

Madame Giry's eye dipped closed, inching darkness before her. When she opened them, her wish hadn't been granted. The note was still there. "Where did you get that?"

"I took it from Vicomte de Chagny. I'm a gentleman, Madame, but also an investigator and while I despise doing this, I must. Tell me what you know in its entirety, and I'll see you are pardoned for the years you hindered these investigations. If you don't, I'll be forced to act in the manner of my station."

She thought a great burden would have been removed from her, but in the long minutes it took for her to admit her cheat, she felt like Judas betraying a man of whom she felt so deeply a part. And like Judas, she could do nothing but wait until that pivotal moment and beg forgiveness.

Erik slowed as they wound their way out of the labyrinth. He paused and stared toward Madame Giry's door. Christine attempted to push beyond him several times. If her patience was wearing thin, Erik's frayed even more.

"This is madness. I am not about to creep in ghost-like silence any longer." She plowed past him.

Erik reacted with split-second reflexes. Despite his pain, he reached out with his good arm to brace her against the wall. Something was off, he could feel it. "Come now." He released his pressure.

"That is it? You will take me to the vicomte so you can disappear out of my life again? No explanations, no apologies?"

Erik forced her back against the wall, pinning her with both hands. It sent jarring pain up his arm. "Erik answers to no one. Erik need not apologize for anything! What more do you wish from me, Christine?"

"The ability to make my own choice, not the ones you or my title make for me. I choose to have answers I am worthy of, instead of being trapped in some perpetual guessing game. Is that possible?" She glared directly into his eyes. "Or have you flawlessly woven over the image of Death, the *illusion* of a gentleman?"

"So the susceptible child disappears in the woman? Make haste to recall, my dear, I still do not tolerate disobedience."

"Answers!"

"You vain child," Erik criticized around his insufferable annoyance. "Whom are you going to question? Angel, demon or father? Who is it you wish to reply?"

Christine's head tipped to her chest, her display of strength knocked down by his well-practiced reprimand. "Why did you bring me to the house on the lake when you meant to bring me here?"

Erik abruptly loosened his grip and took a step back in horrified unease. Why had he done that? It was where he'd brought her in the past. Where he thought she had, for at least a portion of a fortnight, felt secure. Could it be a source of confusion for her? He shook his head. No. How could Christine understand the reasons he would instinctually flee there? She didn't understand him. He'd made a snap decision and obviously chosen poorly.

"So you dress yourself with an air of discomfort?" she observed. "Perhaps you cling to the past as ardently as I and I look upon a man wishing to redress the choices he has made? Vain child you may call me, but children mature. Possibly you do not love this woman between us as completely as you profess?"

Erik shook his head, weary of her persistent assumption that he didn't understand his heart. A surprising tenderness filled his reply. "Do you recall when you first saw Anna?"

"At the masquerade. Dancing with an exquisite gentleman who was quite enamored by her. Every one could see that. The Holy Ghost Himself could not have cut in on those two."

"No, and I would not have let Him."

Silence lingered until hoarse confusion clung to her voice. "How... how could that have been you?"

Pity made him draw his fingers lightly down her face. "The boy loves you, Christine. Someday may you honestly learn that. Deny the changes all you wish my Persephone. I will not repeat Orpheus' folly and chance a look behind."

Erik turned his attention back to Madame Giry's door. He would see this charade through to its end and then address what he'd been denying. He *could* look toward a future.

He had his grip upon Eurydice—the surface was only moments away.

The door creaked open and Erik found Madame Giry staring into the mirror. The opera seemed to have etched lines deeper into her already wrinkled face.

"Vicomtess, thank Heavens," Madame Giry gasped. Erik grimaced as her gaze landed on his blood-soaked shirt. "Mercy, what happened?"

Removing the satchel still slung over his shoulder, he lowered it to the floor. "Nothing of concern. Keep Christine here and do not leave this room. Barret is looking for her and he has my Anna." Madame Giry caught her breath, pressing her hands to her heart. "I must find her as well as Raoul." He turned to the door.

"Monsieur, wait!"

The warning came too late. The door slammed inward. Knocked off guard, Erik was unable to react fast enough to deflect the man lunging toward him. His back hit the table. The shattered mirror sent bits of glass shooting like tiny daggers around them. Sundries soared across the room.

Erik flung the Inspector off with a feral growl and fought back with a raw, inhuman fury. The remaining guards leapt in, wrestling Erik to the ground with equal fervor. A sharp blow of a rifle butt aimed directly to Erik's injury forced enough submission for the gendarmes to gain control. A bellowing scream bespoke Erik's agony. The gendarmes pulled his arms behind him with no regard to his pain. He grimaced and swallowed a second scream as his shoulder and arm turned deeper shades of scarlet.

Inspector Legard panted like a bellows as he wiped blood from his nose. "Are you ladies all right?" he questioned. Neither answered. The color had drained from Christine's face and Madame Giry kept hers hidden in her palms. The tiny office filled as more guards poured into the room followed by Raoul. His arms were open the instant Christine flung herself into his embrace. He nodded his thanks to Legard.

Erik continued to struggle, the pain making it hard for him to gain any ground. He stared up with a profound hatred at Raoul.

Letting go of Christine, Raoul circled Erik. "The Phantom is at a loss for words?"

"If you want to have words with me, Monsieur, might I suggest we do that alone, man to man?"

"Man to man?" Raoul stripped the mask from Erik's face. The room filled with a fierce cry. Erik instinctively lowered his head, attempting to hide his face. "Hardly." Raoul flung the mask aside.

Legard muttered a string of curses and covered his mouth with the back of his hand. Several of the guards backed away, but the ones holding Erik were forced to remain where they were, gripping a man whose mask of Death held at bay a sovereign anger.

Erik breathed with heavy humiliation. He looked toward the women. For a moment his eyes—the edges pinching under the weight of his sadness—locked with the box keeper's. In all the years Erik had known her, she'd never seen him unmasked. The hands upon her cheeks trembled. Her eyes glistened with moisture.

"Do forgive me, Mother Giry. I apologize for Monsieur le Vicomte's lack of manners. This should not occur before a lady."

Legard intervened, waving for his men to get Erik to his feet.

"Do you care to make this easy and tell us where Barret is?"

Legard tried not to look directly into Erik's face.

"I do not know. He has Anna. She was leading him from Christine."

"Or to me." All eyes turned to Christine. She looked to her husband. "Anna Reneè Barret. That is what he called her."

"I knew they had a connection, but she told me he killed her mother," Raoul said incredulously. "I never thought she could have been blood." Erik ignored the disgust pouring out his lips. "How many more lies are we to be privy to? Your twisted games of manipulation are over. Get him out of here."

Erik jerked against the gendarmes' grip. Writhing in their arms like a reptile, he lunged toward Christine. She buried her face in the comfort of Raoul's embrace.

"Oh, you would betray me again?" Erik snarled. "Your words are nothing but a cheat. It *is* Erik you still fear. Why is it you cannot look on me if your words moments ago were so true? I freed you and now you would imprison me? Why, when I wept upon your breast years ago could you not see I was releasing you? I was releasing us. Is it because you speak only lies, lies as hideous as I?"

"Away with him!" Raoul shouted.

Erik's reply snaked from his lips, "Perhaps, Monsieur, it is not *my* mask you should remove." He locked eyes with Christine, as the gendarmes dragged him toward the door. "You know damn well of Anna's intent."

Christine sadly replied into the security of Raoul's shoulder. "I do not know anyone's intent anymore."

Erik refused to relinquish control. He thrashed and his body arched with pain, but he wouldn't go willingly. The Inspector halted his men in their efforts to usher Erik toward the door.

"Barret and Anna are somewhere in the opera house. If we're fortunate, we'll find them now that the Phantom is restrained. They aren't to leave this theater." He gestured toward Erik. "Deal with him first then join the others. Get him to the wagon and lock him in the cage."

Cage?

Paired with the raging pain shooting down his arm, his normal razor sharp focus disappeared. A brief paralysis washed over him with that one word before mindless panic set in. He was not about to be caged like a common mongrel or shut away in any prison not of his own doing...

Chapter Thirty-one

Oh, if only she'd obeyed Erik and run.

The halls were packed. Throngs of men in evening dress hurried toward the dancers' lounge. Foremen wound their way in the opposite direction, seeking respite from the evening's affair in local pubs. Mingled among them were the leering eyes of gendarmes trying to look inconspicuous while they searched the Opera Garnier.

"Keep your face down, Anna. Have you forgotten everything I taught you?"

Anna's chin jammed against her chest as her father's fingers clamped upon the base of her skull. She stared at her feet, her eyes casting small glances around. The two walked in tandem, artful in the way they moved together.

"See, just like old times, isn't it strumpet?" He tickled the back of Anna's neck with his fingers. "Away from the gendarmes—locate the vicomte."

Could she just run?

If she were able to break free, perhaps she could reach the vicomte and warn him of Barret's intent for Christine. Raoul would certainly have an easier time keeping Christine safe than she.

She stole a glance at her father. She'd managed to dodge him once, but this wasn't the labyrinth. Not heeding his warning about keeping her face down, Anna lifted her head. She made brief eye contact with a distant group of gendarmes. It roused their suspicions. They headed in her direction. Risking a chance to flee, Anna attempted to move toward them. Her father's grip tightened.

Nothing, not a slight of hand, an imperceptible nod or a fleeting glance got past Richard Barret. Too late, she remembered. The hall swirled around as her father spun her toward him and away from the oncoming gendarmes.

It was a gala evening after all, and the corridors of the Garnier were packed with all sorts of gentlemen with various intents. The gendarmes moved on when all they saw was a man bent over a woman in a passionate kiss.

"You son-of-a-bitch," she spit when Richard twirled her away. She swiped viciously at her lips.

Richard licked his. "Don't do anything stupid like that again or I assure you I'll not be so kind next time."

Scrubbing her mouth raw against the back of her hand, she reasoned through the situation. If she ran he'd follow. He always liked a game of cat and mouse. He wouldn't kill her. Anna had called his bluff on that threat too many times in her life. She was all with which he had to bargain.

They continued, two cats gracefully perusing a hunting ground. Each step brought a jarring pain to her thigh. Wincing, her hand crept toward her dress pocket and dipped inside.

Holy hell, the knife!

She gripped it tightly, feeling her pulse in her fingertips. The Brussels street flooded back to her. The memories attached to the steel replayed in her mind. They were still as sharp. Anna touched a finger to the lingering taste of bitter scotch on her lips and looked at her father. She'd done it once. She could do it again.

Crowds were a good thing...

Anna's hand curled around the hilt. She closed her eyes against the sixteen-year-old trembling inside her, pivoted and screamed. She swung with her free arm, the people around her scattering in chaos when they saw the flash of a blade.

Richard was wiser this time. He blocked her blow, taking the brunt of the blade to his forearm. It barely made contact, but served its purpose before clanging to the floor. Anna struggled out of his grip and ran, disappearing in the swirling vat of people. Like a rat scurrying away from light and using the commotion to her advantage, she dodged and wove her way in and out of the fray.

Crowds were a good thing; getting lost in an angry mob even better.

To no avail, Erik struggled the entire way to the carriage house. As they entered, all he saw before him was the wagon with its wooden sides, its iron bar and its lock. The idea of arrest and relinquishing his control to be thrown in a cage like a hideous, monstrous beast closed like a crown of thorns around his mind. The door swung open. The pungent aroma of stale hay hit him in the face. It contrasted sharply with the fresh, clean hay reserved for the horses. The gendarmes shoved him inside. Erik lunged for the door before it was locked shut, but was met with a face full of wood.

His world had bars. Ahead, behind, and to the side of him—his world had bars.

Caged. Imprisoned. This is what he'd avoided all his life—a sentence not of his doing.

Uncontrollable anxiety fueled the pain inside of him. Memories of his youth when he frequented fair after fair with a manager grew like fire to wind in his mind. Even then, at the hands of showmen and under the pity of a public that freely viewed the vulnerability of his unmasked face, Erik had a modicum of control. Here he did not. He was exposed and at the mercy of others.

He clawed at the lock like a cat trapped in a box. He kicked and threw himself at the door. This degradation he wouldn't tolerate. He didn't admit the wrongs of his past and risk his freedom to save Christine, only to be stripped of all the power he had. He wouldn't be locked away and chained to rot in some dark and repulsive prison like a deviant of the underworld. Not when his bleak existence had found a way to the light.

He growled, kicked, and spit obscene and incomprehensible words at the door that locked all chances of fleeing his past.

The door that prevented him from finding Anna.

Shame over his past indiscretions with Christine had waned to resentment over her betrayal. Fury over being imprisoned turned to dread at the thought of his actions causing Anna any harm.

Unspeakable dread took control. His mind closed in around him locking out the world and all facets of reason. The panic pulled him back into the murky elements of his memories, blocking out any chance for light to enter.

"Stop your ruckus!" a guard shouted.

Erik pounded further.

"Stay down, or we will keep you down."

Erik pounded harder.

"He'll rip himself to death at that rate." A gendarme laughed.

"What good it will do him," the second replied. "He's already the living dead."

Murderous vengeance swelled in his chest. His fists thrashed the wooden barrier. Erik heard their cries, but they rang differently in his mind. They transported him to a time and place where he freely stood before the fairgoers as they shouted out their demands: more tricks, more song. The crowds begged for the fantastic. Erik didn't mind—he humored them. In all that time, he'd had the race he so despised completely under his command.

He'd never wavered under those shouts until the demands became intimate and the voice of his manager rang louder than any of them. Seeping words into his soul that began to slowly drown whatever bit of humanity he thought he had. *Behold the Living Corpse.* Words that transformed man into Death and Death into an alluring ally.

And if he had to revisit the madness of Death to save the Love of the Maiden—then so be it.

Erik pounded again.

Chapter Thirty-two

Raoul ushered his wife down the hallway. He shut the door to the manager's office, locking it behind him. Christine moved with unsteady steps to the divan. Raoul crouched in front of her, laying his hand upon her knees.

"I will order my carriage and have you returned to the flat. My *maître d'hôtel* will be contacted to see to it everything is ready for your return to Chagny. I am staying here until we find Barret and Anna." He reached up and fanned her tresses back behind her shoulders. "I am sorry you had to see him taken like that. I know how deeply you once cared for him. But you need to trust *my* love, Christine. Trust I will keep my promise to you. I love you. He will be brought to justice. No one deserves to go through what you have."

"What of Mademoiselle Barret?"

"I do not exactly know what to make of her."

"And his opera house?"

Raoul clamped his jaw and steadied his reply. "It is no longer his, Christine, and it never was. Until suitable replacements can be found the opera house will remain under Chagny guidance."

The idea of taking on such a monumental task filled him with dread. Such a foolhardy act went against everything his title deemed appropriate.

"What are you going to do?" she asked, tiredly.

He smiled faintly. The youthful, uncertain sadness to her voice contradicted how strong he knew her to be. "Whatever necessary. Whatever I need to do to bring you everything you wish in this."

"I am not worthy of you and your heart. You deserve so much more than the choices I make for love." She reached up to brush a line of hair from his forehead.

Raoul lifted her hand to his lips. "You speak foolish things that are pooled from all you have suffered. This *will* end. Erik will no longer possess you. You became my life when I took you to my side. Whatever you need of me in this, I will make it so—my life, my name is all for you. That is my choice. That is my love."

"What will happen to Erik?" she spoke so softly Raoul had to lean forward to hear her plea.

"He will pay for what crimes he has committed in his life. Erik condemned himself to Devil's Island. If not there, then execution. I can only imagine the latter to be more humane." Raoul sat beside her. "You see him now for what he has always been. The man is mad. You cannot deny that. He will certainly pay for what he did to you."

Raoul leaned in to claim her lips and kiss away her sadness. Christine's attempt to return it lacked her usual passion. The door rattled in its jam, breaking their kiss. Raoul rose, holding a hand out to his wife, signaling her to remain where she was. He reached for his pistol. When Christine's lips parted at the sight of him armed, he shot her a stern look not to parry him. Raoul unlocked the door. A pint-sized explosion sent him stumbling backward. Anna shouldered her way in and whirled to slam the door.

"When he finds me no matter what he wants, do it. What he asks for, give it to him. What are you doing here?" Anna yelled at Christine. "You should be with Madame Giry. Barret runs his cons his way and when everyone doesn't play nicely he tends to get unruly."

"You would know, would you not Mademoiselle Barret?" Raoul convicted.

Anna quieted. "How do you know my surname?"

Raoul followed her gaze to Christine. His wife's face had dragged into an assemblage of remorse.

"Where is Erik?" Anna demanded.

"I suspect halfway to a Paris prison by now," Raoul said, decorating his voice with cold suspicion.

Anna lost her breath. The flush on her cheeks faded to white.

"Should you be in that prison along with him?" He didn't get his reply before the door crashed inward. Richard Barret entered, his pistol drawn and a crazed look in his eye.

"Now you've made me angry, Anna." Richard swung the length of his arm around to level the pistol on Raoul. "Go ahead, Vicomte, continue to reach beneath that waistcoat. Anna, get his weapon."

Anna didn't move. Richard gestured angrily with his pistol, waving it between Raoul and his wife.

"Anna this is not Brussels, get it now. Defiance might be worth the risk to your life, but I doubt you want to try my patience and see if it worth the risk to theirs. Now move!"

Raoul glowered at her, the suspicions in his mind slowly confirmed as Anna encircled her hands around his waist. She slid his jacket aside. Spreading his arms allowed her access to his hip.

"I was feeling I betrayed you," he said quietly. "You have played me the fool, Mademoiselle. Quite cunning."

With a sharp jerk, Anna freed his pistol. It rocked him closer into her. "You have lived a sheltered life, Vicomte. In my pedigree," she slightly nodded toward Barret, "you learn to do as you are told when you are told." The pistol slid into her hands and she stepped away.

Richard wasted no time in disarming her. "Now," he continued, "it appears the vicomte owes me some money."

"I gave you what I could. I do not have the funds you demanded in Paris."

"Not my problem." Richard grabbed Christine, snickering at her feeble whimpers. He waved the pistol at Raoul's sudden move toward his wife. Raoul had no choice but to back down. "Before I begin, where is the Phantom fellow?"

Raoul's response chilled the air. "Caged like you will be very soon." He took a bold step forward that prompted Richard to aim the pistol on Christine.

"Caged?" Richard laughed. "Oh strumpet, did you hear that? Your lover is caged. Isn't that just bestial? Thank you, Vicomte, you have made my night. This will flow much easier now. Get me my money."

"It is the middle of the night, I cannot. I will do what you want. Just release my wife."

"Give him the evening's receipts," Anna instructed.

Raoul looked at her. "What receipts?"

She indicated a corner. "The booth agents bring the money here before it can be couriered to the bank. It will be in the safe."

"Strumpet, I do love you." Richard gestured impatiently with the pistol.

Raoul's shoulders lifted along with his hands. "I do not know the combination."

Richard rolled his eyes. "Strumpet, if you will. Really, Vicomte, I believe the wrong person is managing this opera."

It took Anna no effort to break into the safe and take what billfolds she could find. She shoved them angrily into Richard's eager hands.

"Now, this is the part where I leave," he proclaimed. He backed himself toward the door. "I expect safe passage out of Paris and to be certain that occurs, she," he indicated Christine, "will stay with me."

Christine squirmed against Richard's grip. Raoul rushed toward his wife, his actions being brought to a stop with the cock of the pistol's trigger.

"Oh, but I do like them feisty. Don't try anything stupid. Anna!" He pointed the pistol at her and waved her forward. "Come. You don't think I'm leaving you here do you? You need to do what you do so well and get me out of this opera house."

The horses kicked, lunging when he lunged until the harness shattered. Erik crashed against the bars, but his cage didn't budge.

The gendarmes cursed as the team took off down the aisle. Erik watched them race after the horses. Adrenaline pumped as he pounded against the door, beating himself senseless in the process. He sank against the wall of his prison, out of breath, and out of will. He clutched his battered arm.

A shower of splinters shot like wooden bullets toward him. Erik threw his hands over his head as the door snapped and swung open. Shock quickly evaporated and he flew at his opportunity for escape. He landed at the feet of Madame Giry, whose stone hard expression was punctuated by a blacksmith iron and carriage pin in one hand and a mask in the other. Stern determination coated her face—no longer a timid box keeper and servant, but an ally and friend.

"Go, quickly, before they find you." She shook the mask insistently in his face. "Forgive me. Go. Find Anna."

Taking it, Erik sighed with comfort as he placed it upon his curse. Never would he have expected such a daring move from the woman he'd forced to serve him. She risked everything to free him and he found all he could say before darting for a shadow was a simple word.

"*Merci*."

Throughout the course of the evening the opera house drained of patrons and players. Paris slipped into slumber around the Garnier, oblivious to the plight at hand. If Raoul could have evaporated away into a blurry oblivion, he would have. It would have been easier than to face the horror of seeing his wife hauled away while he stood like statuary at gunpoint.

Taking his cue from the adrenaline coursing untamed through him, he rushed through the opera house until he found Inspector Legard.

"Barret has Christine," Raoul shouted.

"Barret is still here?" Inspector Legard said incredulously. "How large is the blasted opera house? Where is Anna?"

"I had no choice but to let them go again."

Legard lifted a hand, silently imparting that Raoul had acted wisely. His console quickly switched to anger. "Whose side is Mademoiselle Barret on?"

Raoul shook his head in defeat and gestured instead toward the gendarme that approached.

"Inspector, he's gone!"

"Who is gone?" Raoul barked to the junior officer.

"The Phantom. He tore that carriage apart..."

Anna crept through hallways, keeping her father and his prize artfully concealed from prying eyes. She knew better than to put up the fuss Christine was. The diva's whimpers only excited her father more. He studied the enormous carriage house, scowling at the gendarmes at the distant end.

"Steal us a horse," he commanded. "You do remember how to steal a horse?"

Some children learned nursery rhymes; Anna learned how to steal horses.

"I think I can recall," she replied, her voice throaty with contempt. She didn't appreciate the horrific look Christine shot her, so Anna leveled a challenging gaze on her, warning the vicomtess not to pass judgment on the only person capable at the moment of handling the situation.

"There's that sarcasm again strumpet." Richard shoved her from the shadow toward the stalls.

"Stop calling me that," she spat.

Richard laughed.

Anna hadn't moved with such stealth since the last time she was employed by her father. The situation seemed remotely familiar. Lurking about, devious intentions, and gendarmes she couldn't do a damn thing about.

They were too far away for Anna to get their attention. In the past when working under Richard Barret, getting the attention of the authorities was the last thing on her mind. Surprisingly, it would've been her last choice at this particular moment as well. It would be preferable to just save Erik's skin leaving Richard to his own devices, but she had to think of Christine.

With great care, Anna silently lifted tack from the wall and headed to a distant stall. How was she going to get Christine out of this? She cursed the life that had returned full circle on her. Tears pulled at the corner of her eyes.

"Easy boy." Stay composed and talk calmly and the horse will be still, she reminded herself aloud as she gave the stallion the bit. Her voice cracked though and being alone, Anna permitted her tears to fall. She leaned her head against the horse's neck.

"Let's go, Anna." A harsh whisper pebbled her skin.

She lifted her head and wiped at her eyes. Shaking hands fumbled as she untied the tether and coiled it in her hand. All she wanted was a normal life. She just wanted—

A pair of hands shot from thin air. They slammed her against the wall of the stall. The pressure of her fear rose against her chest when she saw—

Erik!

Suddenly, her heart exploded with relief. She opened her mouth to speak, but was silenced before the first whisper passed her lips. A moan—deep and guttural came from the depths of Erik's throat. In seconds, his lips crushed against hers, backing her deep against the coarse wall. He devoured her with his kiss and held her lips with intensity she never thought possible.

Forehead against forehead he locked their gazes. A long slow sigh escaped her mouth. Putting a finger to her lips, he slowly pried the rope from her hands.

Anna didn't heed his request for silence. "He has the vicomtess, Erik."

Erik peered from the stall. "That is not of concern to me."

"Erik! You have to get her out of here."

He leaned back into the stall, assaulting her with words as roughly as he did his lips. "Erik does not have to do anything."

Anna had seen him angry before, but this time he seethed. "You're frightening me."

"It is about time."

"She needs you." His detached glare rattled her bones.

Richard's voice broke their stare down. "Anna, my horse."

"I'm working on it," she spat back. She grabbed Erik tightly by the arm and looked him directly in the eye. "What has happened to you? Where did Erik go? Where did this sudden angst toward Christine come from?" She stumbled when he yanked his arm free. "What did she do to you? She's your Christine! Erik—"

"She *was* my Christine! She did nothing to *me*. It is how she betrayed *you*. I am not about to discuss such matters now. I am getting you out of here."

"You're getting *her* out of here." Anna pointed out the stall. "I'm used to taking care of myself. I know you love that woman, and if you let anything happen to her you'll never forgive yourself. I'm used to being second best, Erik, it doesn't bother me."

He followed her gesture toward Christine. The voices of Legard and Raoul got progressively louder and the insistent commands of Richard got bolder.

Erik's stalking carved small circles in the hay around her. "As silent as you may make it, you also have a knack of gnawing your way into my mind. It drives me madder than I already am."

He clawed at the thin flesh on his temples, making what skin showed around his mask pucker in emphasis. He lowered his hands and looked her up and down. The almost imperceptible droop to his shoulders betrayed his defeat. He inched open the door.

Anna eyed the rope he fondled erotically in his hands. “No killing, Erik, please.”

Erik donned a genteel air. “Does Erik kill?”

His smile dripped with sweet sarcasm as he turned his attention out the door. His penetrating gaze caused her to back away. She’d never seen such a tremendous look before; one that was the result of an ordeal to which she hadn’t been privy—a look that demanded her immediate compliance.

Erik leaned his cheek against her ear. “You are not second best.” The tone had him perched precariously on the right side of danger. He coiled the rope he held out of sight and again spoke directly into her ear. “Do you claim to understand me?”

“Yes.” A heat warmed her cheeks and spread down her neck. The inches between them pulsed with her shallow breathing.

Erik teased the nape of her neck with silken tones. “Do you know me?”

“Yes.” Her legs lacked the firmness his voice held.

“Do you trust me?” His voice had turned remarkably husky. He hunched deeply over her, stroking her head with his, temple against temple, chin caressing chin.

“Yes.”

He enveloped her face in his hands and drew her tightly against his chest. The back of her head tipped to her shoulder as he turned her to look up at him. He gazed deep into her eyes with longing more tried than the wind. He gently rocked her face before—in an achingly slow movement—he turned his head to taste her again. He ran his tongue against the seam of her lips, and when she opened for him, he spoke the words directly into the kiss.

“Then let me be the man you dare not know.”

Chapter Thirty-three

The door hung at an awkward angle and thin slivers of wood mingled with the hay. Legard studied the broken carriage and distant renegade team. It was difficult to decipher who was more agitated—the horses or Legard.

Smoldering with impatience, Legard grabbed the gendarme by the arm. "How did this happen?"

"Jules, we do not have time for this," Raoul interjected. "Would logic have Barret heading in this direction if his intent was to get out of here quickly?"

Legard nodded, shoving his incompetent man aside and signaling for the gendarmes at the far end of the stable. "We'll start here first and work our way back to re-cover the opera house. I'll make certain the exits are secure." Legard glanced skeptically at the destroyed carriage. "Raoul, there's no telling where the Phantom might be, I am afraid—"

"That is right Messieurs, where could I be?"

Years of training to expect the unexpected couldn't prevent Inspector Legard from gasping in shock and looking for what cover he could find. He grabbed the vicomte by the arm and yanked the young nobleman within the safety of his reach. The carriage house reverberated with the astonishing menace and jeering chords of an undeniable threat.

The Phantom's voice boomed from every corner preventing Richard Barret from moving forward with his well-planned escape. "What the blazes was that?" he cursed.

Erik's laughter swirled against the undercurrent of the danger Richard heard. The unnaturalness of that voice forced an unwanted submission from him. Richard hated to be submissive. He grabbed Christine, determined to leave the opera house, his plans still intact.

His sanity was another matter.

"That is right, Messieurs, be ready for me." Erik's maniacal laughter engulfed everything.

"Your tricks are useless," Raoul shouted.

"Tricks, Monsieur?"

"Your mind games. You would be wise to note I am bound by you no more."

"How bold, Monsieur."

"Where is that coming from?" Richard shouted. He jammed a finger in his ear and shook it quickly.

Panic set in; the vicomte and Inspector blocked the way out in front of him, and that eerily faceless voice permeated everything. Men he could see and a demon he couldn't, surrounded him on all sides. He had to get out—and fast. His only means of escape would be through the vicomte and the path he blocked. Richard still had a very good reason for Raoul to let him pass. He grabbed Christine and darted from the shadow.

Erik saw Anna from his shelter. The tip of her head barely peered over the rim of the stall door.

"Erik?" she called warily.

He didn't answer. Tempting as calling to her was, a metamorphosis had taken place and he didn't truly wish her to see. Leaning her head out of the stall allowed Erik to see the shock etched on her face. He watched as the inspector and his men turned in bewilderment on one side of her, and spied—as she did—Richard and Christine rushing from their hideaway.

"Vicomtess," Anna shouted. The vicomte echoed her cry.

Erik couldn't resist adding to the confusion. Soft lilting sounds of *Christine* drifted through the air, carried forward by his laughter. It held a hauntingly chilling quality that could have frozen the Seine. It made everyone pause—except Richard. Erik smiled. Precisely what he wished to occur. Nothing could stop a roach scurrying from light, nor a man seeking escape. Who would know this better than Erik?

"Stop right there!" Legard shouted, standing staunchly in his spot and aiming his pistol down the length of the carriage house.

"Such valiant words," Erik complimented.

"Stay out of my way, Inspector, or I will kill her." Richard aimed his pistol at Christine's head. He walked toward the inspector—giving him a wide berth—while searching for the voice pursuing him.

"Such bold acts," Erik critiqued.

Raoul and Legard didn't know where to focus their attention: on the Phantom or Richard. In kind, Richard didn't know where to focus: on the Phantom or the authorities. Erik had complete control over total chaos. Pistols swung wildly in every direction, hands too shaky and minds too deluded to pull any triggers.

Erik laughed again. Was there no way for him to escape the

arrogant stupidity of the feebleminded? "Confused, Messieurs? I am right here. Who wants first try?" Bold and defiant, he appeared as if from nowhere. Spreading his long arms, he arrogantly swaggered down the center of the aisle, his sights set on Richard.

"Nothing to say Monsieur? Your Phantom has arrived."

"I intend to take what is mine and leave," Richard cracked, leveling his pistol on Erik. "Do not follow me."

Erik's voice was his one supreme weapon. The timbre of it switched, his eyes blazing with all the flames of hell as metallic syllables cracked through the building. Under the power of a ferocious voice, nobody dared move. "You cannot take what is not yours, Monsieur."

A stall door exploded outward making Erik whirl toward the sound. Not even a beast as powerful as a stallion was saved from the awesome monstrosity of Erik's anger. Massive horseflesh thundered out of the stall, the force dragging Anna with him. Throwing her hands over her head and curling into a ball was the only thing sparing her from the thrashing hooves. The horse bolted down the aisle momentarily breaking the concentration of the moment. It charged its unsuspecting victims.

"Messieurs!" Anna screamed.

Erik watched the entire scene unfold as he walked the length of the carriage house. Richard spun in time to dodge out of the way of the frantic horse. His doing so momentarily separated him from his prize and tossed him to the ground, his pistol knocked from his grasp. Raoul seized his chance. He ran toward Christine, spinning her into his arms. Richard grabbed for her, but came up empty. When he rounded again, he laid eyes on an opportunity and took off running.

Erik's diversion worked until he caught a glimpse of Richard's rapidly shrinking form. Richard caught Anna's arm when she turned to flee, and given no choice, she was dragged down the length of the carriage house.

The casual command Erik had evaporated. Any control he had was chased away by the rush of wrath filling him. He summoned his rising energy to master his reign of terror.

He would not have Anna harmed...

He would not have her in fear of her life...

He would not have Anna taken from him...

A great black demon visited the carriage house as Erik pursued Barret. This time the very bowels of the opera house shivered and all of Paris trembled from the terrific roar that came from the depths of his soul.

When Raoul thrust Christine into Legard's arms, Erik stopped in his tracks. Momentarily transformed, he took a few steps toward the vicomte to force his distance. Erik's voice changed as he harshly enunciated:

"Beware, Monsieur, the paradox of choice, because I choose at this moment not to kill you."

He glanced over Raoul's shoulder to a white-faced Christine before fleeing in the direction of Barret.

Though he felt Legard's warning shot whiz over his shoulder, Erik didn't turn. He was consumed with one target and one alone.

Anna dug her heels into the ground, anything to slow the manner in which Richard dragged her away. She writhed in his grip. Her size hindered her efforts. He took off down a sharp corner at the far end of the carriage house, hurling both of them into the carriage bay. The dim light caught him off guard. She took the opportunity to force herself against him.

Ramming her shoulder into his chest as hard as she could, she knocked Richard aside freeing a chance to run. She turned up and down aisles of waiting carriages at a breakneck pace, increasing her distance between her and her father with every pivot. Panting, her heart raced and her vision blurred from the exertion. She bent and rested her hands on her knees, gasping for breath to squelch the fire in her lungs.

Footsteps slapping against the floor forced her up, but a sharp cramp knocked her sideways. She grabbed at the stitch in her side, stumbling forward when a hand came from behind, sliding around her waist. Her breath hitched as she was pulled tightly against a solid chest. A second hand emerged to slowly brush the hair from her neck.

"Anna, don't make a sound."

She did as the voice bid. Taking a deep and cleansing breath, she closed her eyes, and melted into her calm. The peace rushed over her like an opium fog before she bucked backward with every ounce of strength she had. Her fist made prime contact with Richard's groin.

"Bitch!"

Anna scrambled away, but he gained the upper hand as she lost her footing on the slick hay. The carriage rocked with the impact as Richard, gnashing his teeth, shoved her against the wood and metal. The wheel jammed into her lower back.

"I've had enough of you, Anna. It's bad enough you've ruined my life, must you ruin my fun as well?"

She caught her breath enough to spit in his face. The back of his hand across her cheek split her lip and forced her submission.

"You always were a spirited one. So bold with everyone, yet so easy to manipulate when it comes to me. Why is that? Move," he commanded.

She did, but not before feeling his flesh peel away beneath her fingertips. Bloody red welts raked across his face.

"I'll not tolerate your disobedience," he growled, pinning her hands to the side of the carriage. "Tell me, strumpet, where is your Phantom fellow now?"

The carriage wheel dug into her back. She moaned against the pain. "I hate you."

"No you don't. You adore me. Don't you feel it, Anna? The thrill of the con? The allure of days gone by?"

His hand wrapped around her neck. Anna shut her eyes at the proximity of his cruel grin.

"That's right, refuse to look at me. It only makes this more exciting. You know how I love a challenge." He yanked open the carriage door and threw her toward it. "A secluded spot, confused police hot in pursuit. It makes the need become great indeed." Richard slid her hair aside and leaned into her. "Where is he, strumpet, not coming to your rescue?"

He nipped the base of her neck, working his lips upward and forgetting the pursuit behind them. Lust fed off of her fear and their improvised hiding spot. He ground his arousal hard against her, backing her into the carriage. Jerking down the steps, he shoved her against them. When she fought back, her cry escaped as a second fist made her flesh sting. The welt swelled as she felt her father's excitement rise.

Blood flooded her mouth as she clamped down on her tongue. Doing so was the only way to block out her father as he fought to satisfy what she most hated.

Erik had whirled in time to see, feel, and hear the impact of that fist. He moved slowly, nary making a sound. His fury closed the distance between them. The rope uncoiled in his hands. That familiar fluttering in his stomach returned with a vengeance.

Richard's mouth stopped to suckle Anna's earlobe, a free hand sliding up her dress and progressing along the inside of her thigh.

"I dare say," Richard crooned, as his tongue darted in her ear and his hand reached deeper toward his prize, "that Phantom's not your type."

Erik's world went crimson. He dropped the rope and his exquisitely stretched lasso, revulsion preferring to course through bare hands.

The carriage bay filled with Anna's howl of shock and Erik's subhuman cry. He wrenched Richard off her. Flinging him around with superhuman strength, Richard flew into the far wall. The board cracked with his impact. Erik pinned him, one hand digging into his miserable neck.

A Punjab lasso would have been more efficient, elegant and impersonal. But Erik desired to watch this. He wanted to see the terror in Richard's eyes, hear him struggle and feel the pressure of collapsing flesh. Erik needed the satisfaction of choking every last contemptible piece of life out of him.

Richard flailed. Erik shook with the effort it took to crush the windpipe. The quiver in his stomach grew urgent. Richard thrashed and kicked and it wasn't until his neck was purple did Erik have enough of seeing his face. He threw him to the floor and reached for his silk. With a quick stroke, Erik coiled it around Richard's neck.

"She is *precisely* my type."

And with two sharp twitches and a loud snap, Richard Barret went slack.

Chapter Thirty-four

"Murderer!"

The shout cracked across the carriage house as Legard and Raoul rounded the corner to witness the final moments of Erik's insanity and Barret's life.

Anna paled.

She staggered from her spot, collapsing against the wall. Her hair caught on the rough wood boards as her knees gave up their strength. Though the air held a chill, her palms dampened with sweat. She couldn't control her pounding heart as Erik placidly coiled the rope out of sight. He drew his frame to its full height and with cool disregard for the deed she'd witnessed, took a few steps closer to her. Anna tipped her chin up to stare into the unfeeling eyes of the Angel of Death.

She yanked her head away from his approach to look into the bloodshot eyes of Richard Barret. She could feel the burning of his advance in her ear and tasted the blood on her lip. Off in the distance she heard Legard barking orders and the vicomte voicing his rage. Anna reached out in a confused daze and barely touched the awkward angle of her father's neck. Her eyes inched over the length of black boots and trousers until she met the mask and Erik's unemotional stare.

Anna had watched him kill.

She'd witnessed the same terror he'd instilled in the Paris Opera House years ago. Saw in him that murderous vengeance he kept in constant check. The demon he battled with every waking moment.

She felt his madness.

Looking at her father, she squinted and bucked into the sickness that knotted her stomach. Erik stood over the body, his stance unwavering, his unremorseful gaze on her challenging.

He killed, but he hadn't murdered. His hands may have slain, but his soul had saved.

The shouting grew. Palm over palm, she inched her way up the wall, never taking her eyes off Erik.

An invisible metronome ticked between them. His voice filled with age-old sadness. "Make your choice. I am who I am."

Anna's hand crept along the wall, knocking against a lantern. She lifted it from its hook without a moment's hesitation. Erik didn't flinch as it flew past him. Oil and fire coated the floor as it shattered, igniting hay and sending flames leaping into the carriages. Flinching under the sudden power of heat around her, Anna extended her hand. His lips slipped open in silent affirmation.

She would set herself on the same path as he.

Erik hesitated. The barrier of flames grew. Anna watched as his eyes locked on Christine. She was protectively cradled in Raoul's embrace.

Through the rising smoke Anna wondered if Christine would have done the same.

Erik's eye never left Christine's confused gaze as he entwined his fingers apprehensively around the ones extended to him. As the shouts rang out behind him and the fire roared, Erik firmed up his grip.

Christine made her choice. Anna made hers. Now Erik looked toward a shadow and ran.

The fire spread, making the primary need to get the horses to safety before the ceiling collapsed. A small army was enlisted: gendarmes, stable hands, men upon the street—it mattered not who as long as they had a back to spare and the courage to douse the flames. Sparks lit up the night as the Paris streets filled with an acrid and swirling smoke. A curious crowd converged on the site while horses neighed in terror and men shouted among the confusion.

For a blissful moment, no one sought a Phantom.

Erik and Anna watched from the cloak of a distant alley. When it was clear the mayhem would keep him safely cloaked, Erik turned.

"I will return." He headed toward the flames.

"Are you out of your mind? You can't go back there."

"There is something I must do. I will be fine. Stay here."

"I don't have to stay here."

"Anna, please," Erik pleaded. "There is something I need. Stay, and hold this." He shoved the bulging billfold he'd deftly lifted from her dead father's pocket into her hands. Anna's face contorted. Erik hated asking what he did next, but he found he had no choice. "I need you to steal a horse."

Inspector Legard watched the flames coil in the night air as he paused to shuck his smoldering jacket. The carriage house would be a complete ruin, but thanks to the army of men dousing the surrounding area, the flames wouldn't touch the opera house.

Legard cursed the events leading to this mayhem. Every passing moment he lost was a moment lost in his pursuit. He turned, a grim expression tugging on the corners of his mouth. The vicomte approached with an equally dour expression, brushing ash from his jacket and slapping the sparks as they landed on his clothing.

"It's over Raoul," Legard regretted dejectedly.

"For this evening it is over."

Legard stared at the fire. "You're going to pursue this? It's useless, can't you see that? We can never win."

"Jules, in all the years I have known you, your goal has been to see justice served. Do you tell me you admit defeat?"

"It's easier." Tiny pinholes singed the fine linen of the vicomte's dress and a light dusting of ash turned the young man's blond hair a premature gray.

"I need you, Jules. I will not rest until I see him pay."

"You may have to rest, Raoul. Show me the evidence of Erik's previous crimes. Show me proof of any crime Erik committed here tonight."

Raoul's jaw slacked. "I could see your commission stripped for that, Inspector. We all witnessed another murder tonight, arson as well."

"Arson, yes. A murder, however, a court could prove self-defense in coming to another's aid. You saw Mademoiselle Barret and how she was dragged away. We don't know the circumstance."

"Murder is murder. Have you forgotten Wischard and Laroque?"

"Were they by his hand?"

The air between them throbbed with tension.

"You know as well as I there are crimes of which Erik is guilty. So long as he is out there, this opera house is some bizarre catalyst for him. I made the mistake of not seeing this through once and I have lived with the guilt of that for too long, not only because of Christine but because of all the others involved. Now more murders have been committed. I am not saddened Barret is dead, but murder is still murder. Tell me you do not think of Erik as guilty."

Legard stared at the swirling smoke, speaking around the set to his jaw. "I believe he's guilty."

Raoul grabbed him by the shoulder. "You are a genuine man, Jules. I cannot see this through without you. Say you will be there for me. Say you will be there for Christine."

Legard quieted, not knowing on what path his service would take him, but knowing deep in his heart he had to follow the one he felt was just and right. "I will."

"Then we continue at dawn and each dawn thereafter."

Raoul had the final word. Legard watched with unorganized emotions as the vicomte wove his way through the crowds, taking total command of the cause Legard deemed lost. He cleared his head and prayed he would have the same will and strength this time as well.

Madame Giry ignored the late hour—ignored everything. She thought to go to the carriage house when word of the fire reached her, but she was exhausted. She'd heard enough. Raoul and Christine were safe and Richard Barret was murdered by the Phantom.

The Phantom.

That name was once again a common whisper, causing the walls of the opera house to tremble. She closed her eyes, giving in to the sensation that she felt aged.

She opened her eyes. She didn't jump, yell, or even wonder how Erik got in. "You're safe," she said on a heavy sigh. He nodded. "You're leaving, aren't you?" He nodded again. "Where will you go?"

"I do not know," he remarked with quiet authority. "But this time it is clear I cannot remain here. I need you to tend to my opera house. I may still return for her."

"What of Anna?"

She heard admiration and longing in his voice. "She wishes to come with me."

"Good. Good," Madame Giry replied.

"I owe you more than my gratitude, Madame." Erik reached to calm her fumbling hands. His long fingers contrasted vividly with her plump, stubby ones. Erik covered them with sincere gentleness. "I owe you my life and my deepest apology for everything I—"

"Erik, stop."

She bit her tongue. Addressing him by name was a moment of which she'd thought on for years. Madame Giry looked hesitantly into his eyes for any reprimand, but a smile inched across his lips.

"Will you be in contact?" she asked quietly.

"If you wish." Erik withdrew his hand and headed to the door, spying the satchel that lay there. He slung it over his shoulder. Madame Giry wondered if more than the bag made him heavy with sorrow.

"Monsieur, wait." Madame Giry left the room and returned, draping Erik's opera cloak across his arms. "For when you reclaim your theater."

She didn't hide her misty eyes. Trying to fight the fountain of emotions the Opera Ghost commanded at his will was impossible.

"You have always been a faithful servant, Madame, and a silent friend even if it was my bitterness which prevented it from being pursued." Erik reached for her hand again. A tear found its way out of her eye. He brushed it away with his thumb. "*Merci, mon ami.*"

With those words he disappeared as quickly as he'd appeared. For one final time, she marveled at how indistinguishable Erik was between the shadows and the opera house. Touching the still chilled echo of his hand upon her cheek, she felt for the first time the gentleman he truly was.

Anna watched in dumbfounded shock as the flames came under control. Her hand had caused such mayhem? Disagreeable acts were frequently her bedfellows, but this was simply unheard of. The stolen horse stood tethered out of sight. Stealing the beast was—to her at least—a much lesser offense. She jumped when Erik approached.

"I was getting worried," she admitted. "Where did you go?"

"Just saying goodbye to an old friend."

"The opera house or Madame Giry?"

Erik extended his hand. A frown filled his voice. "Come."

She turned from the scene, amazed at how they could stand so close to the havoc they'd unleashed and go unnoticed. Or so she thought.

"You cannot leave," the vicomtess said.

"I do not see as I have much choice this time, Christine," Erik replied. "Do you intend to turn us in?"

"What good would that do? Either way you will find a means to leave."

The distinct sadness in her whisper made Anna hang her head in sympathy.

"If you wish to do us good, then tell your vicomte what you know is truth. What you know Anna did in that labyrinth."

He gently nudged Anna to urge her ahead. Without protest, she left, knowing this was a moment in which she had no part.

"Tell him the truth?" Christine stammered. "What is that, Erik? It has been twisted in my head for so long I do not understand it anymore."

Anna hesitated. She glanced over her shoulder.

"The truth, Christine," Erik parroted. "The truth that I kept my word, then and now. I let go of you. I allowed you to move on without my interference. I allowed you to choose your life. The fact that you cannot accept the choices you made, or that you now wish to choose differently is not my concern. There is one critical point you must remember. You returned to me. You came back into *my* life. I did not return to yours."

"You came back into my life the instant you rose from the dead,"

Christine said defiantly.

"I did not do that to come back into your life. I did that to come back into mine. You will never be able to fully understand the man that lies behind this mask."

"Was I permitted the chance?" she asked boldly. "Do not abandon me to tread unrealized waters alone, Erik. I am drowning in a whorl of affection I hold for *two* men, and I cannot swim. You are responsible in part for this charade between us. You cannot just walk away."

Erik pointed down the alleyway. "Let me walk away, Christine. You had your choice long ago. Let me choose now."

Anna nearly tripped upon those words. She heard his footfalls follow hers, but stop again.

"All I asked you for was love. That is all I asked from anyone. All I desired was a chance—just one chance—to be equal among men when it came to the simplest need. I wanted to be loved for *myself*, but no one allowed me the dignity to prove who I could be. I gave you the only thing in my life that loved me in return. That never denied or betrayed me. I gave you my *music*—my soul."

Anna glanced over her shoulder in time to see Erik gesture angrily at his mask.

"I cannot take back this face! I cannot exchange the atrocities of my past. Nor can I risk madness any longer by trying to rotate my life to make my imperfections fit with perfection." Christine jolted backward when he indicated her. "I cannot change to suit mores that will not have me. I am a product of what man has made me to be, what rejection caused me to be. I have lived too long in a dark and unhappy world, pouring everything I desired into music—hoping someone would unravel the melody and listen. I thought you had. But you only heard what you wished to hear."

As she continued to walk away, Anna peered toward the vicomtess, who stood paralyzed under Erik's impassioned plea.

"When it came time to choose, Christine, you chose to love your ideal and my music. That destroyed me. My music is the one thing once I gave you I could never take away. The melodies I compose, the ones reflecting the man beneath the mask are complex. If you had truly listened, and if I had known how to allow you to do so back then, you would have heard the counterpoint. I told you once, I will tell you again so you can move on as I. I want to live like anybody else. I do not want to be left to weep alone. You can still my breath, Christine. But for all our carefully woven illusions and lies, we cannot find what we need to complete each other. Forget me. Forgive me. I will always be a part of you. I will *always* love you. But I am seeking the missing part of me. My *happiness*..."

Anna stiffened as she heard Erik rush toward her. Her heart pinched when he passed her. She called his name, but he refused to meet her eyes. She was certain the pain coiling his stance wasn't from the wound in his arm.

Glancing from him to the opera house, Anna saw Christine standing staunchly against a backdrop of dying flames. A profound ambivalence shone behind her eyes as she watched Erik mold himself into the night. Anna looked to him before backing away from Christine and into the shadows.

As she did, Christine's eyes leveled upon her and carried all the betrayal and jealousy in the world.

Chapter Thirty-five

The depths of evening ended in a dusty vagabond's camp far on the outskirts of Paris. The jumble of misfits cluttered around campfires, their only goal for that night—to look out for one another. For Erik, the camp had the faint echo of his years spent wandering from fair to fair.

They inched along its outskirts. The night they intruded upon was a lively affair of shared meals, music and dance. It seemed in these outlets no one had a past. The idea of such was nothing more than an obsolete narration of days gone by.

The fire Anna built added to the winking lights of the camp. Off in the distance the fires of other travelers danced like fireflies in a vast meadow. Erik's eyes locked in the direction of Paris and his opera house. The smell of ash and smoke on his clothing added to the illusion he was closer than actuality.

In his lifetime, he'd committed a number of atrocities that caused him to live like a fugitive. But no horror seemed as disconcerting as the final way he'd bid his beloved Paris goodbye. Every time he fled his transgressions, he managed to find some place to settle where his word became law. None was quite as comfortable as the Opera Garnier. No place was as steeped in music, as yielding to his creative genius, as safe from the persecuting and judging eyes of man—or as close to Christine.

A shower of sparks caught his eye. Anna had tossed another log on the fire. She hadn't said a thing to him in an unbearably long time. He faced her. "You are cross with me."

Her look was tipped with poison.

Anna threw another log and bent to stoke the flames. "I'm not cross. Now take off your shirt."

"Mademoiselle!" Erik crossed his arms, his face contorting in shock beneath his mask. "I most certainly will not!"

Her face puckered unpleasantly, a clear indication he'd tipped her temper. That anger she claimed she didn't have vibrated the air between them. "You're still bleeding. Unless you want every four-legged animal following us as well, you need to rinse that shirt."

A curt nod directed his attention toward the brook. He followed her gesture and reluctantly looked at his wounded shoulder. Blood seeped through both bandage and shirt. The last few hours made him forget the pain and looking at his blood made it all too vivid. Although hesitant, he grudgingly peeled off his shirt. He winced as flesh stuck to blood-soaked fabric.

She paid him no mind, an observation for which Erik felt fortunate. Being exposed made him self-conscious and vulnerable. He stared toward Paris again, wringing the blood out of his sleeve. The motion made his face pinch and he swallowed a grunt of pain. Fresh blood broke through the barrier of Anna's bandage and seeped from the wound. The icy water he splashed on his shoulder and arm felt worse than being stoned. He forced the pain from his mind and picked at the areas of dry blood, certain the water was turning crimson.

"Come here," Anna demanded.

He turned slightly. "Erik will not."

"Erik."

"Erik does not wish to."

"Get over here now!"

Lest he scorn her—women, he was coming to understand, were not to be defied when in moods—he moved to her, laying the shirt before the campfire to dry. Usually she wasn't this sullen. She stoked the fire with the blade of the knife and jerked her head indicating he should sit.

He approached with caution. "Why are you so angry?"

Anna let the blade she'd been tending cut through a coal.

"I'm not angry. I'm confused. Now sit still."

Erik followed the glowing knife as she removed it from the fire. It lit the determination on her face.

"Why are you confused?" The red hot blade quivered with heat.

She looked up from the knife. "Why?" she asked incredulously. "*Why?* Over the last several days I have been thrust into an affair I still cannot figure out. I am a fugitive—again—having taken part in events beyond my comprehension." She gestured wildly forcing Erik to dodge the knife more than once. "I've left behind the Paris streets, the only place I ever called home, where there are people who will be wondering where I am. I am pursued by a good portion of the French authorities as an accomplice for kidnapping, robbery and murder over events that apparently span both past and present. I burned a carriage house and stole a vicomte's prized stallion!"

Erik gasped and took a good, hard look at the beast. He swallowed his mischievous grin to cringe at the tones her voice achieved.

"I watched you kill my father, so please, *do* pardon me if these concepts are a little confusing. Not to mention, I'm traveling this path with a man who I'm fairly convinced loves another woman more than I initially estimated."

Erik looked away as Anna positioned herself behind him. She wasn't gentle when removing his bandage.

"Here. Bite on this. Hard." She shoved a stick in his face.

He sharply shook his head, mindful to keep from looking at the knife. "No."

"Bloody hell, Erik, do it."

"I said, no!"

The finality in his voice could have knocked the stars from the heavens. She didn't argue further and he didn't provoke her. He recognized a stalemate when he saw one. She snatched his bicep. He jolted, schooling his anger.

"Are you ready?" she roared.

"Just. Do. It."

Under the circumstance there was only one way to treat his entry and exit wounds. Cauterization would clean and seal them—thus stanch the bleeding—but the pain would be extraordinary. He barely took a final moment to compose himself before Anna laid the heat of the knife against his open skin.

Erik arched into the blinding pain and screamed in tones that defied his usually melodic voice. The air hissed as hot metal scorched flesh. Two more times the knife moved. He bucked backward and shoved Anna to the ground.

The bottomless pit of agony radiated down his arm and shot fire out his fingers. The scent of burning flesh turned his stomach. Erik heaved in and out in deep gulps as he rolled to his feet. His world spun out of control and if not for the tree he collapsed against, he would have hit the ground in peaceful blackness.

A few more gulps of air as he clawed at the bark of the tree marked the passing of time before the seared flesh waned to a tolerable level. He jerked his arm trying to throw off the burn.

"I'm sorry," Anna said remorsefully. "The bleeding had to be stopped."

Erik nodded through clenched teeth, but offered no sort of comfort in return. She sighed and turned the knife on herself. She cut a swath of cloth from the hem of her dress. Ripping a long piece off and dabbing her smoldering hemline, she indicated for Erik to sit once more. This time she bound his wound with greater care.

"We'll need to find some cleaner cloth," she mused. "The first dwelling we come across I'll steal what laundered clothing I can find for bandages and get you a new shirt." Anger dominated her voice. "I refuse to use the money you pressed upon me. We'll bury the old shirt when we can. I'll find what provisions may be useful. We must be ready for anything given all that has transpired."

"I did not want this, Anna. There are things one cannot control. My past will always be a part of me. There is no escaping it. What would you have me do?"

Anna kept her focus on his arm.

"I do not love her like I once did." He winced as she dug deeper into his wound. Perhaps it was purposeful. "Not in the same way," he added, though he recalled the moments in the labyrinth. He dared not confess the feelings he knew Christine held for him. He tossed a stray twig into the flames and watched it shrivel to ash.

She sighed weakly. "It has been a long journey, has it not?" She wrapped the bandage around his shoulder and arm.

He would rather not think about it.

The fire cracked, breaking the silence. No matter how far they'd traveled from Paris in one night he was chased by his final words to Christine. What was happiness? It was something he wove an intricate web to catch, but never glutted upon. Christine had been his world. Anna was so very different.

He moved his head slightly to stare at her as she tended his wound. Was this right? His physical wound would heal, but what of the scars ripped open by the past? Was he not destined to be with Christine? That is what he'd thought for so many long and lonely years.

Long and lonely.

The weight of his cheat hit Erik hard, making his chest deflate. He was tired of lonely thoughts, lonely conversation, and a lonely bed. No matter all the ways he loved Christine, he was always—alone. Christine had Raoul, the source of some form of happiness for her. Could he not have his? Could he be happy hunted by the Vicomte de Chagny and the woman they both loved?

Feeling disjointed and out of place in a world he couldn't control, he gave up reasoning through the sordid affair that brought him to a vagabond camp smelling of smoke, ash and blood. Instead, he concentrated on the woman beside him whose gentle affections were seeing to his every need.

The mere thought of such made him fidget. An unexpected surge of emotion overtook him. The closer his feelings for Anna came to the surface, the more foreign they seemed. He became self-conscious without his shirt.

"Erik, stop fussing. You're making this difficult."

"Erik wants his shirt."

"It's wet, you'll catch the death." She tried to tie the bandage, but he shifted too much. "What is the matter with you?"

"Anna, please." He yanked his arm from her grip.

She opened her mouth as if to berate him, but pursed her lips and chose silence. He watched her cheeks pink. It blended with the orange color the fire cast against her face. It took quite a bit to make a lady such as Anna blush. He clutched his upper arm and turned from the awkward situation.

"Erik, forgive me. I didn't mean to cause discomfort. I had to—"

"You had to do what you had to do," he bit back. Erik didn't like vulnerability and he was falling prey to it. Tired and confused, he tried to suppress all that had him teetering dangerously close to the edges of madness. "It was inevitable that you had to see what you had to see," he sneered, swinging to face her. He gestured up and down his body. "Now you understand all the ugly reality as to why I live as I do." He gave a sharp nod back in the direction of Paris. Anna looked him directly in the eyes. It infuriated him.

"Go ahead," he growled. "Looking at me to tend to my needs is one thing. Looking on me now as you do in morbid curiosity, seeking the weakness in the monster is another. But by all means continue if you must."

She continued. Erik couldn't hide his anguish. He didn't waver through her scrutiny, though his chest heaved under her intense gaze. Their eyes met briefly before she looked away. He found it fitting she should hide her opinion. He knew the unjust ugliness he was built with extended beyond a mask.

"Erik." Anna reached for his hand and urged him to sit. "I see nothing but a strong and capable man."

He stared at their intertwined hands before looking into the campfire. What was he to do with those words? With her free hand she prodded gently at the fire. Lifting an orange tipped stick, she gestured east.

"*Österreich.*"

The statement struck him dumb. Anna grinned. Her eyes twinkled. It seemed she enjoyed toying with him.

"You're not the only one with a colored past, Erik. Austria, remember?"

He cautiously nodded. He recalled a distant conversation over their nights in the labyrinth.

"I was born there. My mother was Austrian. You'll like it."

Erik bit his tongue in his haste to protest. "Absolutely not. I cannot, and I will not speak German. It is a vulgar, horrid language. I dare say there is no music to it."

Anna spread the coals. Her laughter tumbled around him. "The language is beautiful, Erik. Besides, France is out at the moment."

He rubbed his arm as if trying to rub the idea off of him.

Gently she poked him and smiled as he shook his head. "We best get some rest. We'll need to move as soon as this camp breaks."

He nodded and watched as she took command of the situation with renewed purpose. He marveled at her versatility and willingness to be with him despite the circumstances. It roused his emotion. She leaned into him and gave him a soft peck on the leather of his mask. Those emotions took over with a ferocity Erik found he couldn't contain. He abruptly shifted, moving in such a way to capture her lips.

A small cry of shock escaped her. He muffled it by deepening his passions for her. She relaxed into his affections. He welcomed the warmth found in her lips. He kissed with an urgent command as if nothing else in the world mattered. And, for a moment nothing else did. Anna leaned into him and started to return his kiss with the same passion when Erik suddenly pulled away.

"No," he whimpered, jumping to his feet.

"Erik?" Anna fell forward. She braced herself to keep from falling into the fire.

He circled the campfire, rubbing his temples, trying hard to stop the tingling in his lips and body. "Anna, I cannot."

"You cannot—what?" Confusion decorated her face.

With a groan, he pushed the palms of his hands to his eyes, trying to maintain control. This was not how he'd envisioned such desire and passion to be roused in him. Not like this, not here, not in this way.

"I...you..." He had to stop to find the words.

Slowly he knelt by the fire. Anna studied him out of the corner of her eye. He turned, and let his gaze roam over her. Her cheek and lip were bruised. They'd most assuredly be purple by morn. Her temple had turned a fiery shade of red and her untamed hair a sooty gray from ash. Testimony to all she'd gone through over the last several days.

The warm glow of the fire defined a fit woman capable of taking care of herself. But her eyes drove Erik mad, for there was nothing simple in the way they questioned; nothing simple in how they absorbed every detail of every moment to lock it away as some memory to be recalled later. That other fluttering in the pit of his stomach he oft identified with surfaced once more. Anna raised an eyebrow. It begged him to finish his sentence. He blurted it out as fast as he could.

"You ignite in me a passion unlike any I have ever felt. There are certain desires..."

Erik balled his hands into fists to control the surging in his body. Her eyes softened to him and the slight tilt to her head portrayed her plea for him to continue. His usually bell-like voice turned gruff. A small sound escaped from deep within his throat and he turned from her, clenching his fists until his nails dug in.

"Desires that I have had before, but have never fully acted upon."

He faced her as she nodded her understanding and reached for his hand. Her touch put him on fire.

"Anna, stop." He had to get this out. "Never have I felt so complete of a man than when I am with you. I want nothing more than to take those desires and act upon them." Erik couldn't ignore the way his melodic tones turned husky. "Selfishly, I want nothing more than to make everything that has happened disappear and for one blissful moment grant myself the liberty of every seduction and every allurement I have oft explored in my mind but never felt in my flesh. Just once I want to love and love with the ardor and intensity I have slept with in my dreams, but I cannot. I cannot put you through that."

He took a deep breath and held his hands in front of his lips, shaking his head as he glared into the fire. It wasn't the only thing burning.

The fire kept cadence with the sounds of the night. Erik watched Anna gaze into the fire. Desperation that she didn't think the same things made his vision blur. She could look upon his face with no fear or revulsion. But what of all of him? He turned away to focus his gaze elsewhere when she quickly lifted her eyes to steal a glance at his bare chest. Erik stiffened under such appraisal. She turned away. He couldn't blame her.

"Erik, what are you telling me?" she asked, rejection edging into her voice.

He breathed heavily. He lowered his hands and spoke unblinking toward the fire. "Men have always taken that from you. In your life there have been men who used you to enact their desires and to play out their lust." He couldn't meet her eyes. Those moments he knew of, though few, repulsed him. "With the urges—the *affections*—I feel now, and my inability to control all I feel, I will be just like them. I will not do that to you. I cannot make you revisit those places—not ever. Not after all you have been though. All I have witnessed."

Would she be willing to stay with him if he refused her in such a way? That sacrifice he would make for her honor. The crack of the fire was the only sound until Anna's tears joined the popping wood. She reached for his hands.

"Erik, no. You're right in that men have done things. But they didn't want what you do. They took control, power; they wanted to hurt. They did hurt." Anna reached up and made him look at her. "You want to bring a life of passion, connection, love."

Erik shook his head sadly. "I am not a normal man. I have yet to bring those things properly to the company of a lady. I do not know how. I do not wish to hurt you with the affections I realize. There are ways a gentleman should behave before a lady and as much as I try..." The words would not come. As much as he tried—he knew he was different. "Do not make this seem so simple. Nothing in this is so."

"Erik, we are both naïve in this. In many ways I have never experienced what you most desire either." She reached to him and pulled one pathetic strand of hair out of his face. "This friendship has been through many changes, so much has gone on. Everything is still so raw. When the time is right—and if you still wish—I will be here. I have waited my whole life for you."

Anna's eyes lit up with her small, but weary smile. She turned to the fire, lazily poking the dying embers. Sparks twisted into the night. Erik followed their spiraling dance. His breath hitched.

He was loved for himself.

He closed his eyes and gave in to his emotions. It would not be easy for Anna to be with him, he knew this, but he also knew she had made her choice. She wanted him.

She had waited her whole life—for *him*.

He rose, pacing away from the fire, and then turned. He opened his mouth to speak, but shut it again. He repeated this pattern as his heart turned over in his chest. Erik kept his focus on the gold band around his pinky. A drum line in his mind kept beat with his heart. He could bear the agony no longer. The wind and his whisper merged as one.

"I drifted through the dark for many years wondering if it were possible for ghosts to cry tears." He glanced over his shoulder. Anna had stopped poking at the fire to stare at him "I had become one in my own lifetime. Ordinary men have *reasons* for living." Beneath his mask, it wasn't heat that moistened his cheeks. Erik reached to his face. The mask dropped to the ground. "What reason did I have? I thought I had found my reason in Christine. But she was not my reason for living. She was my distraction from dying. My past filled me with such sorrow, my face with such bitter loathing, I buried all hope that the glad tidings of men could pertain to me. And through time, I had gathered all the illusions I created and tried so hard to make them fit together. I never imagined the perfect fit would be the one most mismatched and the only illusion I did not create." He reached into his pocket and held out a shattered remnant of an ink bottle, a once perfect piece of china and a broken scrap of mirror. "If I had known I could one day have the most exquisite dream and not fear waking, I would not have poisoned my life with regret."

He knelt to Anna's level and palmed the pieces together. Anna gasped as they slipped out of sight before her eyes. He slid his ring from his pinky.

"Distractions in time fade. In you I find my beauty. I am not afraid of living. The moment you hugged my violin to your chest and learned my Madrigal—you held me. And it is in those arms I would wish to die. If you will have me—and all I can and cannot give you—I will love you ardently. I will worship you mind, body and soul." Erik shifted his gaze from his ring to her eyes. "Be my reason, Anna. Complete me?"

The breeze carried her sigh of yes and swirled it around the camp. The ring glided onto her finger as he dragged her into his arms. He hunched deeply over her, burying his tears in the nape of her neck. He cared not where their travels would lead so long as he had his Anna he had music.

Erik pressed his lips to her ear and whispered his love in such a way the dying flames of the camp seemed to flare in reply and all of France seemed to sigh.

"Je t'aime avec tout mon coeur. Je t'adore... "

Chapter Thirty-six

There are steps to acceptance, the first being an awareness of one's past. And though nothing can be brought back from it—with acceptance the past can be transcended. Had I been the purveyor of such wisdom years ago I would not have lived sedated by an ethereal black pool of misbegotten desire. If I had known my past would be embraced, I would have been aware of the possibility for a future.—Erik

Dawn rose, as reliable as ever. As it struggled to wipe the sleep of night from the sky, Erik mounted the stallion then lifted Anna up. He held her like blown glass as if the previous night could be shattered and lost in an instant. Most wanderers headed west, Erik turned the stallion toward the sun. He headed them down the paths of the indigents and vagrants, following only where the road would lead. Focusing ahead, he made no effort to glance toward Paris. With no possessions, their burdens were light. Nothing to their names except a horse and a small satchel containing various random items: an exquisite violin, an elegant cloak, and an odd assortment of seemingly meaningless things.

The warm sun and the rhythmic clip of the horse's hooves made Anna sleepy. She rested lightly, her head fitting easily between Erik's shoulders. He relished the arms of the mismatched companion wrapped artfully around his waist.

Erik rolled his ring around Anna's finger. His head swayed in fluid motions to the composition being written in his mind. He sighed at the sensation of her head against his back as the sway of the horse moved her in rhythm to the patter of the hooves. It warmed him in a way he'd never known.

A louder clip of a less elegant steed came up behind them. Anna stiffened. She lifted her head. A graying old man on an equally aged mare trotted up beside them.

"Good day, little lady, mind if an old traveler shares the road?"

Anna greeted the ridiculous visitor, while Erik chose to react with more caution. He refused to look at the man.

"Quite, Monsieur," Erik responded, none to happy to have his music interrupted or to have someone intrude upon the rather amorous images the woman resting upon his back painted in his mind.

Anna jabbed him in the ribs and replied for both of them. "Not at all."

Erik turned to offer his *bonjour* as well.

"Good God! What's with the mask?" the crass old man blurted.

Tension shot an arrow straight up Erik's spine. He clicked to the horse and urged him into a faster trot. The old man was not deterred.

"Oh, come on, old chap. I didn't mean anything by it. Everyone has a story. It defines who we are and makes the journey ahead more interesting."

Erik yanked the reins, jolting Anna and sharply wheeling the stallion around. The horse danced nervously with the sudden change in his master's temperament. Anna gripped Erik's waist both to save herself from falling while urging calm in him. Erik took his cue. He lifted Anna's palm to his lips and let his kiss linger. Pressing her hand to his chest, he turned the stallion in a small circle. The horse's hooves drummed to the staccato beat of his voice.

"My story? I am a murderer: a murderer and a Maestro, a magician and a mastermind. I have slept in the far corners of hell with my face as my shackle and my voice my only respite. I have dreamed of beauties far beyond the reaches of earthly imagination only to be held hostage to the nightmares of my past by the restlessness of my deranged mind. I awoke from an inhuman world to defy my fate and embrace my past because of paper, ink and figs..."

Author Information

If one is going to query a publisher, Jennifer suggests not doing so in pink ink. Her first, written when she was twelve, was nothing if not colorful. She is a member of the Historical Novel Society and the Romance Writers of America in addition to being a writing mentor. She writes historical fiction and historical romance with unusual themes and locations, such as autism and the social mores of the mentally ill in the 19th century. She has a passion for Austrian culture and is often found searching for stories and romance in long forgotten histories.

It was her love of research and classic literature that brought her to expanding Leroux's *The Phantom of the Opera*.

She enjoys hearing from her readers. Email her at author@jenniferlinforth.com.

She can be found on the web at
www.jenniferlinforth.com.

Action/Suspense: *Eric Fullilove*
The Zero Day Event

Romantic Suspense: *Candace Gold*
A Heated Romance
Jo Webnar
Saving Tampa

Young Adult: *R.R. Smythe*
Into the Woods
Anne Kimberly
Dark Well of Decision

Anthologies: *Michèle Ann Young/Kimberly Ivey/*
Billie Warren Chai
Brides of the West
Deborah MacGillivray
Cat O'Nine Tales
Deborah MacGillivray/Rebecca Andrews/Billie Warren Chai/
Debi Farr/Patricia Frank/Diane Davis White
Love on a Harley
Zoe Archer/Amber Dawn Bell/Gerri Bowen/
Candace Gold/Patty Howell/Kimberly Ivey/Lee Roland
No Law Against Love 2
Jacquie Rogers
Faery Special Romances
Holiday Romance Anthology
Christmas Wishes
Holiday Romance Anthology
Holiday in the Heart
Romance Anthology
No Law Against Love
Romance Anthology
Blue Moon Magic
Romance Anthology
Blue Moon Enchantment
Romance Anthology
Recipe for Love
Deborah MacGillivray/Leanne Burroughs/
Amy Blizzard/Gerri Bowen/Judith Leigh
Love Under the Mistletoe
Deborah MacGillivray/Leanne Burroughs/Rebecca Andrews/
Amber Dawn Bell/Erin E.M. Hatton/Patty Howell/Isabel Mere
Romance Upon A Midnight Clear

Praise for Highland Press Books!

THE CRYSTAL HEART by Katherine Deauxville brims with ribald humor and authentic historical detail. Enjoy!

~ Virginia Henley, NY Times bestselling author

* * *

RAPE OF THE SOUL – Dawn Thompson clearly shows just what an amazing talent she was by instantly giving you a dark, suspenseful tale of horror. She described the book as 'Anya Seton meets Stephen King' and that is a fair assessment of its style. I would also say she added a touch of Daphne du Maurier and Arthur Quiller-Couch. Rape of the Soul is one of those books that will linger on bookshelves, and be read again and again.

Thompson delivers on all levels. When Jean Maitland enters the abandoned glass house of Craigmoor, you have a Hitchcock style, 'dark at the top of the stairs' foreboding that pure evil can exist and can reach from the past to destroy the future. Thompson delivers with this spellbinding tour de force, her legacy to her fans. It's a keeper.

~ PRN Reviews

* * *

THE SENSE OF HONOR - Ashley Kath-Bilsky has written a historical romance of the highest caliber. This reviewer fell in love with the hero and was cheering for the heroine all the way through. The characters are multi-dimensional and the secondary characters bring life to the story. Sexual tension rages through this story and Ms. Kath-Bilsky gives her readers a breath-taking romance. This reviewer was very pleased with how the author handled all the secrets. Sometimes it can be very frustrating for the reader when secrets keep tearing the main characters apart, but in this case, those secrets seem to bring them more together and both characters reacted very maturely when the secrets finally came to light. This reviewer is hoping that this very talented author will have another book out very soon.

~ Valerie, Love Romances

* * *

HIGHLAND WISHES by Leanne Burroughs. This reviewer found that this book was a wonderful story set in a time when tension was high between England and Scotland. The reader can feel this author's love for Scotland and its many wonderful heroes.

This reviewer was easily captivated by the story and was enthralled by it until the end. The reader will laugh and cry as you read this wonderful story. The reader feels all the pain, torment and disillusionment felt by both main characters, but also the joy and love they felt. Ms. Burroughs has crafted a well-researched story that gives a glimpse into Scotland during a time when there was upheaval and war for independence. This reviewer is anxiously awaiting her next novel in this series and commends her for a wonderful job done.

~Dawn Roberto, Love Romances

* * *

I adore this Scottish historical romance! ***BLOOD ON THE TARTAN*** by Chris Holmes has more history than some historical romances—but never dry history in this book! Readers will find themselves completely immersed in the scene, the history and the characters. Chris Holmes creates a multi-dimensional theme of justice in his depiction of all the nuances and forces at work from the laird down to the land tenants. This intricate historical detail emanates from the story itself, heightening the suspense and the reader's understanding of the history in a vivid manner as if it were current and present. The extra historical detail just makes their life stories more memorable and lasting because the emotions were grounded in events. The ending is quite special and bridges links with Catherine's mother's story as well as opening up this romance to an expansive view of Scottish history and ancestry. ***Blood On The Tartan*** is a must read for romance and historical fiction lovers of Scottish heritage.

~Merri, Merrimon Reviews

* * *

I can't say enough good things about Ms. Zenk's writing. ***CHASING BYRON*** by Molly Zenk is a page turner of a book not only because of the engaging characters but also by the lovely prose. In fact, I read the entire thing in one day. Reading this book was a jolly fun time all through the eyes of Miss Woodhouse, yet also one that touches the heart. It was an experience I would definitely repeat. I'm almost jealous of Ms. Zenk. She must have had a glorious time penning this story. As this is her debut novel, I hope we will be delighted with more stories from this talented author in the future.

~Orange Blossom, Long and Short Reviews

* * *

MOON OF THE FALLING LEAVES is an incredible read. The characters are not only believable, but the blending in of how Swift Eagle shows Jessica and her children the acts of survival is remarkably done. The months of travel indeed shows hardships each much endure. Diane Davis White pens a poignant tale that really grabbed this reader. She tells a descriptive story of discipline, trust and love in a time where hatred and prejudice abounded among many. This rich tale offers vivid imagery of the beautiful scenery and landscape, and brings in the tribal customs of each person, as Jessica and Swift Eagle search their heart.

~Cherokee, Reviewer for Coffee Time Romance

* * *

Jean Harrington's ***THE BAREFOOT QUEEN*** is a superb historical with a lushly painted setting. I adored Grace for her courage and the cleverness with which she sets out to make Owen see her love for him. The bond between Grace and Owen is tenderly portrayed and their love had me rooting for them right up until the last page. Ms. Harrington's ***The Barefoot Queen*** is a treasure in the historical romance genre you'll want to read for yourself! Five Star Pick of the Week!!!

~ Crave More Romance

* * *

IN SUNSHINE OR IN SHADOW by Cynthia Owens - If you adore the stormy heroes of 'Wuthering Heights' and 'Jane Eyre' (and who doesn't?) you'll be entranced by Owens' passionate story of Ireland after the Great Famine, and David Burke - a man from America with a hidden past and a secret name. Only one woman, the fiery, luscious Siobhan, can unlock the bonds that imprison him. Highly recommended for those who love classic romance and an action-packed story.

~ Best Selling Author, Maggie Davis,
AKA Katherine Deauxville

* * *

ALMOST TAKEN by Isabel Mere is a very passionate historical romance that takes the reader on an exciting adventure. Readers will watch in interest as Deran Morissey, he Earl of Atherton, and Ava Fychon, a young woman from Wales fall in love and overcome obstacles. This is a very sensual romance that wins the heart of the readers.

The character's personalities will fascinate readers and win their concern. Ava, who is highly spirited and stubborn, will win the respect of the readers for her courage and determination. Deran, who is rumored in the beginning to be an ice king, not caring about anyone, will prove how wrong people's perceptions can be. ***Almost Taken*** by Isabel Mere is an emotionally moving historical romance that I highly recommend to the readers.

~ Anita, The Romance Studio

* * *

Leanne Burroughs easily will captivate the reader with intricate details, a mystery that ensnares the reader and characters that will touch their hearts. By the end of the first chapter, this reviewer was enthralled with ***HER HIGHLAND ROGUE*** and was rooting for Duncan and Catherine to admit their love. Laughter, tears and love shine through this wonderful novel. This reviewer was amazed at Ms. Burroughs' depth and perception in this storyline. Her wonderful way with words plays itself through each page like a lyrical note and will captivate the reader till the very end. Read ***Her Highland Rogue*** and be transported to a time that is full of mystery and promise of a future. This reviewer is highly recommending this book for those who enjoy an engrossing Scottish tale full of humor, love and laughter.

~ Dawn Roberto, Love Romances

* * *

PRETEND I'M YOURS by Phyllis Campbell is an exceptional masterpiece. This lovely story is so rich in detail and personalities that it just leaps out and grabs hold of the reader. Ms. Campbell carries the reader into a mirage of mystery with deceit, betrayal of the worst kind, and a passionate love that makes this a whirlwind page-turner. Mercedes and William are astonishing characters that ignite the pages and allows the reader to experience all their deepening sensations. This extraordinary read had me mesmerized with its ambiance, its characters and its remarkable twists and turns, making it one recommended read in my book.

~ Linda L., Fallen Angel Reviews

* * *

REBEL HEART by Jannine Corti Petska - Ms. Petska does an excellent job of all aspects of sharing this book with us. Ms. Petska used a myriad of emotions to tell this story and the reader quickly becomes entranced in the ways Courtney's stubborn attitude works to her advantage in surviving this disastrous beginning to her new life. This is a wonderful rendition of a different type which is a welcome addition to the historical romance genre. I believe that you will enjoy this story; I know I did!

~ Brenda Talley, The Romance Studio

* * *

SOUTHERN FRIED TROUBLE - Katherine Deauxville is at the top of her form with mayhem, sizzle and murder.

~ Nan Ryan, NY Times bestselling author

* * *

INTO THE WOODS by R.R. Smythe - This Young Adult Fantasy will send chills down your spine. I followed Callum and witnessed everything he and his friends went through as they attempted to decipher the messages. At the same time, I watched Callum's mother, Ellsbeth, as she walked through the Netherwood. Each time Callum deciphered one of the four messages, some villagers awakened. Through the eyes of

Ellsbeth, I saw the other sleepers wander, make mistakes, and be released from the Netherwood, leaving Ellsbeth alone. There is one thread left dangling, but do not fret. This IS a stand-alone book. But that thread gives me hope that another book about the Netherwoods may someday come to pass. Excellent reading for any age of fantasy fans!

~ Detra Fitch, Huntress Reviews

* * *

BRIDES OF THE WEST by Michèle Ann Young, Kimberly Ivey, and Billie Warren Chai - All three of the stories in this wonderful anthology are based on women who gambled their future in blindly accepting complete strangers for husbands. It was a different era when a woman must have a husband to survive and all three of these phenomenal authors wrote exceptional stories featuring fascinating and gutsy heroines and the men who loved them. For an engrossing read with splendid original stories I highly encourage reader's to pick up a copy of this marvelous anthology.

~ Marilyn Rondeau, Reviewers International Organization

* * *

CAT O'NINE TALES by Deborah MacGillivray. Enchanting tales from the most wicked, award-winning author today. Spellbinding! A treat for all.

~ Detra Fitch, Huntress Reviews

* * *

***FAERY SPECIAL ROMANCES* - Brilliantly magical!** Ms. Rogers' special brand of humor and imagination will have you believing in faeries from page one. Absolutely enchanting!

~ Dawn Thompson, Award Winning Author

* * *

Christmas is a magical time and twelve talented authors answer the question of what happens when ***CHRISTMAS WISHES*** come true in this incredible anthology. ***Christmas Wishes*** shows just how phenomenal a themed anthology can be. Each of these highly skilled authors brings a slightly different perspective to the Christmas theme to create a book that ensures to leave readers satisfied. What a joy to read such splendid stories! This reviewer looks forward to more anthologies by Highland Press as the quality is simply astonishing.

~ Debbie, CK2S Kwips and Kritiques

* * *

RECIPE FOR LOVE - I don't think the reader will find a better compilation of mouth watering short romantic love stories than in ***Recipe for Love***! This is a highly recommended volume–perfect for beaches, doctor's offices, or anywhere you've a few minutes to read.

~ Marilyn Rondeau, Reviewers International Organization

* * *

HOLIDAY IN THE HEART - Twelve stories that would put even Scrooge into the Christmas spirit. It does not matter what *type* of romance genre you prefer. This book has a little bit of everything. The stories are set in the U.S.A. and Europe. Some take place in the past, some in the present, and one story takes place in both! I strongly suggest that you put on something comfortable, brew up something hot (tea, coffee or cocoa will do), light up a fire, settle down somewhere quiet and begin reading this anthology.

~ Detra Fitch, Huntress Reviews

* * *

BLUE MOON MAGIC is an enchanting collection of short stories. You should have no problem finding a tale to suit your mood. ***Blue Moon Magic*** offers historicals, contemporaries, time travel, paranormal, and futuristic narratives to tempt your heart.

Legend says that if you wish with all your heart upon the rare blue moon, your wishes were sure to come true. True love is out there if you just believe in it. In some of the stories, love happens in the most unusual ways. Angels may help, ancient spells may be broken, anything can happen. Even vampires will find their perfect mate with the power of the blue moon. Not every heroine believes they are wishing for love, some are just looking for answers to their problems or nagging questions.

Blue Moon Magic is a perfect read for late at night or even during your commute to work. The short yet sweet stories are a wonderful way to spend a few minutes. If you do not have the time to finish a full-length novel, but hate stopping in the middle of a loving tale, I highly recommend grabbing this book.

~ Kim Swiderski, Writers Unlimited Reviewer

* * *

Legend has it that a blue moon is enchanted. What happens when fifteen talented authors utilize this theme to create enthralling stories of love?

BLUE MOON ENCHANTMENT is a wonderful, themed anthology filled with phenomenal stories by fifteen extraordinarily talented authors. Readers will find a wide variety of time periods and styles showcased in this superb anthology. ***Blue Moon Enchantment*** is sure to offer a little bit of something for everyone!

~ Debbie, CK²S Kwips and Kritiques

* * *

NO LAW AGAINST LOVE - If you have ever found yourself rolling your eyes at some of the more stupid laws, then you are going to adore this novel. Each story deals with at least one stupid or outdated law. Let me give you an example: In Florida, USA, there is a law that states 'If an elephant is left tied to a parking meter, the parking fee has to be paid just as it would for a vehicle.' No matter how many times you go back and reread them, the words will remain the same. The tales vary in time and place. Some take place in the present, in the past, in the USA, in England...in other words, there is something for everyone! Best yet, profits from the sales of this novel will go to breast cancer prevention.

A stellar anthology that had me laughing, sighing in pleasure, believing in magic, and left me begging for more! Will there be a second anthology someday? I sure hope so! This is one novel that will go directly to my 'Keeper' shelf, to be read over and over again. Very highly recommended!

~ Detra Fitch, Huntress Reviews

* * *

LOVE UNDER THE MISTLETOE *is a fun anthology that infuses the beauty of the season with fun characters and unforgettable situations. This is one of those books that you can read year round and still derive great pleasure from each of the charming stories. A wonderful compilation of holiday stories. Perfect year round!*

~ Chrissy Dionne, Romance Junkies